CW01499166

1

LONDON, SEPTEMBER 1904

Flora stood before the gilt-framed mirror in her townhouse entrance hall and tilted her hat further to the left, examining the result with a critical eye.

'I like it the other way.' Bunny's reflection appeared over her shoulder, his focus on a pasteboard card in his hand.

'Why do you keep staring at that invitation? The words won't change.' Flora returned the pigeon-wing-grey velvet hat to its original position and met his gaze in the mirror.

'I still find it strange we've been invited to tour a hospital neither of us has heard of.' He tapped the card against his thumbnail before tucking it into an inside pocket.

'I asked Lydia about St Philomena's Hospital.' Flora tweaked a stray strand of hair into place. 'She says it was founded by a wealthy philanthropist to provide medical care for the children of the poor.'

'An admirable endeavour, I'm sure. But why have we been invited?' Bunny pushed his spectacles further up his nose with a middle finger. 'If Arthur became ill, we're not likely to take him to a hospital in Southwark.'

'I suppose not.' Flora suppressed a shiver at the thought of illness in connection with their infant son, who enjoyed chubby, good health. 'Charities are always looking for funds, so it stands to reason they might regard Mr Ptolemy Harrington, Solicitor at Law, a viable proposition.'

'I suppose that makes sense.' Bunny joined her by the front door held open by their butler. 'Are you sure you wouldn't rather go in the motor car?'

'It's too late to change your mind.' She nodded to where a square motor taxi idled at the kerb. 'The taxi is already here.' Turning towards him, she flicked a toast crumb from the corner of her husband's mouth. He submitted to the fuss, his downcast expression so like Arthur's, she experienced an urge to kiss him; an impulse she resisted with Stokes present. 'Besides, Southwark is not a suitable place to leave your beloved Aster, no matter how many street urchins you pay to watch it.'

'I suppose so.' Bunny released a disappointed sigh and followed her onto the top step. 'Taxi it is then.' He guided her through the front door with a discreet but firm squeeze of her waist. Thankful her coiffure was saved from Bunny's enthusiasm for open air driving, Flora turned back at the front gate, giving the house a slow, appraising glance of appreciative pride.

The elegant Portland stone façade rose four floors from the street; a brace of Doric pillars flanking a black front door. Behind black painted railings, a set of stone steps descended into basement kitchens equipped with the latest innovations; something Flora had insisted upon. As a former governess, she endeavoured to make her own servants' lives easier; a sentiment voiced in the presence of her mother-in-law, Beatrice Harrington; whose resulting contempt still made Flora's cheeks burn.

* * *

DEATH BY THE THAMES

THE FLORA MAGUIRE MYSTERIES BOOK 4

ANITA DAVISON

Boldwood

First published in 2017 as The Forgotten Children. This edition published in Great Britain in 2024 by Boldwood Books Ltd.

Copyright © Anita Davison, 2017

Cover Design by Head Design

Cover Illustration: Shutterstock

The moral right of Anita Davison to be identified as the author of this work has been asserted in accordance with the Copyright, Designs and Patents Act 1988.

All rights reserved. No part of this book may be reproduced in any form or by any electronic or mechanical means, including information storage and retrieval systems, without written permission from the author, except for the use of brief quotations in a book review.

This book is a work of fiction and, except in the case of historical fact, any resemblance to actual persons, living or dead, is purely coincidental.

Every effort has been made to obtain the necessary permissions with reference to copyright material, both illustrative and quoted. We apologise for any omissions in this respect and will be pleased to make the appropriate acknowledgements in any future edition.

A CIP catalogue record for this book is available from the British Library.

Paperback ISBN 978-1-83518-869-9

Large Print ISBN 978-1-83518-870-5

Hardback ISBN 978-1-83518-868-2

Ebook ISBN 978-1-83518-871-2

Kindle ISBN 978-1-83518-872-9

Audio CD ISBN 978-1-83518-863-7

MP3 CD ISBN 978-1-83518-864-4

Digital audio download ISBN 978-1-83518-867-5

Boldwood Books Ltd
23 Bowerdean Street
London SW6 3TN
www.boldwoodbooks.com

For my sister Jan. Thank you for everything.

The motor taxi ambled along Victoria Street, the almost silent engine strangely unsettling as they passed the Catholic cathedral and drove around Parliament Square, past monumental buildings that represented the might of the British Empire. On the far side of Westminster Bridge, Portland stone and red brick gave way to the wood and steel of the industrial area of the city, which deteriorated a little more with each mile. The taxi's route took them in a wide circle and back to the river again, where sat the sparkling new structure of Tower Bridge. The sky had been overcast when they left, darkening steadily until by the time they reached Quilp Street and passed beneath the wrought iron archway that displayed the sign 'St Philomena's Hospital for Sick Children', light rain pattered the vehicle's roof.

'It's hard to comprehend we're only three miles from Belgravia.' Flora stared at the soot-stained red brick and faded paint of the surrounding houses, shops and warehouses; all in various stages of neglect. The hospital, a solid, rectangular building with a mansard roof, squatted amongst its less imposing neighbours, like an elegant woman who had known better days; the red brick having faded to a dirty russet colour by forty years of coal smoke from the surrounding factories and tanneries.

Bunny helped Flora from the taxi, they put their heads down against the rain and, with their arms around each other, ran for the entrance.

'I can smell baking.' Flora sniffed appreciatively at an enticing smell of burned sugar as they exploded into the hall and brushed water from their clothes.

'That's because the Peak Frean's biscuit factory is in nearby Bermondsey. It's one of the larger employers in this area.' Bunny gave his hat a shake as they approached a large desk at the far end of an imposing entrance hall filled with white-capped nurses, lumbering porters and serious faced doctors who strode purposefully across the tiled floor and disappeared through various sets of double doors located on both sides of the hall.

'Mr and Mrs Harrington, is it?' the man at the desk squinted at the square of pasteboard Bunny handed him. 'As you can see, we have quite a few visitors today, but someone will be here shortly to show you round.' He nodded to where a group of ladies in wide-brimmed hats conversed in low tones with black-suited gentleman in homburgs; their level of animation ranging from bored disinterest to fake laughter.

'I hope we won't have to wait too long,' Bunny whispered, nodding to where some people were being ushered through a set of swing doors, but which made little effect on the remaining crowd.

'Don't be such a stuffed shirt.' Flora cuffed him lightly. 'I hoped you might enjoy a few hours away from your office for a change.'

'Hmm, this wasn't quite what I had in mind when I said I needed a break from paperwork.' Bunny adjusted his tie in the reflection of a framed print of Southwark cathedral.

'It's quite an impressive building though, don't you think?' Instead of the disinfectant and carbolic soap she had expected, Flora inhaled the fragrance of late summer flowers mixed with beeswax and warm bread. 'As a charity, this place doesn't look short of funds, either.' She tilted her head back to where a glass lantern four stories above flooded the marbled entrance with daylight, a slate grey sky visible through the rain-streaked glass. Half panelled in polished wood, the walls sported a border of ceramic tiles at shoulder height with flower designs, their Latin names written in flowing script underneath.

Flora crossed the monochrome tiled floor to where an alabaster statue of an adolescent girl was set in a curved niche in the wall. She was in two-thirds scale, and dressed in a loose gown of expertly carved folds to her feet, a posy of flowers held against her cheek.

DEATH BY THE THAMES

THE FLORA MAGUIRE MYSTERIES BOOK 4

ANITA DAVISON

Boldwood

First published in 2017 as The Forgotten Children. This edition published in Great Britain in 2024 by Boldwood Books Ltd.

Copyright © Anita Davison, 2017

Cover Design by Head Design

Cover Illustration: Shutterstock

The moral right of Anita Davison to be identified as the author of this work has been asserted in accordance with the Copyright, Designs and Patents Act 1988.

All rights reserved. No part of this book may be reproduced in any form or by any electronic or mechanical means, including information storage and retrieval systems, without written permission from the author, except for the use of brief quotations in a book review.

This book is a work of fiction and, except in the case of historical fact, any resemblance to actual persons, living or dead, is purely coincidental.

Every effort has been made to obtain the necessary permissions with reference to copyright material, both illustrative and quoted. We apologise for any omissions in this respect and will be pleased to make the appropriate acknowledgements in any future edition.

A CIP catalogue record for this book is available from the British Library.

Paperback ISBN 978-1-83518-869-9

Large Print ISBN 978-1-83518-870-5

Hardback ISBN 978-1-83518-868-2

Ebook ISBN 978-1-83518-871-2

Kindle ISBN 978-1-83518-872-9

Audio CD ISBN 978-1-83518-863-7

MP3 CD ISBN 978-1-83518-864-4

Digital audio download ISBN 978-1-83518-867-5

Boldwood Books Ltd
23 Bowerdean Street
London SW6 3TN
www.boldwoodbooks.com

For my sister Jan. Thank you for everything.

Her eyes were demurely cast down and the words 'Saint Philomena' were etched onto a plaque fastened to the base.

'Do I see the work of Carlo Marochetti in this statue?' she asked. 'If this is an accurate portrayal, this saint was only a child when she died.'

'Probably not an accurate portrayal, then.' Bunny wandered further along the hall, his attention on a landscape. 'Most likely a romantic recreation.'

'It is indeed Marochetti's work.' A low, resonant female voice spoke at Flora's shoulder. 'He fashioned the late Queen's statue for her mausoleum.'

Flora spun round to face a woman in her mid-forties regarding her calmly; her stance and demeanour were that of the archetypal angel of mercy: slender hands encircled by stiff white cuffs clasped serenely in front of her, and her head slightly bowed. Her delicate, symmetrical features told of beauty in her youth, with slight traces of crow's feet visible beside her blue-green eyes. Only the soft, golden aura was missing.

'I'm sorry. I didn't realise anyone had heard me.' Flustered, Flora's voice trailed off as a strange sensation coursed through her that felt like recognition. Had she seen this woman somewhere before? A memory hovered at the back of her mind, but she couldn't place it. If it *was* a memory.

'It's a skill I find useful occasionally.' The woman's warm smile held a hint of mischief. 'Allow me to introduce myself. I'm Alice Finch, the matron here.' Her austere black uniform dress clung flatteringly to her still-girlish figure, and her dark honey-coloured hair was worn swept up, beneath a stiff white cap from which trailed a matching strip of linen trimmed with a double row of tiny pleats that fell to her hip.

'Flora, Flora Harrington. Nice to meet you.' She cleared her

throat noisily to attract Bunny's attention. 'That gentleman over
there is my husband, Ptolemy Harrington.'

At the sound of his name, Bunny turned from his study of the
poster and strode towards them, taking the lady's outstretched
hand.

'What an unusual name.' Miss Finch gave his hand a brief,
business-like shake.

'We don't call him that,' Flora began. 'He's known as—'

'Quite.' Bunny interrupted her, one hand raised to adjust his
spectacles. 'What does this statue represent?'

'Our patrons named the hospital after her.' The matron's eyes lit
with amusement at Bunny's self-conscious flush. 'If you are interested, Philomena is the patron saint of children and young people
who lived in the fourth century. She's quite beautiful don't you
think?' Her gaze swivelled towards Flora with a penetrating look.

'Er...' Flora's tongue felt clamped to the roof of her mouth, and
she was aware she was staring. 'Yes, yes, she is.'

'At the time of her martyrdom, she was thirteen, or so legend
says,' Miss Finch said, seemingly oblivious to Flora's discomfort.
'Philomena was a Greek princess who was tortured and killed
because she scorned the advances of a Roman emperor. Her
remains were found inside the catacomb of Saint Priscilla in Rome
about a hundred years ago.'

The bustle of the entrance hall diminished to an indistinct
murmur as Miss Finch's melodious voice stirred another place and
time in Flora's head. She had heard that voice before, but where?
And when? She tried to remember, but nothing came.

'Are you all right, Flora?' Bunny said, breaking the spell. 'You
seem – distracted.'

Flora started; aware they were looking at her. 'Er, no.' She
massaged her left temple, self-consciously. 'Just a slight headache.'

'Let me get you something for that?' Miss Finch offered. 'We have an excellent pharmacy here.'

'Th–that's kind, but won't be necessary.' Guilt heated her cheeks at the lie. 'Please, tell us more about your saint.'

'It's quite an interesting story.' She turned back to the statue. 'Philomena's remains were moved to Mugnano, near to Naples. There, several miracles occurred which prompted the Roman Catholic Church to grant her sainthood. A nun there claimed to have seen a vision in which Philomena recounted her entire life story, including her ordeal at the hands of her persecutors.'

'How fortuitous,' Bunny said, his tone sceptical. 'That these revelations should have come from a nun, I mean.'

'Precisely.' Miss Finch sliced a sideways look at him, their thoughts evidently in accord. 'There have been similar claims, but I'm not entirely convinced of their provenance.'

'Well, even if it isn't true,' Flora interjected, relieved to find her voice sounded normal again. 'I quite like the notion of a saint dedicated to babies and children. Is this a Catholic hospital?'

'Not at all. We accept children of all faiths. We even have a separate ward with a kitchen for preparing meals for our Jewish children.' Miss Finch glanced around the now deserted entrance hall with a perplexed frown. 'Oh dear, you appear to have missed the last tour group. Never mind. If you have no objection, perhaps I might show you our facilities myself?'

'We'd be honoured, wouldn't we, Flora?' Bunny prompted.

'Um, yes, of course we would,' Flora agreed, unable to tear her gaze from the woman, who quite fascinated her.

'Splendid!' Miss Finch clapped her hands together. 'Now, where shall we begin?' Then in answer to her own question added, 'The Primrose Ward, I think. It's for patients close to recovery, so you'll be less likely to be exposed to infection.' She gestured them through a set of double doors and led them along an internal corridor painted a cheerful yellow to offset the lack of windows.

Nurses in pristine uniforms bobbed curtseys as they passed, while porters pushing squeaky-wheeled trolleys acknowledged them with respectful nods. A man in a dark overcoat emerged from a door on their right and strode towards them. Solidly built, though not fat, his salt and pepper hair sprouted thickly from a low hairline; a heavy gold watch chain looped across the front of his paisley waistcoat added to his overall air of affluence.

'Ah, Miss Finch.' He lifted his silver-topped cane in salute as he drew level. 'I've left my group in the conference room, availing themselves of the refreshments.' He directed a neutral smile of acknowledgement at both Flora and Bunny. 'I believe we impressed them with our work here, thus I'm optimistic about new subscriptions.'

'That's excellent news,' Miss Finch replied, turning to Flora. 'Allow me to introduce you. Mr and Mrs Harrington, this is Mr Raymond Buchanan, who is a member of our Board of Directors. Mr Buchanan, Mr and Mrs Harrington.'

'It's a pleasure to meet you both.' He shifted his bowler hat into the hand that held the cane and shook Bunny's hand. 'Are you interested in becoming a patron of St Philomena's?'

'Um, well we aren't sure as yet,' Bunny said. 'Although I'm interested to hear how the subscription system works.'

'Well, it's straightforward. Depending on the generosity of your donation, you may have a cot in one ward named after you.' His eyes slid sideways, as if the conversation had served its purpose and he was eager to be off. 'Miss Finch will furnish you with the details. Now, I'm afraid you'll have to excuse me. I'm late for an appointment.'

'Mr Buchanan, before you go, might I have a brief word?' The matron drew him to one side, her head bent close to his as she talked, one hand clenched in a claw-like grip on his arm. He frowned slightly and nodded once or twice in acknowledgment, but his expression remained fixed longingly on the door.

'Come away, Flora.' Bunny tugged her to one side, his voice lowered. 'They obviously wish to talk privately.'

'Not so much a talk, more an argument.' Flora sneaked a look over Bunny's shoulder. 'At least on her part. Whatever she's saying it's important to her. He's not saying much and looks eager to get away.'

'It's none of our business,' Bunny said in a harsh whisper. 'Now stop staring. You've been doing that since we arrived. Which is most unlike you.' His frown dissolved, and he blinked. 'Come to think of it, it's not actually, but you aren't usually so obvious.'

'I know, and it's odd, but I cannot help it. There's something familiar about Miss Finch. Almost as if we've met before but I can't place her – oh, look out, she's coming back.' Flora pretended to study a notice on the wall that explained the dangers of a lung infection from polluted air.

'I'm sorry about that.' Miss Finch rejoined them, though her face was visibly paler, her lips drawn together into a thin line.

'Is everything all right?' Flora asked. Bunny pinched her inner elbow, and she stiffened but her smile stayed fixed.

'Perfectly.' Miss Finch exhaled slowly. 'Simply a minor difference of opinion. Now, where were we? Ah yes, Primrose Ward.'

2

Primrose Ward proved to be a room of almost a hundred feet long across the entire length of the building. A row of square, multi-paned windows ran along one side in walls decorated in pale green and cream, and there was a row of metal bedsteads on each side.

'I've never seen a room with four fireplaces before,' Flora said, impressed.

'We light them all when the ward is full,' Miss Finch explained. 'If not, we can partition it and heat only the required section.'

'How practical.' Bunny acknowledged the three nurses who had sprung to their feet when they entered, striding forward to shake each of their hands, accompanied by one of his charming smiles. Two girls dipped curtseys and flushed a deep red and giggled, while the third girl remained rigid and stared at the floor.

A group of six children played on a brightly coloured rug set before the hearth of a single blazing fire, in front of which a dappled rocking horse was being ridden with enthusiasm by a curly-haired boy of about six. A row of teddy bears sat lined up for a tea party, watched over by two of the nurses, who appeared to be little more than children themselves.

'They don't look ill.' As she took in the children's bright eyes and pink-cheeked faces, Flora wondered how many times they had had to jump to attention that morning for visitors.

'I agree, although you'll find most of them are small for their age,' Miss Finch said. 'Their diet is barely adequate in most cases. These children are about to go home, which is why they are not in their beds. I wish I could keep them here and build them up with clean water, good food and warmth. However, I have no choice but to return them to their homes.' She lowered her voice slightly. 'Most live in dreadful conditions; damp and cramped in most cases, with little heating, and unsanitary water.'

'Can nothing be done?' Bunny's question was almost a challenge.

'A great deal is being done, Mr Harrington.' The matron levelled her steady gaze on him. 'Both by the Salvation Army, and ourselves. It is simply never enough. The pollution from the factories and tanneries in this area makes full health impossible. Most of these children are malnourished and contract infections easily.' Her tone became slightly bitter. 'Then there is the problem of drink. I understand a glass or two is the only respite their parents have.' She exhaled in a long sigh. 'The times I have been forced to hand over a still fragile child, barely able to walk, into the hands of its drunken mother...' Miss Finch's eyes met Flora's and held. 'To watch him cling to her skirts while she plunges from one side of the street to the other. It's a hard sight to banish from one's mind.'

'That must be awful,' Flora said. 'For both you and the child.' Her sympathy rose for an experience beyond her understanding.

'The nurses in pink aprons are the students we train here,' Miss Finch said, regaining her amiable expression.

A girl of about sixteen sat cross-legged on a rug, feigning to drink from a miniature cup and saucer for the benefit of a small group of enraptured children.

'That nurse looks young,' Bunny observed.

'The Board once regarded nursing as a disreputable occupation. That we contaminated young minds by the work we do here.'

'I never thought of nursing as being disreputable,' Flora said.

'You should read what Miss Florence Nightingale said about the abuse her nurses received at Scutari.' A cloud passed across Miss Finch's features. 'But don't pay any attention to me. I can be a bore on the subject when I get started.'

'Not at all. It's fascinating, and noble, if I may say so,' Bunny said, making her smile again. 'What are the primary illnesses you deal with here?'

'Chest complaints mostly. Whooping cough, pneumonia, bronchitis and tuberculosis. We treat a fair number of work-related accidents too; mishaps with machines or delivery boys who fall off carts is something we see regularly.'

A ball rolled across the floor and landed at Bunny's feet. He bent and returned it to a tiny boy who toddled on unsteady legs towards them. He accepted it shyly, all the while staring up at Flora in wonderment.

'It seems cruel for such young children to go out to work,' Flora said.

'Unfortunately, yes. But it's legal for them to be employed nine hours a day from the age of ten.' Miss Finch guided the child back into the circle with a gentle hand.

Flora frowned, embarrassed at her ignorance, and resolved to learn more about the factories south of the river.

'Are these the youngest patients treated here?' Bunny asked, tousling the curls of the boy with the ball, who appeared to have taken a liking to him.

'At one time the governors didn't permit patients older than twelve, or under two years old, but now we treat all ages.'

'Why ever not?' Flora asked, shocked.

'Infants cannot voice their symptoms accurately and require constant monitoring.' Miss Finch shook her head sadly. 'We did not have enough staff. However, that rule has been relaxed in the last few years.'

'I'm glad,' Flora said. The thought of Arthur being denied medical help if he needed it made her blood run cold.

'Even so,' Miss Finch continued. 'Certain illnesses render us helpless. Diphtheria and tuberculosis, for example. All we can do is let the disease run its course.'

Flora blinked rapidly at the thought. How did the staff who faced this harsh reality every day remain optimistic? Her dismay must have shown on her face, for Bunny grasped her hand in a firm, reassuring grip. Miss Finch gave the nurses a 'carry on' gesture, then ushered Bunny and Flora towards the double doors, which opened to reveal a junior nurse. She sent pleading glances to Miss Finch from vivid cornflower-blue eyes. Her distinctive pink apron clashed with a mass of curly red hair caught untidily beneath her cap; hair which, judging by its thickness, must have been a chore to dress each morning.

'Yes, what is it, Nurse Prentice?' Miss Finch turned back to the door.

'Could you spare me some time this afternoon, Miss Finch?' A tinge of desperation lifted her voice.

'I expect so,' she lowered her voice. 'Is it related to what we discussed the other day?'

The girl nodded, her gaze sliding to Flora and back again. 'It's quite urgent.'

Miss Finch's reply was drowned out by a burst of noisy tears from the ward they had just left. The flap of double doors preceded a woman in the black uniform and white cap of a senior nurse. Miss Finch and Bunny set off along the corridor, deep in conversation. Flora was about to follow, then hesitated and hung back when

Nurse Prentice gave a start at the sight of the newcomer. The woman's hand shot out and gripped Nurse Prentice's upper arm, her lips moving and her expression angry.

The nurse flushed a deep shade of red and stared at the floor, but offered nothing in return. The exchange ended as quickly as it had begun. Dismissed, the young nurse bobbed a swift, if awkward, curtsey and fled.

The woman turned an angry gaze on Flora, her chin lifted in neither remorse nor embarrassment. She was younger than Flora had first thought, with dark eyes and an oval face which would have been pretty but for a sour expression.

Refusing to feel shame, Flora returned her defiant stare.

'Are you coming, Flora?' Bunny called from further along the corridor where he and Miss Finch had paused and looked back at her.

'Yes, yes, of course.' Flora pushed the bad-tempered nurse from her mind and hurried after them down a short flight of steps into a half basement. A row of shoulder height windows lifted the gloom, the space filled with the savoury smells of cooked meat and the clang of pots and pans.

'The main kitchen is on this floor,' Miss Finch said unnecessarily. 'The door at the end leads to a rear yard which contains separate buildings for the wash house, a disinfecting oven, and a post-mortem room.' She stopped short as a young man in a faded waistcoat over a striped shirt, the sleeves rolled to the elbows, stepped smartly into their path.

'Pardon me, Miss Finch. I didn't see you there.' A lock of floppy brown hair in need of a cut slipped over one eye. 'I was on my way to—' He paused and frowned up at the ceiling. 'Oh dear, I appear to have forgotten where I was going.'

'This somewhat fey young man is Dr Albert Reeder, our radiologist,' Miss Finch said with an indulgent smile, adding, 'and don't let his air of distraction mislead you. He's a genius and responsible for our X-ray room.'

'Have you brought more visitors to admire my domain?' Dr Reeder rocked on his heels, both hands thrust into his trouser pockets.

A bed occupied the centre of the room beside a series of poles, attached to which was a camera larger than one Flora had ever seen before; the contraption apparently allowed its change to the required height. Attached to the top was a round glass ball that contained what looked like a cylindrical light bulb.

'How intriguing.' Bunny stepped closer. 'I've read about this new technique of photographing bones. I would be most interested to see how it's done.'

'Splendid!' Dr Reeder ushered Bunny inside, though Flora did not move, sensing Miss Finch was also reluctant to enter.

'Is it safe?' Flora whispered.

'I have my reservations.' At Flora's start, she added. 'I accept that progress in diagnostics is valuable in medicine. However, the full effects of these Rontgen rays are still unknown.'

'It doesn't look too intimidating.' Displaying no such doubts, Bunny joined the young doctor where he examined the contraption more closely. 'How does it work?'

'This glass is vacuum-sealed and electricity is passed through this tube here,' Dr Reeder gushed with enthusiasm; his words accompanied by extravagant arm gestures. 'X-rays, or to be accurate, electromagnetic energy waves, are released at the positive electrode. The high-energy rays are synchronised with the camera shutter, so they pass through soft body tissue, but are absorbed by dense material such as bone.' He held up what looked like a sheet of black glass within a metal frame with cloudy white shapes on it. 'That's what the shadowing is on the photographic plate.' He placed a firm hand on Bunny's shoulder. 'I'd be happy to give you a demonstration.'

'That would be excellent, I—' he caught Flora's brief shake of her head, then took in Miss Finch's fixed expression. 'Perhaps another time.'

'I see our esteemed matron's misgivings have made an impression.' Dr Reeder sighed. 'This is an innovation. A major step forward for the medical profession.'

'Tell me, Doctor,' Miss Finch said carefully. 'Do you still pass your hands beneath these rays when you take your pictures?'

'Of course!' He held up his hands, twisting them back and forth in front of his face. 'See? No signs of damage. The rays are invisible and therefore harmless.'

Miss Finch's lips formed a hard line. 'I advise caution with that light, Doctor.'

'It's not merely a light, it's a cathode ray within an evacuated glass bulb, which—'

'I'm cognisant of the science,' Miss Finch cut him off firmly. 'Only that we don't know enough about the long-term effects to be complacent.'

The doctor's shrug dismissed her. 'Whilst we are on the subject, is there any news about moving my X-ray department to a higher floor?' His eyebrows rose into his hairline in eager anticipation. 'The damp down here is injurious to the equipment. We have to spend the first hour of every day drying it out.'

'I've submitted your request to the Board of Governors.' Miss Finch's patient tone implied she had been asked this same question many times. 'All I can do is await their decision.'

'Ah well, I suppose I'll have to be patient.' Dr Reeder released a long-suffering sigh and brushed back the errant lock of hair. 'However, from a diagnostic viewpoint, I make the surgeon's lives easier.'

'I cannot argue on that score,' Miss Finch conceded. 'Now,

please don't let us detain you. You appeared in a hurry to be somewhere a moment ago.'

'Ah, yes.' A light seemed to ignite behind his eyes. 'I remember now. I was on my way to the pharmacy. Good day to you, Miss Finch, Mr Harrington, Mrs Harrington.'

'Are you really worried about him?' Flora waited until he was out of earshot to speak, her gaze on his back as the windows played light and dark patterns on his retreating back.

'I am.' Miss Finch chewed her bottom lip. 'Although I'm a lone voice on the subject. Not in treatment terms, you understand. The ability to take images of bone damage is invaluable. What worries me is the amount of exposure to which men like Reeder put themselves. He works with that equipment for ten hours every day and feels he's immune to what has befallen others. Ernest Wilson for instance.'

'Who?' Flora asked.

'I've heard that name.' Bunny held up a hand as if a thought had just struck him. 'He works at the London Hospital. He's had articles published in the British Medical Journal about X-rays. Fascinating subject.'

'Ernest Wilson is a pioneer of the technique. He's quite brilliant.' Miss Finch sighed. 'But his methods have become careless. He's gradually losing his fingers.'

'You believe these machines do that?' Flora gasped and cast a fearful look at the room behind them.

'Indeed, I do. Unfortunately, not everyone agrees with me.'

'I had no idea.' Bunny massaged his chin with one hand. 'That's quite worrying.'

'Do you use these machines for the children?' Flora asked.

'Rarely, I'm glad to say.' Miss Finch lowered her voice. 'The department is still experimental. Dr Reeder has an agreement with the Board to do his research here but he is not let loose on the children.'

'Glad to hear it.' Flora suppressed a shiver. 'What of his request to move the X-ray room to another floor?'

'And allow his damaging rays to infiltrate the entire hospital?' Miss Finch raised a single sardonic eyebrow. 'Not while I'm matron here. Now, I imagine the other visitors must have left by now, so might I invite you to my office for some refreshment?'

Without waiting for an answer, she mounted the stairs again to the main floor.

'I had no idea you knew about x-rays.' Flora tucked her arm beneath Bunny's as they set off after her.

'I know lots of things.' He pulled her to a halt and slanted a look downwards. 'By the way, you still haven't explained your apparent fascination with the woman.'

'Fascination is a strong word. Perhaps I admire her dedication.' Flora feigned ignorance. She glanced to where she waited for them at the end of the corridor. 'Look sharp, or she'll think we've lost interest in her tour.'

3

Miss Finch's office was at the rear of the ground floor, with a window that looked onto a small garden; a spacious room that was still cosy. A sturdy oak desk sat at right angles to a dresser that took up the whole of the opposite wall, the shelves tightly packed with serious looking leather-bound books.

The same nurse whom Flora had witnessed upbraiding Nurse Prentice turned away disinterestedly as Flora and Bunny were shown in, and with a half sneer, she returned to arranging ledgers in a glass-fronted cabinet.

'Ah, Sister Lazarus.' Miss Finch greeted her. 'You may leave that until later. Would you be so kind as to fetch some tea for both myself and my visitors?' She gestured Flora into an upholstered chair that proved more comfortable than it looked.

Sister Lazarus wore her straight black hair pulled into a severe bun from a centre parting, presenting a narrow, heart-shaped face and exacerbating protruding ears. The black uniform dress on her angular frame, long bony arms, and close-set pebble eyes reminded Flora of a spider. The stiff white cap perched on the back of her head did nothing for her pale complexion and yet she wasn't an unattractive girl, simply awkward; as if uncomfortable in her own skin.

'As you wish, Miss Finch.' She dropped the last ledger onto the desk with a thud and left the room, flint in the glance that she swept over the company. This was the first sign of animosity Flora had detected from a member of the staff towards the matron. Either that, or Sister Lazarus regarded making tea beneath her?

'Please excuse my colleague's manner.' Miss Finch caught Flora's contemplative look at the closed door. 'Sister Lazarus has an unfortunate manner, but she means well. Most of the time.'

'I admire young women who follow a career,' Flora said as she arranged the folds of her skirt. 'I took the first post I was offered as a governess. I never thought to look further.'

'We all come to our station in life through different routes.' The matron's soft gaze settled on Flora. 'I should imagine you were a most capable and conscientious governess.'

'She was.' Bunny broke off from his examination of a row of certificates displayed on a wall and winked at her.

'Where was this?' Miss Finch took her seat behind the large desk, her hands clasped on the tooled leather inlay.

'In the country,' Flora replied. For reasons she could not yet fathom, she was unwilling to reveal too much about herself. 'My former charge is an impressive young man of seventeen now.'

'You must be proud of him, having contributed to building his character?'

'You're right, I am.' Flora certainly felt possessive pride in Eddy's achievements as well as hope for his future.

'Young women these days have more independent spirits, though I fear they venture into dangerous territory,' Miss Finch continued, apparently happy to share confidences. 'Several of my nurses flirt with joining the Women's Social and Political Union.'

'Do you disapprove of votes for women?' Flora addressed Bunny.

'Not at all.' He turned from his scrutiny of the pictures and folded his arms across his chest. 'I encourage this modern thinking, and see women as capable of using the privilege of a vote wisely. Some men believe women would select candidates purely on a handsome face or a well-turned-out suit.'

'If the former were true, Arthur Balfour would never have become Prime Minister,' Flora said.

Miss Finch's resulting laugh was joyous and uninhibited, bringing an admiring smile to Bunny's face.

Flora frowned, transfixed by the sound, struck with a feeling she had heard that same laugh before. But where? And when? Her inability to recall it one way or the other frustrated her.

'I find the militant manifesto of the WSPU causes me some concern,' Miss Finch said when the moment of hilarity passed. 'Mainly because they appear to have commandeered my favourite tea room in Ebury Street, which makes me less than sympathetic.'

'I know of it,' Flora said eagerly. 'Is it called Martell's?'

'The same,' Miss Finch replied, a world of anticipation in the look she levelled at Flora across the desk.

'Is Sister Lazarus a supporter of the suffragists?' Bunny placed his hands on the back of a chair.

'Not that I am aware,' Miss Finch said, thoughtful. 'Though now I think about it, her character is entirely suited to throwing bricks through windows. Perhaps I should suggest she join Mrs Pankhurst's ladies?'

Flora smiled at the image, while Bunny let out a throaty laugh, interrupted by the return of Sister Lazarus with a loaded tray.

'I'm sorry I took so long, Miss Finch.' She paused on the threshold and split a baleful look between them, as if aware their laughter was directed at her. 'A valve stuck on the boiler and I couldn't get the pilot lit for ages.' She plonked over-full cups of murky brown liquid haphazardly on the desktop.

'Er, thank you, Sister.' Miss Finch jerked back her chin, her expression convincing Flora she would have liked to roll her eyes as well, but fought the impulse.

The nurse withdrew, leaving wet footprints on the boards between the door and the rug. Flora surmised the kitchen must be in another building and a trip outside in the rain had been necessary. No wonder she looked bad-tempered.

'Sister Lazarus is an excellent nurse,' Miss Finch flinched as the door slammed shut with a resounding bang. 'She's a stickler for the rules, but lacks warmth, which I find is vital when dealing with children.'

Flora took a sip of the hot, if stewed, tea when a sudden, piercing shriek made her jump. 'My goodness, what was that?' Her cup leapt in her hand, but she settled it without spillage just as the sound of running feet approached.

'It sounded as if it came from the rear yard.' Miss Finch deposited her cup on the desk followed by Flora and then Bunny. 'I'd better see what has happened.'

Flora exchanged a look with Bunny in a silent signal and followed the matron down the hallway.

Halfway down, Miss Finch had stopped at an open door leading into a walled yard surrounded by a jumble of brick buildings. The rain had eased off a short time before but had left tiny puddles between the cobbles.

Miss Finch eased her way to the front of a crowd that had already gathered. Two men in white coats emerged from the main building, both with identical leather aprons which bore ominous stains that Flora assumed were dried blood; one of the men she recognised as Dr Reeder. They took immediate command of the situation and instructed the onlookers to stand aside. No one left their vantage point but simply crowded closer together, blocking whatever had drawn their attention from Flora's gaze.

Flora wondered if they had been summoned, or had they too heard the scream and dashed to investigate?

Doors opened at intervals, revealing curious nurses and kitchen workers who drifted into the yard to see what the fuss was about.

Miss Finch eased her way to the front, issuing impatient requests of 'Excuse me' and 'Let me through,' while Flora and Bunny took advantage of the pathway she had carved to the front of the crowd and eased behind her into a clearing.

The figure of a girl in the distinctive pink apron of a student nurse lay on the ground; face up, arms spread wide and one leg bent at the knee. A wide pool of blood had gathered beneath her head and spread into surrounding rain water, red rivulets moving along the seams in the cobbles in a wide arc.

'It's Nurse Prentice.' Flora inhaled sharply and grabbed Bunny's arm. 'The nurse from Primrose Ward.'

'Don't look.' He pulled her into his side as if to shield her, but his warning came too late and Flora could not tear her gaze away.

'Someone do something! She's been hurt,' whimpered a girl with wild eyes and wispy brown hair. She wore the same pink uniform dress and white apron, her arms wrapped around her waist.

Miss Finch bent and lifted the girl's wrist, then laid it down again. 'How did it happen?' she demanded of the girl, who shook her head but did not respond.

'She weren't here when I went to take me dinner,' a man in overalls said loudly as he eased forward to get a better look.

A wide-hipped female with a ruddy complexion shushed him, while gasps erupted from newly arrived spectators. Murmurings went up among the growing crowd and two student nurses comforted a third who had burst into noisy sobs.

'Didn't anyone see what happened?' Miss Finch demanded.

More mutterings and denials came, and a man in brown, mud-stained coveralls carrying a hoe stepped forward. 'I came through the garden gate a minute ago and saw her lying there.' He looked up as if inviting further comments, but was greeted with only blank stares and shaken heads.

'Looks like she slipped on the wet and hit her head on the kerb there.' Dr Reeder pointed to a raised stone border that enclosed the yard. One of the rough-hewn stones bore streaks of blood on the edge.

'Rubbish, man!' The second doctor had squatted beside the body where he prodded the back of the girl's skull with his fingers. 'There's a depressed fracture of the parietal bone. At a guess I would say she was hit.'

'Hit with what?' Dr Reeder asked, both arms splayed across the yard, empty but for the curious onlookers. 'There's nothing here to have caused it. She must have tripped.'

The walled space was about fourteen feet square, containing nothing but a couple of rain barrels and a small wooden tool hut. The body lay between two low rectangular flower beds with the stone borders Dr Reeder had mentioned.

'I will investigate further when I get the body to the mortuary. The police will have to be informed,' the more senior of the doctors addressed Miss Finch.

Nodding, Miss Finch issued instructions to the porter, then eased backward through the crowd, drawing Flora and Bunny with her. 'It's best you both leave before the police arrive.'

'Don't you want us to wait and talk to them?' Flora chose not to mention it wouldn't be the first time she had had to explain her presence at a scene of death to the police.

'There's no need. You cannot tell them anything. I'll deal with it.

Make your way back to my office and wait there. I'll ask the porter to order you a cab and join you shortly.'

'Don't worry about that,' Bunny said. 'I'll flag one down on the road.'

'You're not likely to find one out on the street.' Miss Finch's raised eyebrow showed the impossibility of this suggestion. 'Cabbies don't wait around in this neighbourhood. I'll ask Forbes to send a runner to fetch one for you.' She ushered them away from where the doctors had been joined by a third, their voices raised in emphatic argument. Dr Reeder gestured to the crowd to go back inside the building, his arms waving as if he were directing traffic.

Slowly the onlookers drifted away, though some took more persuading.

In the matron's office, Flora had resumed her chair while Miss Finch who had since joined them restlessly paced the floor, her jaw clenched tight.

'Miss Finch, if you need to be elsewhere, we quite understand.' Bunny remained standing; an elbow balanced on the mantelpiece. 'Miss Finch?' he prompted when she did not appear to hear him.

'I–I'm sorry?' She swung to face them with a start, her eyes clouded with inner thoughts. 'I beg your pardon, and no, of course I'll remain here until the police arrive. You are my guests.'

'Dr Reeder and that other doctor appeared to differ in their opinions about how the nurse died,' Bunny ventured.

'I shouldn't read anything into that.' Miss Finch leaned a hip against her desk whilst she drummed the surface with restless fingers. 'The doctors here lock horns frequently. It's their way of asserting themselves.'

Flora found her apparent lack of emotion over Nurse Prentice's death surprising. Had she forgotten she had spoken to that same nurse a little while before? Or was that what was troubling her now?

'What do you really think happened, Miss Finch?' she asked unable to shake the feeling there was something wrong about the scene they had just witnessed. At first sight everything seemed uncomplicated. A young girl runs across a rain drenched yard, slips and hits her head on a cornerstone. In most cases it would cause little more than a sore head or momentary unconsciousness. Rarely death.

Flora resolved to look up the term 'parietal bone' when she got home.

'The safety of all the students here is my responsibility. Nor does it make my job any easier that Lizzie Prentice was an orphan.' Miss Finch looked stricken.

'You cannot be held responsible for an accident.' Bunny's brow furrowed, as if he sensed there was more to Miss Finch's distress than she revealed.

'I know, but...' she plucked at the pages of an open ledger on the desk.

'The dead girl was the same young woman who asked to speak to you in the ward,' Flora said. 'She wanted to speak to you urgently.'

Bunny's eyebrows drew together, and he gave a tiny shake of his head, which Flora ignored. She knew that look; it warned her not to ask awkward or leading questions. Not that she ever took any notice.

'I know.' Miss Finch sighed. 'I wish I had not dismissed her. She obviously had something on her mind.'

'Might it have been important enough to get her killed?' Flora asked.

'Flora,' Bunny murmured in warning.

'I really don't know.' Miss Finch wandered to the window again. 'One thing could be entirely unrelated to the other.'

Flora perched on the last three inches of the squab. Did Miss

Finch already know what Lizzie wanted to discuss?

Just then, Sister Lazarus arrived, flinging the door open so hard, the metal knob banged against the wall, forcing Bunny to take a rapid sideways step to avoid being hit. 'The police are here, Miss Finch. They insist on speaking to you. Immediately.' Her pointed chin lifted as she stressed the last word.

'Already?' Miss Finch pushed herself upright. 'That was quick.'

'Mr Forbes went to fetch them. A carriage had overturned on the corner of Marshalsea Road, so they were already close by.'

'Are they in the yard now?'

'No, Miss Finch. The body – I mean Nurse Prentice – has been taken to the morgue, so they have gone there.'

'She was moved?' Miss Finch stared at the nurse with a mixture of annoyed surprise. 'Who presumed to give that instruction?'

'I did.' Sister Lazarus' eyes narrowed. 'I simply thought—'

'You shouldn't have done that, Sister.' Miss Finch massaged her forehead with one hand. 'Don't you know anything? The police need to see where Nurse Prentice died.'

'I apologise.' Sister Lazarus' eyes held no regret. 'Dr Reeder said it was an accident. Anyway, it didn't seem right to leave her lying there for everyone to stare at. It would have been... disrespectful.' Her bland expression didn't reflect the sentiment.

'I suppose there isn't much we can do about it now.' Miss Finch's jaw clenched. 'I'd better come and explain it to the detective in charge of the case.'

'There isn't one.' Sister Lazarus shrugged, her gaze sliding away when Miss Finch glared at her. 'Just a sergeant and a couple of constables.'

Miss Finch closed her eyes briefly but said nothing.

'If it helps,' Bunny said, 'Flora and I will speak to police if it's required.'

'That won't be necessary.' The matron's knuckles whitened as she gripped the edge of the door, lowering her voice. 'Mr Harrington, Mrs Harrington, I apologise for this unfortunate turn of events.' Her straightforward gaze shifted to Flora and held. 'I hope we shall meet again. Perhaps one day later this week at my favourite tea room? It's my custom to go there in the afternoons.' With a last nod, she pulled the door shut behind her, leaving them alone with the inhospitable nurse.

'That sounded like an invitation,' Bunny whispered. 'Will you accept it?'

'I'm not sure.' Flora flicked a look at Sister Lazarus, who clattered the crockery as she re-loaded the tray. The opportunity of meeting Miss Finch again was too strong to resist. What did she wish to say that could not be expressed in front of Bunny? Or was it Sister Lazarus' presence which had prompted her to issue her oblique invitation?

'What a dreadful thing to happen,' Flora gathered her gloves and bag as a prelude to leaving. 'Was that poor girl a friend of yours, Sister?'

'Nurse Prentice was a student, whereas I'm a qualified ward sister.' The stiffening of her shoulders was the only sign she resented being questioned as she hefted the loaded tray in both hands and swung round slowly. 'Fraternisation is not conducive to discipline.' Her upper lip curled, implying Flora had suggested something untoward.

'My apologies.' Flora blinked, wondering if she meant all students, or this one in particular. 'Although we assume you knew her.' She glanced at Bunny, who said nothing, though appeared to study the nurse thoughtfully.

'I did,' Sister Lazarus replied grudgingly. 'She was barely competent as a nurse and was a gossip. I had to reprimand her frequently. Miss Finch can be an excellent administrator but is lenient where the students' behaviour is concerned.'

'I see.' Flora concentrated on buttoning her gloves, having learned from experience that to keep eye contact often stifled confidences. 'I'm sorry we didn't drink your tea after all the trouble you went to.'

'It's no bother. The staff kitchen is only two doors along the hall.'

Whenever Sister Lazarus looked her way, Flora experienced the odd sensation she was being judged by a critical head. A notion which struck her as odd, seeing as Flora had not attended school. Then again, the only headmistress she had met in her life had turned out to be a murderous spy, so perhaps that was the source of her unease?

'I'd better go. The police will probably wish to talk to me.' Sister Lazarus eased backward through the door with the tray, only to be replaced by the porter.

'Your hackney is here, sir, madam.' He hovered for a moment, then when neither Flora nor Bunny made any show of leaving, he inclined his head and set off back the way he had come.

Flora hesitated. 'Are you sure we should leave, Bunny?'

'Normally, no. However, in this case, Miss Finch may have a point.' He grasped Flora's arm and guided her along the corridor towards the main door. 'The police might think it too much of a coincidence that you are in the vicinity when yet another body is found. Discretion is the better part of valour and all that.'

'You know.' Flora quickened her steps to match his on the way back to the front entrance. 'I've never subscribed to the premise of that saying. Discretion means you miss all the most interesting events in life.'

'It doesn't look as if there is anything interesting in this case.' Bunny acknowledged the porter's nod as he held open the door.

Inside the cab, Flora adjusted her skirt over her knees, her attention briefly caught by another hansom which had drawn up beside them. The driver flicked the rein and pulled away, just as Flora got a glimpse of the occupant's profile.

'Bunny,' she said, once he had climbed in beside her. 'That man who was just leaving, didn't Miss Finch introduce him to us? Mr Buchanan, wasn't it?'

'Can't see now. He's gone, but I'll take your word for it.' He closed the wooden flaps with one hand whilst with the other, he knocked on the trap above his head and gave their address to the driver. The hansom jerked forward, pausing at the gates for a carter to pass by, by which time the other hansom was out of sight.

'Didn't he say he was in a hurry to keep an appointment over an hour ago?' Flora asked.

'Come to think of it, he did, yes. Funny that. I saw him in the crowd when Miss Finch suggested we leave.'

'Did you?' Flora turned her head and stared at him. 'How odd.'

'Not really. Perhaps his "I have somewhere to be" was simply an excuse not to have to stand around in corridors making polite talk. He said he had spent the morning showing visitors round. Perhaps he simply needed an excuse to get away.'

'Possibly.' Then what had niggled at the back of Flora's mind resurfaced. 'Did you notice Sister Lazarus' skirt and shoes were wet when she brought in the tea?' At his frown she went on, 'Not all of it, just a few inches of the hem at the front. If the staff kitchen was only two doors from Miss Finch's office, why did she need to go outside in the rain?'

'Most likely because she had to fetch a handyman to fix the pilot light on the boiler.' Bunny braced a hand against the doorframe as the taxi took a sharp corner. 'You aren't the only one who pays attention, you know.'

'I had forgotten that.' Flora slumped against the upholstery, mildly disappointed there was such a simple explanation. 'She's a strange, cold sort of person, didn't you find? For a nurse.'

'Sister Lazarus? I imagine it's necessary for survival in that profession. High emotions must be counterproductive to what they must see. Especially with children.'

'I suppose so.' Flora tried to recall if Sister Lazarus' face was among the crowd gathered round Lizzie Prentice in the yard, but couldn't remember.

'Stop looking for shadows, Flora.' He slid his arm around her shoulders and pulled her closer. 'Don't misunderstand, I enjoy these sojourns into crime, but not everyone you meet is a villain. Accidents happen occasionally.'

'Yes, I suppose you're right.'

By the time the hansom had reached Westminster Bridge, she had resolved to call Lydia when they got home and invite her to tea at Martell's the following afternoon.

4

Flora planted a kiss on Bunny's cheek as she joined him for breakfast the next morning. Soft autumn sunshine flooded through the casement window, with no sign of the previous day's rain lifting her spirits.

He gave her a brief smile before returning his attention to the sheaf of letters in his hand. 'There's a report on Lizzie Prentice's death in this morning's paper if you want to look.' He pushed the newspaper towards her, folded open at the page.

Flora poured herself a cup of coffee, then gave her attention to the *Morning Post*, where a bold headline announced the death of a student nurse at St Philomena's Children's Hospital. In words which suggested they had come straight from Dr Reeder, the journalist reported the girl had slipped on wet cobbles and hit her head on a stone kerb. Below it sat a fuzzy drawing which only vaguely resembled Nurse Prentice.

'Anything interesting in the post?' Flora pushed the paper away and stirred milk into her cup.

'I've received a notice of these Motor Car Act rules that came into force this year.' Bunny tapped the page beside his plate. 'I have to register the new motor.'

'I thought you had already registered the Panhard?' Flora helped herself to a roll from a silver lattice basket the butler had placed beside her hand.

'The system doesn't work like that, I'm afraid. I have to do it all again so they can send me a new number plate to attach to the car.'

'What an odd and cumbersome system. I never see more than one or two motor cars at any one time in the city, so why do they feel the need to keep track of them all? They didn't do that with carriages.' She broke off as the tantalising smell of hot bacon announced their butler's arrival with Bunny's breakfast. 'Are you going to camp out all night like Earl Russell to secure a number you like?'

'That was different. He did that because he was determined to secure the first number issued for any motor. My number twenty-six isn't nearly as prestigious as his A1. Anyway, the fact this system is in place at all shows the combustion engine is here to stay.' He waved his fork in the air as he talked. 'I told you they weren't a fad.'

'Indeed, you did. Just coffee and toast for me, please, Stokes.' Flora stared longingly at the sausages, bacon, tomatoes and fried eggs glistening with butter loaded onto Bunny's plate.

The butler gave her a look loaded with disapproval with his bow of acquiescence as he withdrew.

'Not hungry?' Bunny looked up at her briefly before attacking a sausage.

Flora waved him away. Since the birth of their son, Flora's clothes fitted too snugly for comfort. If she was to return to her former coltish figure, some restraint was necessary.

'About yesterday,' she began, avoiding his question. 'I cannot help thinking we should have waited and talked to the police after that nurse was found.'

'Whatever for?' he said between mouthfuls. 'They would have kept us hanging about all afternoon and it was an accident. I'm not unsympathetic, but we had nothing to tell them.'

'Apart from her brief but intense argument with Sister Lazarus, which no one saw but me,' Flora said, too low for him to hear. She reached for the sugar bowl, but then changed her mind and pushed it away.

'Did you say something, darling?' Bunny looked up briefly from his plate.

'Just agreeing with you over the accident theory. That older doctor didn't concur with Dr Reeder, did he?' Flora sipped her coffee, relaxing as the hot, potent brew revived her laggard spirits.

'I think we have been here before.' Bunny looked up, his blue eyes sparkling behind his glasses.

'Been where before?' she asked, bemused.

'You remember. Our first meeting aboard the *Minneapolis*. When the captain said that chap van Elder had died from a fall, and you insisted he'd been murdered?'

'And I was right, wasn't I?' Flora plucked a triangle of toast from the rack and scraped it with an almost invisible layer of butter. 'Maybe I am on this occasion too?'

'This occasion?' He lifted his knife in her direction before applying it to a slice of bacon. 'Ah, I see how your mind is working. That nurse died a short while after she expressed a wish to talk to Miss Finch and the person who didn't want that to happen disposed of her? Is that what you are thinking?'

'It that so ridiculous?' She nibbled the toast, and tried to pretend it was a hot, meaty sausage, but failed.

'You cannot turn everything into a crime, Flora. Nurse Prentice could have been about to ask for a day off, or an advance on her salary for all we know. For a crime, you need evidence and facts. We have little of either in this case.'

'We?' Flora shifted her voice down an octave. 'You feel there might be a case, then?'

'No, I don't.' Bunny put down his knife and fork and reached for his coffee cup. 'It was an unfortunate, even a tragic death, but nothing to do with us.' His tone remained calm, but a tiny tick appeared in his temple.

'Not yet,' Flora murmured, her gaze on the tiny pulse, which gave a sudden rapid jump.

'I remember what happened the last time you started poking into matters of death and conspiracy? You were almost killed.'

'But suppose—'

'It's not as if you knew her.' He cut her off with a wave and reached for the butter dish.

'No, no, I didn't.' She returned her cup to the saucer with a firm click. Flora hadn't known Marlon van Elder or Evangeline Lange either, but that fact had not prevented her from taking an interest in their respective murders.

She resolved to let the subject of Lizzie Prentice drop for the time being. Then a thought which had occurred to her the day before resurfaced. Discarding her unfinished toast, she rose and approached the bureau that stood in an alcove beside the fireplace.

'I think this registration scheme is good if they can get it right.' Bunny reverted to their previous conversation. 'I predict a time when everyone will use petrol engine vehicles instead of horse-drawn ones.'

'Surely not in our lifetime!' Flora looked up briefly from her crouched position at the bottom cupboard.

'The world is moving faster than we think. I'm not so sure about these other rules the Motor Car Act is trying to impose. Like fines for reckless driving.'

'Isn't that a good thing?' She tutted as several items tumbled out onto the floor, none of which was what she sought.

'Perhaps, but I would like to know who decides what is reckless and what isn't. The good news is that the speed limit has been increased from fourteen miles an hour to twenty.'

'That's good news?' Flora piled the objects haphazardly back into the cupboard, unbent with a grunt, and opened one of the upper drawers.

'What are you doing, Flora?' Bunny twisted to face her with an exasperated sigh. 'Have you lost something?'

'The box of photographs I keep in here. I haven't seen them for a while. It looks as if they might have been moved – ah, no, here they are.' She withdrew a pasteboard box from the second drawer and brought it to the table.

'Those belonged to your fath—I mean Riordan, didn't they?' Bunny wiped his mouth on his napkin and pushed his plate away. 'What do you want with those?'

Flora registered, but didn't react to his slip of the tongue. Occasionally, she too forgot that Riordan Maguire, the man who had raised her as his own, was not a blood relative, so could hardly chastise Bunny for making the same mistake.

'They called them "carte de visit" when I was a child.' She sifted through a pile of sepia images mounted on a thin card, found the two she was looking for and returned the rest to the box.

Bunny rose and skirted the table, studying the pictures over her shoulder.

'That's your mother, isn't it?' He pointed to a photograph of a fair-haired woman perched on a chair in what was obviously a photographer's studio. Lily Maguire met the camera lens with confidence and a hint of a smile, her tightly corseted figure held stiffly upright, her delicate hands demurely clasped in her lap. 'She was a beautiful woman.'

'Yes. She was.' Flora ran a fingernail across another image, this one also of her mother, her legs stretched out in front of her beneath her skirt, one hand on her wide straw hat and her gaze fixed on the far distance. A slightly blurred outline of the house revealed the picture was taken on the ha-ha in the garden at Cleeve Abbey. Flora knew every line and blemish of both photographs, but couldn't remember the woman who had posed for them.

'Why do you keep them in a box? Wouldn't they be better framed and put on display?'

'These are the only copies I have. In the daylight, they will fade and then I will lose her forever.'

'I didn't think of that. What made you want to look at them today?'

'You'll think I'm being ridiculous.' She looked up into his eyes and summoned her courage, willing him not to dismiss her.

'Oh, I don't know,' Bunny mused. 'Ridiculous was when you ordered the removal of a perfectly functional kitchen range and replaced it with one of those new-fangled Windsor models. However, if you recall, I didn't utter a word.'

'You didn't have to.' Flora lifted one eyebrow in his direction. 'The week-long muttering under your breath was clear enough.' She sighed. 'All right, I'll tell you. When I saw Miss Finch for the first time yesterday, I had this strange feeling she was my mother.'

'That's not likely, Flora.' The enquiring light in his eyes faded immediately to scepticism. 'Lily Maguire went missing nearly twenty years ago. No one knows what happened to her.'

'I know that.' She tapped the image with a fingernail. 'But take another look. Don't you think Miss Finch looks like an older version of this woman? There's something about her eyes which struck me as familiar. Unnervingly so.'

'You've always said you didn't remember your mother.' He sighed, took the photograph from her and peered at it as if he hadn't seen it a dozen times. 'I suppose this could be what Miss

Finch might have looked like when she was younger. Which doesn't make her the same person.'

Flora bit her bottom lip, wishing she hadn't broached the subject at all, but what she had felt yesterday was too strong to be ignored and she needed him to understand.

'I suppose the shape of the face is similar.' He studied the photograph again. 'I cannot recall the colour of Miss Finch's eyes but it's hard to see a similarity in a sepia photograph.'

'They were blue-green.' Flora's hope that he might have seen something in the woman's face faded to disappointment. 'You think I'm imagining it don't you?'

'I agree there's a resemblance, but no more.' Handing the photograph back to her, he massaged her shoulder with one hand. 'It's possible that having become a mother yourself recently, you think about your own mother more?'

'You've been reading those psychoanalysis articles again, haven't you?' She cut a swift sideways look up at him.

He bent so his cheek rested against her hair. 'How can a stranger have affected you so strongly?'

'I cannot explain it. When I saw her in that hall, so serene, almost angelic in her uniform, I recognised her. I knew exactly how her voice would sound too.'

'And did it? Sound as you expected?'

'You'll think I'm mad, but yes. Yes, it did. That's why I was so taken aback.'

'I see.' His tone intimated he was about to persuade her otherwise. 'Even when the housekeeper at Cleeve Abbey explained about the night your mother died? What was her name?'

'Amy Coombe,' Flora replied, conscious he was not taking her seriously.

'That's the one. Her father argued with your mother the night she disappeared.'

'Everyone thought Amy's father had killed her in a drunken rage and hidden the body.'

'What other explanation could there be?' His arm tightened around her; his voice lowered to a little above a whisper. 'If she still lived, why would she have stayed away from you for so long?'

'I don't know.' She leaned into him, comforted by the smell of his skin and the cologne he wore. 'What if she survived Sam Coombe's assault?' Bunny inhaled as if about to interrupt her, but she rushed on, 'No, listen. Coombe was questioned by the police, but he maintained she had simply left. They couldn't charge him with anything because her body was never found, and naturally he wouldn't admit to it.' She took a deep, shuddering breath as the half-formed hope surged inside her. 'What if she – I mean perhaps —' she broke off, unable to finish the thought.

'She's dead, Flora. She must be. I don't want you harbouring false hope. It will eat away at you.'

Dismayed, she returned the cards to the box and replaced the lid just as a discreet knock preceded Milly, the nurserymaid, who paused in the doorframe, her face as expressionless as a mannequin in Selfridges shop window. Didn't the girl ever smile?

'Master Arthur has been dressed and fed, Mrs Harrington, if you wish to visit the nursery.' She bobbed a brief curtsey and waited; her gaze fixed somewhere above Flora's head.

'Thank you, Milly. I'll be up in a moment,' Flora replied, dismissing her.

'What was that about?' Bunny scowled as the door closed. 'You aren't usually so terse with the servants? Has she annoyed you?'

'I have arranged set times for my visits.' At his incredulous look, she shrugged. 'It's the only way I ever get to see the baby. She would keep me out of the nursery altogether if she could.'

'What do you mean?' Bunny's brusque tone demanded an explanation. Stokes could have set up a wine shop in the cellar, for all Bunny would have noticed, but anything concerning the well-being of their son required his full attention.

'Her manner makes me feel as though our son is like a new toy I'm not allowed to play with. Milly chooses his clothes and decides which toys he plays with and when.'

In Flora's opinion, Milly was too young to bear the responsibility of their precious new baby, though Bunny had insisted she was well qualified. If only she was more animated; surely babies needed smiles and happiness around them?

'He's not yet five months old, darling,' Bunny chuckled. 'He doesn't play with toys yet apart from the soft and furry kind.' He returned to the table and shuffled his papers into order, apparently having lost interest in the subject.

Flora sighed in frustration. The teddy bear Flora had bought was missing from his crib when she visited, replaced by a surprised looking bunny rabbit. Its appearance always made her feel rejected, although the baby could not know the difference.

'I took him to the park in his perambulator the other day,' Flora persisted, conscious she sounded petulant. 'On my return, Milly informed me I kept him too long in the London air.'

'Should I discharge her?' He peered at her over his spectacles, though a smile twitched the corner of his mouth.

'Er, no, don't do that.' The idea had instantly appealed, only to be rejected again, replaced by practicality. 'Good nursery staff aren't easy to find. Besides, she's efficient, and even I have to admit, Arthur's thriving.'

'Then you mustn't let her bully you.' He slid the papers into a well-worn leather briefcase that sat on an empty chair.

'Sally tells me the same thing. She doesn't like Milly much either.' Flora's lady's maid was a forthright young woman engaged partly because her mother-in-law disapproved. Flora had never regretted her decision, for Sally Pond had proved an asset during an encounter with a murderer the previous year. She couldn't imagine life without her now, despite the girl's forthrightness.

A discreet knock at the door, followed by a cough, preceded the return of Stokes.

'Mr Osborne has arrived, madam. I've shown him into the study to await your convenience.'

'Thank you, Stokes.' Flora glanced at the ormolu clock on the mantle as the butler withdrew. 'He isn't due for another half hour.'

'Where is William taking you on this treat?' Bunny hefted the briefcase in one hand and made for the door.

'You've just answered your own question. He says it's a surprise.' Flora moved to the window that overlooked the street. 'Now I know why he's early. He's come to show off his new acquisition.'

Bunny crossed the room in three brisk strides and gave a sharp intake of breath at the sight of a gleaming motor car that stood at the curb. 'Good grief, it's a Spyker!'

'A what?' Flora blinked at the admiration in Bunny's eyes, which reminded her of an intensity he normally reserved for her.

'I suppose it is quite pretty,' she said, feeling a need to show some enthusiasm for the motor car, which now had several passers-by gathered around to admire it. 'I like the emerald green colour with the black outlines on the doors.'

'She's more than pretty. Beneath that bonnet is an eighteen-horsepower engine, a pressed steel chassis with solid axles and an advanced suspension system of elliptic leaf springs.'

'Well, of course, that makes it all so much clearer.' Flora rolled her eyes and reached up to plant a kiss on his cheek. 'And now I know you'll be happily occupied with William's new toy. I can spend a few moments with Arthur before we leave.'

'You still cannot bring yourself to call him Father, can you?' His words halted her at the door, but she did not reply, simply sent him a warm smile and left the room.

She adored William and revelled in his company, but to give him the status Riordan Maguire could no longer claim struck her as a betrayal. It would be as if she had negated all the memories of the man who had loved her. William was, well, William; the dashing young man who had made flying visits during her childhood to his three nieces, his arms full of gifts and always with a ready story to tell four girls entranced by the handsome, romantic man who flitted in and out of their lives. Riordan may not have been her blood, but he deserved the respect due to a loving parent, which was how she would always remember him.

Flora paused at the landing window just as Bunny descended the front steps onto the street and joined William. Though the day was warm, her father wore a full-length camel overcoat, a long yellow scarf wrapped around his neck and a flat leather cap with a pair of driving goggles perched on the peak.

William gesticulated as they circled the machine, while Bunny, a hand cradling his chin, gave an occasional nod.

The sight of his handsome face made Flora wonder what he would think of her theory about Lily Maguire. If the two came face to face after all this time, would he recognise the girl he had once loved?

A more insidious fear intruded as she stared down at William. What if these unresolved feelings about her mother were turning to an unhealthy obsession? Or had she been reading too much of Bunny's copy of Sigmund Freud's *The Psychopathology of Everyday Life*?

'Who are you really, Alice Finch?' she murmured, her breath forming an opaque film on the window glass.

5

The heat of London's summer with its glaring sunlit pavements and wilting trees had changed to crisp autumn air beneath a pale blue sky. Flora settled onto the buttoned leather bench of the Spyker, a blanket over her knees, while William cranked the starting handle.

After several false starts, the engine purred and spluttered into life, prompting William to throw up a fist in triumph then dash around the bonnet and into the driving seat.

'Where are we going?' Flora snuggled into the blanket he had thoughtfully provided.

'It's a surprise.' He pulled his goggles down over his eyes and grabbed the wheel in both hands. 'All I will reveal is that it's not far away.'

The motor car lurched forward into the centre of the road, took a sharp left turn into Lyall Street, then a screeching right into Sloane Square, narrowly missing the rear wheel of a horse-drawn hansom.

'Manoeuvres well, doesn't she?' William shouted above the

discordant honk of an irate motor taxi driver forced to the side of the road.

Flora flinched as a hansom veered across their path. 'I'm not accustomed to travelling at this speed.' She bit down on her bottom lip, hoping the couple taking a leisurely walk in Sloane Square would not choose that moment to cross the road. 'We pass everything so quickly that I cannot focus. I sense a headache coming on.'

'Don't be so grumpy, Flora.' William took one hand off the steering wheel and give her shoulder a friendly shove. 'Not like you to be so unadventurous. I thought you would love it.'

'Sorry, I don't mean to be miserable, and I'm enjoying the ride. In a way.' Her heartbeat raced as a green and gold Harrods delivery van made a last-minute dash for a gap in the traffic. 'Could you slow down a teeny bit before we hit something?' The thought of a resultant tangle of spindly equine legs mixed in with wheel spokes made her stomach knot. London horses led a hard life and were, without exception lean and nervous looking. One advantage of motor vehicles was that fewer animals would have to spend their days pounding hard roads for hours, never seeing a field or a hill, only to die from overwork far earlier than they should.

A gust of wind lifted Flora's scarf and blew the end across her face. 'What prompted you to arrange this mysterious excursion?'

'It's an expression of my gratitude.' He grinned wryly at her, his eyes sparkling from behind his round driving goggles. 'I never imagined that I would become a grandfather, and I'm so delighted. I wanted to spoil you.'

His words scraped at her heart, and an image of Riordan Maguire loomed into her head. She tucked the errant scarf back in place, avoiding his eye so he wouldn't see the tears that had sprung in her own. Whenever she felt her baby's soft cheek beside hers, she was struck again with fresh pain that Riordan would never see him. 'He's watching over you,' people told her, but the words meant little. Death was stark, inevitable and eternal. Riordan was gone. Just like poor Lizzie Prentice.

'Did you hear me, Flora?' William shouted above traffic noise as they idled at a crossroads.

'What? Oh, of course I did.' She forced her thoughts back to the present. 'And it was hardly necessary. Your mother's diamond necklace was thanks enough.' Flora's first thought had been what William's late mother would have thought of his giving the precious Osborne diamonds to his illegitimate daughter. 'And you realise Arthur is nearly five months old?'

'Indeed, but I needed time to arrange something different. Hedges Butler came up trumps in the end.'

'Who is Hedges, and what has his butler got to do with anything?' Flora called to him over the noise of the engine and multiple clops of hooves on the surrounding road.

William laughed as the motor car sprang away from the corner and took another stomach lurching turn. 'That's his name. Frank Hedges Butler. I've said enough already. Wait until we get there. It's not far now.'

'This is Chelsea Bridge Road.' Flora stared round at the street they had turned into. 'Are you taking me to watch the polo at Ranelagh Gardens?'

'No, I am not, but you are half-right. Now be patient. You'll see soon enough.' They rolled through a set of iron gates and negotiated a long gravel drive, where William brought the vehicle to a halt.

'There! Wasn't that a splendid run?' He relaxed against the leather upholstery and removed his gloves. 'What are you smiling at?'

'You.' Flora giggled. His boyish enthusiasm was infectious, making times like these easier. Their relationship could still be awkward, lacking the shared memories that accompanied a lifetime's parenting. She hoped this occasion might be a special moment she could store away to be relived in the future.

'At least the weather hasn't let us down.' William cocked his chin at the sky, but offered no explanation. 'Not a cloud in sight and little wind.'

'Which applies to what exactly?' Flora felt warm in her heavy coat and unwound her scarf from her neck. 'Shooting birds?'

'They haven't shot a pigeon here for a long time.' He shoved his goggles onto the peak of his cap, patting her knee through her coat. 'All will be revealed soon. Just you watch.'

'Watch what? There's nothing here, apart from those people in that field over there.' She nodded to where a group of men surrounded something laid on the grass between them that resembled a misshapen sheet, large, flat and shapeless. Then her idle glance turned to fascination as the sheet billowed slowly from the ground and rippled along the entire length as if it were breathing.

'Goodness, what is that?' Her breath caught as the object bulged, filled and lifted off the ground in a massive teardrop shape as it grew. Below it hung an oversized square basket attached to the base by a series of ropes. The entire contraption rose several feet into the air before settling back onto the grass.

'It's a balloon!' Flora stared, transfixed.

'Welcome to the Aero Club.' William grinned, evidently pleased with himself. 'She's called The City of New York. Hedges Butler's pride and joy.'

'He gave his balloon a name?' Flora stared, entranced, at the massive inflatable as it strained against a network of ropes slung over it like a giant fishing net. 'How does it just hang there like that in mid-air?'

'The envelope, which is the technical term for the canvas part, is filled with coal gas. It's lighter than air, so as long as it's full, the balloon stays afloat,' William said. 'The view from sixty feet up is magnificent.'

'You intend going up in that thing?' Flora turned an incredulous look in his direction.

'Of course.' He opened his door and leapt onto the ground. 'And you're coming with me.'

'Me?' Flora froze in place, but excitement stirred inside her. Could she?

Flora stared in wonder at the now fully inflated balloon that hovered ten feet off the ground, its elongated shadow spread across the grass. The crowd stood around it in a semi-circle, necks craned as if the object were a divine deity to which they paid homage.

'It's perfectly safe.' William walked around to her side of the car and opened her door. 'Besides, it's tethered to the ground, so only goes in one direction. Up.'

'That's what I was afraid of,' Flora murmured, taking the hand he extended to assist her onto the running board.

Still stunned, she offered only mild resistance as he drew her across the grass that squelched beneath her boots after that morning's rain. A handsome man who looked to be in his late twenties occupied a folding wooden seat set on the grass, his knees splayed and several coiled hemp ropes piled up beside him.

He rose when he spotted them approach and kept rising until he towered over them. Bunny was almost six feet tall, but this man must have been half a foot taller. His thick, dark brown hair matched his heavily fringed eyes, lightly tanned skin, and a full moustache over a sensual mouth.

'Flora, allow me to introduce you.' William nudged her forward. 'Charles, this is my daughter, Flora Harrington. Flora, the Honourable Charles Rolls.'

'Ah, so this is the lady about whom I've heard so much?' Flora's hand was clutched in his large, firm one, her skin prickling through two layers of gloves. 'Delighted to meet you at last.'

Flora's cheeks warmed as she stared up into deep brown eyes. She inclined her head, but her tongue wouldn't work and she only murmured something unintelligible.

'Charles is a motor car fanatic, just like Bunny and me,' William said. 'He has a keen interest in balloons and aeroplanes as well.'

'Bunny imagines a ride in the quiet streets of Richmond an adventure,' Flora said. 'But an aeroplane!'

'Osborne here says you might like a trip up in The City of New York?' Mr Rolls clapped his gloved hands together with a muffled thump.

Flora was about to inform him that 'like' wasn't a word she would have used, but Mr Rolls did not appear to expect a response. He led her firmly towards the basket, the side of which almost reached her shoulders, a row of sandbags hanging at intervals from the rail.

'Not nervous, are you?' He gestured she mount the short set of wooden steps.

'What an idea.' Her voice shook slightly, but she was determined not to appear nervous in front of this impressive man, nor disappoint William when he had gone to all this trouble.

Suppressing a shiver, she hitched up her skirt and stepped over the rounded edge of the basket, her hand immediately grasped by the male occupant who helped her inside. Now she knew what a cat in a basket felt like.

'Mrs Harrington, meet Frank Hedges Butler.' Mr Rolls drew her attention to the solidly built, middle-aged man in an overcoat. 'He's the owner of this magnificent example of scientific engineering.'

'Nice to see another young lady take to the sport.' His fleshy face creased into a welcome smile, then widened as he caught sight of William climbing in behind her. 'Osborne, my dear man, glad you made it.'

'Do you take many ladies up in your balloon, Mr Hedges Butler?' Flora asked as Mr Rolls leapt in beside them with remarkable grace for such a tall man.

'Indeed, yes, my daughter Vera adores sky-sailing, and Charles' sister, Lady Eleanor Shelley is also a keen balloonist.' He slapped the rail of the basket with something like affection. 'There'll be just the four of us, my dear,' he continued, then as if sensing her unease added, 'Don't worry, we shan't be going anywhere. The balloon is tethered.'

Despite hearing this assertion twice in quick succession, Flora was not reassured.

'The atmospherics are perfect right now with no ambient wind, so you won't be buffeted about too much.' Mr Rolls' smile revealed even teeth.

'I was hoping not to be buffeted at all.' Flora attempted a light laugh, though no one appeared to hear her.

A man in workman's overalls and a flat cap gestured from the other side of the basket. Hedges Butler patted Flora on the shoulder. 'Excuse me, my dear, my engineer wishes me to help him check the ropes. Sometimes I think they don't trust me with my equipment.' His wide shoulders shook with a baritone chuckle as he turned to Mr Rolls. 'Charles, would you help me look at the envelope? It's stretched a little on one side.' With a last nod, the pair climbed back down the steps again.

'Don't look so panicked,' William whispered in Flora's ear. 'They're simply being cautious.'

Flora smiled weakly, irritated that he seemed to sense an anxiety she was doing her utmost to hide. 'Though I quite like your Mr Rolls.' She nodded to where he stood with Mr Hedges Butler, his impressive frame bent towards the older man.

'He's a remarkable fellow, isn't he? Did I mention he's walking out with Vera? The daughter of Hedges Butler?'

'How interesting.' It occurred to her she and William were alone in the basket, which could leave the ground at any moment. 'Not that I'm interested in Mr Rolls. I'm a married woman, remember?'

'Really? No interest, eh? Then why did you blush when he held your hand?'

'Nerves. And what exactly have you told them about me?'

'Not much. Other than when you're around, there's usually a body somewhere close by.'

Flora gasped in protest, but his wide grin told her he was joking. However, this rendered any mention of Nurse Prentice's death out of the question.

'Everyone ready?' Mr Hedges Butler's enthusiastic inquiry was greeted with a loud and keen agreement from the men, but a strangled groan from Flora. 'Release the winch!' he ordered the two workmen who guarded the ropes.

Flora held her breath as the basket gave a sharp sideways jerk, then eased away from the earth and rose slowly into the air. She squeezed her eyes shut and clung to William's arm with one hand, the fingers of the other hooked over the edge of the rail.

'Isn't it exciting?' William's tone challenged her to contradict him.

'I don't know, I can't bear to look!' Flora huddled closer, inhaling the rich, spicy scent of his cologne, hoping the wicker floor was sturdy enough not to collapse under her feet and send them all plunging to the ground.

William chuckled. 'I haven't spent four guineas on tickets for you not to see anything. Look at this magnificent view!' He wrapped an arm around her shoulders and drew her close into a rough hug.

Slowly, Flora prised open her eyes, and instantly her breath caught in her throat. The rectangular gardens lay beneath them like a green blanket crisscrossed with trees and hedges. A grey-brown ribbon wound around the perimeter on which toy-like cars and horse-drawn vehicles raced along at speed.

'Well?' William asked gently. 'What do you think?'

'I cannot think,' Flora exhaled in a rush. Her fear dissolved and exhilaration filled her chest. 'It's amazing.' The wicker creaked beneath their weight, and a chilly breeze caressed her cheeks, making her nose run.

The basket jolted as the thick rope tether went taut, then thankfully held as its upward movement halted sharply, leaving the entire contraption suspended above the ground. Flora craned her neck to study the vast bulge of the balloon that hung above them, its base level with the tops of trees where the leaves had changed their summer colours to shades of gold, red, and brown.

'It doesn't seem real.' Flora stared at the ground far below them. 'It's so quiet up here and everything looks like a toy model.' Wide-eyed, she located the River Thames, on which rafts of barges and tugboats jostled for position between the Chelsea Embankment and the Middlesex side.

A seagull appeared in line with her shoulder, its wings spread and head turned to stare at her in quizzical surprise as it glided by.

'I don't know what I'm doing up here either,' Flora whispered, a giggle in her throat. The bird gave a shriek of protest, banked higher and disappeared into a tiny silver 'v' in the distance.

A light tap came on her shoulder, making her jump. She turned to see the handsome face of Charles Rolls beaming down, a full champagne glass held out to her.

She summoned the confidence to release her grip on the rail and took the glass with murmured thanks. 'When I got up this morning, I never imagined I would drink Champagne in a balloon.'

'Can you think of a better way to spend an early autumn morning?' Charles grinned and handed the second glass to William.

'I wish Bunny was here!' she whispered, once Charles had moved away. 'He would love this.' She took her first sip, her eyes closed as the bubbles fizzed on her tongue and once settled, the velvety, sweet apple and slightly floral taste followed.

'I invited him, actually.' William tapped the rim of his glass gently against hers. 'He said he wanted us to enjoy this first experience together. Next time, perhaps.'

Flora's smile froze on her face at the thought Bunny knew exactly what William had planned. She would have a few strong words for him when she got home. Or maybe it was better this way, or she might have found an excuse not to come.

After two glasses of champagne, she no longer felt the sting of the wind on her cheeks, experiencing a sense of disappointment when the balloon was lowered to the ground.

'I would love to do that again,' she declared as William helped her climb out of the basket. She staggered slightly but blamed that on the sense of light-headedness the balloon had given her as opposed to the champagne.

'I knew you would.' William squeezed her shoulders before drawing her towards Mr Hedges Butler, Charles Rolls and others whose names Flora couldn't remember to take their farewells.

'I liked your Mr Rolls,' Flora observed again on their way back to Eaton Place. 'He's quite an adventurous character. I hope Mr Hedges Butler's daughter is of the same mind.'

'Indeed, she is, although I doubt they'll take their friendship as far as marriage.' William turned a corner so fast, he startled a horse pulling a cart on Chelsea Bridge Road.

'It's not unheard of for young people who share the same interests to forge a life together.' Flora responded.

'Charles is far too focussed on his adventures,' William replied.

'He's got a scheme in mind to go into partnership with some chap called Royce. Charles claims he's the best engineer in the world and together, they plan to build the most luxurious motor car ever seen.'

'He sounds like Bunny. Or at least the way Bunny used to when he still hoped to make his living from the manufacture of motor cars.' Had they not married and had a child, perhaps he would have been free to follow his own fate.

'I know what you're thinking, Flora.' William took his eyes off the road to glance at her. 'Don't torture yourself. Bunny is the happiest young man I know.'

'Really?' She hoped she didn't sound too desperate.

'He's found his rightful place in that law firm. He told me he would like to move from corporate to criminal law and try actual cases. When the next grisly murder takes place, you'll be seeing his name in the papers.'

Flora gave a short, nervous laugh. 'Defence or prosecution?' With an effort, she pushed away the image of Lizzie Prentice, whose death she was still not convinced was an accident.

'Ah, now that I cannot tell you, you'll have to wait and see.'

William braked hard, as a man in a Homburg had stepped smartly off the kerb and into the road without looking.

Flora gasped, causing her to grab the edge of the windscreen to prevent being thrown against it.

William stood up in his seat and shook his fist. 'We no longer have to employ a man carrying a red flag to walk ahead of cars, my good man! Might I suggest you look where you are going?'

'William! You don't have to abuse the poor man.' Flora giggled as she offered the culprit an apologetic smile, shocked at how aggressive William had become while seated behind a wheel. He was normally so passive. 'This isn't Hyde Park Corner. I don't expect he sees a motor car in these streets often,' Flora ventured as they set off again, leaving the astonished man staring after them from the pavement.

'I suspect that's going to change.' William pulled the car up outside the Eaton Place house and turned off the engine. 'Well, after the best surprise outing ever, am I going to be invited to luncheon?'

'Of course you are.' She climbed out onto the pavement, wondering why everything seemed to move. 'Perhaps I should have more adventure in my life?'

'Or less champagne.' William laughed as he guided her up the steps to the front door.

6

Once Bunny had gone back to his office after luncheon, Flora had asked Stokes to serve their coffee in the conservatory, which overlooked the walled town garden. She and William settled in white painted chairs warmed by the winter sun and a pot-bellied stove set at the far end.

'That girl seems to like you,' Flora observed with a hint of resentment when Milly had complied with her request to bring the baby down to see his grandfather. 'She actually blushes in your company and forgets what she's about to say.'

'The fact you refer to her as "that girl" tells me you have not warmed to her.' William lifted the baby level with his face and through pursed lips blew bubbles against Arthur's rounded cheek as he squirmed and babbled excited, incomprehensible noises.

'Is it so obvious?' Flora said, dismayed she was so readable. She had hoped to present an enigmatic façade to her staff, but it appeared she had failed.

'Has it occurred to you she's intimidated by you?' He lowered Arthur and attempted to set him on his lap, but the baby's chubby legs refused to bend, leaving him precariously balanced on

William's thighs. He winced as a small hand gripped the hair behind one ear and tugged. Head bent, he carefully prised chubby fingers away, but thinking it was a fine game, the baby let out a shout and grabbed a forelock with his other hand.

'By me?' Flora bit her bottom lip to prevent a laugh. Apparently, all it took was a small baby to render an impressive man like William totally helpless. 'Why would she be? I give her a free hand in the nursery.'

'Silly girl. You're her employer, the mistress of this elegant house with every advantage in the world. This is her first position, and she wants to make a good impression.' William held onto the wriggling small body as Arthur enthusiastically mouthed his chin.

'He's teething.' Flora had imagined no one would be intimidated by her. Even a maid.

'So I see.' He set the baby back on the blanket laid out for him on the floor. Arthur wobbled a little at first but soon righted himself. 'Goodness, he's sitting up on his own.'

'His latest achievement. That and two bottom teeth.'

'I must come around more often.' He bent over Arthur's thatch of thick, red gold hair. 'He grows so fast.'

'You would be very welcome, you know that.'

'You've been quiet since luncheon, Flora. Is something wrong?' He adjusted his jacket where it had been rucked up by the baby's feet. 'Apart from stern-faced nursery maids, I mean.'

'Have I? I didn't realise. And not wrong exactly, but something has been on my mind lately. Would you be offended if I asked you to tell me about my mother?'

'Your mother?' His expression was unfathomable. 'What do you want me to say?'

'I know that you both wished to marry, but Lady Vaughn had other plans for her younger brother and persuaded you to leave the country. Which was pretty poor of you though I have since forgiven you.'

'Glad to hear it.' He chuckled as Arthur banged two wooden bricks together with a loud rhythmic clack. 'I've regretted my actions so often since then. I should have had the strength to defy society and make her my wife.'

'You were young, only nineteen, and Mother was younger. It's easy to do what's expected of you at that age and not have the courage to defy convention. I understand that. I know the sad, hard part, William. What I'm more interested in are the times the two of you were happy. What was my mother really like when she was young and daring enough to seduce her employer's brother?'

'Is that what she did?' An amused frown appeared between his brows. 'Lily, well she was impulsive, adventurous, even rebellious.' His lips twitched into a smile as if he recalled memories. 'Much like you, actually.' Flora's cheeks warmed at what he obviously meant as a compliment. 'I spent the summer after my first year at university at Cleeve Abbey when Venetia was still recovering from the birth of Jocasta.' A shadow crossed his features as his mind drifted back over the years. 'My sister had a rough time and George was worried about her. She had lined up the servants on the front drive to greet me, but all I saw when I climbed out of the carriage was this devastatingly pretty fair-haired girl leaning out of an upper window staring at me. When our eyes met, I gave her what I thought was my most charming smile, but she poked out her tongue and slammed the window shut. I was completely smitten from that moment and determined to find out who she was.'

'And when you discovered she was your sister's lady's maid? What then?'

'It didn't matter a jot. All I wanted was to spend every moment in her company. Lily's role had been temporarily usurped by a stern martinet of a nurse, so Lily and I were largely left to our own devices. I don't think anyone noticed we spent all our time together. Or if they did, no one said anything to me.' He reached for his coffee cup, but didn't drink from it, simply held it in his slim, tanned fingers. 'The Abbey was a country idyll then, where the hot summer days were clear and bright,' he went on in a voice softened by happy memories. 'We would sneak into town on the governess cart for afternoon tea, or go for long walks in the woods, making sure we returned separately, of course. There was no need to ask for trouble.'

'When did it end?'

'Christmas.' His brow furrowed then, as if the wonderful memories had turned sour, released a long sigh and stared off over the garden. 'The smell of pine needles still makes me sad. Anyway, George threw a lavish party to celebrate the season and Venetia's recovery. He invited the entire neighbourhood, festooned the house with candles and a massive tree was set up in the front hall. The sour-faced nurse was no longer in residence, and Venetia had put on a little weight, so Lily was kept busy making alterations to her best gowns.'

'Something I have been trying to avoid.' Flora patted her own midriff.

'Rubbish! You're as slight as a schoolgirl.'

'That's kind, but not accurate,' Flora said, though the compliment pleased her. 'Go on, you were telling me about the last time you saw Lily.'

'It wasn't the last time, but we parted on Christmas Eve 1876. We arranged to meet in the orangery after dinner, but when I arrived, she had obviously been crying. That's when she told me she was expecting.'

Flora was tempted to ask how he took the news, but knowing what came afterward, resisted.

'I was shocked, of course,' William went on. 'Delighted too, although I knew there would be hell to pay. Lily insisted she must go away, but I didn't see it was necessary when I could leave university and we could live perfectly well on my allowance.'

'Which didn't happen.' Flora sighed as she contemplated how different her life might have been if it had. Different, but not better. Lily had married Riordan Maguire, who although devoted to Flora, wasn't her real father.

'No. George's mother was alive then and the old harridan simply wouldn't hear of her daughter-in-law being related to a lady's maid. Venetia was outraged at the idea as well, but given time I might have been able to convince her. The trouble was, my sister wasn't strong enough to resist the dowager Countess, mainly because she had already disgraced herself.'

'Disgraced?'

'She had given George three daughters in five years, but no son and heir to continue the Vaughn name, which was considered a failure as far as the family was concerned.'

'Did you even attempt to persuade them?'

William blinked in shock. 'Of course I did! I argued and cajoled all that holiday, but there was no shifting them. They saw it as a youthful indiscretion, which had to be swept aside so I might lead the life they all had envisaged for me.' He exhaled in a sigh. 'The life I saw for myself too I suppose. While I was still fighting the family, I was told Lily had married Riordan.'

'She was having a child; she couldn't wait for you to decide.' Flora couldn't keep the frustration out of her voice.

'I know that, but I was angry and upset. I blamed her for giving in and marrying someone else. I was young, arrogant and stupid.' William's eyes clouded as he followed the progress of a sleepy bumble bee which hovered over a clump of lavender. It was as though he had forgotten she was there. Finally, he spoke again. 'George suggested I go to Boston to complete my education and then run the family business. I jumped at the idea. I had this misplaced notion I was the victim; the one who had been abandoned and rejected as not good enough.' He propped an elbow on the arm of the peacock chair, leaned his cheek against his hand and slid his gaze towards her. 'Why do you want to know all this, Flora?'

'I thought it was time.'

Arthur grabbed the hem of her skirt, apparently tired of being ignored. Flora bent to disentangle his fingers, swapping the fabric for a stuffed penguin, which the baby attempted to shove into his mouth, making both Flora and William laugh. 'Would you rather not talk about those days?'

'I don't know.' William nudged the baby gently with the toe of his shoe, sending Arthur into an outburst of delighted chuckles. 'I never have, so it's a novel experience for me. I don't come out of it well, do I?'

'No, you don't.' She injected a hint of rebuke into her voice. 'Mainly because having you as a father means I'm not descended from the Ulster Scots when I had woven this romantic Celtic heritage around myself.'

'Ah, sorry about that. I'm purebred Home Counties and your mother was born in Surrey.'

'Exactly.' Her smile faded as another thought struck her. 'William? Would you rather have distanced yourself from me when the truth came out? After all, you chose not to have a family of your own.'

'Of course not!' He leaned across the space that separated their twin chairs and grabbed her hand in both of his, his eyes pleading. Eyes so like her own, she experienced a slight shock each time she looked into them. 'I came to an agreement with Riordan that I wouldn't interfere. Lily had made her choice, and I accepted it, finally. I returned to Cleeve Abbey as often as I could when you were growing up. More so after Lily disappeared.' He didn't elaborate, but the implication he found it difficult to talk about Lily sent a cloud across his face. 'In fact, Venetia had to rein me in occasionally, told me to stop spoiling you. She said if I treated you differently to her girls it would be noticed.'

'I noticed.' Flora returned his smile, though his kindness had confused her. With hindsight, it made perfect sense. 'Why did you never marry?'

'It's quite simple, and maybe even a little ridiculous.' A slow flush crept up his neck. 'I have met no woman since who could compare to Lily. I've met lots of lovely, accomplished and intelligent women, but none who made me feel the way she did. I think of her often.'

Flora swallowed a sudden instinct to blurt out what she was thinking, but resisted. It wouldn't be fair to share her fantasies about Alice with him. Though sorely tempted, she was saved from doing so when Arthur flailed his arms and grizzled, his features crunched up to prepare for a full-blown wail.

'Oh dear, we're in for tears.' Before Flora could react, Milly reappeared, bobbed a curtsey to both of them and scooped Arthur into her arms, murmuring gentle endearments. Thus soothed, the baby's wail did not materialise.

'It's time for his nap, Mrs Harrington,' she said, retreating with a final curtsey.

'See what I mean?' Flora whispered when the glazed door clicked shut. 'It wouldn't surprise me if she was waiting outside the door on alert for the first cry.'

William grinned, but said nothing. He drew his half hunter from his vest pocket and peered at it. 'Much as I relish your company, I had better be off. I have an appointment at four.'

Flora was about to say she had one too, but this was not the right time to mention Alice Finch.

'By the way, Flora.' William paused at the front door as Stokes helped him on with his coat. 'I'm going away for a little while.'

'Are you taking a holiday?' Intrigued, she held his driving cap in both hands, ready to hand it to him.

'Uh, no, it's work related.' He tied his scarf round his throat as he talked. 'More ambassadorial dinners I expect. Lots of hand pressing and small talk.'

'This isn't about the Serbians again, is it?' A pang of fear tightened her hands on the cap. 'How long is a while?'

'A few weeks. And take that frown off your face. I plan to be well received and pampered in some of the best drawing salons in the world.' He took the cap from her, nodded to Stokes, and moved onto the front step. 'I'll be back before you know it.'

She waved him off with a smile that hid a niggling worry. Why did he wait until the last minute before telling her? Was his trip so dangerous he didn't want to discuss it?

7

Martell's Tea Room stood at the junction of Ebury and Lyall Streets, its front window a curved bay with bottle glass panes among a row of similar shop properties. Flora's arrival was accompanied by the excited dance and jangle of the bell over the door and the magical appearance of the proprietor in his customary black-tailed suit that he always paired with a brightly coloured and embroidered waistcoat. Today, he displayed a glaring canary yellow masterpiece with tiny birds poking their heads out from green leaves.

He looked up as she entered the shop, his dark eyes alight with pleasure at the sight of her.

'Madame 'Aarreengton.' Skirting the counter, he eased between the marble-topped tables towards her, his hands held palms upwards in welcome. 'Yet again you honour me by gracing my 'umble establishment.'

'I find it impossible to stay away, Mr Martell,' Flora replied, smiling. 'I'm ashamed to say your delicious madeleines keep drawing me back.' Her swift glance around the busy room located Lydia at a table for two, though there was no sign of Miss Finch.

'You're so kind, and the charmant Mademoiselle Grey awaits you.'

'Don't bother to escort me to the table, Mr Martell.' Flora halted him with a hand on his forearm. 'I can see how busy you are. I'll have my usual.' An enticing smell of baking wafted through from the back room and made her mouth water.

'Absolument, ma chère madame.' He clapped his hands theatrically to attract the attention of a pert waitress in a crisp white apron.

'Have you been flirting with our host?' Lydia's laughter-filled voice rose above the clatter of crockery and the low murmur of conversation as Flora reached her. 'He always makes such a fuss of you. I think you must be his favourite.'

'It's all I can do not to laugh whenever I see him.' Flora looked in the mirror above Lydia's head and adjusted her hat before she took the chair opposite. 'He's such a caricature of the archetypical French waiter.'

'Here he's a prince among the teacups instead of the wine cellar. Though one never knows quite what people are hiding.'

'You think Mr Martell has secrets?' Flora frowned. Lydia's imagination was more vivid than her own.

'Well.' Lydia shuffled forward on her chair, though there was little chance of being overheard amongst the cacophony of the busy tea room. 'Not him, but I've heard,' she paused for dramatic effect, 'that a certain tea room owner in Piccadilly runs a brothel in the apartment above the shop.'

'Where do you hear such things?' Flora widened her eyes as she tugged off her gloves and laid them on the white tablecloth.

'Here and there.' Lydia shrugged. 'The ladies sit demurely sipping tea as they wait to be selected by the gentleman who arrives on the pretence of taking tea. Shocking, don't you think?'

'And distasteful.' Flora didn't know whether to believe her, though Lydia had always had a firm grasp on the grittier side of London life. Their friendship had grown during the exposure of Lydia's employer as a Serbian spy the previous year. Elena Lowe had been the headmistress of the Ladies' Academy where Lydia worked as a teacher. Since then, Lydia had run the school with an aplomb that had surprised everyone.

'What about that woman in emerald green sitting below that mirror over there?' Lydia nodded at the object of her fascination. 'She's alone, and no one has approached her. Do you think she's waiting to be chosen by some predatory man who—'

'Lydia!' Flora pressed her knuckles to her mouth to suppress a sudden burst of laughter.

'Maybe not a house of ill repute then,' Lydia conceded with a sniff. 'However, our Frenchman encourages Emmeline Pankhurst's acolytes.' She nodded at a group of women at a table in the bay window, their heads close together in earnest conversation. 'They come in here all the time. I'll wager they're plotting to wave banners outside Parliament and throw eggs at the politicians.'

'I cannot approve of the Women's Political and Social Union,' Flora said, frowning. 'They are so fierce with their notions of civil disobedience. Such tactics will surely put the suffragist movement back years. Millicent Fawcett must be so disheartened. After all her years of reasoned argument and gentle persuasion, her cause has been ambushed, and just when the more liberal politicians have considered the issue seriously.'

'I believe Mrs Pankhurst has been dragged away by the police several times this year for her public protests.' Lydia cocked her chin at the group of earnest looking women. 'I could not bring myself to harass politicians in the street. I would die of embarrassment if anyone I knew saw me.'

'Then perhaps you shouldn't stare at them like that,' Flora

warned. 'They might take us for potential recruits. Or worse, parliament spies.'

'Don't!' Lydia gave an exaggerated shiver, then straightened. 'Come to think of it, you haven't been to a NUWSS meeting for weeks.'

'I know. I'm a dreadful slacker.'

As well as being an independent, professional young woman, Lydia was also a member of the National Union of Women's Suffrage Society, where Flora had gone to enquire about a potential murder victim. Lydia's self-assurance and quiet dignity had marked her out as someone Flora would like to know, and during the past year, she had not been disappointed.

'I didn't mean to sound hard.' Lydia's hazel eyes rounded in mortification. 'You have little Arthur to look after as well as that delicious husband of yours. It's no wonder you have no time for the NUWSS.'

'More like laziness, I'm afraid. It's not as if I'm busy either. I have so much help in the house I twiddle my thumbs these days.' Milly's disapproving face jumped into her head, but she pushed it away. 'Are you still an avid supporter now that you and Harry are engaged?'

'I could never marry a man who did not support the movement,' Lydia replied. 'Harry wouldn't want me to abandon the cause either, though he's been distracted lately.' Her hand flew to her mouth. 'Didn't I mention it? Harry's uncle left him a house in Kensington and he's spending all his time lately talking to architects and builders.'

'What about your own house in Kinnerton Street?' Flora loved the compact, three-story villa Lydia had inherited from her parents. 'Or isn't that grand enough for the clan Flynn?'

Lydia grimaced. 'I think you've summarised it perfectly. His uncle's house is twice the size of mine, but is old-fashioned. It doesn't even have gas lighting, let alone electricity.' Lydia broke off, mid-sentence, her features softening into a delighted smile at the sight of Mr Martell who approached their table, a tray balanced on one hand.

'I've brought your tea personally, Madame 'Aareengton.' With exaggerated care, he laid an arrangement of crockery in front of her, together with two madeleines on a doily. 'And 'ow is your husband and that adorable bébé?'

'They're both well, thank you.' Flora wished he wouldn't keep mangling her name. It grated on her ears each time she heard it. Also, as far as she could recall, Mr Martell had not laid eyes on either Bunny or their infant son. 'Our son is thriving. How kind of you to ask.'

'I take a keen interest in my clientele, chère madame.' His shiny black eyes surveyed the room as he spoke. 'I like to think of you all as more than mere patrons.'

Flora inclined her head in acknowledgment, while Lydia feigned interest in a flower arrangement on the table. An awkward pause developed until Flora came up with a way to distract him. 'Perhaps you might put aside two of your mille-feuille cakes for me to take away, Mr Martell.'

'But of course, chère madame. Not your usual taste so they must be a treat for that perky little maid of yours who often accompanies you?'

'You have been paying attention.' Flora's eyes widened in surprise.

The Frenchman made no move to leave, until the silence became awkward, then finally the Frenchman took the hint, bowed and backed away. 'I wasn't rude, was I?' Flora asked. 'But he can be quite intrusive.'

'I said you were one of his favourites. And if I ever have to take a post as a lady's maid, I shall come to you, Flora. Cream cakes indeed.'

'It was all I could think of to distract him. Which will delight Sally, though goodness knows what my mother-in-law would say if she knew. She believes servants need little more than gruel and day-old bread to survive.'

'She's not alone.' Lydia glanced past Flora's shoulder. 'He's still staring at us. Perhaps he's simply bored taking orders for tea all day and needs a distraction? Though I have to say he's equally attentive to all the ladies.'

'You've been shopping, I see?' Dismissing the Frenchman, Flora changed the subject. 'How are the plans for your wedding progressing?' She took a sip of her tea, closing her eyes briefly as the hot, fragrant liquid relaxed her.

After the investigation into the murder of Evangeline Lange, which had brought Flora and Lydia together, Lydia had become engaged to Evangeline's fiancé, a development which had not been entirely unexpected to all who knew them.

'Slowly. It won't be a grand affair, and we don't even have a date yet.' Lydia gazed back at Flora over the rim of the teacup she held in both hands. 'I've no living relatives other than my aunt in Holborn. Besides, Harry's more distant family might not even come to the ceremony.'

'I take it they disapprove?'

'Not openly. But I cannot blame them. I'm not the catch Evangeline was. I'm a schoolteacher, not an heiress.'

'You're a headmistress at an establishment where every parent clamours to enrol their daughters. The school could easily have folded after the scandal of the spies incident, but thanks to you it did not. You should be proud of yourself. I know Harry is.' A charming flush entered Lydia's peach and cream cheeks. Her confidence partly restored; Flora was determined to reassure her.

'Besides, Harry's engagement to Miss Lange was arranged by their families. He wasn't passionately in love with her, not the way he is with you.'

'Do you really think so?' Lydia's high cheekbones turned a darker pink, followed by a shrug intended to be nonchalant but also conveyed an air of despair. 'You should have seen how his parents reacted when we considered Caxton Hall for the ceremony instead of some medieval ancestral church in the wilds of Norfolk.'

'Hmm. I can see that wouldn't be received well.'

'We compromised eventually and settled on St James', but there are still some discontented murmurings about the whole thing. Which reminds me,' she glanced up at the wall clock above the counter. 'I'm meeting him in half an hour.'

'Don't for a moment intimate you see yourself as not good enough or you'll be lost forever.' Flora topped up her cup from the pot, aware she was handing out advice she hadn't heeded herself. Beatrice Harrington's frequent asides that blamed Flora's every inadequacy on the fact that she was raised by a country house butler still rankled. That Riordan Maguire was a widower only made things worse, as if this misfortune was Flora's fault. Since the discovery that Flora was in fact related to Lord Vaughn, albeit tenuously, her attitude had undergone a subtle change.

'Anyway.' Flora dropped a lump of sugar into her tea, creating ripples across the surface. 'You have the perfect excuse to buy new clothes, no matter how small the wedding, so make the most of it.' She plucked a shell-shaped sponge from her plate, her attention caught by a chair at the table to her right.

The couple who had occupied it since her arrival had departed, leaving a copy of that morning's paper behind. The page had been left folded open, the sketch of Lizzie Prentice's face uppermost. This stark reminder rekindled Flora's uneasiness about the nurse's death.

'Flora? Are you going to eat that cake or simply wave it about?' Lydia asked.

'What? Oh, sorry.' Flora replaced the sponge on her plate. 'I was thinking about yesterday.'

'You and Bunny planned to visit that children's hospital in Southwark if I remember correctly.'

'We did, yes, and something unpleasant happened. Someone was – died.'

'Oh, my!' Lydia brought a hand to her mouth. 'What happened?'

'A student nurse was found dead in the rear yard.'

'How awful.' Lydia's delicate hand drifted to her throat. 'Don't tell me you were there when it happened?'

'I'm afraid so. We heard a scream, not from the girl herself, but from someone who found her. Bunny and I rushed into the rear yard, but there wasn't much to see. She was just lying there on the cobbles. It was worse for Miss Finch.'

'Who is Miss Finch?' Lydia stirred her tea faster, the spoon clicking against the china.

'The matron. One doctor declared the girl's death an accident, but I got the distinct impression she wasn't happy about it.'

'One of them? Was there a conflict of opinions amongst the medical staff?'

'Nothing gets past you does it, Lydia?' Flora smiled and bit into a madeleine, almost groaning, as the soft sponge melted on her tongue. 'These get better each time I come here.'

'Don't change the subject.' Lydia helped herself to a cake. 'You wouldn't have mentioned this Miss Finch at all unless there was more to it.'

'Why do you think that?' Flora feigned innocence, although she had been longing to bring up the subject of Alice Finch since she arrived. She could always rely on Lydia to ask all the right questions.

'Don't flutter those eyelashes at me. Now tell me about this Miss Finch.'

Flora hesitated, but knew if she confided her half-baked theories to Lydia they would go no further. 'Beforehand, I overheard the nurse ask Miss Finch if she might speak to her.'

'The nurse who was killed? Do you know what she wanted to talk about?'

'Her name was Lizzie Prentice. No, but she said it was important.' Flora wiped crumbs from the corner of her mouth. 'Now I look back on it. I got the impression Miss Finch already knew what it was about.'

'What made you think that?'

'I don't know, really. Her lack of surprise, perhaps?' She would have to ask Miss Finch about it when they next met. If they did.

'That sounds intriguing enough to warrant further investigation.' Lydia stared off as if pondering the thought. 'But coincidences, as well as accidents, happen sometimes.'

'Now you sound like Bunny, and I need a more sympathetic ear for this next part.' She inhaled a deep breath and set her cup down. 'This might sound ridiculous, but the second I saw Miss Finch, I felt I knew her.'

'Knew her from where?' Lydia delicately pulled a madeleine apart with slim, delicate fingers, placing a minuscule piece between her lips. 'And what does this have to do with the nurse's death?'

'Well, nothing really, but please hear me out. Miss Finch looks exactly like a photograph I have of my mother when she was younger.'

'This Miss Finch looks like a twenty-year-old photograph? Is that so surprising? I'm sure lots of people look alike.'

'It's more than that.' Flora tried to keep the frustration from her voice. 'She looks exactly how I imagine my mother would look now.'

'Flora.' Lydia sighed and replaced the half of her cake on her plate, fastidiously brushing crumbs from her fingertips. 'I love you dearly, but listen to yourself. A woman you have just met looks like your mother might have looked had she lived? That doesn't make sense.'

'Bunny said the same thing. He thinks I'm looking for answers where there aren't any. He wasn't unkind, just – logical and, well, dismissive. Thank you for not laughing, anyway.'

'I would never laugh at you. You've never really talked about your mother before.' Lydia gave Flora's hand a gentle pat and lifted her teacup to her lips. 'How long ago did she die?'

'When I was a child. At least everyone assumed she had died, but in fact, she disappeared.'

'Disappeared? How fascinating. I gather you haven't accepted that she might be dead?' Lydia was nothing if not perceptive.

'I grew up believing that, but recently I discovered her body was never found. Since then, I think about her a lot and wonder what really happened.'

'Goodness, how dreadful for you!' Lydia pressed her index finger to a crumb on her plate and brought it to her mouth. 'I gather these thoughts of yours will not go away until you have unearthed the truth?'

'You know me too well.' Flora regretted having broached the subject, but acknowledged she had become increasingly preoccupied with the matron of St Philomena's hospital. Even her exciting trip in a balloon had not banished the woman completely from her thoughts. At least she had resisted telling William that she believed his first love was alive, well, and working in South London. It was bad enough that her own imagination took flight, like Mr Hedges Butler's balloon, let alone giving him false hope.

'I was strangely tongue-tied during the tour and Bunny told me off for staring at her. Does that sound fanciful?'

'That Bunny would tell you off, oh, absolutely.'

'You know what I mean.' Flora smiled at Lydia's expression of feigned shock. 'He thinks it has something to do with my new motherhood. He hasn't been able to put down Dr Freud's *Psychopathology of Everyday Life* since he obtained a copy last year.' Flora's uneasy laugh failed to hide her irritation. 'When I use a wrong word or say something out of context, he snatches off his spectacles with a triumphant "Ah-hah" followed by a lengthy explanation on why I had said it.'

'I do so adore Bunny.' Lydia's uninhibited laugh brought enquiring glances from nearby tables. 'His devotion to you shines from his eyes whenever he looks at you. Makes me quite shivery.'

'Harry looks at you like that. I've seen him.'

'Maybe.' Lydia released a heartfelt sigh. 'Though sometimes I wonder if he's thinking of Evangeline. He was distraught when she was killed, so much so he and her father haunted the police station for days demanding to know what they were doing to find her killer.'

'That's understandable. They suspected Harry for a while, and he had to clear his name.'

'You don't think it was more than that?' Lydia's eyes pleaded for reassurance. 'Suppose he never gets over her?'

'He already has, Lydia. You mean more to him than Evangeline ever did. Theirs was an engagement of assets, not hearts.'

'I suppose so.' Lydia applied a silver cake fork to her second madeleine. 'I can always rely on you to make me feel better, but don't think I haven't noticed the way you keep glancing out of the window every few seconds. Are you expecting someone?'

'No. Not at all.' Flora was reluctant to insult Lydia by admitting she had invited her as a subterfuge. She owed her more than that. 'What did you say earlier about meeting Harry?'

'My goodness, I almost forgot.' Lydia gasped and her gaze flicked to the clock again. 'Oh dear, I'm late and I promised I wouldn't be.' She took a last bite of the cake and then discarded it onto her plate. Her chair screeching across the floorboards, she leapt to her feet and gathered her parcels together. 'Let me leave you some money.' She scrabbled in her purse, which she fumbled and dropped onto the table.

'Don't worry about that. It's my turn, anyway.' Flora waved her away.

'You're so kind, Flora.' She crammed the purse back into her bag and backed towards the door. 'We must do this again – soon.'

The doorbell jangled as Lydia hurried out, colliding with a top-hatted gentleman who was forced to swerve in order to avoid her, dislodging his hat. Flora heard his annoyed muttering as he passed her table. She glanced back at the street where Miss Alice Finch pushed open the door. Flora's stomach performed an odd flip of excited anticipation. It wasn't like looking at someone she had known for less than a day, more recognition of a face that had featured in her life over many years.

She wore a grey coat the colour of a pigeon wing, and a dusky pink scarf tucked in at her neck, the shade mirrored by the ribbon wound around the crown of her grey hat, which was turned back at the front and had a jaunty pheasant feather tucked into the side. Buttoned from neck to mid-thigh, the flared hem of her tailored coat swayed with each step as she pushed through the door. A bag on a cord at her side swung as she walked, her head held high and a half smile on her lips as Mr Martell showed her to a table in an alcove.

The low buzz of conversation, the repeated jangle of the shop bell and the clatter of crockery filled the crowded room, which felt uncomfortably hot. Flora debated whether to draw attention to her presence, or wait for Miss Finch to notice her? Undecided, she lingered over her rapidly cooling tea, conscious of Mr Martell, who threw her brief, suspicious glances, as if a lone woman was something which required scrutiny.

'What are you waiting for, Flora?' she muttered to herself, picking up her bag and gloves. 'Isn't this why you came?' Rising, she crossed the room and halted beside the table where Miss Finch consulted the menu. 'Good afternoon, Miss Finch. May I join you?'

8

Miss Finch looked up from her scrutiny of the menu with a look of mild inquiry that transformed to warmth. 'Mrs Harrington, how nice to see you!' She gestured to the empty chair opposite with an elegant wave of her hand. 'I would be delighted for you to join me.'

'Thank you.' Flora sat, conscious the exchange smacked of a performance as she waited for her companion to summon the waitress and change her order, though more tea was the last thing Flora wanted.

'I hope you enjoyed your visit to the hospital yesterday,' Miss Finch said, when the waitress had left. 'And your handsome husband, of course, he of the unusual Greek name.'

'He did indeed, and although he interrupted me when I was about to call him Bunny.'

'Ah, I see.' Her eyes flashed with laughter. 'A schoolboy nickname, but a constant source of embarrassment?'

'Exactly, although most people say it suits him.' Flora busied herself arranging her skirt and bag while studying her companion's features from beneath her lashes. Miss Finch had a nose not unlike her own and a similar symmetrical arch to her eyebrows above the same wide, expressive eyes which confronted Flora in her mirror each morning.

'She looked charming, your friend,' Miss Finch said, revealing the fact she must have watched Lydia leave, and if so, had she loitered outside until Flora was alone?

'She is. And a professional woman like yourself. She is head-mistress at an academy for young ladies.'

'Admirable.' Miss Finch gave the now crowded room a sweeping look which lingered for a second on the beaming face of Mr Martell. 'Forgive me for hurrying you and your husband away from the hospital yesterday. I thought it best to keep you both away from the police.'

'That makes us sound as if we had something to hide, but I assume it was because we had nothing to contribute?'

'Exactly, and I would also like to apologise for my indiscreet comment about Lizzie being killed.' Miss Finch leaned forward slightly; her voice lowered. 'It was unwise of me to voice such thoughts in your hearing.'

'There's really no need for an apology, Miss Finch.' Flora did not accept this as a viable excuse, but she could be patient.

'Oh, please call me Alice. I have a feeling we're going to be good friends.' She broke off to acknowledge the waitress who placed a tray on the table between them. If the girl noticed Flora had changed places and was about to embark on another afternoon tea, she gave no sign but there was an extra cup on the tray.

'Do you live near here, Mrs Harrington?' Alice asked, once the girl had left, handing Flora a full cup to which she had added milk. 'Oh, I'm sorry I forgot to ask. Do you take milk or do you prefer your tea with lemon?'

'No, this is perfect. Thank you.' Flora sipped the excellent but unwanted tea. 'I live a short walk away. Yourself?'

'I have lodgings in Birdcage Walk.'

'Near St James' Park?' Flora's eyed widened. 'That's quite a way from Quilp Street.' In more ways than one, making her a neighbour of the king.

'It's quite a simple journey by omnibus.' She twirled a spoon in her cup. 'I like the distance it puts between me and my work. It gives me time to marshal my thoughts in the mornings.'

'How long have you been matron at St Philomena's?' Flora asked, unsure where this conversation was headed. Why had Miss Finch seemed so keen for them to meet again? To swap trivia about their lives or something else?

'I trained at the London Hospital where I was a ward sister for several years before I was offered the post at St Philomena's.'

'Quite an achievement. Do you have a family?' Flora halted; conscious she was prying. 'I'm so sorry. How rude of me to bombard you with questions when we hardly know one another.'

'Not at all. And no, I don't. I have no parents and had I married, I would have had to give up nursing, which was something I was not prepared to do.' She offered Flora a plate of almond biscuits before taking one herself. 'Actually, there was another reason I hoped we could meet here sometime.'

'Go on?' *Ah, here it comes.*

'I have a problem at the hospital.'

'Yes, I know.' Flora plucked a biscuit from the plate and nibbled at the edge, mainly for something to do rather than from hunger. 'One of your nurses died violently.'

'No, not that. Well, yes, it is that.' She discarded a half-eaten biscuit on her plate with a grimace. 'I meant what I said yesterday. I believed then that Lizzie Prentice was killed. I have no reason to change my mind now.'

'I'm listening.' Flora returned her cup to the saucer with a click. She tried to recall whether her mother had disliked almonds, but that was hardly something of which a six-year-old child would be aware.

'Indeed, and you are remarkably calm. Exactly as you were yesterday.' Her blue-green eyes met Flora's steadily. 'Most young ladies would have a fit of the vapours at the sight of a body, but you didn't so much as flinch.'

'Yesterday wasn't my first encounter with violent death, Miss F— Alice.' The woman's eyes widened a fraction, but the gesture appeared more contrived than genuine. Then, as if she had decided, she exhaled slowly. 'I have a confession to make, Flora. I hope I might call you that?'

'I should be delighted. What sort of confession?'

'I read about your involvement in the Evangeline Lange case last year where you helped expose a killer.'

'You flatter me. It was more a coming together of events where I almost misjudged the situation completely.' Flora buried her nose in her cup, giving this some thought. Her name had indeed been in the newspapers, but as she had remarked at the time it had been included at the bottom of a column on page five of the Evening Post. That Alice had not only seen it but remembered her name stirred a trickle of excitement that crawled up her spine.

'So tell me, Alice, why do you believe Lizzie's death was not an accident? Was it something the police said?'

'Those dolts!' Alice's perfectly shaped upper lip curled in contempt. 'Dr Reeder was adamant Lizzie had simply slipped on the wet cobbles in the yard and struck her head. Dr Marsh disagreed, as you heard, but the police accepted the loudest voice and the most obvious solution, seeing as there was no evidence to suggest otherwise.' She chewed a fingernail, though this gesture seemed out of character with her immaculate appearance. 'I understand their dilemma. What else could it have been? I mean, who would have a reason to kill a student nurse?'

'What conclusion did they come to?'

'A bright spark of a constable had suggested she must have discovered a thief stealing morphine from the pharmacy, which is about twenty feet from where she was found and whoever it was most likely panicked and hit her to get away before she raised the alarm. They appear to suspect the whole of Bermondsey of being opium addicts!'

'Was there anything missing from the pharmacy?'

'Apparently not.' She sighed. 'Which our most senior physician declared proved nothing, other than Lizzie must have disturbed the burglar when he broke in. That he attacked her and ran away empty-handed. But with no evidence the police concluded it was likely an accident.'

'Which brings us to your reasons for believing Lizzie was murdered.'

'No but I'm certain Lizzie was about to tell me something important, and was prevented from doing so.' Alice winced and massaged her forehead with one hand. 'Or do I sound overly dramatic?'

'Not at all,' Flora's curiosity piqued. 'Do you know what she was about to tell you?'

'Vaguely. But let me start at the beginning or none of this will make any sense.' Alice eased forward in her chair. 'As I explained yesterday, the children brought to St Philomena's are often ill because of their living conditions. Some have chronic illnesses which cannot be cured in a few days, while others simply need a clinic visit to check their illness has abated. In this way, we offer long-term care when they are discharged from the hospital with the offer of clinic visits to help keep them healthy.'

'That sounds like a good policy.'

'It is, though attendance is spasmodic as some parents cannot keep the appointments, or don't see the benefit. However, recently,

Lizzie alerted me to several children having missed their appointments.'

'You've just explained why that isn't unusual. Perhaps their parents didn't feel it was worth bringing them to the hospital once they were well?'

'Which is exactly what Mr Buchanan said when I broached the subject with him.'

'I'm sorry. I didn't mean to imply you are being an alarmist.' Embarrassed heat spread into Flora's face until she was sure her cheeks burned. What was she doing interrogating this woman? They were strangers, weren't they?

'You're right.' Alice waved away her apology. 'I assumed their parents were too indolent or disinterested to bring them in again. Usually, we're too busy dealing with sick children to worry about the ones who have gone home. Excuses which I deeply regret now, because six of these children haven't been seen in over a week.'

'They've been reported missing?'

'No, that's the problem. I contacted the police, but they said no reports have been made.'

'You aren't to blame for what happens when children leave your care.'

'Maybe not, but I'm convinced something strange is going on. Lizzie was too. She told me she had seen the same man loitering outside the hospital the last few weeks.'

Flora's interest sparked, and she leaned forward slightly, her tea forgotten. 'Go on.'

'Lizzie was young and pretty, and maybe not the brightest of girls, but she had good instincts. She grew up in Grotto Street; a dreadful place where survival to adulthood is a battle.' She took a deep breath before continuing. 'Lizzie said the man's appearance coincided with each of the children being discharged.'

'Did she observe them in his company?'

'Not as far as I know. But it was at her insistence this meant something, that I visited the homes of each of these children. In each case, we were given a plausible explanation why they weren't there. Two of the boys had begun apprenticeships with a builder. A girl of eleven had been taken into service in Bristol and one was visiting an aunt. I got no response at the other two houses, but in each case the neighbours told me the child no longer lived there.'

'Something tells me this didn't satisfy you.'

'Six children?' Alice raised a sceptical eyebrow. 'All living within half a mile of each other, leaving home in the same week? Indeed, it didn't. Also, the stories I was given by the families seemed too perfect, as if they had been told what to say and recited it by rote. When I tried to delve further, they simply repeated themselves.'

'That sounds odd.' Flora picked at the tiny pieces of almonds on her plate. 'Did Lizzie say who the man was? The one she saw at the hospital?'

'Only that she didn't know him, but I suspected she wasn't being candid with me. As I mentioned, she grew up locally, so there's a possibility she knew him, even if it was only by reputation. I didn't press her, but I warned her to stay away, at least until I could look further into the matter.'

'Do you think she listened to you?'

'I have no way of knowing, but she was adamant she knew what she was talking about.'

'Then it was likely she approached him.' Flora sighed. 'Did she tell you what he looked like?'

Alice shrugged again. 'Only that he was an ordinary-looking chap, neither old nor young, who wore a flat tweed cap and a brown moleskin overcoat. I cannot help feeling she found out something: either his identity or something about the whereabouts of the children. Whatever it was I think she was about to tell me on the day she died.'

Miss Finch gave the room another swift glance, then stiffened. Flora followed her gaze to where Mr Martell observed them from the other side of the counter. When he saw her watching him, he turned swiftly away and addressed the nearest waitress.

'He's too far away to hear us if that's what's worrying you,' Flora tried to be reassuring.

'I'm sorry, I'm being unreasonable.' Alice tore her eyes away from the Frenchman. 'Why would he care what I say?' Despite this assertion, she leaned closer, lowering her voice. 'Lizzie told me she was going to the Antigallican, a public house on Tooley Street where this man was known.'

'Antigallican...' Flora tried the name out on her tongue. 'That sounds like a name contrived by someone who is averse to Frenchmen.'

'That's exactly what it is. Several public houses were called that, although not their real names, by the locals during the Napoleonic Wars. Most have changed their names to something less confrontational, especially now we have an Entente cordiale over the French foreign territories.' She gave an irritated wave with one hand. 'But that's incidental.'

'Did you report all this to the Governors?' Flora took a sip of her tea and grimaced when she discovered it was cold.

'I did, yes. As far as they are concerned, the police are satisfied Lizzie died as the result of a fall, and those children are no longer our responsibility.'

'I cannot believe they would ignore you completely.' Flora's stomach tightened as a thought struck her. *Unless one or more of them had something to do with it.*

'Alice, what do you think is happening to these children?' Flora signalled to the waitress to bring them a fresh pot of tea. Not that she wanted one, but they couldn't sit there with empty cups, not when the tea shop was so busy.

'I cannot imagine, and please excuse my directness, but their bodies haven't turned up in the immediate neighbourhood either, so I must assume they are still alive. As for the long term, well, I dare not think what might become of them. We need to find some evidence, then the police might be interested in my theory.'

Her use of the word 'we' made Flora smile. She had used it unconsciously and did not retract it or apologise. As if she knew Flora would agree.

'Is that why you hoped we would meet here, so you might enlist my help?' Their joining forces would also be a perfect opportunity to discover more about Alice's past.

'I hope I haven't angered you.' She hunched her shoulders in a shrug, which made her seem much younger. 'I knew I couldn't deceive you with my clumsy attempt at appeal. I didn't know what else to do, not after the police dismissed everything I said. Then, when your name appeared on the visitor's list of prospective subscribers to the hospital, well...' She leaned forward over the table. 'If you want nothing to do with this, I quite understand. It was wrong of me to spike your interest. I hope you aren't angry.'

'No, you haven't angered me. I'm intrigued,' Flora mused. 'What do you plan to do next?'

'I thought I might pay another visit to the children's homes, but I wasn't exactly subtle with my questions, so doubt a second time would produce better results. The families won't talk to me.'

'I'm not sure how I can be of any help. Although...' Flora bit her lip as a thought struck her.

'You've thought of something. I can tell. What is it?' Alice wrapped an errant curl around her middle finger, a gesture which made Flora's heart skip. She did the same thing herself when she was nervous.

'What if I volunteered to go in your stead?' The thought was only half-formed, but when Flora voiced it aloud, it made perfect sense.

'You?' Alice blinked and lowered her cup, though Flora doubted her suggestion was entirely unexpected. 'That's quite a clever idea, if I may say so. No one in the area knows you. Though, you don't look much like a slum sister.'

'I beg your pardon?'

'That's what they call the Salvation Army nurses and midwives who visit needy families. Are you sure you want to do this? Bermondsey is not exactly Fitzrovia.'

'I'm well aware of that, but why not?' The details crystallised in Flora's head as she spoke. 'I could take food with me to help things along. If these families are as poor as you say, they won't suspect my real motive.' She brought a hand to her mouth. 'I'm so sorry; that sounded awful.' Her rationalisation had not seemed so bad inside her head.

'Not at all, and you're right. As long as you aren't too persistent with your enquiries. They're a wary lot down there and hiding things from those in authority is a way of life to them.'

'I hope you don't think I have no empathy with these people?' The last thing Flora wanted was Alice to think she regarded this enterprise as a game. 'I'm also a mother and know how I would feel if my child had been taken from me and no one was looking for him.'

'Yes, you are, aren't you?' Alice blinked. 'A mother, I mean.'

Flora couldn't recall when exactly she had told her about Arthur. Though she must have done. 'Well, what do you think?'

'It's an excellent idea. But you shouldn't go alone. I would hate to be responsible for anything happening to you.'

'I'll take my maid with me. I also have a friend who might be persuaded to come too.' Lydia would definitely be eager to help if missing children were involved. The mention of Sally reminded her to collect the cakes she had asked for when she left.

'I'm not sure how much you should reveal to your friend. I wouldn't wish to alarm her.'

'You don't know Lydia.' Flora smiled. 'Besides, she'll get every detail out of me in minutes, none of which would discourage her.'

'I really appreciate your help.' Alice rummaged in the small handbag she had placed on the table between them, from which she withdrew a sheet of paper. 'The addresses are here, as well as the names and ages of the children.'

'You came prepared, I see.' Flora reached to take the paper, but at the last second, Alice retracted her hand. 'Oh, I have completely disregarded your husband. What would he say about this scheme of ours?'

'Leave Bunny to me.' Flora plucked the page from Alice's fingers, barely looking at it before she tucked it into her own bag. Something told her she had been manipulated, which only reinforced her conviction that she and Alice had some kind of bond which transcended the polite reserve of strangers.

Alice consulted a fob watch attached to her lapel. 'Goodness, is that the time? I must get back to the hospital.'

'Yes, I must get home too.' Flora scraped back her chair, the sound bringing Mr Martell to their side with the speed of a magician.

'Have you 'ad a pleasant afternoon?' The Frenchman eyed them both with interest, whilst handing Flora the packaged mille-feuille.

'Perfectly, thank you.' Alice's lips did only twitch as she continued past him to the counter at the front of the shop.

Flora gave a weak smile and followed, annoyed when he remained firmly attached to their side.

'I 'ad no idea you ladies were acquainted,' he persisted, unabashed.

'Did you not?' Flora placed a handful of coins on the counter, refusing Alice's attempt to do the same.

'Such dreadful goings on at the 'ospital, I hear, Mees Feench.' Mr Martell stepped in front of them as Flora reached to open the door. 'One of your nurses met with an accident, did she not?' He inclined his head, so shiny with pomade it reflected the overhead gaslight.

'Accidents happen, Mr Martell.' Flora eased past him and grasped the brass handle. 'Good day to you.'

'That's the last thing I need.' Alice sighed when they gained the street. 'Gossip about the hospital won't help the donations. The slightest scandal can discourage people from having anything to do with us.'

Flora resisted the temptation to look back, though experienced an unnerving sensation that Mr Martell was watching them through the window. Had he overheard their conversation? Or did he read the newspapers like everyone else? 'I wouldn't take any notice of him. He's renowned for his nosiness.'

'So, I've heard.' Alice glanced towards the road. 'Ah, here's my horse bus. I really must go. If I have to wait for the next one, I shall be late.'

'Perhaps I could come to the hospital tomorrow and let you know what I find out?' Flora said.

'Excellent. I'll warn Forbes, the porter, to expect you.' She climbed nimbly onto the platform of the horse bus and turned back with a smile that made Flora's breath catch.

'My dear Flora, I believe we have a plan.'

9

Flora suppressed a shiver as a gust of frigid air swept along the hall from the rear door, which had been left open. When Bunny had insisted on the installation of the telephone at the Eaton Place house, she had imagined reclining on a chaise beside a fire to chat to her friends, not shivering in a draughty rear hall. She would have to convince him to buy one of the candlestick models she had seen on her visit to New York.

'Lydia, I wanted to ask your—' the line crackled in her ear and she broke off, wincing. When it cleared, she tried again. 'How do you feel about doing some poor visiting?'

'Even with this noisy line, I detect a conspiratorial tone in your voice, Flora.' Lydia sounded as if she was in a tunnel. 'Is this yet another murder investigation?'

'Not exactly, and it's not dangerous. At least I hope not.' She bit her lip, glad that Lydia couldn't see the lie in her eyes.

The line went quiet apart from the odd hiss and crackle. The silence went on so long Flora was convinced Lydia had hung up the telephone. 'Are you still there, Lydia?'

'I'm thinking,' Lydia said. 'Where exactly are we going on this charitable visit of yours?'

'To Southwark, it's an area known as St Saviour.'

'Why would you want to go down there?' Lydia's shock came down the line clearly. 'Those docks south of the river contain some of the city's worst slums.'

'I thought that was the point of distributing charity to the poor.' Flora tried to keep the sarcasm from her voice but doubted she had succeeded. 'Are you familiar with this area?'

'Don't sound so surprised. I teach a class on the history of London, so naturally, I'm aware of places like Jacob's Island, Bermondsey and Deptford. Are you sure that's where you want to go?'

'Positive. Are you coming with me or not?'

'Wouldn't miss it. In which case, we'd better take Abel Cain with us.'

'What a biblical name. Who is he?'

'A carpenter who lodges at the end of my street. He does odd jobs for me and my neighbours for a few shillings. I'm sure I could persuade him to spare us a couple of hours.'

'Why do you think he would be useful?'

'You'll see when you meet him. When do you wish to go?'

More crackles and hisses meant Flora had to repeat the arrangements for the following morning – twice. When she finally hung up the receiver, she turned to find Sally watching her from the doorway to the kitchens.

'You weren't thinking of going without me were you, Missus?' Sally's brown eyes narrowed with suspicion as she wiped her hands on her apron. 'Can't have you going to a place like that on yer own.'

'You're as bad as Lydia. Am I being naïve for wanting to go at all? I'll keep my purse well-hidden and I won't wear any jewellery.'

'Then you are ny-eeve Missus, whatever that means. There are far worse villains in that quarter than the odd pickpocket. But I wouldn't mind seeing that Abel again.'

'You've met him?' Flora examined Sally's face for clues, but Sally kept her head down.

'He was at Miss Lydia's place fixing some pipes when I took that note round last week.' Sally picked at the paint on the doorframe. 'He lives with his Mam and works as a handyman doing jobs in people's houses.'

'I'm pleased to hear he looks after his mother. What's he like?'

'You'll see for yerself, Missus.' Sally concealed a smile behind her hand, just as a high-pitched shriek came from the depths of the servants' hall.

'Sally!' the voice called. 'Have yer brought Miss Flora's linens down yet? I want them in this tub or they'll have to wait till Wednesday.'

Sally rolled her eyes and scampered away, leaving Flora smiling to herself.

* * *

'Since when did you take up charity work?' Bunny asked, when they had adjourned to the sitting room with their coffee after dinner.

'I might have.' Flora picked at the silk bookmark in a copy of *Sense and Sensibility* on the table at her elbow. 'Would that surprise you?'

'Not at all. Immersing yourself in good works is an admirable way for a married woman to spend her time. And my—'

'—mother would approve,' Flora finished for him. The reason she had resisted such activities was because Beatrice Harrington liked to pontificate on how Flora ought to spend her time. The last thing Flora wanted was to give her the satisfaction her advice had been taken. 'I'm putting my spare time to good use.'

'Really, Flora, how long are you going to keep up this charade?' Bunny's glance flicked up at her as he added milk to his coffee. 'This is connected with Miss Finch at St Philomena's, isn't it? Did you see her at Martell's this afternoon? She implied she was there often.'

'I thought you'd forgotten.' Flora pretended to study a hangnail.

'No, but I was hoping you had.' Leather creaked as he adjusted his position in the wing-back chair beside hers. 'Are you still convinced she might be your long-lost mother?'

'Forget I ever mentioned that.' Flora waved him away. 'She's a charming woman, and we got on so well, we might have known each other for years. Does that never happen to you?'

'I had the same instinct about my dentist.' Bunny sipped from his cup and swallowed. 'Amiable chap. We might have been separated at birth.'

'Stop mocking me.' Flora narrowed her eyes at him, lifted her coffee cup, then set it down again without taking a sip. 'She's asked if I would involve myself in some charity work.'

'Teasing perhaps, but I would never mock. You shouldn't put too much importance on it, my love.' He softened his tone. 'What I was trying to explain is that it's possible to feel connected to a stranger without being related to them. And why do you keep fidgeting? You've picked up your coffee cup twice but not drunk any of it. Is something bothering you?'

'Possibly.' She clasped her hands on her lap and took a deep breath before continuing. 'We discussed the possibility that Lizzie Prentice was hit over the head by someone.'

'Have the police changed their opinion?' Bunny leaned his head back against the upholstery and stared at her. Then realisation dawned, and he sighed. 'Oh Flora, you aren't trying to change it for them!'

'Why not? Someone might have had a reason for wanting her dead.' She related a censored version of her conversation with Miss Finch that afternoon, finishing with details of the missing children.

To his credit, Bunny listened intently, with not a sigh or a rolling of eyes to betray his real feelings. She liked to think it was the mention of the children which had altered his attitude. Since the birth of their son, his perspective towards them had changed as much as her own.

'You've made an excellent case for Miss Finch, who evidently contributes a great deal to the Bermondsey community. They get precious little help down there. What is this work she's asked you to do, and how is it connected to Lizzie Prentice and these missing children?'

'We're going to visit their homes tomorrow to distribute food parcels and see if we can find out anything.'

'I see, and you thought I might forbid you to go?' His expression remained serious, though his lips twitched. 'Is that why you've been as nervous as a cat all evening?'

'I would have mentioned it before, but the telephone rang just after you arrived home and then Stokes announced dinner, so...' She shrugged. 'I needed to approach the subject diplomatically.'

'You know how I feel about you wandering the London streets alone.'

'I won't be alone. Lydia is coming with me, and she's bringing someone called Abel.'

'I was about to suggest taking a policeman, but he'll do just as well. That area down by Tower Bridge is dangerous.' Bunny reached for the biscuit dish, which Flora moved within his reach. The wafer-thin biscuits dusted with cinnamon were Bunny's favourite. Flora had ordered them specially.

'I doubt even you could get into too much trouble delivering food.' He chewed a biscuit thoughtfully. 'However, where Miss Finch is concerned, I don't want you to be distraught when you discover she's been married to a banker for twenty-five years and has six children.'

'She never married, and has no family to speak of.'

'My, you have been busy.' His eyes sharpened behind his glasses. 'Is being a wife and mother not enough and you feel the need to keep looking for your mother?'

'This has nothing to do with her.' The pain in his face brought her out of her chair and to his side. 'I love a mystery, as you well know, and now I have two to keep me interested.'

She stood behind his chair, locked her arms around his neck, and pressed her cheek to his. 'I love being married to you. You've spoiled me entirely, and the staff run this house with little help from me. Milly doesn't need me at all where Arthur's care is concerned.'

'If you're feeling undervalued, my love, I could discharge them all?'

'Definitely not.' She hugged him tighter. 'I like the way things are.'

'What else did you and Miss Finch discuss apart from missing children and nurses who die in mysterious circumstances?'

He lifted her hand from where it lay on his collarbone and planted a kiss on her palm.

'That there could be a perfectly reasonable explanation for the children not being in their homes. And Lizzie Prentice's death could have been an accident. In which case, there's no reason for my involvement, and Miss Finch and I will simply spend a congenial hour together.'

'You're going to see her again?'

'I'm calling on her at the hospital tomorrow afternoon to give her a report on our charitable expedition into Bermondsey.'

'From anyone else, that would sound a perfectly harmless suggestion, but not where my wife is concerned.' Bunny snapped open the copy of the *Evening Standard* the butler had left for him 'All I ask, is you take care.'

'Of course I will.' She planted a kiss on his cheek. 'And thank you for understanding.' Then something he said came back to her. 'Do you know Abel Cain?' Was she the only one in her household who had never heard of this man?

'We enjoy a passing acquaintance.' Bunny concentrated on his newspaper.

'What is he like?'

'You'll find out,' he murmured, without looking up.

'Why does everyone keep saying that?' Miffed, she retrieved her copy of *Lady Rose's Daughter* and settled to read in a room silent apart from the tick of the mantle clock and the rustle of Bunny's paper.

After the first page, Bunny's joke about Alice being married with six children returned and she could not take in another word of her novel. Suppose he was right, and Alice Finch was just what she purported to be? What if there was no convenient answer to what had happened to her mother all those years ago? Was she tilting at windmills, as Riordan Maguire liked to say?

Somehow, the room seemed a little darker and cooler than a moment before. She released a sigh and rose. 'I think I'll go to bed.'

'Is your novel not interesting enough for you?' Bunny asked without looking up. 'I thought Augusta Ward was a great success in America.'

'I'm not sure why.' Flora fingered the cover. 'The heroine is a woman called Julie, the daughter of a couple who left England in order to be together. Her mother was married to someone else, thus they cannot marry, a situation which puts Julie at a disadvantage. I've reached the part where she takes a position with an aristocrat who hates her.'

'Echoes of your own life, perhaps?' His gaze lifted to hers and held.

'No, and I certainly don't have a cruel employer.'

'I wondered if you had cast my mother in that role?'

'Your words, not mine.' Flora halted with her hand on the doorknob and turned back. 'Are you going to join me?'

'I'll be up in a moment,' Bunny replied without lifting his head from the page.

10

'Abel Cain, meet Mrs Flora Harrington.' Lydia's eyes sparkled as she made the introduction on Flora's doorstep the next morning.

He looked to be in his twenties, with wide, expressive brown eyes and a slightly flattened nose that gave character to his regular but unremarkable features; although it wasn't his face which made Flora stare, but the fact he stood well over six feet, with shoulders as wide as a door, so she had to crane her neck to meet his gaze. A brown and mustard tweed jacket strained over his well-defined chest, while hands as big as shovels rested on the stone pillar. In comparison, even Charles Rolls could have been described as being of average size.

'Pleased to meet you, Missus.' His voice was softer than Flora expected. He snatched off a brown cap to reveal toffee coloured hair brushed back from a square brow with what appeared to be little help from pomade.

'And I you, Mr Cain.' Flora exhaled a slow breath. 'Well, I doubt anyone will give us any trouble with him present,' she said out of the corner of her mouth.

'Which was precisely why I asked him to accompany us,' Lydia said, beaming.

Sally bustled forward, ostensibly to help Stokes manoeuvre the cumbersome food basket through the gate, but on reaching the young man's side, she halted. Her cheeks turned bright pink, and she stammered a greeting. No wonder she had been so keen to come.

Flora eyed the cab that waited on the road, glad she had requested Stokes summon a four-wheeled 'growler' cab with two horses and room for four passengers, instead of a one-horse hansom.

Having stowed the basket beside the driver's feet, Abel climbed into the cab and squeezed into the seat opposite. Sally eased into the corner, her hunched shoulders pressed up against the window. The growler left Belgravia behind and bowled towards Westminster Bridge and a minute into the journey, Flora was about to enquire if Sally was quite comfortable, but changed her mind. From the sideways looks her maid shot at Abel from beneath her lashes, Flora decided her concern was unwarranted.

'Where should we begin our search?' Flora asked as she consulted her handwritten list.

'One address on Miss Finch's list is in Wild's Rents, though I doubt the driver will take us to the door. We'll get him to drop us off on the Old Kent Road and walk the rest of the way.'

'I see.' Flora swallowed, suddenly nervous that even a London cabby might be reluctant to enter a place she intended to go on foot.

Her trepidation increased once they crossed the river, where the buildings became shabbier with drab colours muted to various shades of brown and grey, overlaid with a layer of soot. The streets were crowded with grim-faced hurrying figures who trudged rather than walked, their eyes cast to the ground and shoulders hunched.

Their route followed the railway line for a mile or so, then took a right turn, where the driver pulled the cab to a halt but did not climb down and open the door.

Abel, who had not uttered a word for the entire journey, leapt onto the pavement, his hand extended to help Lydia down.

'I 'ope you knows what you're doing bringing these ladies down here,' the driver addressed Abel from his seat above them.

Abel's engaging smile was accompanied a 'what can you do' shrug as he handed the man his fee. He placed the basket on the pavement, then helped Flora and Lydia down onto a road filled with horse-drawn carts, handcarts and trams that rattled along, their whistles blowing to warn pedestrians to get out of the way.

Sally only just made it onto the pavement before the driver pulled smartly away.

'Charming,' she said with a sniff. 'Good job we didn't ask him ter hang about.'

'Which wasn't at all likely.' Lydia led them down a side street, leaving the clamour of the main road behind them as they ventured into narrow streets lined with high red brick walls darkened to a sooty black, the street lamps non-existent.

Flora had imagined rows of neat cottages separated by low stone walls – shabby and utilitarian, but cosy – not a double row of tall, depressing tenement buildings that blocked out the sky on either side of a dirt road filled with stinking rubbish. Between them ran rows of back-to-back houses that resembled crooked paperboard boxes, the streets little more than dirt alleys.

Women stood around in groups with an occasional grubby child at their skirts, their shawls clutched over creased, patched skirts glaring in morose silence at the small party who passed.

'I'm feeling conspicuous,' Flora complained, unaccustomed to such scrutiny from the bold, impertinent stares that came her way.

'Keep a sharp look out,' Lydia whispered. 'Or you'll be missing a pair of gloves or your hat before you can turn around.'

'It's that bad?' Flora's eyes widened.

Lydia laughed. 'I'm exaggerating – but it pays to be on your guard. Strange faces stick out here and we don't fit, so it makes them suspicious.'

'You make them sound like wild animals,' Flora grimaced as she skirted a pile of horse droppings that looked so old, even the flies had lost interest.

'In a way they are. Having to live on your wits to survive can change a person.'

'But we're here to help.' Flora said nervously. Instead of stepping aside to let her by, they squared their shoulders and stood their ground, or simply glared at her as she passed.

'I tried to warn you,' Lydia said. 'Your eyes will feel sore from the discharge from the factories. It goes away after a while.'

'Do most people who live here work in the factories?' Flora blinked, though more from anticipation than real discomfort, as they entered a row of identical scruffy houses of three storeys high, the lower level half below ground.

'Some do. Others try to make a living by casual work on the docks or the railway. Secure work around here is hard to find.'

'The houses aren't very well maintained,' Flora whispered, observing the paint that peeled from window frames, broken railings and doors that hung lopsidedly from rusted hinges.

'The landlords don't care.' Lydia snorted. 'As long as their rent comes in, why should they spend money on paint and window glass?' Her voice took on a cynical edge. 'Those fortunate enough to qualify for rooms in The Peabody Buildings have a better life.'

'Peabody what?' Flora picked her way over a pile of debris from discarded packing crates that threatened to twist an ankle. She cast a look behind her to ensure Sally and Abel were keeping pace, the pair engaged in conversation. Abel's loping stride made Sally almost skip along beside him to keep up.

'There are Peabody's all over this end of town,' Lydia eased round a deep puddle in the cracked and uneven pavement. 'Blocks of flats built by some American philanthropist about thirty years ago, where families who qualify can rent sets of rooms, depending on what they can afford.'

'Like St Philomena's hospital you mean?' Flora said. 'What do you mean by qualify?'

'It's not simple. You must have a secure job, be of good character and be able to prove you're married to the partner you want to live with. Don't look so shocked, Miss Prim. You'd be surprised how many couples here aren't legally spliced.'

'You're right, I probably would be. What are these buildings like?' Flora couldn't imagine they would be worse than the crumbling, shabby buildings she had seen that morning.

Lydia shrugged. 'Fairly basic, though at least they have indoor plumbing, even if it is a communal standpipe in the hall. Most people rent two rooms but four is not unheard of, though when the flats were first built, two or even three families had to share a sink on the landing. Changes have been made though, and proper kitchens have been installed since then. There are rules though, harsh ones. They cannot hang wallpaper as it might harbour vermin.'

'Which sounds sensible.' Flora wondered briefly how Lydia knew so much about them.

'Have you got vermin in your wallpaper at Eaton Place?' Lydia shot her a hard look.

'I doubt it, oh, yes, I see what you mean.' Flora swallowed, chastened.

'No nails are to be put in the walls, and if a tenant is ever found to be drunk, he's out. The superintendent keeps an eye on everyone and is quick to report rule breakers.'

'I see.' Flora fell silent, feeling she had insulted Lydia but was unsure quite how.

A group of ragged children stood at the corner, huddled around what at first glance Flora thought was a man slumped in a wooden crate. On closer inspection, she realised it was a pair of trousers and a torn jacket stuffed with rags and straw. The head was a stuffed sack with a face drawn shakily on it, two bushy eyebrows with eyes fixed on a remote point, and strands of brown wool looked like hair sticking out from beneath a faded flat cap.

'Penny fer the guy, miss?' A child with a dirty face pleaded.

'This is a tradition I know something about,' Flora whispered as she delved into a pocket of her coat where she had carefully placed several small coins, among them some threepenny pieces and a few sixpences for just such an occasion. 'Where do they burn the guys? Not in the streets, surely?' She stared round at the narrow streets with their dilapidated houses, brick walls and cobbled alleys full of rubbish.

'They'll find a patch of waste ground somewhere to build their bonfire.'

'S'only a penny, miss,' the smallest of the group said. 'Don't need no discussion 'bout it.'

'Don't you go cheeking the lady!' Sally snapped, sending him back a pace.

Flora tossed a threepenny piece into the air, and the boy's eyes followed the course of the dull brass-coloured coin as it spun in the air towards the hat, his mouth breaking into a wide smile.

'Cor thanks, Missus!' He pushed up the brim of his hat with a wide smile.

'You're too soft, Flora.' Lydia tucked her arm through hers and pulled her away. 'You'll see a lot of that before the morning is over. Don't be too generous or you'll run out of coins in no time.'

'You said yourself, it's a tradition.' Flora could hardly grudge a few pennies. 'And I don't regard a penny for the guy as begging.'

'I suppose not. They put potatoes under bricks in the bottom, and when the fire burned down they were cooked.' Lydia brightened a little at the memory. 'I still don't think baked potatoes without that hint of ash are quite the same.'

The row of terraced houses on the next street was in a far worse state of repair than the ones they had just left. The plaster had broken away in places, leaving patches of lathe showing through. Windows grimy with dirt made them almost impossible to see through and some had no glass at all, only a sheet of sacking fixed with nails to rotting frames. Lopsided steps led to cracked and split wooden front doors, which offered little or no protection from intruders. Shabby, faded clothes in dull colours hung from lengths of string slung between windows.

The slippery ground underfoot dipped in the middle, where rainwater and rubbish had accumulated and spread. The smell of damp wood, ordure and boiled cabbage dominated, overlaid with more earthy, feral smells which made her eyes water.

Flora's foot slipped in a pool of greasy water and she stumbled, steadying herself with a hand on the nearest wall.

'Have you hurt yourself, Miss?' Abel sprang forward from his place beside Sally, a frown between his penetrating eyes. Besides the man's imposing size, his gentle manners endeared him to Flora, making her feel safer on these alien streets.

'A minor slip, that is all, but thank you.' She waved him away, watching as he dropped back to walk with Sally, her face turned up to him in infatuation.

'I cannot wait to get home and have a hot bath.' Flora shuddered as she picked her way across a dirty puddle. Not a blade of grass or even a weed broke up the flat grey buildings, where a tree would suffocate among these streets. How she pitied those forced to live in such depressing surroundings.

'Which is a luxury most people down here don't enjoy.' Lydia's voice took on a sharp edge. 'Have you any idea how much it costs to heat coal for hot water? Let alone the price of soap in relation to an ordinary family's weekly income?'

'I didn't mean to suggest anything.' Flora slowed her steps, startled by Lydia's tone.

'This is the first address on your list.' Lydia didn't appear to notice or chose not to as she pushed open a lop-sided gate with its middle spars missing.

The house was narrow, little more than the width of a door and a small window set between two waist-high walls which marked their neighbours. The bowed step bore the indentation of many feet, and in the absence of a door knocker, Lydia rapped her fist hard on the split wood.

'It's so quiet.' Flora stared up at the blank windows, sensing silent watchers on the other side. 'Almost sinister.'

'Most people will be at work at this time of day,' Lydia said, as the front door remained stubbornly closed against her onslaught, its peeling paint showed it had once been a darker colour. 'Those who have jobs that is. Women and children too.'

'Even the children?'

'Children to us, maybe, but to the factory owners, a nine-year-old can work a ten-hour day at the ovens.'

'I thought the 1880 Education Act put them in school where they belong at that age?' Flora said.

'Legally, yes. But plenty are forced to earn a living to help support their families. It's the way of the world.' Lydia heaved a sigh. 'The way of this world, anyway.'

'You appear to know a great deal about life here, Lydia.' Flora studied her profile, which she kept averted. Before Flora could ask her more, the door squeaked open on rusty hinges to reveal a man in shirtsleeves and waistcoat who narrowed his eyes at them in suspicion. 'What do ye want? Me rent's paid up till the end of the week.'

'It's not about that, Mr Flavell, I assure you.' Flora pretended to consult the list Miss Finch had given her, although she had memorised it. 'Is this where Albert Flavell lives?'

'Bertie is me sister's boy. She passed away three years ago. May she rest in peace.' The scepticism in his voice suggested this was in debate. 'I'm Joe Briggs.'

'My apologies, Mr Briggs.' Flora summoned her most winning smile. 'I was given this address by St Philomena's Hospital. We believe Albert recently suffered a severe case of bronchitis.'

'He did that, but they fixed him up at the 'ospital. What do you want wiv 'im?'

'I'm glad to hear your nephew is better, Mr Briggs.' At Flora's signal, Abel handed her the basket before returning to the gate where Sally waited. 'We brought some food to expedite his recovery.'

'Well, then.' Mr Briggs cast a swift glance at the alley, nodded and stepped back. 'Ye'd best come in.'

Sally and Abel remained outside, but even with just the three of them the tiny front parlour still felt cramped. The house comprised one room with a door in the rear, left open to reveal a tiny scullery with a cracked porcelain sink beneath a grimy one-paned window. A step in one corner with a rickety wooden door that only just covered the opening led to a narrow staircase that wound sharply upwards. Flora speculated that there was only one room above and apart from the scullery, only an outside privy in a paved rear yard.

A set of uneven shelves had been nailed to the wall above a scarred dresser that contained a meagre collection of mis-matched pots and a pair of dull pewter candlesticks with snubs of burned down candles. The walls had been papered in the distant past, the ghost of a pattern still visible in the corners.

A worn wooden table and three mismatched chairs sat under the front window, and a homemade rag rug was set before a tiny grate, now empty. Though the autumn day was mild, damp still leached from the walls to make the room smell musty.

'Take a weight off.' Mr Briggs cocked his chin towards two wheel-back chairs which needed some beeswax polish. 'I'd offer yer tea, but this ain't the Savoy 'otel.'

'We don't expect it, Mr Briggs.' Flora licked her lips, and debated how to begin.

'The matron at the hospital told us Bertie had missed his clinic appointment,' Lydia said, displaying no such reticence. 'We trust he hasn't suffered a relapse?'

'He din't need no appointment. Not now, he's better, and the cough has gone. He didn't go 'cos I don't have time to tek 'im. I 'as to work ya knows.'

'Of course, although you're not at work now.' Lydia nodded pointedly at an enamel faced clock that sat on the mantelpiece.

'Nay, well. Me shift don't start till three.' His bland expression gave no sign he had just fallen into his own trap. Clinic appointments were always in the mornings, so he could well have brought Albert.

Flora plucked a wood-framed sepia photograph from the tiny dresser; the room so compact, she only had to reach a hand to touch virtually everything in it. 'What a handsome boy.' She studied a fair-haired child of about ten with enormous eyes and an unsmiling, full mouth. 'Is this your nephew, Mr Briggs?'

'Aye.' His eyes narrowed again, the fingers of one hand flexing as if he would snatch it away from her. 'Everyone says he's a good-looking lad. Most people thought he was a girl until he were five.'

'May we see Bertie?' Flora asked though she could detect no sounds that a ten-year-old boy occupied the tiny house.

'Nay. He ain't 'ere. He's gorn to stay with me sister.' At Flora's enquiring look he checked himself. 'I mean, me other sister.'

'How nice for him.' She replaced the photograph gently. 'And where does she live?'

'Sussex.' He shifted his feet as if the subject made him uncomfortable. 'I thought the air would do 'im good.'

'That's considerate of you. And your sister.' Lydia glared at him; suspicion clear in every plane of her face. 'I know that county well. Whereabouts in Sussex?'

'Uh, well.' He performed an awkward twist of his mouth, accompanied by a quick jerk of one shoulder. 'By the seaside it is. He'll get some clean air and be right as rain when he gets back.'

'I'm sure he will.' Flora's softened her tone to counter Lydia's harsh one. 'And when is he due to come home?'

'I dunno. When me sister sends him, I expect.' He advanced on the basket Flora had set on a shaky table, its surface scarred by years of use. 'So what ye got there, then?'

'Since Albert, I mean Bertie, isn't here, we may as well go.' Lydia hooked the handle over one arm and moved towards the door. 'Good day to you, Mr Briggs.'

The man's face fell and Flora's conscience got the better of her. She withdrew a brown paper wrapped packet from the basket and held it out. 'Take this anyway, Mr Briggs. And I'm sorry we missed Bertie.'

His expression softened, and he muttered his thanks as he shut the door on them.

'Sussex, my hat,' Lydia grumbled when they gained the street. 'I doubt that man has the first idea where the boy is.' She glared at Flora. 'Why did you give him the food? He made it quite obvious he didn't want to speak to us.'

'I felt sorry for him,' Flora replied, giving the façade of the sad little house a last look. 'Besides, there's not a lot of point taking it home again.'

'I suppose you're right, and I shouldn't be ungenerous.' Lydia set off at a swift pace down the path. The fact she didn't believe Briggs' story any more than Flora did was implicit in the set of her shoulders.

11

The next address on Flora's list was in an adjoining street, which was even less appealing than the last. The door was opened by a surly, uncooperative woman who might have been any age between twenty and thirty-five. She smoothed work-reddened hands down a patched skirt, which was gripped firmly by a small child with a face so dirty, it was impossible to determine the sex.

When pressed with a combination of Flora's persuasion and Lydia's shortness, she became vociferous in her insistence it was none of their business where her girl was.

'We were merely enquiring how your daughter fared after she left the hospital, Mrs Fox.' Lydia used her best schoolmarm tone. 'She hasn't been well lately, and we thought some nourishing food would aid her recovery.'

'Martha ain't me daughter. She's me brother's girl.'

'Where exactly is your brother?' Flora asked.

'Went ta find work up north, 'cos there's been none here for weeks. Not for him anyway, what with his liking for the beer and the foreman at the docks sayin' he ain't reliable. He don't send me nothing for Martha's keep, neither.' She wiped her hands again, but it seemed to make no difference to the caked dirt embedded in her ragged fingernails. 'St Phil's fixed her up, and when she got home, a lady called and offered her a place in service, so I let her go.'

'What lady was this?' Lydia demanded.

'I don't recall what she called herself. She came to the door and said she needed a tweenie.'

'And you let Martha go, just like that?' Flora said.

'It were a good position.' She gave the shabby room an icy stare. 'Better'n I can offer her here.'

'Where did this woman take her, Mrs...?' Lydia left the sentence hanging.

'Flaherty's me name. And I dunno, do I? I've never been further than Deptford, so it meant nothing ta me. It were somewhere in the country.'

'Where in the country?' Flora asked more gently, hoping to dilute Lydia's confrontational tone.

Mrs Flaherty shrugged. 'Don't 'ave an address, but Martha promised to write when she could. Now, are you going to give us some of what's in that basket or what? Martha might have fallen on her feet but I've still got three nippers under four ter feed.'

'Of course.' Resigned, Flora beckoned Sally forward, though she suspected the chances of Martha being able to read or write were slight – a thought she kept to herself.

'You're too soft-hearted, Flora,' Lydia said when the door was closed smartly on them. 'That food was in exchange for information.'

'She looked as if she could do with a decent meal.' Flora glanced back at the house they had just left. 'Even if she sent an eight-year-old to work as a domestic servant.'

'It's not unheard of.' Lydia kept her attention on the list of addresses in her hand as they walked. 'Most tweenies are older than twelve, but those not old enough to handle the work upstairs are kept below stairs until they are trained.'

'I know what a tweenie is, Lydia,' Flora snapped. 'I have two.'

'Oh, of course.' Lydia sneaked a look at her. 'I don't mean to be patronising. But some children are worked hard in these big house kitchens. Some don't leave the basement for several years.' She held out the list, a gloved finger pointed at a line of the script. 'Is that a three?'

'Looks like it,' Flora muttered, then added, 'Did you notice that Flaherty woman said 'they fixed her up'? Mr Briggs used that same expression in relation to Albert.'

Lydia shrugged. 'It's a common enough figure of speech.'

'Maybe. But Alice said the families she spoke to seemed coached when she had spoken to them. The same thought occurred to me in there.'

'You could be right. Let's see how we get on at the other places.'

No one answered their knock at the next cottage, and at the penultimate address they found a young girl of about ten, who stared at them with round eyes but claimed to know nothing at all about a boy named James. In a fit of nerves, she suggested they return when her mother was at home and slammed the door in their faces.

Flora gave up in frustration but left a parcel of food on the windowsill where she was sure the girl would see it.

'Where next, Lydia? Though I feel we are wasting our time.'

'There are only a couple more, the first one just two streets away. It might seem as if we have gained nothing, but Miss Finch was right. There's something odd going on here.'

They found the tenement building comprised dark stairways that smelled of boiled cabbage and stale urine, the steps so caked with dirt, their boots hardly made a sound on the treads. The girl who answered the door on the second floor was not long out of her teens and wouldn't allow them inside. Perhaps this was prompted by the sight of Abel, who lounged with his back against the wall, with muscled arms crossed over his massive chest straining the arms of his jacket.

'I told you, he's gone away,' the girl insisted. 'He don't live 'ere no more.'

Defeated, Flora beckoned Sally, who had taken charge of the basket. Her maid was less lavish than Flora in doling out the packets of food.

'I cannot stay here any longer,' Flora whispered, drawing Lydia further down the hall. 'I need to get out of this building. I'm finding it difficult to breathe.' Taking quick breaths to lessen the worst of the stink was making her light-headed.

'This block is worse than some, I agree. I could do with some fresh air myself.' They had almost reached the main door when a shadow detached itself from the wall and loomed in front of them.

Flora gasped, more in shock of the unexpected than fear, for she had not heard a sound.

'What do you think you are doing?' Lydia spoke from behind her, her voice hard but with a tinge of fear that wobbled her last word. 'Get away from us immediately.'

'Just give us yer purse and we won't 'arm yer,' snarled a man wrapped in a shabby black coat, his words slurred together in a growl which made it difficult for Flora to make out what he said.

'And you, Missus,' another rough-voiced male addressed Lydia. 'We want yours as well.'

Flora's mouth dried as two more dark-clad figures emerged from the gloom beneath the staircase. One was smaller than the first, though all three looked to be young and undernourished; their caps pulled down to hide the top half of their faces.

Had they seen them go into the building and had waited for them to come out? How stupid of her to have left Abel behind.

These thoughts flashed through Flora's head as instinct made her clutch her purse tighter to her body, which made little sense as it contained only a couple of pounds at most.

'C'mon, don't hang about. We ain't got all day.' The first youth stepped closer. His chin was chiselled and youthful with no stubble, but his voice was hard, pitiless. He hooked one hand onto Flora's forearm. She stared down at his thin fingers, the nails rimed with black grime. Indignant, she was about to demand he remove it when something glinted in his other hand.

'He's got a knife!' Lydia whispered.

The words, 'I know', formed on Flora's tongue but she could not speak. Where was Abel?

The inactivity must have made the others nervous, as one of them gave an impatient grunt and lunged forward, a hand outstretched towards her purse. Flora froze, her instinct was to hang on to the bag, thus creating an undignified tussle.

'Let go of it, Flora. It isn't worth it!' Lydia begged.

Her words made sense but Flora couldn't move, her fingers cramped onto the bag as if it were a lifeline. A tussle ensued, ending when Abel appeared from nowhere and with a furious growl, shoved the youth to one side. With a hand on the collars of the other two, he tossed them across the hallway so they landed on their friend. All three ended up in a jumbled heap on the stone floor where Abel laid into them with fists and feet. Their answering blows were more defensive than an actual fight, resulting in a series of surprised yells, grunts, and thumps.

After mere seconds, their attempts at resistance ceased. One boy on the floor scrambled onto all fours away from the melee, his face a picture of blind panic at the sight of his two friends pinned to the floor by the massive form of Abel, who now stood over them, his clenched hands on his hips as he stared down at them.

The smallest of the boys, the one who had not felt the worst of

Abel's wrath scrambled to his feet and with a last glance into Abel's angry features, bolted through the door that slammed back into place with such force, the frame rattled.

Another youth curled into a foetal position where he lay, moaning and clutching his shoulder where a blow or a kick had landed. Beside him the one who had ordered Flora to hand over her purse was on his knees, bent over and retching.

'Go on, get off out of here before I call a constable.' Abel cocked his chin at the door and tugged down his jacket.

'Can't—' The youth on his knees held an outstretched hand towards Abel in a feeble effort to ward him off. 'Can't-get-me-breaf.'

Abel grunted, grabbed him by the scruff of his neck with one hand, and propelled him towards the door that he held open with the other. Either it was deliberate, or Abel didn't care when the youth collided with the doorframe, tripped and fell onto his knees. Abel merely hauled him to his feet again, his boot connecting with his rear as he sent him on his way.

The third youth scampered across the floor on all fours and made a lunge for the door, ducking to avoid a final cuff from Abel as he disappeared into the street.

'Thank goodness!' Lydia exhaled noisily. 'I thought you'd never get here.'

'I heard them from the landing.' Abel retrieved the knife from the floor and examined it, his upper lip curled in disgust. On closer inspection, Flora saw it was a light, badly made and cheap object which looked less threatening than it had a moment before, dwarfed by Abel's massive hand.

'If I hadn't been so frightened, I might laugh at what you just did, Abel.'

'Leastways, it was more interesting than carrying a basket all day.' Abel pushed a hand through his brown hair, which now refused to stay in place and flopped over his forehead, and grinned. 'Are you ladies all right?' he asked, almost as an afterthought.

'Perfectly.' Flora brushed grime from her purse with a gloved hand. 'I'm surprised the entire building hasn't come running to see what all the noise was about.'

'Doubt it,' Sally said from halfway up the flight of stairs, the basket slung between both hands. 'More likely they'd lock their doors and take no notice.' Her brown eyes shone with admiration as she sauntered past Abel, throwing him a shy look from beneath her lashes.

Abel returned her smile, and gave the knife a last look before slipping it into his pocket.

'We are both unhurt, thanks to you, Abel.' Flora re-entered the street, her fists clenched to stop them shaking. She wasn't going to admit to the nausea that gripped her lower belly. If Lydia hadn't brought Abel, they would have been robbed or attacked.

Never again would she dismiss Bunny, whose repeated warnings she should not wander London streets alone she had brushed aside as unnecessary fussing. For the first time it came home to her that London was not all elegant squares and fine houses interspersed with green spaces. It was hard, dark and dangerous and life was worth little.

'I told you he'd be useful, didn't I?' Lydia displayed no trace of nerves as she adjusted her hat and followed Flora into the street. 'Not that I expected that to happen.'

'Nor did I.' Flora released a relieved breath as the door slammed shut behind her.

'Well, I suggest you stay close to me in the future,' Abel said, herding the three of them in front of him like a sheepdog. 'Tough neighbourhood is this.'

12

Flora released a long sigh as the door of the last place they visited was closed on her. The young woman who lived there had told them her brother had been accepted into an apprenticeship but seemed to know little about it.

'She was more interested in what we had to give her,' Lydia said.

'She looked scared.' Sally rested the basket on the ground and re-arranged the parcels inside, separating them from the fruit.

'Abel might have been responsible for that,' Lydia said. The way he lounged against the doorframe and picked his fingernails with a file was enough to frighten anyone.

'No, Missus,' Sally shook her head slowly. 'It were more than that. She was told not to talk.'

Flora glanced at Lydia, who shrugged.

'She could be right,' Lydia said. 'I have the same feeling. Although it appears not everyone finds us unwelcome.' Lydia nodded to where a girl of about eleven leaned against a gatepost on the other side of the road, watching them.

She wore a faded green dress a size too large for her, beneath a shapeless cardigan that hung unevenly, caused by a rip above the pocket. Her scrawny legs stuck out from an ankle-length skirt, ending in bare, dirty feet. Shrewd brown eyes looked out at them from beneath toffee coloured hair that could have used a wash.

Flora hesitated to approach her, assuming she would run and be swallowed up by the maze of alleys. Instead, the girl pushed away from the low wall and sauntered towards them, her chin stuck out belligerently. She halted in front of Abel, her head tilted back as far as it would go without losing her balance.

'You was the one who saw off those Clay boys didn't cha? Never seed 'em so scared. They won't stop till they reach London Bridge at the rate they was going.' She folded her scrawny arms across her chest without a trace of nerves. 'What they bin feeding you, then?'

Lydia snorted and Sally giggled behind her hand.

Abel's smile exhibited surprise and admiration, and he muttered something which might have been, 'cheeky mare'.

'Are you from St Phils?' the girl asked Flora.

'You could say that.' Flora bent towards her so their eyes were on a level; the girl's wide and suspicious.

'You been askin' about the kids who went to the 'ospital and didn't come back?'

'Do you know something about it?' Flora asked, conscious that Lydia had moved up beside her to listen.

'My friend Annie lives over there.' The girl nodded towards a building with a lop-sided wooden door that might once have been painted green, but showed mostly bare wood. 'She's not there no more. I bin looking for her.'

'What's your name?' Flora asked gently, though at the same time took a step back to avoid any lice which might have taken up residence in the girl's thatch of hair.

'Ada, Ada Baines.' She swiped a grubby sleeve beneath her nose.

Lydia consulted the list, but when she looked up at Flora again, shook her head.

'Have Annie's parents asked the people at St Philomena's where your friend is now?' Flora mentally crossed her fingers. Perhaps Annie had died, and no one thought to tell Ada.

'Ain't got no parents.' Ada's eyes glinted. 'She took herself. She didn't need no nursemaid. She's twelve, like me.'

'I see.' Flora concealed a smile at the child's irrepressible confidence. 'When did you see her last?'

'Two weeks since. Pr'aps longer.'

'She could have gone somewhere to convalesce,' Flora said, remembering Alice mentioning the home on the south coast where they sent children to regain their strength.

'Dunno what that is.' Ada shrugged. 'Huggins told me she'd gone, but he wouldn't say where.'

'Who is Huggins?' Lydia asked.

'Her uncle. Or that's what he calls hisself. Took up wi Annie's mam a year ago, but she scarpered last Christmas. Annie doesn't like him.'

'Is there a possibility Annie ran away?' Lydia asked.

'She wouldn't do that.' Ada's eyes narrowed as if Lydia had insulted her. 'A Sally Army bloke came to see Huggins with another man.'

'What Sally Army bloke?' Lydia pushed into the gap between Flora and the girl. 'What was he like?'

'I dunno. He wouldn't even look at me.' Ada's eyes looked suspiciously wet but didn't develop into full-blown tears. 'The bloke with him said Annie had gone into service at some big 'ouse north of the river. I told him Annie and me were going into service together, but he didn't care. Said she was happy where she was and told me ter clear off.'

'Maybe Annie needed the work and didn't have a choice?' Flora thought her story sounded odd. If Annie had gone away, that wouldn't explain why she hadn't said goodbye to her friend, or been seen since.

'I don't believe it.' Ada's jaw jutted forward. 'Anyway, the fella said Annie's grandma had gone with her. He was lying. She don't 'ave no grandmother. Besides, she wouldn't 'ave left me without a goodbye. We're best friends.'

'Have you seen the Salvation Army man before, or since?' Lydia eased closer.

'Seen him about a few times.' Ada shrugged. 'Short, stocky bloke in a brown coat. He's got funny eyes. Like this.' With unnerving skill, Ada made one eye slide inwards.

'What else do you know about him?' Flora persisted.

Could he be the man Lizzie Prentice saw at the hospital? A stocky man with a squint shouldn't be hard to locate. Or was she being optimistic?

'Only that he drinks at the Corks.' Ada eyed the basket Sally held, which made her pull it protectively closer.

'Corks?' Flora frowned. 'What's that?'

'The Cork Galleon, down that way.' She hooked a none-too-clean thumb towards the main road.

'She means The Antigallican,' Lydia said. 'It's what the locals call the public house on Tooley Street.'

'Alice mentioned that place to me the last time we spoke,' Flora said, surprised that Lydia not only knew of it, but also its colloquial name.

'His name's Swifty Ellis,' Ada said, bringing all eyes swivelling in her direction. When no one spoke, she blew out a frustrated breath. 'The man wiv the funny eyes.'

'Why didn't you tell us that in the first place?' Lydia shook the girl by one shoulder, hard enough to make her wobble on her feet.

'Di'nt ask.' Ada rolled her shoulder out of Lydia's hold, unconcerned.

Lydia's unsympathetic manner puzzled Flora, first the boy Bertie's uncle and now this scrap of a girl whose only concern appeared to the whereabouts of her friend. Why was she being so harsh?

'I see, well, thank you, Ada. We'll be sure to ask about Annie.' Flora turned away, dismayed that not only had they got nowhere, but they had another name to add to their list.

'Missus?' Ada called her back. 'Can I have some o' them little oranges?' She pointed at the basket hooked over Sally's arm. 'You're giving 'em away aren't cha?'

Ashamed she had not thought of it herself, Flora reached in and retrieved four tangerines from the basket she handed to Ada, together with a paper-wrapped parcel. 'There are some sausages in there. Ask your mother to cook them for you.'

'Don't be daft.' Ada dropped the fruit into a pocket and tucked the parcel under one arm. 'Me mum's doing a double shift at the biscuit factory. I'll cook 'em meself.' She gave Abel a slow wink before darting through a rickety gate into the faceless building opposite.

'Remind me not to patronise young children again, Lydia,' Flora gestured to Sally to retrieve the basket. 'We may as well go home.'

'At least we can go home.' Lydia's melancholy had returned. 'We aren't trapped in this place like that poor scrap.' She cocked her chin at the door of Ada's building.

Their slow walk had brought them to a short parade of shops with peeling paint, ancient posters and dusty windows, which made it impossible to see what was stacked behind the glass. Wooden boxes of gnarled vegetables, fruit, and racks of second-hand clothes were spread out on the pavements in front.

'Then again,' Lydia said after a moment. 'Ada could have made up the story about this Annie to encourage you to hand over some food.'

'Surely not!' Flora gasped.

Lydia shrugged. 'You don't know these people. They're not naturally cruel, but a stranger's finer feelings play no part in their fight for survival. They do what they have to. I'm not judging, them. It's the truth.'

Jolted by Lydia's pragmatism, Flora acknowledged the harsh realities she had never had to face before. Poor did not mean a lack of luxury, fewer choices and sparser homes; real poverty was insidious, hardening the spirit, and deadening any joy in life that grabbed the soul and never let go. Flora could walk away whenever she chose, but Ada and many like her had no choice. They were trapped.

'I don't really care if Ada made up that story about Annie,' Flora said after a moment. 'At least she'll get a decent meal inside her tonight.' She slowed her steps. 'Lydia, how do you know so much about this place and these people?'

Lydia looked about to make some throwaway remark but checked herself. She bit her bottom lip, then cast a quick look over her shoulder to where Abel and Sally had fallen behind.

'I haven't always lived in Kinnerton Street.' Lydia stared ahead, so all Flora could see of her expression was her profile. 'I was brought up in Peabody Buildings between East Lane and the rope factory less than a mile from here.'

'I had no idea.' This was the last thing Flora had expected. How had soft-spoken Lydia come from these slums to a neat little house in Belgravia?

'Why should you?' Lydia shrugged. 'I got out. Many don't. I put the past behind me so it wouldn't colour the rest of my life.' Her tone was flat, emotionless as if she spoke about someone else.

'What was it like?' Flora tried to imagine Lydia as a child with wayward hair and dirty bare feet like Ada, but the image refused to form.

'My father was a foreman at the Peek Frean factory when I was a nipper. He earned a regular wage, so my parents qualified for the Peabody. We rented four rooms on the first floor.' Lydia paused in the road and lifted her face to the sky. 'Can you smell that?'

Flora took a tentative breath. 'Sulphur, soot and manure?'

'No, not that.' Lydia laughed. 'Beneath it is a sweet baking smell.'

'I noticed that earlier. At first I thought it was a restaurant or a bakehouse?'

'It's the biscuit factory. That smell is part of my childhood. It carries all the way back to Jamaica Road. The factory is a mile away, on the other side of the railway line. That or the jam factory. The smell is stronger on some days, depending on the direction of the wind.

'In the summer, we walked home from school past the open doors of the factory where the girls in their white aprons packed the biscuits. They'd bring out paper bags of broken ones and we'd gorge ourselves on the waste ground.' Her smile turned wistful. 'I cannot look a garibaldi in the face to this day. Too many memories.'

'I'm sorry. Perhaps I shouldn't have asked you to come with me this morning.' Flora tucked her arm through Lydia's and pulled her closer.

'I wanted to. If children are being taken, this is an ideal place to do it. Most people here are good and hardworking who live for their families and care for them as they should. Then there are the others. The children keep coming and they don't know how to stop it. And when they do, they are in the way. Another mouth to feed or sometimes another pair of hands to send out to thieve for them. There's no one for them to complain to, much less care.' She slowed her steps, her chin lifted as she met Flora's gaze. 'I don't ask for sympathy, Flora, I thought I had left all this behind, but seeing young Ada was a reminder of things too much a part of me to forget.

'I was lucky. My parents loved me and I was an only child, so I didn't have to share a pallet bed with three or four others. Some children at the school where I taught came from homes like Ada's.'

'You taught school here?'

She nodded. 'I began my teaching career in Bacons Free School, founded by the guild of tannery workers on Weston Street.' She glanced back over her shoulder to where Abel and Sally walked about ten paces behind; the top of Sally's head bobbed in line with Abel's shoulder, her face animated as she chatted, the basket slung between them.

'If you want to know what life in a place like this really means, ask Sally. She was raised in Whitechapel, so her childhood must have been like mine. Probably worse – at least there are jobs to be had here.'

'Perhaps I shall.' Flora had dismissed Sally's outrageous sounding claims as an exaggeration, or a call for attention. Something she would never do again. 'I wish you had told me, Lydia. Why did you feel the need to hide your upbringing from me?' Flora asked, hurt she was being condescended to. 'I'm hardly gentry. I was brought up in a servants' hall.'

'You were a governess, an upper servant, which isn't the same thing. You also lived in the country, with fresh air, clean water, space to run and play and the best food available. Now look at you. The daughter of a gentleman, married to a solicitor and with an earl for an uncle!'

'Maybe so, but I would never have judged you for your past.'

'I know, but it was more about me than you. I found it hard enough telling Harry.'

'How did he take it?' No wonder Lydia felt inadequate to Harry's previous fiancée, who had been a considerable heiress.

'Wonderfully well.' Lydia laughed. 'His family is high society now, but he told me when he was a boy, he discovered his great grandfather earned his fortune from cotton mills and mining. He was a self-made man who treated his workers abominably. The family don't want it talked about, but Harry refuses to be ashamed of his origins. Why else do you think they were so keen for him to marry Evangeline?'

'Harry doesn't have anything to apologise for.'

'That's what I said, but somehow, he feels he owes something to the common working man. He's been to listen to the Member of Parliament for West Ham talk. What's his name now? Keir Hardie. His mother was scandalised when she heard he had joined the Labour Party.'

'I imagine she is.' Flora giggled as they halted at the corner, where two equally shabby streets meandered off in different directions.

'I think that's enough about me for one day,' Lydia said. 'We have more important matters to deal with. What about the man Ada mentioned who visited Annie's stepfather? Swifty, was it?'

Flora nodded. 'He could be a local bully boy working for someone with money and influence who can afford to hire a henchman to do his dirty work.'

'Exactly. And if he's the same one seen outside the hospital, he's the procurer.'

'Who is he procuring these children for?' Flora said, unwilling to ask 'why' out loud, though she had her suspicions.

'We'll have to think about it more,' Lydia said, waiting for Abel and Sally to catch them up. 'We'd better make our way back to the Old Kent Road if we want to locate a cab. We won't find any down here.' Her delightful smile, absent all morning, returned. 'Besides,' she adopted an accent that mimicked Ada's, 'me plates of meat are sore, what wiv tramping ruddy pavements all morning.'

13

Locating a hackney in the bustle and noise of the wider thoroughfare of Jamaica Road proved more difficult than Flora had imagined, even with Abel doing the hard work for them.

Thunder groaned ominously ahead, and a sudden burst of rain drove them to shelter beneath a shop awning.

'Never mind a cab, Abel. We can take that. It's going our way.' Lydia waved towards a horse bus that had pulled up several feet away.

'I've never been on one of those before,' Flora stared up at the open upper deck, where the four men in suits brave enough to sit in the open air all raised umbrellas against the rain.

'Then it will be a novel experience.' Lydia dragged her through a rapidly forming stream of water that ran along the gutter onto the platform. Their feet had barely reached the first row of seats before the driver pulled away.

Flora gasped and turned to scan the road behind them, only to relax again as she spotted Sally and Abel behind her. He had lifted her bodily in one arm while the other held onto the half-empty basket.

Flora followed Lydia down the narrow aisle, avoiding elbows and wide hats as she went, finally collapsing onto an empty seat.

'Abel appears to have taken a liking to your Sally,' Lydia whispered.

'So I see.' Flora watched as Abel settled her maid into a seat, then slid in beside her, the basket perched on his lap.

The thirty-minute ride proved to be more enjoyable than Flora had expected, despite a steady rainfall that flowed in rivulets down the windows, obscuring the view. By the time they reached Hyde Park Corner, the deluge had stopped as quickly as it began, carving a rainbow into the sky where clouds parted to reveal patches of blue.

'We'll walk the rest of the way,' Flora said, appreciative of the cleaner air, made refreshing by the rain after the cloying atmosphere of the ugly, rubbish strewn streets they had recently left.

At Eaton Place, where Flora invited Lydia to take luncheon, the two availed themselves of Flora's well-appointed bathroom to remove the street grime from their face and hands, leaving Sally to entertain Abel in the kitchens.

'Harry will have to make do with a bowl and pitcher to shave in when he moves into my house.' Lydia giggled, patting her face with a fluffy white towel. 'I haven't even told him about the outside privy.'

'Won't the renovations on his uncle's property in Kensington be finished by the time you are married?'

'I doubt it,' Lydia said, as she followed Flora downstairs to the dining room. 'The house is in a poorer state than even poor Harry imagined, though it was a wonderful surprise. Harry doesn't mind, but his mother says he's lowering himself by starting our married life at my house.'

'Your house is darling, Lydia, and that's a ridiculous attitude.'

Flora smiled at Stokes as he placed a plate of hot, sliced pork and potatoes on the table between them. 'I'm glad to be home. I'm still shaky after that encounter with those men in the stairwell. I don't know what I would have done had Abel not been there.'

'It was nice of you to invite him to take his meal in the kitchens with Sally.' Lydia spooned vegetables onto her plate.

'Sally looked fit to burst with happiness, didn't she? I expect she'll be on her best behaviour for the rest of the week. How long have you known him?'

'Abel? He's lived in the house at the end of our street since we moved in. He was so kind to Mother during her last illness, and would even look in on her occasionally when I was teaching at the Academy.' At this mention of her mother, Lydia stared at her lap, her mouth working as she fought for control. Lydia's mother had been ill for over a year, but her death five months before had still come as a shock.

'I must remember to recompense Abel for his time,' Flora said briskly, aware Lydia was not the type to indulge in public emotion and wouldn't welcome platitudes. 'I'm glad the rain held off until we were on our way home.'

'You don't have to distract me, Flora. I'm all right, really.' Lydia applied her cutlery to the meat on her plate. 'I'm sorry I was so maudlin, but I didn't expect Bermondsey to generate that kind of emotion in me. This might sound odd, but I didn't see the filth and squalor in quite the same way when I was younger. It was simply home, and I knew no better.'

'Don't feel you have to talk about it if you don't want to.' Flora slid the condiment dish towards her.

'I've never been one to pretend, and as I mentioned before, Harry knows all about it so it's hardly a dark secret.' Lydia picked at her food with a fork. 'Life wasn't so bad at the Peabody.'

'Remind me again – where did that name come from? It seems an odd choice for people's homes.'

'Mr George Peabody was an American philanthropist. A banker, I heard, who built several estates in London for poor working folk. The emphasis being on "working". Mother was thrilled when we found out we were eligible for rooms there. I recall making a fuss about having to be vaccinated against smallpox before we could move in.'

'Was that a rule or something?'

'Yes, everyone had to be. They scrape a layer of skin off your arm and rub it with a quill. Quite painful, actually.' She rubbed her upper arm through her sleeve as if recalling the pain. 'I still have the scar. It must have worked, as there wasn't one case of smallpox in the buildings all the time we lived there.'

Flora poured water into her glass while contemplating whether she ought to have Arthur vaccinated. 'I expect the Peabody Buildings were more comfortable than one of those draughty little cottages?' Flora recalled the bare walls and cracked doorframes and the mildew smell that made her nose itch.

'In relation to what?' Lydia snorted. 'The flats were basic, with a cast iron range, an oven, and a boiler. No bathroom, though. We had to share a toilet block with other families. Our treat for the week was when Dad took Mother and me to the public baths built for the dockers in Spa Road.'

'You had to go elsewhere for a bath?' Flora asked, astonished.

'Oh Flora, what a sheltered thing you are. This is London. Even well-off families use public baths. Better than a tub in the scullery. The hot water is pumped through pipes, not heated in pots on a range. Far more convenient.'

'I suppose so,' Flora mused, wrestling with the concept.

'We had to walk through the railway tunnel to get there.' Having taken the first step in recalling her past, Lydia appeared to get into her stride. 'If there was a train coming when we were on our way back, I refused to enter the tunnel until it had gone by in case I got dirty again.'

'It was the dirt which struck me too,' Flora said. 'The air seemed to be thick with grime that clung to everything. I'll make sure Sally gets that coat properly cleaned before I wear it again.'

'That's because of all the factories. My clothes were always stiff from dirt that became ingrained in the fibres. Washing them in a tub could never quite get it all out. I remember Mother had a friend who lived in the Peabody in Blackfriars Road. We would walk there on a Sunday to see them. I used to love going there because they had a patch of grass at the back for the children to play in. It was only a square of green, but it was paradise to me. At East Lane, all I had was a triangular concrete yard.'

Flora gave her a weak smile, recalling the rolling fields and rose garden she had had to play in as a child. Surroundings she realised now she had always taken for granted.

'When did you move to Kinnerton Street?' she asked carefully, eager to know how Lydia's fortunes had altered so drastically, but not wanting to pry. Bermondsey to Belgravia was quite a leap.

'That was unexpected.' Lydia toyed with a carrot on her plate but did not eat it. 'When I was thirteen, Father's mother died. It seems they didn't get on, for reasons which were never revealed to me. I knew nothing about my grandmother and we had never met, but Father was her only relative, so her house came to him when she died.' Her eyes glowed at the recollection. 'The first time I saw that little townhouse, I thought we were rich. Eight entire rooms for the three of us and bedrooms with real fireplaces. The basement kitchen had hot water, and a proper cooking range. Even the outside privy was a luxury, as it was only for us. We could even afford to hire a maid. I was in heaven. I did so much better in school too, as I had somewhere private to study. Father was so proud when I became a teacher.'

'What happened to your father?'

A cloud passed over Lydia's face, and she stared at her plate. 'An accident at the factory. An oven door wasn't closed properly and—' She twirled her fork above her plate as if she needed time to compose herself. 'He, uh, he was burned. Badly. He took three days to die.' She looked up and gave a shaky smile. 'The factory took care of the funeral and looked after Mother and me. We didn't suffer.'

'I'm so sorry.' Flora covered Lydia's hand on the table with hers. 'And naturally you suffered, just not in the way you mean.'

'It was a while ago.' Lydia shrugged, then straightened abruptly, sliding her hand from beneath Flora's. 'Now. You promised I could see that lovely baby of yours. I expect he has grown since I last saw him.'

They adjourned to the sitting room, where the nursemaid arrived promptly in response to Flora's summons, her arms full of a boisterous, beaming Arthur.

'Did you really name him after Arthur Conan Doyle?' Lydia's question was delivered with a dose of scepticism.

'Of course not. We both liked the name, although I'm fond of the Sherlock Holmes stories.'

'He's adorable.' Lydia cuddled the squirming baby, while Milly faded into the background, apparently reluctant to withdraw entirely.

Flora suppressed a sigh. 'Milly, why don't you take a break and have a cup of tea in the kitchens?'

'I've not long had my luncheon, Miss Flora.'

'Just fifteen minutes. I think we can be trusted with Arthur for that long.'

The girl dropped a swift, if grudging, curtsey and obeyed, though her expression remained sullen.

'You still don't like her, do you?' Lydia unbent Arthur's fingers from her bottom lip.

'I don't have to like her as long as she's conscientious.' Flora was reluctant to give Lydia the impression her nurse didn't trust her with her own child. 'He grows so quickly, which was the first thing William said when he was here the other day.'

'How is William, and how does he enjoy being a grandfather?'

'He's a little bemused.' Flora smiled as Lydia caught Arthur's hand in mid-wave and planted kisses on the palm, eliciting delighted baby chuckles. 'He still feels he needs to shower me with gifts he's so thrilled.'

'I wouldn't complain about that.' Lydia blew bubbles into the soft folds of Arthur's neck while he made grabs at her hair.

'Lydia, about our visit to Bermondsey this morning,' Flora said slowly. 'Did it strike you that none of the people we talked to were actually the children's parents?' When Lydia remained silent, she went on, 'Albert Flavell lived with his uncle, as did the second girl, Martha, was it? Elsie with her grandmother and that girl Ada told us – Annie – lived with a stepfather.'

'Annie wasn't on the list Miss Finch gave you.'

'I know, but if Ada is to be believed, she's still missing. It all points to the fact these children were taken from their homes, but not by force. Their families gave them away.'

'Or sold them.' Lydia absently smoothed the baby's golden hair away from his face.

'I was trying to come up with another explanation, as that one is too horrible to contemplate.'

'We need to face it, Flora. It's possible this man Swifty offered the families enough money for not only the children, but also their silence.'

Flora's hand froze on its way to stroke Arthur's cheek. Hearing her say it aloud chilled her.

'Those children we asked about were nephews, nieces, and grandchildren,' Lydia said. 'They were specifically chosen because the families wouldn't be hard to persuade to hand them over.'

'How could anyone sell a child?' Arthur started to grizzle and Flora held out her arms and the baby lurched into them, only to demand immediately he go back to Lydia, where he padded his feet on her lap like a cat.

'I doubt the families understood what they were doing.' Lydia tucked her hand beneath the baby's knees, giving him no option but to sit. 'My guess is, this Swifty person promised to secure positions for them on the condition they told no one about it.'

'Maybe they are too afraid to go against him?' Flora said.

'Whatever their reasons, there are no apprenticeships, or servant's places in grand country houses.'

'Those poor children.' Flora bit her lip as stark reality made her stomach knot. 'We have to do something.'

'That's the problem. Where do we begin to look when no one has complained?' The baby's eyelids fluttered closed and his head lolled against Lydia's bodice. In seconds, his chest rose and then fell again in a gentle rhythm.

'How does he do that?' Flora looked on at her son in amazement. 'One moment he's wide awake and lively, the next he's fast asleep.'

'I don't know, but I envy him.' Lydia cradled the baby in the crook of her arm. 'Now, what were we saying?'

'How do we get the police to open a proper investigation?' Flora broke off as the door opened to admit Milly, who glided forward and relieved Lydia of the sleeping baby. Had she been waiting behind the door?

'Miss Flora?' Stokes appeared in the doorframe just as Milly passed him on the way out. 'There's a telephone call for you.'

Lydia rose. 'If you're busy, I ought to go.'

Flora waved her down again. 'Not yet. We need to make a plan.' She entered the hall as the sound of Milly's footsteps receded up the stairs. 'Just wait a moment until I have taken this call.'

'That wasn't bad news, was it?' Lydia asked when Flora returned to the sitting room. 'You look pale.'

'It was Alice Finch at the hospital. Another child has gone missing.'

'Oh, no.' Lydia stood, her face a mask of anguish.

'Alice didn't want to discuss it over the telephone, so I'm going to St Philomena's to talk to her. I was planning to go anyway.'

'Now?' At Flora's nod, she said, 'Then I'm going with you.'

14

When they arrived at St Philomena's, Forbes, the porter, had evidently received his instructions, for Flora was hardly inside the front door before he carved the way for them, through a crocodile line of visitors, to the office where Alice awaited them.

Alice leapt to her feet and greeted Flora with the warmth of an old friend, which she extended to Lydia.

'Lydia was the friend I told you about who came with me to Bermondsey this morning,' Flora explained as they took their seats opposite the vast desk. 'She has a comprehensive knowledge of the neighbourhood which proved useful.'

'How kind of you, Miss Grey.' The strain of the last hours stood in Alice's eyes as she grasped the younger woman's hand. 'I apologise for involving you in this affair, but despite what some people might think, I believe this latest disappearance is connected to the others.'

'As do I, Miss Finch,' Lydia said. 'In fact, I was treated here for bronchitis when I was eight. I'll always remember how kind the nurses were.'

'Indeed?' Alice's shrewd gaze slid over Lydia in her fashionable and expensive clothes, the surprise she must have felt well concealed. 'I'm always happy to be reacquainted with former patients. Not that I was here then.'

Flora fidgeted in her chair. 'Alice, tell us about this child who has gone missing. I've been fretting in the cab all the way here.'

'Yes, of course.' Alice folded her hands on the desk in front of her. 'Her name is Isobel Lomax. Her parents went to Leeds to visit relatives and left the child with a nanny, who brought her to the hospital because she was running a fever.'

'What happened?' Flora asked.

'A misunderstanding, from what I can gather.' Alice said. 'Isobel had only a mild chest congestion, but it was frightening enough for the nanny. When she returned for Isobel yesterday to take her home, she was told she had been collected the day before. Sister Lazarus thought she had been discharged, but the nurse on duty said there was nothing written in the discharge book. No one missed the child for an entire day.'

'Did anyone see Isobel leave?' Lydia asked.

'Forbes said a child matching her description was escorted through reception by a respectable-looking man he assumed was her father. They got into a hansom cab and left, but he had no idea where.'

'He thinks it was her,' Flora said. 'Isn't he sure?'

'Who can say?' Alice lifted her hands, palms upwards. 'We have sixty to a hundred children here at any one time, most of whom stay for an average of four days. He cannot possibly remember them all.' Alice leaned back in her chair, defeated. 'Isobel is an attractive little girl of seven with fair hair and blue eyes. That alone makes me doubly concerned for her welfare.'

'That doesn't sound encouraging.' Flora chewed her bottom lip, the implications of Alice's words raising the hairs on her arms. 'Can the porter describe the man she left with in more detail?'

'All he could tell us was that he wasn't tall, dark-haired, with a moustache and he wore a black overcoat and top hat.'

'Which covers about half the men in London,' Lydia observed, unhelpfully.

'It doesn't sound anything like the stocky man with a squint Lizzie saw when the others went missing,' Flora said. 'We think we've discovered his name. Swifty Ellis,' she added.

Alice frowned. 'Not a name that's familiar to me. Perhaps one of the nurses knows who he is. It might be worth asking them.'

'Is the nanny certain the man who came for Isobel wasn't a member of her family?' Lydia asked.

'She insists she told no one Isobel was here,' Alice replied. 'She was too frightened her employers would find out she had let her fall ill.'

'She must be in a terrible state now the child is missing,' Lydia said.

'Indeed, she is. The police are dealing with her. The poor girl is only sixteen, and this is her first position.'

A discreet knock at the door preceded Sister Lazarus, who strode in without waiting for a response. 'Dr Reeder wishes to speak to you, Miss Finch,' she announced shrilly, looking through Flora as if they had never met.

'Would you tell him I'll be along when I'm finished here?' Alice clenched her fists on the desk with barely suppressed impatience.

'He says it's important,' the nurse insisted. 'I told him you would come straight away.'

'Is it a case of life or death regarding a patient, Sister?' Alice regarded the woman steadily, a nerve twitching at the corner of her eye.

'Well, not as I understand it, but—'

'In that case, I'll be there in due course. You may go.' Alice inflated her chest with a slow breath, which thinned her nostrils.

Sister Lazarus swung round abruptly, causing a jingling sound which came from somewhere in the folds of her skirt. She glared at Flora through black pebble eyes, then hauled the door shut with a firm bang, which was not quite a slam. Sister Lazarus not only possessed the demeanour of a bad-tempered nun, it appeared she equipped herself like a chatelaine. Did she jingle like a gypsy horse as she strode around the hospital? If so, at least the students could hear her coming.

Lydia stared at Flora with a 'what was that about?' look, to which she responded with a hand gesture that conveyed she would explain later.

'I apologise for that.' Alice cleared her throat while avoiding their eyes. 'Now, as I was saying, this time, the police are involved because Isobel has been reported officially missing.'

'What exactly are they doing about it?' Flora asked.

'They refuse to tell me anything.' Alice fiddled with the buttons on one cuff with the fingers of her other hand. 'Only that they have begun door-to-door inquiries in Greenwich.'

'Greenwich? But that's miles from here.' Lydia exclaimed. 'Why did the nanny bring her to St Philomena's?'

'It seems Isobel fell ill whilst they were on a visit to the Tower of London. In a panic, she summoned a cab driver and asked for the nearest hospital, and he brought them here.'

'Oh, I see. That makes sense.' Flora was thoughtful. 'But why search her own neighbourhood? Whoever took her is hardly likely to take her home.'

'My dear, that's exactly what I told them.' Alice sighed. 'The police said they have procedures to follow. With a missing child, they always begin in the home neighbourhood because children often simply wander off and get lost.'

'Procedures?' Flora fisted her hands in her lap. 'Why are they wasting time? Don't the police have any common sense?'

'It seems not,' Alice said. 'There's nothing we can do to dissuade them but we can hope for the best. Did your own enquiries produce better results?'

Flora sighed, disappointed. 'I'm afraid not, apart from the name Swifty Ellis. Which may or may not be relevant.'

'There was also the girl, Ada Baines,' Lydia reminded her. 'She asked us if we had seen a friend of hers who was treated here but has also gone missing.' Flora handed over the handwritten list with Annie's name added to it.

'Oh dear. Another one?' Alice regarded the page with dismay.

'No one wanted to talk to us.' Flora sighed after giving a recap of their investigations. 'We didn't learn any more than you did.'

'But you did, my dear.' Alice patted Flora's hand. 'I hadn't realised those children weren't living with their parents. That could be significant. Tell me about Annie.'

Flora smoothed the sheet of paper out on the desk and withdrew a tiny silver pencil from the bag. 'She lived in Wild's Rents and according to Ada, was brought here about three weeks ago.'

'Let me see.' Alice consulted a thick ledger on her desk, flicked back a few pages and ran a finger down the left-hand page. 'There was an Annie Sims treated for a chest infection early last month. She was discharged after three days.'

'That could be her.' Flora added the word 'Sims' and a question mark to Annie's name and wrote Isobel Lomax below it. 'We met a young friend of hers this morning who said she hadn't seen her since she came to the hospital.'

Alice released a long breath. 'This situation seems to get worse. Are we the only people who care about these children?'

'We need to find out more about this Swifty person,' Lydia said. 'If he's been hanging around the hospital, someone must know something about him.'

'The police had spoken to the rest of the staff already,' Miss Finch said. 'I'm reluctant to suggest I don't believe them.'

'Then we must think of a more subtle way to enquire,' Lydia said.

'What about that public house Ada mentioned?' Flora turned to Lydia.

'The Cork Galleon?' Lydia nodded slowly. 'The locals call it the Antigallican. Ada said he was a regular there.'

'I cannot see you young ladies going into that establishment,' Miss Finch said, her expression mildly incredulous.

'Not us,' Flora said slowly, turning possibilities over in her head. 'But we know someone who might go unnoticed.'

'You mean Abel?' Lydia asked.

They were interrupted by a sharp knock at the door which preceded the return of Sister Lazarus, apparently in no better mood than she had left. 'Dr Reeder says—'

'I know, thank you, Sister. I shall be along directly.' Alice rose and eased around the desk. 'Sister, would you mind escorting Mrs Harrington and Miss Grey back to the main entrance?'

'If you insist, Miss Finch, but I have work to do.' Sister Lazarus' eyes hardened as she watched Flora refold the list and return it to her bag.

'As do we all, Sister. However, I'm sure you can spare a few moments.' Alice closed the door behind her, leaving the three of them alone.

'Sister Lazarus,' Flora began, unable to rid herself of the feeling she addressed a nun. 'What do you think about these strange goings on at the hospital?'

Lydia tactfully wandered a few feet away and studied a photograph of a row of student nurses on the wall, though the set of her shoulders revealed she heard every word.

'I assume you mean those children Miss Finch is always talking about?' Sister Lazarus replied with a sniff. At Flora's nod, she shrugged. 'If Mr Buchanan or any of the other governors were worried about them, there would be a cause for concern, but they aren't. Miss Finch must have got it wrong.'

'Is Miss Finch inclined to exaggerate?' Lydia asked, her expression innocent.

'Well, not that I'm aware.' Sister Lazarus' cheeks turned a deeper pink. 'She's used to a more refined life than most of us.' She gathered files from the desk into a thick pile, apparently having forgotten the important work she had to do. 'As for those children, if their families didn't care about them, they wouldn't have brought them to the hospital at all.' She hefted the pile into her arms like a shield. 'Better not keep that cab waiting, Mrs Harrison. It's not easy getting them to come here at all.' She swept out of the room, leaving the door open as if she expected them to follow.

'It's Harrington,' Flora corrected, following her into the corridor.

'My mistake.' The ghost of a smile appeared on Sister Lazarus' face, confirming Flora's suspicion she had done so on purpose, but subtlety did not sit well on her sharp features. She looked more like a ferret about to pounce on a rabbit. 'Isn't this your second visit in as many days?' she asked, the question more like a reprimand. 'You must like it here, which surprises me, as we are only a charity hospital. I would have thought Guy's would have been a more suitable place for ladies like yourselves.'

'Miss Grey and I are considering making donations,' Flora lied, hurrying to keep up with the nurse's brisk pace. 'You do such excellent work here and my husband likes the idea of having a bed with his name on it.'

'Very admirable, I'm sure.' Sister Lazarus hugged the ledger close to her chest as she walked, but did not try to slow down.

'Did you treat Isobel Lomax when she was here?' Lydia put on a spurt in order to draw level with her other side. They must have presented an odd sight with the stern sister flanked by two well-dressed ladies skipping to keep up.

'Well, no. My job is mostly supervisory and I have a lot of administration to do. The actual nursing is done by others.'

'I can see you have a good deal of authority here.' Lydia wasn't going to be put off, it seemed. 'What do you think happened to her?'

'The child most likely wandered off because her nanny was late arriving to fetch her.' She shifted her feet, eager to get away. 'I blame the parents. How careless to leave a child in the sole care of a servant.'

'Will you attend Lizzie Prentice's inquest, Sister?' Flora asked, determined not to let her ignore them.

'Whatever for?' They had reached the entrance hall where she halted abruptly, the ledger held up to her chest like armour. 'It's a waste of my time when I could do more important work here.'

'You don't think it was possible she was attacked?' Flora asked.

'I haven't really thought about it.' Her thin lips curled. 'Members of the public come and go all the time through the rear yard. The gate is never locked.' Her narrowed eyes slid to Lydia and then back to Flora. 'Now you must excuse me. I have duties to perform.'

Without waiting for a response, she turned and strode away.

'She has no idea of anything,' Lydia murmured, her hard gaze on the woman's retreat.

'Or says she hasn't.' The nurse's comment about Miss Finch being accustomed to a more refined life came back to her. She wished she had asked her to explain, but doubted she would have got a straight answer.

15

'I do apologise, Mrs Harrington.' Forbes greeted them in the entrance hall with both arms held out in supplication. 'I'm afraid your taxi was claimed by another visitor. However, I sent a boy to fetch another one. He shouldn't be long if you wouldn't mind waiting.'

'It cannot be helped.' Flora concealed her frustration beneath a smile.

Lydia claimed a bench seat to the right of the porter's desk, but Flora was too restless to sit and paced a hall where nurses, hospital workers and visitors formed a constantly moving stream.

She paused in front of the statue of St Philomena, pondering the question who had collected Isobel from the hospital and how he or the elusive Swifty character were connected to Lizzie Prentice's death?

If the coroner decreed it was an accident, how could they convince the authorities to take the case of the other missing children seriously? Without official help there was so little they could do.

The sound of the front door opening, followed by Forbes'

enthusiastic greeting brought Flora's attention to where Mr Buchanan strode into the entrance hall, one hand lifted in salute to the porter while with the other, he accepted a thick white envelope the man handed him.

Mr Buchanan nodded in greeting to a passing doctor as he absently opened the letter, while displaying only mild curiosity as he perused the contents, which appeared to be two small slips of paper. As he read the first, his brows knitted together and he gave a sharp gasp and stared at it. He didn't appear to register the second slip which had fallen to the tiled floor, his focus on what looked to be a handwritten note.

Flora stepped forward and retrieved the fallen slip of paper, reading it rapidly before handing it back. 'Yours, I believe, Mr Buchanan?'

'Uh, thank you, Mrs...?' He nodded vaguely and reached for it, his other hand clenched in a fist around the note.

'Mrs Harrington,' Flora prompted. 'Miss Finch introduced us the other day.'

'She did?' He stared at the paper clutched in one hand as if it might bite him. 'Oh, yes, I think I remember. Er, now if you'll excuse me.' He marched over to the porter's desk, one hand slapped on the surface to gain the man's attention. 'Did you see who left this for me?'

'No, Mr Buchanan.' The porter stared vaguely at him. 'It was on the desk when I arrived this morning. Is there no return address?'

'Never mind.' Mr Buchanan shoved both papers and the envelope roughly into his pocket and pushed away from the desk, turned and headed for a door on the right.

'Flora!' Lydia called, 'Our taxi is here.'

'I'm coming,' Flora dragged her gaze away from the governor's back and turned around and collided with Sister Lazarus. Something small but hard hit Flora's thigh, but was hidden beneath the nurse's skirt.

'Oh, excuse me. I wasn't looking where I was going,' Flora said.

'It's of no importance.' Sister Lazarus acknowledged her with a curt nod and a sneer, not pausing in her stride.

Flora observed the woman's retreat, and spotted what looked like a shiny gold ball swinging from a chain attached to the nurse's skirt as she walked. She squinted to get a closer look, just as the nurse looked down in annoyance, and tucked the object into her pocket before walking on again.

'Flora,' Lydia's voice rose in mild impatience. 'Come along or we'll lose this one as well.'

'Coming.' Flora joined her, still frowning.

'What was that all about?' Lydia asked as the porter showed them to their cab and closed the wooden shutters over their legs.

'Do you like music?' Flora's thoughts raced as the incident in the hall ran through her head.

'Of course, doesn't everyone? What sort of music in particular?'

'There's a concert recital at the Bechstein Hall tomorrow evening.'

'I heard about that, some German pianist. He's reputed to be a musical genius.'

'Austrian, actually. It's his London debut with the Hallé Orchestra.' Flora grasped the brim of her hat as the driver urged their horse over the bump between the gates and the main road.

'Really?' Lydia's right eyebrow lifted slowly and her lips formed a tiny smile. 'Do you know what he will play?'

'Actually, I do. Brahms Piano Concerto No. 2, Opus 83 in B Flat Major.'

'And you got all that from a slip of paper?' At Flora's start, she laughed. 'I saw you hurl yourself across the floor at whatever fell out of the envelope that gentleman was holding. Not subtle, Flora.'

'Maybe not, but effective. I only caught a glimpse, but it was enough to remind me of an article I read in yesterday's paper about Mr Schnabel.'

'Are you going to tell me who the worried-looking gentleman was, and why you're so interested in a foreign pianist?'

'Mr Raymond Buchanan. He's one of the hospital governors, and something tells me that concert is the last place he wants to be. When he saw that ticket, he looked as if all his worst fears had been realised.'

'What has he got to do with anything?' Lydia asked, her voice raised above the clop of hooves and the rush of traffic passing them on both sides.

'Mr Buchanan is on the Board of Governors at St Philomena's.'

'Does Miss Finch think he's involved in the children's disappearance?' Lydia asked, going straight to the heart of the matter.

'No, quite the opposite. She seems to admire him.' The implication that Alice may also be involved was something Flora refused to contemplate, although experience had told her anyone could be a suspect until proven otherwise.

'Then why does he worry you?' Lydia tilted her head to one side.

'When Nurse Prentice's body was found, Alice, I mean Miss Finch, insisted Bunny and I leave before the police came. I saw Mr Buchanan in a cab beside us. I didn't think anything of it then, but seeing him just now reminded me.'

'I'm sorry, I still don't see the connection.'

'He was in a hurry to keep an appointment, so why was he still at the hospital an hour later? And why leave within minutes of a dead body being found on hospital grounds? Wouldn't he have been eager to remain and take command of the situation?'

'It's not exactly conclusive, Flora. And if he was trying to be discreet, he would hardly have got into a cab at the front entrance where everyone could see him after establishing he wouldn't be there.' Lydia tapped her finger tips against her lips. 'Has Sister Lazarus got anything to do with these instincts of yours? Your Mr Buchanan almost jumped out of his skin when he saw her just now.'

'Really? I didn't notice that.' Lydia's powers of observation were enviable. 'I assume it was a concert ticket in the envelope?' Lydia made a grab for the strap above her head as the cab took a sharp right turn. 'Where you intend to go in order to spy on him?'

'Something like that. I might be wrong about him, but if so, I'm sure Bunny would enjoy a musical evening.'

'I hate to say this, Flora, but you might be out of luck. That concert has been sold out for some time. Harry tried to buy tickets a month ago.'

'I have my ways of obtaining these things.' Flora flicked her a knowing look. 'Perhaps I'll get a box and keep a surreptitious eye on the man.'

'There are no boxes at the Bechstein Hall,' Lydia said with authority. 'There isn't even a gallery. It's only a five hundred seat theatre on one level with a raised stage. I imagine it might be difficult to watch someone without their noticing.'

'I'll have to think of something else then,' Flora said dejectedly and stayed silent for a while.

Their pace slowing into a right turn into Grosvenor Square, Flora spoke again.

'Lydia, what did you think of Miss Finch?'

'I thought her charming, as well as professional.' Lydia leaned closer, her voice raised above the noise of the traffic. 'There appeared to be some animosity between her and Sister Lazarus.'

'I'm not over fond of that woman either, especially when she put Alice's concerns about the missing children down to fussing. I would expect a nurse to have more compassion.'

'Perhaps Sister Lazarus has an inflated opinion of her own abilities and is simply jealous of Miss Finch?'

'That's one theory I suppose.' Flora gritted her teeth as the cab negotiated the clamour of vehicles which careered round Hyde Park Corner like they were on a racetrack. 'That wasn't why I asked. Do you think Alice and I look alike?'

The hansom pulled sharply to the side of the road outside Lydia's townhouse, slamming Flora's back against the upholstery. Flora pushed up the wooden flap and re-thought her usually generous tip.

'You don't still think Miss Finch could be your mother, do you?' Lydia asked.

Flora let the half-open flap fall back into place. 'I do, yes. Is that completely ridiculous?'

Lydia chewed her bottom lip before answering, while the horse whinnied and shifted its hooves as if impatient to be moving again.

'There is a certain resemblance between you. In the shape of your eyes, but it's fleeting.'

Flora's heart leapt then settled again. Was she willing to latch onto anything, no matter how slight, which might link her to Alice?

'Flora, I know you want this, but it's not logical. Why would she go by a different name and leave you to be raised by a man who wasn't a blood relation?'

'Maybe I simply want her to be my mother in order to answer all the questions I still have about why she disappeared.'

'You might have to face the fact you may never have those answers.' Lydia rested her hand on Flora's forearm. 'Can't you leave the past alone and enjoy your life now? You have so much.'

'You make me sound ungrateful and self-pitying.' A wave of shame flooded through her. 'But you're right. I have a lovely home, a wonderful husband and the sweetest baby in London. I should treat Alice Finch as a welcome new acquaintance, not a solution to the mysteries of my own past.'

Even as the words left her, Flora's mind screamed a denial. No, it wasn't enough. She felt incomplete not knowing why her mother had abandoned her. What could a six-year-old child have done to drive her own mother away?

'As a concert appears to be out of the question,' Flora said. 'Would you like to bring Harry to supper tomorrow evening? If we combine resources, we might come up with some strategy. I assume you have mentioned it to him?'

'I have yes, but he seems as clueless as any of us. Supper would be nice, though.'

'Bunny has some Lord Mayor's dinner tonight. At this short notice it won't be anything elaborate but I'm sure cook will come up with something.'

'It will make a nice change for Harry, who has never mastered the tiny stove in his rooms.' Lydia removed her hand and pushed open the doors again. 'Now I really must go. I have a deputy head-mistress who manages well without me, but I still have a mountain of administration.'

The cab moved off again and Flora raised her hand in a vague wave, her thoughts returning to Mr Buchanan. Why would a ticket to a piano recital evoke such an angry reaction? Was the man not a music lover?

* * *

'How did your visit to Bermondsey go this morning?' Bunny shrugged out of his shirt in his dressing room and slung it over a nearby chair, leaving the door open to the bedroom as he continued their conversation.

'Not particularly well.' Flora propped her chin on her crossed

hands on the brass bedpost. 'The families all had a plausible explanation why the children aren't there.'

She relished these intimate moments in the day, which were
theirs alone, with no Stokes or Milly likely to interrupt. Though
tonight, her thoughts kept returning to the closed faces they had
encountered that morning.

'I gather you didn't believe their explanations?'

'Not just me, Lydia didn't either. Nor did Sally.'

'Oh well, that's conclusive, then. If Sally—'

'Don't tease. Sally has good instincts for people. She thinks
they've been warned not to talk to us.'

'I don't like the sound of that.' Bunny appeared, a white towel
slung over one naked shoulder. The short, blond hairs on the back
of his neck glowed gold in the flame from a wall of light. For a man
who spent most of his life at a desk, he was built like an athlete,
with slim hips a neat, tight waist and a washboard stomach.

'I met Abel Cain today,' Flora said. 'I see now what you meant
about him, and he certainly proved his worth.'

'I realise that finding out what happened to those children is
important, but I still don't like you being so involved.'

'I hope nothing has happened to them yet. I need to find them
before it does.'

He dipped a wet badger hair brush into a bowl of solid shaving
soap, working up a lather, then turned to look at her, frowning. 'I
was on the verge of telling you not to go, but knowing he was with
you gave me confidence.' He paused, the brush held in mid-air.
'What do you mean he proved his worth?'

'Um, only that the curious kept their distance.' Flora slid off the
bed and wandered closer, leaning a shoulder against the doorframe
to watch him. If she revealed their encounter with the youths in the
stairwell, Bunny would forbid her to go anywhere near the place
again. 'Lydia and I aren't sure what we should do next.'

'Maybe you should wait for the inquest verdict on that nurse.' His eyes met hers in the mirror as he swiped the brush over his face, spreading a layer of creamy white suds over his chin. 'What was her name?'

'Lizzie Prentice.'

'Yes, of course. I should have remembered.' He retrieved a freshly sharpened straight razor from the box that had arrived from the barber's that morning. 'If the coroner decides it was an accident, there may be nothing else you can do. Unless you can find some connection between her death and those children to interest the police.' He stretched his neck and moved the razor upward across his skin in swift, well-practised movements.

'Actually, there might be.' Flora's fingers itched to stroke his smooth back, but she pushed down the curl of desire that unwound in her belly, unwilling to distract him from what she was about to say. 'Alice Finch telephoned this afternoon when we got back. Another child has gone missing. Her name is Isobel Lomax and when her nanny went to fetch her from the hospital, she wasn't there.'

'Oh no, really?' He twisted at the waist to look at her, shaking excess suds from the razor into the bowl. 'How dreadful. When you say missing...' He left the word hanging.

'Officially missing. This time, the police have a description of the man she left with.'

'I see. Well, that's good, isn't it? That the police are now involved. I hope they find her, and soon.' He turned back to the mirror and applied the razor to his face again.

'I hope so too.' Flora was about to tell him that did not help the other six children when he said something she didn't catch. 'I'm sorry. What did you say?'

'I said, what made you invite Lydia and Harry to supper tomorrow?' His speech was slightly distorted by the finger he held against his nose, the straight razor applied to his upper lip. 'It's not like you to be so spontaneous.'

'I've been meaning to ask for ages and she was so kind coming with me today.'

'Excellent idea. I look forward to it. Haven't seen Harry for too long. Though I hope the evening won't turn into a propaganda exercise. I hear he's considering standing for Parliament as a Liberal.' The razor clicked against the side of the ewer as he rinsed off the soap. 'And I'm sorry to desert you this evening, but I cannot get out of this dinner.'

'I understand that these social occasions are important to your career.' She gave him a bright smile. 'Sally has the night off, so I'll probably help Milly bath Arthur and have an early night.' This was not the right time to mention that she had arranged for Sally and Abel to pay a visit to The Antigallican to see what they could discover about Swifty Ellis. Sally had needed little persuading with the promise of an evening in Abel's company in the offing.

'Much as I hate to admit it,' Bunny was still speaking. 'The chasm that exists between the affluent and the poor leaves the weaker members of our society at risk. Especially the children. London is a dangerous place.'

'Now *you* sound like a politician.' She drifted back to the bed, lowering her chin to the bedpost, her gaze on the crease of his back which disappeared below his belt. At some point, the leather had dipped low enough to reveal the dimples on either side of his spine.

'Not me, though I admire Harry's principles. We all declare these activities are scandalous, but console ourselves it's happening in Southwark and not on our own doorstep.' He flicked the towel from his shoulder and strolled into the bedroom, wiping traces of soap his razor had missed.

'Isobel Lomax didn't live in Southwark. She was there by accident.' Flora shifted position to face him, her feet dangling a few inches above the floor. 'Lydia has a theory that the children's families are being paid well to look the other way. That's why they haven't been reported missing.' She was about to ask if he had any idea that Lydia had been brought up in Bermondsey, but changed her mind. She hated keeping secrets from him, but repeating Lydia's story to someone else, even Bunny, would feel like a betrayal of confidence.

'If you're right,' Bunny paused withdrawing a clean shirt from a drawer, 'then it's a well-organised operation and dangerous people are likely involved.' He shook out the shirt and slipped it over his shoulders. 'I don't want people like that even knowing you exist, which they soon will if you go around asking questions.'

'But what if Nurse Prentice knew something about who took the children?'

'Are you saying she was killed to get her out of the way?'

'Or because she knew something? Which is possible isn't it?'

He straightened, his expression stern, though his eyes without his glasses looked soft and more vivid than usual. 'I'm afraid so. However, this time, I hope you'll be sensible and leave it to the police to discover who killed her and why.' He frowned as he fastened his collar studs, but fumbled them and the left side of the collar came free. 'Damn.'

Flora slid off the bed, gently slapped his hands away from the collar, and fastened the studs for him.

'I'm serious, Flora.' He selected a silk bow tie from the dresser and slung it around his neck, the ends flat against his shirt. 'It's not your responsibility to provide the police with evidence.' He pointed at his tie in a 'would you mind' gesture.

'But that's exactly what I must do, or those children will be forgotten.' She knotted the tie beneath his chin into a symmetrical bow, folded his collar down over it and tugged the ends out gently.

'If we can make the police investigate not just Isobel but the other missing children properly, we may stand a chance of finding them.' She retrieved his spectacles from the dresser and slid them onto his nose, then placed her hands flat against his chest. His eyes darkened with a mixture of what she knew to be concern and frustration. 'Go on, admit it, you want to solve this puzzle as much as I do, but you also have this need to keep me out of harm's way.'

'You know me so well.' He wrapped his arms around her and rested his chin against her forehead.

'I understand you worry about me, but if we do nothing, how can we live with ourselves knowing that young children have been taken from their homes and are...' her voice trailed off as unimaginable images crowded her mind. With an effort, she pushed them away. Sentimentality wouldn't help her now. 'Think of Arthur.'

'I am thinking of him.' He released a long breath into her hair. 'Perhaps I could find someone in authority willing to examine the case more closely. Someone who has influence and resources.'

'Oh, would you?' She jerked backward and stared up at him, incredulous and yet conscious she had been waiting for him to offer. 'Thank you.' Her eyes welled, and she blinked away tears.

'I'm not promising anything,' he began gently, 'but the Chief Constable and half the senior ranking police officers in the city will be at The Guildhall tonight. There must be someone among them I can convince this situation is worth pursuing. I only hope the criminal fraternity don't find out that the police stations will be empty this evening.'

'Well, I certainly shan't tell them.' Flora pressed her face into his shirt and breathed in the starched linen and shaving soap that, predictably, sent her blood rushing through her veins. Her arms slid up his back with a will of their own, then aware her eyes were still wet, she broke away suddenly. 'I mustn't ruin your shirt. Now, where's your dinner jacket?'

As she turned away, Bunny caught her hand, pulling her back into his arms, his head bent and his lips against the skin below her ear.

'Forget the jacket.' His voice vibrated through her. 'We have a little time before the cab arrives.'

'Actually.' Her eyes closed as she wound her arms round his neck. 'I was thinking the same thing.'

'You'll have to retie my tie.' He lifted her a few inches off the ground and backed her towards the bed.

'I could probably manage that.'

Flora ate her supper from a tray in the sitting room, pondering the fact that although she appreciated Bunny's understanding earlier, thus far it had brought them no closer to identifying who was responsible for Nurse Prentice's death. Nor had they the smallest clue as to the whereabouts of the missing children.

Once Stokes had removed the tray, she attempted to read the latest H G Wells short story, 'The Country of the Blind' in *The Strand Magazine*, but could not concentrate. Instead, she discarded the magazine and made for the nursery, having reached the first landing when the jangle of the front doorbell resonated through the hall, followed by the butler's brisk footsteps beating a smart tattoo across the tiled floor.

'Thank you, Stokes,' Beatrice Harrington's voice drifted up to where Flora stood, her hands tensed on the banister. 'Inform your mistress I'll await her in the sitting room. I hope you've set a good fire in there as it's bitter cold outside.' The feathers on her voluminous black hat bobbed across the hall. 'I shall require tea, Earl Grey and don't let it stew. Oh, and don't let that red-haired kitchen maid bring it, she always manages to slop milk in the saucer or drops the teaspoons onto the floor.'

Flora released a long sigh, her head against the wall as she allowed herself a moment to compose herself. Then abandoning her plans for a cosy interlude with her infant son, she dragged her feet to the sitting room, where Beatrice was comfortably ensconced in a wing-back chair beside the fire.

'Good evening, Mother-in-Law,' her bright greeting belied the stone in her stomach. 'I wasn't expecting you to call this evening.' Bunny's mother might lack tact, but she could detect disrespect in a heartbeat.

'That's because I didn't inform you I was coming.' Beatrice tugged off her gloves and slapped them onto a side table, her hands held towards the flames. 'I took an excellent early supper with April Groves in Lennox Gardens, and knowing Ptolemy would be at The Guildhall this evening, I decided you could benefit from my company.'

'How kind,' Flora said, while offering thanks that she was no longer required to share a house with her mother-in-law. Bunny had always understood the prickly relationship between his wife and his mother and when their move to the city had become imminent, he had encouraged Beatrice to share the charming villa she had bought in Chiswick with a widowed cousin.

The arrangement had suited them all, especially when Beatrice revelled in her new-found ability to socialise with her friends whenever she pleased. The only disadvantage being that the convenience of a private carriage enabled her to call on her son and daughter-in-law unannounced, and usually at the most inconvenient times.

'Actually,' Flora said. 'I was about to go up and bath the baby. Would you like to come?' As the words left her lips, Flora knew they had been a mistake.

Beatrice Harrington's hat feathers quivered as she directed a look of utter confusion at Flora. 'Whatever for? That's the nursery maid's job.'

Flora had seen grown men cower in her presence, not all of them tradesmen. With her penetrating blue eyes and perpetually pinched mouth she could have taken lessons in intimidation from the late Queen.

'I enjoy bathing him myself.' Flora took a seat on a hard-backed chair, hoping her guest would take it as a sign not to get too comfortable. 'It helps me get to know him, and more importantly, for him to know me.'

'You fret about such trivial things, Flora.' Beatrice sniffed. 'Naturally, he'll know who you are. His nanny will tell him. A child's duty is to its parents, not the other way round.' She wrapped the fur collar of her coat tighter around her throat. That she had not removed the garment at the door encouraged Flora she wouldn't stay long. Not for the first time, she wondered how Bunny had turned out to be such a loving, considerate man with this woman for a mother. The only explanation she came to was that he had a devoted nursemaid?

'I enjoy my time with Arthur.' Flora refused to be intimidated. 'This way he'll know to come to me when he's upset or worried. He needs me.'

'It's enough to keep him disciplined, clothed and fed without worrying about how he feels,' Beatrice went on, oblivious to Flora's stiff shoulders. 'A short visit before bedtime is quite adequate to check he is well and knows his manners. Anything else is merely fussing.'

'Don't you want to see your grandson?' Flora's voice took on a sharp edge which Beatrice did not miss.

'Once he's been bathed and is sleepy for bed, yes of course.' She threw Flora a disbelieving look. 'How can you ask, when you know how much I adore him?'

Flora rolled her eyes, an action she covered quickly as the door opened. 'Ah, here's Stokes with our tea.' She waited until he had set down the tray. 'Stokes, would you ask Milly to bring Master Arthur down?'

While they sipped tea and waited, Beatrice peered at the cover of The Strand Magazine, plucked from where Flora had placed it.

'"Detective stories",' Beatrice read aloud with the same inflection she might have given to the word, 'Blasphemy'. 'I hope you aren't wasting your time on such nonsense, Flora?'

'They're entertaining. Everyone reads Conan Doyle, he's well thought of. Bunny has a subscription,' she added, though regretted her attempt to justify herself.

'Oh well, if Ptolemy allows such publications in the house, it must be acceptable.' Beatrice wrinkled her nose at her first sip from her cup, then lifted the teapot lid and peered inside. 'This is quite weak. How many scoops does that maid of yours put in this teapot?'

'I've never had a reason to ask.' Flora bit her lip hard, relieved when Milly arrived at that moment with Arthur; his hair damp from his bath and his skin pink and sweet smelling. Flora took immediate possession of this irresistible bundle of soft chubbiness, to which his grandmother appeared immune.

Beatrice's display of affection took the form of holding his tiny hand between finger and thumb for a moment before removing it fastidiously in favour of her teacup and saucer.

Flora settled the baby on her knee and listened with growing frustration while Beatrice embarked on an account of her week, which seemed to consist of several excursions to her contemporaries, all of whom had allowed themselves to sink into desultory old age, and whose children had made less than advantageous marriages.

Flora made occasional appropriate responses but kept stealing looks at the clock whose hands seemed to crawl slower than usual. Once the baby was cursorily inspected and declared hale and healthy, Beatrice pre-empted Flora and dismissed Milly with instructions on how many blankets the baby required and a final warning to keep the windows closed. 'October is a brutal month, I find. I can never get sufficiently warm.' She gave an exaggerated shudder and stretched her liver-spotted hands towards the fire again.

'I like that girl,' she added as the door closed on Milly, who had shown no resentment at all to receiving orders from Beatrice. 'She's silent and yet both respectful and vigilant.'

'That's one way of putting it. More tea?' Flora asked, more out of politeness than a desire to prolong the visit.

Beatrice opened her mouth to reply just as the rattle of the doorknob announced the arrival of Sally, who burst into the room, her hat awry and her curly dark hair in her eyes.

'Miss Flora, you'll never guess—' she halted, blinking when she caught sight of Beatrice and gave a little bob. 'Oh, I'm sorry Ma'am, I didn't know you was here.'

'Really, Sally, do you normally enter your employer's sitting room without knocking?' Beatrice snatched her gloves from the table and pushed herself awkwardly to her feet. 'You never could control your servants, Flora. Speaking of which, would you instruct Stokes to tell my driver I shall be out in a moment.'

'You've left your carriage in the road?' Flora asked, incredulous. 'It's a cold night, Mother-in-law. Why didn't you send your driver to warm himself in the kitchens while he waited. Or some refreshment?'

'Whatever for?' Her nose wrinkled and she glared at Sally before she swept into the hall.

Flora followed close behind ignoring Beatrice's complaints all the way down the front steps. 'I could break an ankle on those steps, that street lamp is far too dim. I must talk to Ptolemy about it.'

Flora returned to the sitting room, where Sally had made herself comfortable by the roaring fire. 'Sorry about barging in like that, Missus. If I'd known she was here, I would have waited in the kitchen.' She blew into her hands and huddled closer, her feet braced against the brass fender.

'That's all right, Sally. What is it you have to tell me that I will never guess?'

'We found him.' Sally's eyes glinted, and she hunched her shoulders. 'Swifty Ellis. The man Lizzie Prentice saw at the hospital. The one who was there when each one of the children went missing.'

'Where?' Flora lowered herself into the chair Beatrice had recently vacated.

'I'll start at the beginning.' Sally twisted in her seat to face Flora, her hands thrust into the folds of her skirt. Her skin now glowed a soft pink as the blood flowed back into her face, making her quite pretty. 'We went to that pub in Tooley Street. The Antigalliciyan.' She mangled the pronunciation, but Flora chose not to correct her. 'Abel bought me a port and lemon and we got talking to the barman about boxing. It turns out he used the same gymnasium as Abel when he was younger, the Lynn Boxing Club on Borough High Street.' Sally's shoulders hunched as she talked, showing she enjoyed herself. 'Most of the local thugs use it as a meeting place for, well, for their shady deals and such. Swifty's name came up as he's handy with his fists.' She plucked a biscuit from the tray, but saw Flora looking at her and grimaced. 'Sorry, Missus, I wasn't thinking.'

'Help yourself. Perhaps I should ask Stokes for a fresh pot and an extra cup?'

'Ooh, yes please, Missus.' Either Flora's sarcasm had passed Sally by, or she deliberately ignored it. 'I could do with a cuppa.'

Smiling to herself, Flora tugged the bellpull beside the fireplace.

'Abel did some pokin' about too and the barman said Swifty ain't his real name, they call him that 'cos he's light on his feet,' she said through mouthfuls of biscuit.

'*Isn't*, Sally, not ain't. And I had already gathered that.'

Stokes entered just then with a fresh teapot and cup, unable to hide his start of surprise when instead of Beatrice he saw Sally.

'Put it down there, Mr Stokes. I'll have a refill in a mo.' Sally winked at him.

'You shouldn't goad him, Sally,' Flora chided, once Stokes had withdrawn, stiff-backed.

'Ah, he'll take his revenge later,' Sally said resignedly. 'Anyway, the barman got wary what with all the questions, though he did say Swifty's a casual at St Saviour's.'

'I don't know what that means.' Flora frowned.

Sally eyed the biscuits again and Flora pushed the plate closer.

'Dockers offload sacks and crates onto barges which bring the goods to the city from the ships at Tilbury and Gravesend. They stand on the stones with dozens of others every morning for the call.'

'The call?'

'It's when they are taken on for the day.' Sally took a biscuit and bit into it. 'They don't work a regular job, only when they are needed, so they get a day's work here and there. The bosses turn away three times as many as get work. Swifty isn't big enough to be a stevedore who unloads the ships, so he works on the docks.' Sally slurped her tea, grimaced and added two sugar lumps to the brew. 'Abel bought the barman a drink and asked him to tip him the wink if he walked in. And would yer believe it, just as we was about to leave, he said Swifty was in the other bar.'

'My goodness.' Flora sank down onto the edge of a chair. 'What did you do?'

'Nothing.' Sally shrugged. 'We got a butcher's at him though. That girl Ada was right, he has got funny eyes.'

'I was worried for a moment that you might have become over enthusiastic and challenged him.'

'What do you take me for, Missus? I've got more nous than that. I'd recognise him again, though. He's younger than we thought, and he wears a hat pulled down over his face, but the way he scouted the bar told me he don't miss much. That long coat he wears is top quality too, and it's got a bright yellow lining, like posh people wear. He's a villain, all right. Like as not he keeps the tools of his trade in the pockets.'

'What sort of tools?'

Sally laughed. 'Who knows, but I'll wager there's a knuckle duster in there somewhere.'

'I shan't even ask what that is.' Flora gave an embarrassed cough.

'Abel didn't like him much either.' Sally sniffed as if this vindicated her.

'I'm beginning to like Abel more and more,' Flora said. 'You did well, Sally.'

'There's more.' Sally's eyes gleamed, as if she was about to come to the good part and wanted to savour it. 'The barman said he was short-handed because his part-time barmaid had a nasty accident a few days ago.'

Flora gasped. 'He meant Lizzie?'

'Lizzie.' Sally gave a slow, conspiratorial nod. 'She did the odd evening behind the bar to earn a few extra shillings, what with the wages at the hospital being poor.'

'If Lizzie knew Swifty through the public house, why did she deny knowing him to Miss Finch?'

'Prob'ly 'cos if the hospital knew she worked in a pub they would have sacked her.'

'I wonder how well she knew him?'

Sally grimaced. 'The barman didn't think she did. Said a respectable girl like Lizzie wouldn't have had anything to do with the likes of 'im. That Lizzie had an up and downer with someone that night.'

'A what? Oh, you mean a fight? Which night was this?'

'The last night she worked at the Corks. 'Bout a week ago. Then Abel said we had to go as the barman was getting antsy with all these questions.' In response to Flora's puzzled frown, added, 'You know, ants in yer pants. Fidgety.'

'Oh, I see.' Flora cleared her throat. 'Who did Lizzie argue with?'

'The barman didn't know. Whoever it was stayed in the scullery. He said she was going at poor Lizzie something terrible.'

'She?'

Sally nodded, shoved the last piece of biscuit into her mouth and slapped her hands together releasing crumbs onto the floor. 'A Salvation Army couple were in the public bar that night rattling collection boxes. One of them was telling some drunk to change his evil ways, you know how the Sally Ann do, but the man didn't take kindly to him and a scuffle started. By the time the barman had sorted them out, Lizzie was back in the bar. Next thing he heard, Lizzie was dead.'

'Did he tell the police about this argument?'

'You're such an innocent, Miss Flora.' Sally gave her a sideways glance loaded with derision. 'Nobody says nothing to the police. That's the way it is in Bermondsey.'

Flora relaxed back in her chair with a defeated sigh. Was it a woman who had killed Lizzie in the hospital yard? 'Sally, would you be willing to do some more investigation for me?'

'What sort?' Sally's brown eyes narrowed.

'Follow a man tomorrow night. I want to know who he talks to and what he does. He'll recognise me, but he doesn't know you.'

'Can I take Abel with me?'

'That might be a good plan. A couple will raise fewer questions. We'll finalise the details tomorrow when I've thought it through.'

'You'll have ter put it straight with Stokes, what with me having two nights off in a row.'

'Don't worry, I'll handle him.' She glanced at the clock on the mantelpiece. 'I might as well go to bed. Mr Bunny won't be back for hours.'

Sally rose slowly. 'I'll get your night things ready.'

'I'll be up presently. Oh, and Sally, there's an envelope on my dresser. It's something to thank Abel for his help tonight. Could you have it sent round to him in the morning?'

'No need for that, I'll take it meself.' Sally's broad smile suggested her evening with Abel Cain had gone well.

She sat for a while after Sally had gone, watching the fire burn down to glowing red coals, and the room darkened.

Who had Lizzie been arguing with and what about? Could having Mr Buchanan followed provide more answers or confuse the issue? And what was the connection, if any, between him and Lizzie Prentice? Frustratingly, she had more questions, but fewer answers.

17

The fire in the bedroom Flora shared with Bunny had long since burned to silvered ash, the temperature rapidly dropping until her nose felt cold to the touch. The nocturnal noises of the house combined with a strong wind that rattled window panes and moaned down the chimney for most of the night. Shivering, she wrapped the thick counterpane between her bent knees, fighting to stay awake so she might relate everything Sally had told her about her excursion to Tooley Street to Bunny when he got home from his evening out.

After the hall clock struck twelve, she must have fallen asleep, for the next thing she was aware of was Sally's discreet knock at her door. She groaned and turned over; the dent in the mattress and a lingering smell of her husband's favourite cologne were the only evidence he had slept there.

Flora winced at the glare of daylight as Sally tugged open the curtains on a rattle of brass rings. 'Where's Mr Bunny this morning?' She yawned and stretched her arms above her head. A glance at the mantlepiece clock made her gasp. How had she slept so late?

'He's downstairs with a visitor.' Disapproval stiffened the maid's shoulders.

'Who?' Flora bolted upright, threw off the coverlet and shielded her eyes with one hand, observing Sally's pinched mouth with amusement. It wasn't often her maid took an instant dislike to anyone, but when she did, there was usually a reason. The last man who elicited that look had proved to be a Serbian spy.

'It's that Inspector Maddox. Him what gave you all that earache about the Miss Evangeline Lange case?' She scooped a petticoat and drawers from the floor. 'Not that he would have caught the fella if it hadn't been for us. I've run yer bath, Missus. Best get to it before it goes cold.'

'Thank you, Sally,' Flora said absently, her thoughts elsewhere.

If Inspector Maddox was prepared to come to the house, surely he must have some information to give them? That or he was prepared to open an investigation. Curiosity, together with the layer of ice on the window, made Flora rush her bath. She tried not to fidget while Sally pressed hairpins into the soft sausage curls piled on her head and fastened the tiny row of button on her dress. Finally released from Sally's deft hands and gentle admonitions to keep still, Flora hurried downstairs.

The dining room contained only a maid stacking plates and dishes onto a tray in a lingering smell of hot fat and coffee. Flora carried on past into the sitting room, where a handsome man in his early thirties with coal black hair and eyes to match beneath fine arched brows leapt to his feet as she entered.

'Ah, Flora, there you are.' Bunny approached from beside the fireplace. 'You remember Detective Maddox.'

'A pleasure to see you again, Inspector.' Passing Bunny on her way to the sofa, he whispered, 'Sleepyhead' in her ear.

'You should have woken me,' Flora whispered back, striding forward to take the inspector's hand.

'I was hoping we wouldn't meet again, Mrs Harrington.' Maddox shifted his feet as if embarrassed, but his handshake was firm and confident. 'At least, not at this end of an investigation.'

'We ran into one another at the Law Society dinner last evening,' Bunny said, making Flora wonder just how much of a coincidence that was. 'He works out of Camberwell Church Street these days, don't you, Inspector?'

'Camberwell?' Flora frowned.

'Bermondsey and Southwark are in his patch,' Bunny said, then as if to emphasise his point. 'He's investigating the disappearance of Isobel Lomax.' He gave her a pointed look which conveyed clearly how hard he had worked to instigate that conversation.

'Oh, I see.' Realisation dawned, and she perched on the edge of the sofa, her attention on the policeman's face. 'How interesting.'

'I'm not supposed to discuss ongoing investigations, you understand.' Maddox coughed into a fist, then flicked up his jacket flaps as he resumed his seat. 'However, your husband said you were friends with the matron of St Philomena's Hospital and might have some relevant knowledge, thus my early call.'

Acknowledging that most of what she knew was supposition and theory, Flora exchanged a nervous look with Bunny. 'Did you mention the other children who are missing?'

'I did.' Bunny lowered himself onto the seat beside her. 'Also, that we are aware none of them were reported missing, thus there is no official investigation underway.'

'Does that mean you don't intend to search for them?' Flora asked, wondering if this was going to be a waste of time after all.

'Perhaps it sounds incomprehensible to you, Mrs Harrington,' he said. 'However, at this stage, the force has no cause to commit resources to a search.'

'Even though these children are all under eight years old and might be at grave risk?'

'My dear,' Bunny cleared his throat noisily. 'Shall I ask Stokes to bring you some coffee?'

'No, that's all right.' Flora waved him away. 'I'll have something later, I—' She broke off as she caught his warning look. 'I'm sorry, Inspector Maddox, you have procedures to follow and many aspects of this case don't fit.'

'Indeed, but please don't think I'm unsympathetic.' His voice softened, losing much of its clipped formality, and his eyes darkened to a deep chocolate colour. 'I'm concerned about the plight of these children who are treated like commodities by their own families. Rumours began last year of a similar incident, but the investigation went nowhere as the families refused to talk. As far as we are aware, the children never returned. I'm still haunted by what might have happened to them.'

'What do you think happened to them?' Flora asked.

A look of mutual understanding passed between Bunny and the policeman but was gone in an instant. Bunny fidgeted and Maddox stared at the floor, but no one ventured an answer.

'Inspector.' Flora sighed. 'I realise you feel you must protect my sensibilities, but there really is no need.' She directed an accusing glance at Bunny to include him in the statement.

'I beg your pardon, I'm sure.' The inspector's face flushed and he rubbed both hands along his thighs; unlike Bunny who sat relaxed, one ankle crossed over the other.

'This case is not straightforward.' Inspector Maddox perched on the last four inches of his chair, his shoulders hunched forward. 'If what we suspect is true, these children have been taken with the consent of their families.'

'Consent? You mean they were given away?' Bunny's confirmation of what Flora had already surmised made her stomach churn. 'Surely that isn't legal if the authorities have no idea where they are being taken and for what purpose?'

'It's complicated, Mr Harrington. Since the ratification of the Human Trafficking Act last year, such transactions are criminal. If we can discover where the children are, and who took them, no matter what their purpose, we have the power to ensure those children aren't exploited. Their families could also be liable for prosecution.'

'Last year?' Flora asked, shocked. 'You're saying taking children from their homes for some nefarious purposes wasn't a crime?'

'I'm afraid to say it wasn't.' Maddox ducked his head, embarrassed. 'If a family came to an agreement with a third party to send their child away to work or live with someone else, even if they took money for doing so, there wasn't much the law could do about it.'

Silence stretched as the weight of their combined thoughts mounted, broken only by clearing of throats and the ticking of a clock.

'There's also the death of Nurse Prentice,' Flora said after a moment. 'She brought these children to the matron's notice at St Philomena's. Miss Finch is convinced she discovered something more but was killed before she could do so.'

'That her death was anything more than an accident hasn't yet been established,' Maddox said. 'The inquest has been set for later this morning. As for what she may or may not have been about to impart to Miss Finch, I—'

'I understand, Inspector,' Flora waved him away. Evidently, she would get nowhere with that line of questioning. 'However, Isobel Lomax was seen leaving the hospital with a stranger. Surely that changes things?' Her sharp tone elicited a warning glance in her direction from Bunny.

'I'm not denying that.' Maddox ran both hands along his thighs again as if his palms were sweaty. 'My Superintendent wants that girl found, however, he isn't convinced the cases are connected.' He exchanged another angst filled look with Bunny.

Flora waited for Maddox's full attention, which came after a heartbeat. 'Inspector, have you encountered a Swifty Ellis?'

His eyes narrowed. 'The name is known to us. Might I ask how you heard it?'

'Yes, do enlighten us, Flora.' Bunny raised a sardonic eyebrow.

'I'm sorry, but you weren't here when Sally returned last night. She and Abel Cain were in The Antigallican, and—'

'That's more my patch than yours, Mrs Harrington.' A nerve beside the inspector's left eye twitched. 'Tooley Street is over four miles from here and south of the river.'

'It would take me too long to explain.' Flora stared at her lap. It seemed Bunny had not mentioned her foray into Bermondsey, and she chose to keep it that way. She went on to recount Lizzie's part time job and her argument there before she was killed.

'You have been busy, Mrs Harrington,' Maddox said with barely suppressed annoyance. 'I doubt Swifty Ellis has the nous required to traffic a group of children without someone knowing about it. He's more of a small-time crook who fences stolen goods and pretends to be mentally incompetent when questioned. We rarely get much out of him, but he's got a steady network of thugs who dare not defy him.'

'Isn't that somewhat contradictory?' Flora asked, irritated at his complacency. 'On the one hand, he's too simple-minded to be involved, then you say he has the acumen to run a successful team of crooks?'

'Ah, yes I see your point.' He gave Bunny a 'how-do-you-manage-her' look which Bunny returned with a widening of his eyes.

'How far have you got in finding Isobel Lomax?' Flora asked, annoyed he offered nothing in the way of progress.

'Not as far as hoped.' Maddox's mouth twitched again. 'However, I have spoken to Mr Raymond Buchanan, both about Nurse

Prentice's unfortunate accident and the Lomax girl. He mentioned nothing about other missing children.'

'Because he saw no cause for concern,' Flora said, annoyed. 'Though it doesn't mean there isn't.'

'I agree. You are acquainted with Mr Buchanan?'

'Only briefly.' Apart from a vague feeling of unease, she had no proof the hospital governor knew anything. 'And the barman at The Antigallican? Will you talk to him about Lizzie's argument?'

'If I investigated every confrontation which took place in a south London pub, Mrs Harrington, I would have no time for anything else.'

Flora suppressed a frustrated sigh at the man's patronising tone.

'I'm sorry to disappoint you,' Maddox said, catching her audible sigh. 'And I'm aware you like to dabble in solving crimes, but—'

'Dabble?' Flora stiffened. 'It's not a hobby.'

Bunny brought his fist to his mouth to cover a laugh.

Inspector Maddox flushed, his voice softening. 'I urge you to be careful, Mrs Harrington. If Swifty Ellis is involved, he's doing it for someone far better connected than he is.'

'The dapper man in the top hat seen taking Isobel Lomax from St Philomena's?' From the moment Flora had sat down she'd had the distinct impression he was indulging her for Bunny's sake.

'Exactly.' Maddox slapped his knees and rose. 'Now, if you'll excuse me, I had better get back to the station. However, I assure you, if there's a connection to these cases, I'll find it. Good morning, Mrs Harrington. Mr Harrington.'

Stokes showed the policeman out, leaving Flora pacing in front of the fireplace. 'Tell me he's taking this seriously, Bunny.'

'He is, I made sure of that.' She scooted along the wide sofa and took Bunny's hand in hers. 'Thank you for broaching the subject with the inspector when you were supposed to be smooching with lawyers over fine wine.'

'I know what this means to you but please do as he says, and be careful. I know you, Flora. You rush into situations without thinking. Look at it from Maddox's point of view. Having a civilian poking about in his cases could be embarrassing for him.'

'I'll be careful.' Flora shrugged, but she was also pleased that the inspector was now involved.

'I hear young Sally is squarely involved in this investigation?' Bunny moved to the tray on the sideboard and poured himself a cup of coffee, which despite Flora's refusal he had ordered to be brought in. 'Sending her out to pubs to scout the local colour. I hope you aren't becoming a bad influence on her.'

'Me?' Flora threw him a sharp sideways look. 'It's more likely to be the other way round. I must say she threw herself into it, possibly because it meant an entire evening in Abel's company.' The fragrance of coffee from his cup nudged her sense. 'Might I change my mind about that coffee? I could do with some.'

'You haven't had any breakfast either.' Bunny set his cup and saucer on the table and obliged. 'Maybe I could take you out for an early luncheon?' He set a cup in front of her from which an enticing wisp of steam rose.

'Are you certain the inspector isn't humouring us in return for a good breakfast?'

'Cynic.' Bunny smiled. 'Don't underestimate him. I see him as more a sponge than a fountain, which makes for a good policeman. Give him a chance.'

'I suppose so.' Flora propped her chin in one hand. 'I thought he would do more. All he promised is he'll look into it.'

'And if these children are being taken by a dangerous criminal gang, those sorts of people won't think twice about putting a stop to any meddling on your part.'

'Is that what you think I'm doing? Meddling?' Flora sipped her coffee, relishing the strong taste as an aid to her whirling thoughts.

'No actual progress will be made unless the coroner decides Lizzie was murdered.' She caught his sideways look, adding, 'That's a horrible thing to hope for, isn't it?'

Bunny paced between the fireplace and the window, cup and saucer in hand. 'We cannot link a series of events together based on coincidence alone.' He saluted her with his cup. 'And you know how I feel about those.'

'That they don't exist, I know.' Flora sighed. 'I'm meeting Alice at Martell's this afternoon. I'll tell her about Detective Maddox.'

'Don't go getting her hopes up, Flora. Maddox might find nothing.'

'That's why I intend to help him,' she murmured under her breath.

'What was that?'

'Nothing.'

'And another thing, Flora.' His free hand came down on her shoulder, bringing her head up to meet his eyes. 'I hope you won't use these children to keep you close to Alice Finch? I know how much you want her to be your mother, but it's a small possibility.'

She was about to refute this, but his steady look reminded her it would be useless to lie to him.

'She asked for my help, and anyway, I like her. I think she likes me too. If nothing else, I feel I have made a friend. I won't base too much on it, I promise.' Flora crossed the fingers of her other hand inside the folds of her skirt. The more she saw of Alice, the conviction they were related became more real.

'As long as you are prepared for disappointment.' He ran his knuckles gently across her chin.

'I have some paperwork to do, so I'll be in my office this afternoon.' Bunny returned his cup to the tray and made for the door. 'I'll be back in time to get ready for our evening with Lydia and Harry.'

18

Martell's was unusually busy that afternoon, but the waitress who had served Flora on previous occasions assured her there would always be a table for her. 'Mr Martell insists we never turn you away, Mrs Harrington.'

'How kind.' Flora took a seat at her favourite table with a panoramic view of the street through the wide bay window.

From there she could observe the rest of the room; specifically, a lone woman in an alcove in unrelieved black, who greeted every male patron with a wide smile but ignored the women. She reminded Flora of what Lydia had told her of a Piccadilly Tea Room that ran a house of ill repute on its upper floor.

Her private smile must have been taken as encouragement by Mr Martell, who bustled towards her across the room with purpose in each step.

'Ah, so we have the pleasure of your company yet again, my dear madame.' He held his right hand extended, bent at the wrist, his slight paunch straining an embroidered waistcoat. 'Do you await the delightful Mees Grey, or perhaps Mees Feench will join you today?'

Mildly repulsed by in the anticipation in his gleaming black eyes, Flora summoned a smile. 'I'm flattered you take such a personal interest in your patrons, sir.' Did the man keep notes?

The Frenchman had always struck her as friendly, but lately, his attentions had become cloying, even intrusive. Perhaps his days spent over teacups and cream cakes made him long for some more sophisticated society?

'I like to theenk of myself as a good proprietor, dear lady. I have a keen interest in my patrons.' His oily smile persisted. 'I see you and the elegant 'ospital laydee have become firm friends since coming 'ere.'

'We didn't actually meet in your establishment,' Flora replied, unwilling to give the man too much credit. 'She's an exceptional person, and we have a lot in common.'

'I agree, she is charmant.' He gave a theatrical sigh which to Flora was too contrived to be genuine. 'What a tragedy about that poor nurse who was killed. Such things will do nothing for the hospital's reputation.'

'A tragedy indeed, but not one that could be put at Miss Finch's door.' Flora fidgeted, uncomfortable with the subject. 'As far as I know the nurse fell and hit her head.'

'I did not seek to imply otherwise.' He blinked repeatedly; his eyes surrounded by wrinkles that put her in mind of a myopic turtle. 'And yet that does not disappoint you, madame?'

'I beg your pardon?' Flora frowned up at him from beneath the rim of her hat. 'I don't understand.'

'Mais non? But are you not famous, dear lady? Is not murder of special interest to the brave heroine who confronted the killer of Miss Evangeline Lange last year?'

This statement took Flora so off guard, she floundered for a response. She had not been living in London then, but was on a brief visit to William. Martell must have seen the report in the newspaper though it was indelicate of him to mention it. Alice was right, the man was an inveterate gossip.

Flora was about to deliver a sharp retort when the harsh sound of the bell interrupted them.

'Ah! Here is your companion, if I am not mistaken.' He flicked his fingers at the door as Alice glided towards them, taking the chair he held out for her. With only a brief upturn of his lips in Flora's direction, he returned to the counter where he castigated a waitress who had swept a plate of cakes onto the pristine floor.

'You arrived at exactly the right moment,' Flora said as Alice removed her gloves.

'Oh dear, did I see our garrulous host engaging you in unwelcome conversation?' She wore a flattering shade of sage green; a beautifully cut ankle-length wool coat that accentuated her still-girlish figure.

Flora regarded her with something like pride and hoped she too would look as elegant and youthful as Alice when she reached her forties. And why shouldn't she? Daughters often resembled their mother's, didn't they?

'Flora?' Alice's eyes widened in enquiry. 'Did you hear what I said?'

'Oh, sorry, I missed that.' Distracted, she cast an oblique look at Mr Martell, but he wasn't looking in her direction.

'I said, I haven't been to the hospital today as I attended Lizzie Prentice's inquest this morning.'

'I had completely forgotten. How did it go?' Flora attracted the attention of a passing waitress and issued a request to for some tea, which arrived promptly.

'Dr Samuel's testimony was categorical, in that Lizzie couldn't possibly have injured herself so badly in a fall.' Alice checked her appearance in the wall mirror opposite, adjusting her hat a fraction sideways.

'He's certain about that?'

'His explanation was quite technical, but in simple terms the fracture was too high in the parietal bone to have been caused by a fall. She was hit with something extremely heavy and with some force.'

'So she was murdered.' Flora took a restorative sip of her tea, certain now of what had worried her about the scene in the hospital yard when Lizzie had been found. 'She didn't fall against that stone border, did she? Someone picked it up, hit her and then replaced it, making it look that way?'

'How did you know?'

'Because the bloodstain was on the side of that stone, but there was none on the upper surface. The killer was clever enough to make it look like an accident, but maybe didn't have time to arrange it quite right.'

'The coroner thought the same and his verdicts was that she had been "unlawfully killed by persons unknown".' Alice sighed. 'It doesn't help Lizzie, but at least now the police will have to take the matter more seriously. But we cannot get them to connect her death to the missing children without some hard evidence.' She propped her elbows on the table, her chin balanced on her folded hands. 'Now, I can see you are dying to tell me something. I take it you have news?'

Flora waited until the waitress with the replacement teapot had left.

Over hot, strong tea and a plate of Martell's famous almond biscuits, Flora explained about Sally's visit to The Antigallican, the barman's story of Lizzie's confrontation with an unknown woman in the pub kitchen and Inspector Maddox's visit to Eaton Place that morning.

'That certainly clarifies a few things,' Alice said when Flora had finished. 'I cannot say I'm surprised Lizzie failed to mention she worked at a public house during her time off. The student nurses live in quarters to which we attach certain rules. One of which is a curfew. If Lizzie was working elsewhere at night, it would have been cause for her dismissal.'

'I gathered that,' Flora said. 'Have you no idea of what Lizzie was going to tell you that day?'

'Let me think.' Alice drummed the fingers of her right hand on the table.

'Apart from matters connected to her patients, I don't think – oh wait, there was something.' Alice looked up. 'I came upon Lizzie in the reception hall one morning, a day or so before she died, I mean, before she was killed. She was staring at something, or someone, which froze her right in front of me. So much so, she didn't respond when I spoke to her.'

'What was it?'

'I couldn't tell as the hall was full of visitors and patients that day as well as the staff. When she recovered herself, I asked what had upset her, but she said it was nothing.'

'Did you believe her?' *That must have been about the same time Lizzie had been accosted in the pub kitchen.*

'Not for a moment. Something had upset her badly, but I took the stance that if she wished to tell me, she would choose her own time.' Alice sighed. 'I wish I had insisted. Now it's too late.'

'I see.' Flora released the breath she held. 'That doesn't tell us much, does it?'

'No, I'm sorry. But before Lizzie went off to her ward, she said how odd it was that what you see every day becomes unrecognisable in a different guise.'

Flora frowned. 'A different guise? What did she mean by that?'

'I have no idea. I was immediately taken up with the visitors. Two patients had been booked for the same bed, which put Sister Lazarus into a muddle trying to sort out, so I stepped in. I wish I had paid more attention to Lizzie.' Her voice was tinged with remorse.

'That implies someone at the hospital wanted her dead.'

'Not necessarily.' Taking Flora's cue, Alice dropped her voice to match Flora's. 'Members of the public have access to the building and grounds and tradesmen, visitors, and families. We have visiting doctors and the Board of Governors.' Her eyes widened in disbelief. 'Not that any of them could have been responsible.'

'No, of course not,' Flora mumbled, unconvinced. 'Did Mr Buchanan attend the inquest?'

'Yes, he did. He and Dr Reeder were called to give evidence. I think they were both shocked, as until then, Mr Buchanan was content to go along with Dr Reeder's conclusion that it was an accident.'

'Is Reeder a good doctor?'

'Well, yes.' Alice blinked, as if the question confused her. 'He's a little over-enthusiastic when trying to make an impression, but I doubt he misread the situation on purpose, if that's what you're implying.'

'I wasn't implying anything,' Flora assured her. 'Only that we need to look at everyone involved with this affair. Is Mr Buchanan now convinced these children are genuinely missing? Or does he still dismiss your concerns?'

'I broached the subject with him again recently, but he won't discuss it with me.' Alice sighed and replaced her cup slowly, as if she summoned patience. 'The Isobel Lomax disappearance has affected him badly. Having the police on the premises casts a shadow on the hospital.'

Flora found Alice's reluctance to pursue this Mr Buchanan disconcerting. She did not strike her as a woman easily distracted from a cause that mattered to her. Or was there more to her relationship with Raymond Buchanan than she had confided? He was a widower in his fifties, and not unattractive, so perhaps it wasn't out of the question Alice might be interested in him romantically. 'Have the police learned anything more about the Lomax girl?'

'They appear to be stuck on the theory she went missing from her home.'

'But why then she was seen leaving the hospital with a well-dressed man?'

'Ah, because it transpires the nursery maid has a gentleman friend. The police think he was present when they collected Isobel from the hospital and took her home to Greenwich.'

'Then why isn't she there?'

'Because with the girl's parents away, they concluded that the nursery maid and her suitor were, er, otherwise occupied when Isobel left the house and became lost. It seems the child has sleep-walked occasionally. When the pair discovered she wasn't there the next morning, they then blamed the hospital, saying the staff were covering their own indiscretion. Not to mention negligence.'

'Can the police prove that?'

Alice shrugged. 'They have decided the nursemaid is guilty. She and the young man are being questioned at the police station.'

'What do you think? Could it have happened that way?'

'I don't know, but it sounds like too much of a coincidence. The only difference being Isobel was seen with a gentleman and not this man who fits the description of this Swifty.'

A movement at the corner of Flora's eye made her glance over her left shoulder. She leaned towards Alice and whispered, 'Look out, Mr Martell is coming over. Serves me right for smiling at him.'

The Frenchman paused beside their table, his head tilted and with a comedic expression that lacked subtlety. 'I was just saying before you arrived Mees Feench, that you and Madame Harreengton had become especial friends. As usual, you seem to have so much to talk about.'

'You provide such a charming ambiance, sir, how could we not?' Alice's response was accompanied by a definite tightening of her jaw.

It seemed Flora wasn't the only one who was uncomfortable in his presence.

'I was saying to Madame Harreengton before you arrived, dear lady. About the murder. What a trial that must have been for a professional lady.'

Flora met Alice's eyes, the expression in them displaying the same thought. Did the man have a spy at the Coroner's court?

'News travels fast, Mr Martell,' Alice said. 'I don't believe it has reached the latest edition of the newspapers as yet.' She thrust the hot water pot towards him, leaving him with no option but to take it. 'Would you mind refilling this for us?' Alice requested, despite the teapot on the table being quite full.

He gave a start, then looked around for a waitress, but none were in calling distance. Left with no choice but to perform the task himself, he bowed and with a murmured, 'Certainly, madame,' he backed away.

'That was clever,' Flora said when he was out of earshot. 'I'll have to remember that.' She gave an exaggerated shudder. 'I always regarded his nosiness as ingratiation before. Now it seems he has ears everywhere. I dread to think what he knows about us.'

'Don't worry about it.' Alice lifted the cup to her lips and peered at Flora over the rim. 'I was in here recently with one of my nursing sisters and he prised her history from her in all of five minutes.'

Flora wondered if she meant Sister Lazarus, but couldn't image that lady revealing anything to the fussy little Frenchman.

'Those ladies don't appear to mind his fawning ways.' Alice nodded to where Mr Martell, the hot water pot still in hand, stood deep in conversation with three matrons at another table. 'But then perhaps their lives are less interesting than ours.'

'By the way.' Alice pulled Flora's attention away from the Frenchman. 'Tell your charming husband how grateful I am for his influence with the local constabulary. I got nowhere with the police, but then according to them, I'm an impressionable spinster with an over-active imagination.'

'You are anything but that,' Flora had to raise her voice over the clatter of crockery and a burst of feminine laughter that rose from the table where Mr Martell entertained the ladies. 'What I don't understand is why these particular children are being taken, and why after they have spent time in the hospital? There must be plenty of homeless waifs these people could—' Flora realised what she had said and brought a hand to her mouth in embarrassment. 'Oh dear, that was callous of me. But you know I didn't mean anything by it.'

'I do, my dear.' Alice waved her away and replenished both their cups and added sugar to her own. 'I too have given the same question some thought, and it strikes me that there is a good reason they were chosen from the hospital. The treatment we offer at St Philomena's extends beyond immediate illness. The children are checked for conditions like rickets, skin diseases, eyesight problems, and malnutrition. They leave us healthy, or as much as they can be given their living conditions.' She balanced her full cup in both hands and took a sip. 'None of the children taken are malformed or chronically ill. Without exception they are also good looking; facts which convince me they have been carefully chosen. For what, I dare not imagine.'

Flora's stomach knotted, her gaze fixed on the tiny spoon Alice stirred her tea with a myriad of horrors running through her head. Those poor mites taken from their homes with the promise of a better life only to be forced into... what? Slavery, even prostitution?

The intermittent jangle of the shop bell jarred uncomfortably with the thoughts in her head. How could life be so cruel?

Mr Martell did not return with the water, despatching a waitress to their table instead. After more lamentation of poor Lizzie and idle speculation about Swifty, during which the hot water remained untouched, their conversation dwindled to small talk, as if neither could broach the subject which hung between them.

Finally, Alice looked up at the wall clock. 'Goodness, it's later than I thought. I must go.' She summoned the waitress to settle their bill. 'Mr Buchanan is expecting me.'

'Are you going back to the hospital today?' Flora gathered her bag and rose as the waitress took Alice's money and proffered her change.

'No, I often assist him with paperwork in connection with his other business at his home. He had a secretary at one time, but when she left to get married, he didn't hire another. I think he prefers to work with people he knows, so I agreed to spare him a few hours a week.'

'The hospital isn't Mr Buchanan's only interest then?' Flora tucked a sixpenny piece under her plate as a tip for their waitress.

'His role as a governor only occupies him briefly. His fortune was made in importing items from abroad, especially when Chinese furniture and porcelain became popular.' Alice nodded to the doorman who opened the door for them. 'Then there was that period when everyone wanted an Egyptian room. He has contacts all over the world.'

'He sounds more interesting than I thought,' Flora said as they emerged onto the street.

'When his wife was alive, they travelled everywhere together. Since her death, he sends his agents to buy for him and has the goods sent home on his ships.' She glanced down the street. 'Oh, there's my trolley bus. I don't want to miss it. Goodbye, my dear.'

Alice climbed aboard the vehicle powered by overhead wires, watching as it trundled off towards Hyde Park Corner.

On the short walk back to Eaton Place, Flora's thoughts turned to anticipation of that evening's concert; an excursion she was glad she had not mentioned to Alice. How could she admit she had set her spy team on the man Alice thought so much of? She would face that dilemma later, and if nothing came of it, she wouldn't have to. It was as she reached the path leading to her own front door that she recalled something Alice had said about Mr Buchanan being a shipowner.

* * *

Flora pursed her lips as she held her sapphire pendant up to her throat, her head tilted to assess the effect in her dressing table mirror. Frowning, she returned the item to the box.

'Are you sure it's a good idea having Sally watch this Buchanan chap while he's at the concert, Flora? Is she agreeable to the plan?' Bunny joined her in the bedroom, his skin pink from his bath while rubbing his damp hair vigorously with a towel.

'I thought I had explained,' Flora sighed. 'She's going to sit in the café opposite for the evening. How dangerous can that be? She and Abel will look to all the world like a courting couple having supper. They won't alert anyone's suspicions and if Mr Buchanan is innocent, they will just have enjoyed a pleasant evening.'

'I suppose so.' He lowered the towel and frowned at her reflection. 'Not wearing the sapphire one? It's my favourite.'

'It's not quite the right shade of blue.' Flora looked down at the deep turquoise silk of her dress.

'I'll bow to your superior taste.' He discarded the towel and shrugged into a clean shirt. 'You didn't answer my question about Sally being agreeable to this plan.'

'Sally's excited about it,' she said, in case Bunny thought she had forced her maid to cooperate against her better judgement. 'And more willing when I suggested she take Abel with her.'

'I gather you're paying for their supper?' Bunny laughed.

'And the hackney fare there and back. It's the least I could do.'

'I'll wager five shillings she takes the omnibus so she can pocket the difference.' One perfectly arched right eyebrow lifted slightly.

'I won't take that bet, as I am likely to lose. Sally is enterprising.' A light knock came at the door prompting Flora to hold up a finger in warning to be discreet as she went to open it.

'I'm ready to go, Missus.' Sally slapped her gloved hands together. 'Abel's waiting for me on the area steps.' Smart and pretty in her best outdoor coat buttoned to the neck, she had arranged a pert felt hat jauntily on her wild curls.

'Here's a prospectus for St Philomena's.' Flora handed her a pamphlet she had placed close to hand in readiness. 'There's a photograph of Mr Buchanan on page six. Do you think you could pick him out in a crowd from that?'

'Nice looking man.' Sally held the page at arm's length, squinting, her chin tucked in. 'Shouldn't be difficult.'

'Make sure you and Abel are there well before the performance to lessen the chances of missing him. If he speaks to anyone going in or coming out, I need to know what they look like. Especially if you see Swifty again, but under no circumstances are you to approach him.'

'Cor, this feels like a proper investigation. Do I get paid extra?'

Bunny's amused chuckle reached her from inside the room.

Flora threw him a look, grasped Sally by the arm and eased her into the hall, pulling the door to. 'No, but you can have whatever you like for supper. If Mr Buchanan leaves the performance early, I expect you to notice the time. Do you understand?'

Sally nodded as Flora handed over the money which disappeared into Sally's pocket.

'Off you go.'

She turned from the door to find Bunny, his hands propped on his hips and grinning at her. 'Twelve shillings and sixpence? That's twice what she needs. You spoil that young woman; she'll be getting notions above her station if you aren't careful.'

Unwilling to get into an argument, Flora unhooked Bunny's jacket from a hanger and held it out.

'What exactly has this man done to make you feel this perfectly respectable businessman is involved with these missing children and a murder?' Bunny eased his arms into the sleeves and smoothed the material over his shoulders.

'I'm not sure he's done anything. However, when he opened that envelope with the concert ticket, he looked as if the entire world had descended on him. I know a worried man when I see one.'

'Which may have nothing to do with what is happening at the hospital.' Bunny eased his neck inside his upright collar. 'Besides, if he is involved, he's hardly likely to show his hand at a concert.'

'I disagree. It's the last place anyone would expect strange goings on. Besides, all you have to do is enjoy this evening's supper with Lydia and Harry. I've sorted out everything else.'

'That's what worries me,' Bunny said under his breath. He retrieved his spectacles from a side table and polished the lenses with a handkerchief, just as the chime of the doorbell sounded from the floor below.

'That will be Lydia and Harry.' She plucked the spectacles from his fingers and slid them onto his nose, then brushed her lips across his newly shaven cheek. 'We'd better go down.'

19

Flora and Lydia took their seats in the sitting room, replete from their supper, which none of them had enjoyed more than Harry did.

'I told you Harry would appreciate a home-cooked meal after dining in cafes and restaurants,' Lydia whispered when her fiancé delivered yet another effusive compliment. She wore a shade chartreuse that complemented her fair hair and delicate features. A single drop pearl hung from a gold chain round her throat, her eyes sparkling with happiness, rivalling the diamond on her left hand.

'Are you really going to postpone the wedding?' Dismissing Stokes, Bunny presided over the brandy decanter.

'That's what I've asked her several times.' Harry leaned his forearms on the back of the sofa where the ladies sat. 'I don't care a fig for my parent's disapproval.'

'I see.' Flora said, archly, defensive of her friend, and angry that the Flynns regarded Lydia a poor choice of wife for their son.

'They worked hard to get me affianced to Evangeline, so when she died...' Harry raised both palms off the chair back without completing the statement.

'She was murdered, Harry. By her half-brother.' Lydia accepted the cut glass balloon Bunny held out with its inch of dark amber liquid from which a heady spirit smell emanated. 'Which must have been a shock to your mother. She was very fond of Evangeline.' The implication that she was less so for Lydia was implied.

'More like horror that I wouldn't have access to her fortune.' Harry took a mouthful of brandy, swallowed and gave a slight shudder. 'I've told them countless times I only went along with their plans to appease them.'

'Is the spirit not to your liking?' Bunny asked, his forehead creased in a frown.

'Not at all. It's excellent.' Harry lifted the glass and it caught the light, the transparent gold liquid glowing through the crystal facets. 'It's exquisite. Perhaps I should have sipped it.'

'It's a rather fine Otard XO, matured in the lower vaults of Chateau Otard on the banks of the River Charente. The cellars provide a constant temperature and humidity perfect for the ageing of eaux-de-vie.' Bunny smiled broadly at the three astonished looks directed towards him.

'Eu de vie? Isn't that what the Scots call whisky?' Lydia asked.

'Funny you should say that.' Bunny took his seat in his favourite leather studded chair, one ankle crossed over the other. 'In fact, the Otard family originated from the Vikings, and actually lived in Scotland from the eleventh century. They were Jacobites and followed James II into exile in France after the Glorious Revolution of 1688.'

'How informative, Bunny. I had no idea you were so knowledgeable.' Lydia's eyes shone in admiration.

'Not really. I spent an exceedingly boring holiday in Cognac when I was fourteen with an aunt who dragged me round on a chateau tour. Surprising how certain things sink in.'

'Don't spoil it.' Flora pouted. 'There's me thinking I married a man of the world.'

'Then you might be interested in the only other fact I remember,' Bunny said, ignoring Flora's eyebrow dance. 'Baron Otard was condemned to death in the French revolution, but the night before his execution, the villagers of Cognac broke into his prison and freed him.'

'That's fascinating.' Flora held his gaze in challenge. 'However, we were discussing the postponement of Lydia and Harry's wedding.'

'Oh, yes, sorry. Didn't mean to be a bore,' Bunny said.

'One thing you never are is boring,' Lydia said. 'As for the wedding. It's only being put off until the spring. Harry's father is a dear, but his mother and sisters always look as if they are sucking lemons when I enter a room.'

'Believe me, your efforts will make little difference, Lydia, unless you inherit a fortune. In which case they will forgive anything.'

'Then it's entirely their loss.' Flora patted her friend's hand as an image entered her head. 'It sounds like a Jane Austen moment.' At Harry's confused frown she added, 'You know, Charles Bingley's sisters disapproved of Jane Bennett.'

'Not a reader of romantic novels, I'm afraid,' Harry muttered, his nose buried in his brandy glass.

'Then when we are married, I'll simply have to educate you,' Lydia said.

Harry's lower lip dropped; his discomfort greeted by Bunny with a guffaw of laughter. Lydia scolded them gently while Flora's thoughts drifted to the clock on the mantelpiece which showed it was well after eleven. Surely Sally should have returned by now.

'Flora?' the sharpness of Bunny's tone made her jump. 'I said that the Bennett situation worked out well, so I'm sure this one will. Is there something wrong?'

'Ah, no, of course not. More coffee, anyone?' In response to murmurs of assent she rose and refilled their cups, the action giving her something to do but it did not reduce her growing anxiety. The performance wouldn't go on much after ten thirty, so where was she?

'There is another reason for the postponement,' Harry began, accepting a refill of his glass from Bunny. 'The house my uncle left me in Kensington is in a poor state and I want it to be perfect for Lydia. By any stretch of the imagination the work won't be completed until next April.'

'So long?' Flora set her glass down on a table at her elbow after only three sips. Baron Otard's brandy might be the finest, but it was too fiery for her.

'On another subject,' Lydia interjected. 'Harry is busy flirting with those socialists,' Lydia said, though there was no censure in her voice. 'He's become quite an admirer of Keir Hardie.'

'Isn't he a member of Parliament in some Welsh seat?' Flora asked.

'Merthyr Tydfil, yes,' Harry replied. 'He's a bit of a radical as he insists on attending the Commons in a tweed suit when most MP's wear formal dress.'

'His politics are sound for modern times, in that he advocates women's rights, free schooling and pensions,' Lydia said. 'He's not a supporter of the monarchy either, which upsets the Conservatives.'

'I can see why your parents think Lydia is a bad influence,' Bunny aimed a wink at Harry, which made him laugh.

'Hardie is an interesting man though, and it's about time powerful unions were organised for miners.'

'I feel it's men like him who would be sympathetic to the plight of these children, Flora.' Harry saluted her with his coffee cup. 'There should be laws to protect them.'

'There are, or at least there will be, when the Trafficking Act is ratified next year,' Bunny said. 'Then maybe whoever takes them will face their crimes in a court of law.'

'We need to find them first,' Lydia pointed out, a comment greeted with a sigh from Flora and murmurs of agreement from the men.

'I don't suppose this—' Lydia broke off as the door opened to reveal Stokes.

'Excuse me, sir.' His eyes darted the room before settling on Bunny, while one hand made a vague pointing gesture to his right. 'There's a – person – outside who insists on speaking with you.'

Flora's stomach knotted with disappointment it wasn't Sally. 'Who could call at this hour?' she asked no one in particular.

'You'd better admit them, Stokes. It might be important,' Bunny said, but before Stokes could comply, Abel Cain shoved past the astonished man and strode into the room.

Bunny held up a hand at the butler's shocked protest. 'It's all right, Stokes. You may go.'

The butler bowed and backed away; his reluctance was clear in the way he pulled the door closed far slower than normal.

'Abel?' Flora asked, as everyone's attention fixed on the newcomer, whose impressive build made the room suddenly feel crowded.

He stood with slumped shoulders, his thick brown hair disarranged by the swift and rapid removal of his hat. He repeatedly twisted the brown cap in both hands in front of him until Flora feared he would rip the material.

'Apologies for disturbing you, Mrs Harrington, Mr Harrington.' Abel's brown eyes widened in distress as he looked from Bunny to Flora and back again. 'Has anyone seen Sally?'

* * *

'Isn't she with you?' Flora rose slowly from her seat as dread turned the uneasy fluttering in her chest to panic.

'No, Miss. I hoped she might have come back here.' Abel scanned the room as if he expected Sally might be concealed behind a sofa.

'Well, she hasn't.' Bunny placed his brandy glass on the mantle-piece with a click and came to stand at Flora's side. 'What happened this evening?'

'We did exactly what you said.' Abel's hat received another mangling. 'We sat in that café across the road from the concert hall and saw Mr Buchanan arrive. He was alone, and he didn't speak to anyone we saw. He came into the street during the interval and stood smoking a cigar.'

'What happened then, Abel?' Bunny asked, impatient, as Abel had a slow, contemplative way of speaking.

'He didn't go back into the concert hall again.'

'Where did he go?' Flora clenched her hands to remind herself not to snap.

'That's what I'm trying to tell you.' Abel kept looking towards the door as if he was expecting Sally to arrive at any moment. 'He went round the corner into the Lamb and Flag in St James' Street. He bought a double whisky that he drank straight down, then ordered another. Sally and me watched him, but the pub were busy and we had trouble keeping him in sight.'

'Are you saying he gave you the slip?' Bunny asked.

'No, sir.' Abel shifted his attention to Flora. 'Sally and me got seats at a table by the window, but we didn't dare get closer in case he saw us watching him. But what with all the comings and goings it was hard to keep him in sight all the time.'

'We understand, Abel,' Bunny said gently. 'Did Mr Buchanan talk to anyone?'

'The Sally Army turned up; a man and a woman with collection boxes. I didn't think much of it at first, I mean, them God Botherers like to catch people in pubs and tap them up for a few shillings.'

Lydia giggled, but sobered when she caught Flora's eyes and she mouthed an apology.

'Abel,' Bunny interrupted him. 'Where is all this leading?'

'Sorry, sir.' He ducked his head, embarrassed. 'I don't think he spoke to anyone but the barman. Then Sally got impatient like, and crept closer. When she came back to the table, she said the woman had given Mr Buchanan a note.'

'What did this woman look like?' Bunny asked, one raised brow conveying his impatience.

'I didn't see her properly, sir. She was wearing one of those poke bonnets.'

'She was the Salvation Army woman?' Flora asked. 'Why didn't you say so?'

'I thought I did.' Abel's brows knitted together. 'She had one of those cloaks on over her shoulders. They all look the same, those people. Same clothes, same expressions. Can't tell one from another,' he muttered this last part almost to himself. 'The note made Mr Buchanan angry. He crumpled it up and shoved it into his pocket. He shook his finger at them a couple of times, then ordered another drink.'

'I don't suppose you heard any of the conversation between this pair and Buchanan?' Bunny asked.

'No, sir, I wasn't close enough, and the bar was too noisy.'

'Interesting,' Bunny mused. 'I don't suppose we'll learn what that note was about?'

'I would like to know too,' Flora said.

'Well, that's the thing, Miss.' Abel's neck turned a dull pink. 'I told Sally to stay put at the table while I went to the bar, and, well I... I picked Buchanan's pocket.'

'Without him realising?' Flora asked, both shocked and admiring. How did a man like Abel, who stood over six foot and with shoulders as wide as a door go unnoticed?

'After three double whiskies?' Abel gave her an ironic, sideways look. 'I doubt he would have noticed if I'd taken his ruddy coat off his back.' His cheeks flushed a deeper red. 'Beggin' yer pardon. He just stared into his glass and looked terrible, all grey and drawn.'

'Might we see this result of your sleight-of-hand skills, Abel?' Bunny held out his hand.

'Um, yes, sir. Sorry, I almost forgot.' Abel delved into his coat pocket and drew out a slip of paper which was little more than a mass of creases.

Flora was eager to see what was in it, but Sally was her primary concern. 'Why didn't Sally come back with you?'

'I went to the gents, but I was only gone a minute or two. When I came out again, Sally wasn't in the bar. Nor was Mr Buchanan or the Sally Army couple. By the time I got outside, there was no sign of them.' His shoulders slumped, defeated. 'I told her to wait for me, but you know how she is.'

'I do indeed.' Flora closed her eyes, sympathetic but angry that Abel had allowed Sally to leave without him. 'Where could she have gone?'

'Don't panic, Flora. She isn't likely to get lost.' Bunny laid a hand on her shoulder; a gesture she assumed was meant to calm her, but only made her more agitated. 'London is her home, so let's not worry about her until it becomes necessary.'

Flora nodded, but couldn't help worrying. Sally had plenty of money with her for cabs. So why wasn't she home by now?

'Abel,' Bunny said gently, his grip on Flora's shoulder increasing. 'Think, Abel. What did Sally actually say?'

'I'm not sure now.' Abel's handsome face twisted in anguish like a small boy chastised for some misdemeanour, his brow furrowed as he tried to remember. 'She said she had seen him before, but it was really noisy in that pub.'

'Perhaps this will tell us more?' Bunny unfolded the note and peered at it. '"Eighteen hundred hours, *SS Lancet*, October 4th".' He turned the paper over, frowned then turned it back again. 'That's all.'

'Doesn't "SS" mean steamship?' Lydia said.

'Indeed, it does, with the time and date of its scheduled departure,' Harry said.

'Mr Buchanan is a shipowner.' Flora recalled what Alice had told her. 'It must be one of his vessels, which proves he's involved. He's taking those children out of the country.'

'My goodness.' Lydia gasped. 'October 4th! That's tomorrow.'

Blood rushed through Flora's veins, making her light-headed. 'We must do something, Bunny. Call Inspector Maddox.'

Harry stood, placed his glass on the mantelpiece beside Bunny's and rubbed his hands together. 'Then I suggest we find out where this *SS Lancet* is berthed, then inform the police and have the ship searched.'

'I agree, but we cannot go barging onto a ship without evidence and simply demand to know if they have children on board.' Bunny tapped the slip of paper against his top lip and glanced at the clock. 'It's almost midnight, so we'll have to wait until the morning to do anything. I'll speak to Maddox first thing tomorrow, though he might not take action on the strength of the scant evidence we have.'

'What about Sally?' Flora fought back welling tears. 'The police need to be out looking for her.'

'I know it's frustrating, Flora.' Bunny's voice was annoyingly reasonable. 'Sally hasn't been missing for long enough to cause a police search. Even if I call them now, it's doubtful a lowly night desk sergeant would drag Inspector Maddox out of bed on our say-so.'

'No, I suppose not.' Flora sighed, her thoughts racing. 'Why did Sally go after Mr Buchanan?' *And how could she have seen the Salvation Army man before? Unless he was at The Antigallican the other night?*

'Mrs Harrington,' Abel's soft voice at her side made her jump. 'She didn't.'

'She didn't what?' Bunny demanded.

Every eye in the room rounded on Abel, who swallowed before answering. 'She didn't follow Mr Buchanan. She went after the Sally Army couple.'

20

It was almost two o'clock by the time the party broke up, and with still no sign of Sally, they conceded nothing more could be done that night. Harry had suggested they find out where the *SS Lancet* was berthed and claimed to know someone who worked at the Customs House. Having devised a sketchy plan and a tentative promise to talk again the next day, Bunny and Flora said goodbye to their guests.

'Don't fret too much,' Bunny said to reassure Flora as they climbed the darkened hallway. 'Chances are she'll be back before morning with a colourful tale to tell.'

'I hope so,' she whispered, her concern for her maid growing more intense by the minute. Sally wouldn't leave her worrying like this. Not unless she had no choice.

* * *

After a fitful night, where Flora jumped at every creak of the floorboards or scrape of branches on the window glass, she woke to the clack of the curtains being drawn across the brass pole, flooding the room with sharp white daylight.

She bolted upright in anticipation, only to slump back against the pillows when she saw it was a maid with her morning tea, the whoosh of running water reaching her from the bathroom next door.

'Has Sally returned, Nell?'

'No, madam. Sorry, madam.' Nell placed a cup of steaming tea on the nightstand.

Flora glanced at the bedside clock. Sally had been missing for hours. Was that long enough to prompt Inspector Maddox to instigate a search? Probably not. She could hear his voice in her ear explaining patiently that Sally was a grown woman and was free to stay out all night if she so wished. She could even imagine the moralistic tone of his voice too.

'We're all worried downstairs.' Nell hovered at the door, hoping to hear something of interest she could report in the servants' hall. 'It ain't like her.'

'I've been thinking, Flora,' Bunny emerged from the dressing room, garbed in only a white towel wrapped around his hips to mid-thigh. 'Oops, sorry, I didn't think anyone was—' Nell gasped, her eyes wide above the hand she brought to her mouth, then turned and fled the room.

Flora choked on a mouthful of tea. In the same position, Sally would have smirked and stood her ground, Flora mused, making her stomach knot with sadness. She wasn't here.

Bunny sighed, let the towel slip to the floor, and patted his flat belly. 'I suppose she'll scurry into corners whenever she sees me in the hall now?' He held up a pair of underpants for inspection before putting them on.

'If she gives notice, I'll hold you responsible.' Flora returned her cup to the nightstand. 'Now, what was it you were thinking?' She pushed back the covers and swung her legs onto the floor.

'Sally isn't back?' he asked, catching sight of her face. At the shake of her head, he pulled on a pair of socks and fastened them to red elastic gaiters. 'I'll telephone the police station before breakfast and talk to Inspector Maddox. If he doesn't take what we've discovered seriously, I'll demand an interview with his superior.'

'Inspector Maddox sounded sceptical about children being smuggled in ships by the Salvation Army. That sounds like something from a penny novel.'

'Well, I shan't let him put me off. Not with the weight of evidence that's piling up.' He peered down his nose into a mirror as he clipped his collar to his shirt.

'I appreciate that, Bunny. Thank you.' Emotion thickened her voice. 'I wasn't sure whether you would go against Maddox if he dismissed us.'

'Look, Flora.' He glanced up from fastening his belt, his expression of fierce concentration softened. 'I know I tease you about Sally being pert and disrespectful, but she isn't stupid. She went after that couple for a reason. If she hasn't come back, it's because she's being prevented.' He shrugged into his jacket and blew her a kiss from the door. 'I'll see you downstairs.'

Flora had her bath and dressed, tasks which took on a poignant element without Sally. Not that she minded shifting for herself, but it was on Bunny's insistence she'd employed a lady's maid. Flora had chosen Sally, a bright-eyed whirlwind of a girl who said exactly what she thought and refused to change her East End accent. Despite Beatrice Harrington's warnings of Sally's scant regard for her superiors, Flora enjoyed having her to talk to. Thus, when the tiny buttons on the back of her dress proved too much that morning, causing her to summon a maid to help her, Flora was close to tears.

When she emerged from their room, she heard Bunny's low tones as he spoke on the telephone in the rear hall. In order not to interrupt him, she ascended to the floor above, where, through the half-open nursery door, Nell was in conversation with Milly.

'Even the mistress don't know what's 'appened to 'er.' Nell's sense of the dramatic clear in her high-pitched voice. 'Vanished without a trace, she 'as.'

Flora cleared her throat as she entered the room, but was careful not to look at Nell. Cheeks flaming, Nell dipped a quick curtsey and hurried past her into the hall.

'Little master was up at the crack of dawn, madam.' Milly continued to fold a pile of baby linens. 'He's teething just now, but he copes with it like a trooper.'

'Then I shan't wake him.' Flora leaned over the cot and gently stroked the fuzz of dark blond hair in tiny curls at his neck, just like his father's.

Arthur stirred beneath her hand, flailed a dimpled arm, but settled again immediately, his thumb jammed firmly into his mouth.

'Oh, he won't mind.' Milly snapped a baby vest and folded it against her chest. 'He enjoys seeing you.'

Flora looked up sharply, her gaze on the girl's turned back as the nurse placed the clothes in a drawer. Was it Sally's plight which engendered such unexpected kindness? She welcomed the change and hoped it would last.

Downstairs in the dining room, no aromas of cooking food were detectable, other than the trail of steam that rose from the coffee cup on the table at Bunny's side.

'I told Stokes not to serve breakfast in case we had to go to the police station. There's coffee, though.'

'That's enough for me. I'm too worried to eat.' She approached the coffee pot set over a paraffin flame on its stand. 'What did Maddox say? Are they going to search for Sally?'

'He was remarkably sympathetic under the circumstances.' Bunny discarded his newspaper on the table. 'He accepted everything, including the details of the ship and its departure time.'

'You didn't tell him how Abel had gained those details?'

'Of course not.' His reproachful look silenced her. 'He's going to take some men to search the ship before it sails tonight from Tilbury.'

'That's something, at least.' Flora relaxed her shoulders as the tension of her hard night flowed out of her. 'Waiting is so frustrating. What did he say about the Salvation Army man and Sally?'

'Ah.' Bunny pinched the top of his nose above the bridge of his spectacles. 'That was the less successful part of our conversation. He seemed to think Sally must have misunderstood the situation in the Lamb and Flag. I got the impression he's an admirer of the Army and in his opinion, they're above reproach.'

'Is he a closet Quaker?' Flora murmured, setting down the coffee pot with a thud. 'You said yourself Sally isn't stupid. If she was wrong, and they were genuine, then where is she?'

'Which is exactly what I told Maddox. Finally, he conceded I had a point, and will make enquiries, but also warned me there are many missions in London and tracking down particular members will not be easy. He has asked to be informed if Sally returns on her own.'

'She would be here by now, if that were possible.' Flora sloshed milk clumsily into the coffee. 'I'll wager she's on this ship, the, er...'

'The *SS Lancet*.'

'Why can't I remember that name?' She flapped her free hand in agitation and took the chair opposite him at the dining table.

'Flora,' Bunny's tone dropped to one of conciliation. 'I know you're upset, but I may as well tell you what else Maddox said.'

'Go on.' She stirred her coffee slowly, her eyes fixed on his face, aware she wasn't going to like what came next.

'He agreed to pay a discreet visit to Mr Buchanan this morning. He's not entirely convinced a man of Buchanan's standing could be involved in anything untoward.'

'Buchanan should count himself fortunate he isn't being arrested.' She snorted at Bunny's benign look. 'That man has some explaining to do.'

'Maddox is being cautious. He cannot demand Buchanan's cooperation without first referring to his superior officer.'

'How long will that take?' Frustrated, Flora's voice rose. 'Buchanan could be planning to sell those children. Has Maddox told his superior that?'

'Calm down, Flora. There are still several hours before the ship is due to leave. We're going to have to be patient and trust Maddox knows what he's doing.'

'I don't suppose I have much choice.' She took a gulp from her cup, wincing when the coffee burned the roof of her mouth. 'I feel I ought to call on Alice at her lodgings this morning. She'll want to know about Sally.' Will she be as protective of her friend then?

'Won't she be at the hospital?'

'Not today. She mentioned it was her day off unless there was an emergency.'

'Then I'll come with you. But before we do that...' Bunny rose, took the cup and saucer gently from her hands, and returned it to the table. 'I'm going to take you out to breakfast. No, don't argue. You need your strength to catch dangerous villains.'

'That's not funny.' She glared up at him, where his concerned smile sent a ripple of warmth through her. He was only being Bunny. Worried, protective and loving, but without being patronising. How many women enjoyed those qualities in a husband? She even suspected he admired her determination not to let killers and spies go unpunished, or he wouldn't be so willing to help her. 'All right,' she agreed, though the thought of food still nauseated her.

'To be honest, sitting around here waiting for news is making me restless,' Bunny said as he guided her into the hall.

'I didn't realise you were that fond of Sally.'

'Hmm, let's say I've become accustomed to her. It's quite dull around here without her.' He waved a dismissal to Stokes, who had appeared like a ghost, unhooked Flora's coat from the stand and held it out.

She bit her lip, worried that Alice might be angry Flora had implicated a man she liked and respected without telling her. Suppose Alice refused to see Flora again?

'You need to be prepared for the possibility your Miss Finch knows more about this matter than she admits to.' Bunny shrugged into his coat.

'I don't believe that for a moment.' Flora concentrated on fastening the buttons of her coat, mainly to avoid having to look at him. 'Alice tried to get the police involved, but they refused to do anything,' she reasoned. 'That's why she asked for my help.'

'Which is the story she gave you. Have you thought that she might have had her own reasons for involving you?'

'To what purpose?' Flora put on her hat in front of the hall mirror, where she was forced to meet Bunny's narrowed his eyes in her reflection. 'No, you're wrong. I know you are,' she snapped, though the surge of anger receded quickly. Bunny was simply being cautious, not accusing.

'You're too involved, Flora. In my experience, everyone is a suspect until proven otherwise.' He lowered his voice to a whisper as Stokes, unwilling to be robbed of another of his duties, rushed forward to open the front door. 'No exceptions.'

Flora pouted, but had no answer to that.

Out on the front step, the crisp morning air stung her cheeks and the smell of burning leaves filled her nostrils, evoking afternoons of heavy skies and bonfires in the Gloucestershire countryside.

'I should never have involved Sally.' Flora pulled on her gloves. 'She took such a risk following that man.'

'Really? I wonder who she learned that from?' Bunny cast her a sideways look. 'Don't blame yourself, Sally makes her own decisions. It also strikes me that the collection box bandied about last night was evidently a drop.' At Flora's puzzled frown, he explained, 'An arrangement by which messages are exchanged.'

'You see what you have learned by being married to me?' Flora tucked her arm through his, her shoulders hunched as she leaned into him.

'Some of which I could have lived without,' he murmured as they reached the corner of Belgrave Place where they were more likely to find a passing hansom. 'Didn't the barman at the Antigallican say a Salvation Army couple were in the pub that night. Could it have been the same couple who met with Mr Buchanan last night?'

'And the woman was the one arguing with Lizzie Prentice in the kitchen?' Flora's pulse raced.

'But he didn't see her, only heard the two women arguing.'

'I suppose that would make it too tidy a solution.'

Bunny paused at the kerb, placed a thumb and finger between his lips and issued a piercing whistle. An idling hansom driver parked on the other side of the road touched the peak of his cap to show he understood. He flicked the thong of his whip, swung the cab around and halted the horse beside them.

'It might all be conjecture, but I have an idea about this Salvation Army theory.' Bunny handed her into the cramped interior, which smelled of saddle wax and damp wood. Sliding in beside her, he closed the wooden flaps over their knees with a dull thump.

'You're being very mysterious. What sort of idea?'

'You'll see. Now first things first.' He opened the trap above their heads. 'Claridge's Hotel, if you please driver.'

21

'Are you sure this is the correct house?' Bunny frowned at the black painted double doors of the Georgian mansion on Birdcage Walk, with its gleaming brass furnishings. Reclining stone lions sat atop a pair of gateposts that flanked a wide carriage drive. 'It doesn't look much like a lodging house.'

'This is the address Alice gave me. Or I must have written it down wrong.' Flora bit her lower lip and cast a worried look back to the panoramic view of St James' Park behind them. 'Maybe we could leave before anyone knows we're here?'

'It's too late now. I've pushed the bell.' Bunny sniffed. 'And it's been a considerable time since I've played knock down ginger.'

The left-hand door opened with a click, revealing a butler in a black coat and striped trousers who scrutinised them both. 'May I help you, sir? Madam? Though I should inform you that my master is not at home, but if you would care to state your business with Mr Buchanan, I shall—'

'Mr Buchanan lives here? Mr Raymond Buchanan?' Flora blurted before she could stop herself.

'Indeed,' the man drawled, his curious expression changing instantly to boredom. As if he had no time for unexpected callers.

'Who is it, Fielding?' Alice's unmistakable voice interrupted from behind him.

Fielding continued to block the door; his head turned to address the unseen figure. 'Visitors, madam. They wish to see the master without prior arrangement.' His tone implied it was a minor inconvenience he could handle, and he made to close the door.

Alice appeared in the gap between the double doors, forcing the butler to step back. 'It's perfectly all right, Fielding, these are friends of mine. Please let them in.'

'If you say so, madam.' With obvious reluctance, the butler stood aside, allowing Flora and Bunny into a marble hall large enough to encompass their entire ground floor at Eaton Place. In front of them, a grand staircase levelled off on the next floor, split and went off in opposite directions into a long gallery on the level above them. Gilt mirrors graced the walls, reflecting light from crystal chandeliers on a ceiling twelve feet high, reflecting it back onto the floor below.

Flora's upbringing in the opulence of Cleeve Abbey had not made her immune to the tangible evidence of wealth at every turn. Not just the impulsive expense made amongst gaudy items offered in the London department stores, but the ancient and polished affluence of generations handed down with pride.

'How unexpected, though I'm delighted to see you both.' Alice pressed each of their hands, giving Flora the impression, she would have embraced them had their acquaintance been longer. Her slate blue dress brought out her eyes, her hair, so close to Flora's own was piled in soft curls atop her head which stressed her delicate neck.

'You live here?' Flora said once they were out of earshot of the butler. 'That man said this was Mr Buchanan's house?'

'Come along inside and I'll explain.' Alice led them down a hall, at the end of which stood a glazed door opening onto an orangery that stretched across the back of the house. The ornate metal frame of leaf green with glass panels looked onto a walled garden, its pathways, statuary and mature trees redolent of a country estate.

'This is certainly unexpected.' Bunny stared around, his eyes wide behind his spectacles. 'What a magnificent house.'

'Indeed.' Alice gestured for them to make themselves comfortable in the arrangement of four wickerwork chairs with peacock backs. 'St James' Palace is next door. I believe that during the late fifteen hundreds, King James the First kept aviaries of exotic birds in this spot, thus the name Birdcage Walk. I believe there were camels, crocodiles, and an elephant too, together with a flower garden.' She took a chair opposite, the wide circular wickerwork providing a frame to her head. 'Might I offer you both some refreshment?'

'Ah, no thank you,' Flora replied, including Bunny in her refusal. 'We have just had breakfast.' She almost regretting the fact. The idea of drinking coffee beneath an ancient vine that wound round the iron supports above their heads appealed. The white painted furniture complemented pots of ferns and late summer roses that broke the hard lines of the iron and glass.

'I can see you are both shocked,' Alice allowed her words to sink in, her hands folded in her lap. 'I feel I owe you an explanation.'

'You owe us nothing, Miss Finch.' Bunny flicked up the back of his coat and sat. 'It is we who should apologise for not understanding that you and Mr Buchanan were – um.' He broke off, flushed a deep red and coughed into a fist. 'I mean to say we, er...'

Flora concealed a smile behind a gloved hand at this change of roles, when in most cases it was her runaway tongue which caused them embarrassment.

'We are both intrigued,' Flora said, hoping to save his blushes.

'Naturally, though I wish you to know I am not Mr Buchanan's mistress.'

'Oh, but we didn't think—' Bunny said.

'We would never assume—' Flora added.

'I wouldn't blame you if you did.' Alice cut them both off with another rich laugh. 'Our domestic arrangements appear unconventional to most people. Not those who know us, of course, but to the world at large we are an odd pair. Our only redemption comes from the fact Mr Buchanan's devotion to his wife and his standing in society is above reproach.'

A fact which Flora judged might make Inspector Maddox less diligent than he should be for questioning him. The police were notorious for believing vast wealth meant instant respectability.

'Have you been acquainted long?' Flora offered a weak smile. How could they imply Mr Buchanan's involvement in child trafficking after such an endorsement?

'For many years.' Alice leaned forward slightly as if conveying a confidence. 'His wife, Mary, was an especial friend. When she died five years ago, Raymond was lost and hated the idea of leaving the home where they had spent their married life and raised their children. He didn't want to leave, and the house is too vast for him alone. At his request, I moved in here to look after him. I occupy a separate suite of rooms on the top floor with my own front door. It's an arrangement which suits us both.'

'Is Mr Buchanan at home by any chance?' Bunny glanced at Flora then back at Alice.

'Actually, I'm not sure.' Alice stared round as if puzzled he had not joined them. 'I haven't seen him since yesterday. We had planned to attend a lecture on bronchial diseases this evening, but when I came down for breakfast this morning, he had already gone out. He left me a note saying he couldn't attend the lecture after all, but no further explanation. It's most unlike him.'

'Has his behaviour been unusual recently?' Bunny asked. 'Perhaps he is distracted, or has changed his regular habits?'

'Now you mention it. I believe he has.' Alice fiddled with the clasp of a delicate silver bracelet on her left wrist. 'I thought it was because of the stress of his business and lately of Isobel Lomax's disappearance. She hasn't been found yet, and it's most worrying. When I broached the subject he seemed, well, as you say, distracted.'

'Could something else be worrying him?' Bunny asked.

'Bunny, don't ask enigmatic questions.' Flora became restless. 'Just tell Alice what we came to say.'

Alice straightened in her chair and split a slow look between them. 'I assume this is not simply a social call.'

'No and we would like to ask you some questions about Mr Buchanan. We understand he attended a concert at the Bechstein Hall last evening.' Bunny waited for this information to sink in.

'To hear Mr Schabel play?' Alice's blue-green eyes sparkled with interest. 'Yes, that's correct. How did you know?' She caught the hard edge of Bunny's smile and paused. 'I gather your mention of this isn't a coincidence?'

'No.' Bunny cleared his throat. 'He missed part of the performance because he met with someone. This person gave him a note which contained information about a certain ship.'

'Which ship?' Alice's hand drifted to her throat that trembled slightly.

'The *SS Lancet*.'

'I see.' Alice swallowed. 'I won't ask how this note fell into your possession.' Her gaze remained steady and contained no malice. 'How can I help?'

'The person who observed this exchange was my maid, and she has since gone missing,' Flora said.

'Should I ask what your maid was doing?' Alice's eyes darkened. 'No, of course not. She was spying on Mr Buchanan.'

'Not spying, exactly,' Bunny began.

'That's exactly what she was doing,' Flora cut across him. 'We asked her to, but she hasn't been seen since last night, which is not like her.'

'I'm sorry to hear that. I take it you think Raymond has something to do with these missing children?' She split a worried gaze between them. 'Which explains why he refused to discuss it with me?'

'Not with Sally's disappearance though,' Flora said. 'Not directly, that is. My maid followed the man Mr Buchanan went to meet, and she has yet to return.'

Alice listened in silence as Bunny related the argument Lizzie Prentice had had in the kitchen with a woman, who may or may not have been the same one Abel had seen in the Lamb and Flag with Mr Buchanan.

Flora relaxed slightly as he talked, reassured that he believed Alice was an innocent party in this affair. Either that or he was waiting for her to fall into a trap of some sort yet to be revealed.

'Yes, Flora mentioned Lizzie had argued with someone before she died.' Alice pulled at her bottom lip with a thumb and forefinger. 'And it explains why she wanted to talk to me the day you came to the hospital.' She huffed a breath through her lips, rocking gently. 'Though I cannot believe Raymond would be involved in something like this.'

'We didn't either until last night.' Bunny words showed that he and Flora agreed.

'Oh dear.' Alice twisted her hands together in her lap, then stiffened as if she had decided. 'You had better come with me.'

She rose and led them through a side hall, where she pushed open a door to a room which contained a massive oak desk, its top inlaid with tooled leather set in front of a wide window with a view of the front drive and the park beyond.

'It's never locked,' Alice said in response to Flora's expression when she caught sight of the obviously masculine study. 'We trust each other, you see. Or rather we did – before.' She strode to the desk where she rummaged through a pile of papers, selected one and wordlessly handed it to Bunny.

'This is the ship's manifest, dated three months ago.' Bunny scanned the document briefly, then looked up at Alice and frowned. 'Miss Finch, you must know how this looks? I—'

'Are you sure you want to do this, Alice?' Flora halted him with a hand on his arm. 'We wouldn't want you to discuss anything which makes you uncomfortable.'

'Children are at risk,' Bunny said. 'We have no idea what these people have planned for them, so I'm afraid loyalty and privacy have no place here.'

'Bunny! You aren't in a courtroom now,' Flora snapped.

'No, Flora, he's quite right,' Alice cut across her protest. 'I'm not a fool, Mr Harrington. I'm confident the truth will exonerate Raymond, eventually. However, if he is involved, he must explain, and worse, face the consequences of his actions.'

Flora glanced down so Alice would not see the doubt in her eyes. If Mr Buchanan was so innocent, what was he doing sharing information on his ships with a Salvation Army officer in a public house? If their business were legitimate, wouldn't their meetings be conducted in an office with documents other than scraps of paper?

'You mentioned before that your maid followed a man. Was this the same man Raymond met with – the man from the Salvation Army?'

'Yes, but we don't know yet what the connection is.' Bunny

considered a moment. 'Mr Buchanan talked to a couple who were supposedly collecting for their mission in the pub he went to. It's possible this couple are imposters and not army members at all.'

'Because they were also there in the Antigallican that night when Lizzie had that argument?' Alice said.

'Exactly.' Bunny nodded. 'We aren't certain they are the same couple, but it's more than likely. Other than that, we have no actual idea of who they are.'

'Alice, how did you meet the Buchanans?' Flora asked, her conviction that Alice Finch was Lily Maguire took another dip. Lily Maguire had been a rector's daughter and therefore unlikely to move in the circles the Buchanan's occupied.

'Mary and Raymond Buchanan were good to me when I needed a friend,' Alice began carefully. 'A year before I met them, they lost their twelve-year-old daughter in an accident. Their nephew, who was older, took her out on the Serpentine in a rowing boat. The boy started messing about and somehow the boat capsized, trapping the girl beneath it. Raymond dived in and saved his nephew, but his daughter drowned. Mary Buchanan was distraught and Raymond always believed that she blamed him for losing their child. Mary neither believed nor implied any such thing, but guilt is a powerful master.'

'How awful,' Flora said, though at the same time was aware Alice had not answered her question.

'I can see why you wouldn't think he could abduct children.' Bunny rose and approached a break-fronted glazed cabinet that stood against one wall.

'Exactly.' Alice brought her hands to her cheeks. 'I don't believe it. There must be some other reason for his actions. Raymond is a fierce advocate for the hospital and has sunk some of his own money into it. He's so proud of the work we do there, it simply doesn't fit with what you are suggesting.'

'Excuse me, Miss Finch,' Bunny tapped a glass door with his knuckles. 'Do you have a key to this cabinet?'

'Um, yes, of course.' Alice slid open a drawer in the desk and removed a small bunch of keys.

'Bunny!' Flora reprimanded him. 'Alice was recounting a sad story.'

'And I heard every word,' Bunny said without looking at either of them, his attention on examining each key. He selected the smallest and tried it in the lock.

'Those are Raymond's collection,' Alice said. 'They've been here for years, but I admit I've never taken much notice of them.' Bunny withdrew one of several wooden trays and laid it on the desk. Small objects in what looked to be ivory were arranged in neat indentations in the velvet. A fish with carved scales sat beside a pair of miniature binoculars complete with mother-of-pearl handle, together with a perfect replica of a violin, each one less than two inches long, some even smaller.

'They're miniatures,' Flora said. 'Pretty, but not exactly interesting.'

'That's not all they are.' A superior smile played on his lips. 'They have one thing in common, do you see?'

'Not really, but I know you're longing to tell us.' Flora plucked a tiny fish from the tray, with carved scales and bulbous eyes, turning it over in her hand.

'Do you see that tiny metal circle on one side? Well, if you hold it up to your eye, you can see inside. Each one contains a miniature picture.'

'How can you see anything through that tiny hole?' Flora asked.

'There is a lens inside which magnifies the picture. Go on,' he urged. 'Try it.'

Squinting, Flora held the fish to one eye. Instantly a transparent coloured image jumped out at her; of a grey stone church in minute detail, the words 'Eglise de St Madeleine' below in black script. 'It's beautiful.' She marvelled at the detail. 'It's like a kaleidoscope with the way the light shines through it, but much smaller.'

'Fascinating.' Alice ran her fingers over the tray. 'I always wondered what was so special about them.'

'They are called "stanhopes",' Bunny said, with a triumphant grin. 'Also known as "peeps".' He ran his fingertips over the line of objects, finally selecting a miniature violin that he lifted from the lining and held up to his eye. 'I wonder what this one—' He jerked his chin back, snatching it from his eye as if it burned him.

'What's in that one?' Flora reached to take the object from him. 'Let me look.'

'I don't think—' He jerked his hand away, but she was too quick for him. She held it up to the window and peered through the tiny hole.

'It's a photograph of a woman with – oh!' She pulled back her chin, lowering the object. 'She has no clothes on!'

Alice's lips twitched with the hint of a smile. 'Really? How intriguing.' She selected a peep which was shaped like a ship's wheel, took it to the window and looked through the tiny hole in the centre. 'Goodness me,' she murmured, making no attempt to remove it from her eye. 'I would say this – lady – is a professional model. The photograph was evidently taken in a studio of some sort. The background is carefully staged.'

'It's not appropriate for either of you ladies to be looking at these.' Bunny plucked the fish-shaped stanhope from Flora's fingers and returned it to the box, avoiding her eye. 'This is a gentleman's private collection.'

'I've been a nurse for fifteen years.' Alice laughed. 'It will take more than a naked lady or two to shock me.'

'Really, Bunny,' Flora recovered rapidly from her initial surprise. 'You can buy postcards like this on the Old Kent Road.' At his oblique look, she shrugged. 'Sally told me.' At the thought of her maid, a lump formed in Flora's throat.

'Funny how something so innocent looking can hide such a secret,' Alice said. 'Now I know why Raymond kept them locked away.'

A memory resurfaced in Flora's mind, but it was vague and she couldn't hold on to it. That she had seen something similar before. But where? 'I'm sorry, but I don't think these have anything to do with why you came here.' Alice hefted the tray into her arms and returned it to the cabinet. She turned the key firmly in the lock and returned the bunch to the drawer. 'What are you going to do now? About the *SS Lancet*, I mean.'

'Oh, yes, of course,' Bunny said. 'We informed Inspector Maddox on the contents of the note. He is going to organise a search of the ship before it leaves tonight.'

'And Raymond?' Alice rubbed her hands down her skirt, her face as colourless as her apron.

'It depends on what they find,' Flora whispered.

'I see. Of course.' Alice led them back into the hall. 'Are you sure I cannot offer you something to drink?'

'No, I think we should go.' Flora bit her lip. How could they sit over cups of coffee and make small talk when they had given Alice such devastating news? She would spend the rest of the day worrying that her friend was not only involved in trafficking children, but that she had helped instigate the investigation which might condemn him to a prison sentence.

'I hope this is a misunderstanding and Mr Buchanan is entirely innocent.' She pressed Alice's hand and held her clear gaze.

'I have faith in him.' Alice's eyes looked suspiciously wet. 'You will let me know what happens this evening about the ship? Even if it's bad news, if it concerns Raymond, I need to know.' Bunny looked about to say something, but Alice held up a hand to forestall him. 'Don't worry, if he returns home in the meantime, I will say nothing of our conversation.'

'We appreciate that,' Bunny said. 'Although we know this puts you in a difficult position.'

'I understand, but I still feel that somehow, he's been unwittingly caught up in whatever these activities are.'

'I hope that's the case too.' Flora hoped Alice did not see the doubt in her eyes.

'You will also tell me when your maid is found, won't you?' Alice's eyes softened with compassion.

'Certainly, we shall,' Flora replied, noting Alice did not say, '*if* she is found.'

'Goodness, it's later than I thought. We really must go.' Heat flooded her face as what she had tried so hard to recall earlier came back in a flash. She tugged Bunny by the arm towards the front door. 'Bunny has an appointment. You don't wish to be late.'

'Beg pardon?' Bunny stared at her.

Flora brought her foot down lightly on his instep and he jumped. 'Oh yes, appointment. Of course. I had quite forgotten. This has been a most enlightening morning, Miss Finch.'

'I'm glad you think so, but I don't see how I have been of any help.' Alice escorted them to the front door, where she dismissed Fielding and held open the front door herself.

* * *

'That wasn't exactly subtle, Flora,' Bunny said when they had settled inside a motor taxi that they had hailed near the Cockpit Steps. 'You hurried me out of there like my coat was on fire.'

'Sorry. Perhaps we ought to establish some sort of code which alerts the other to the fact we need to leave.'

'And why exactly? Or was it sheer embarrassment at our suggestion Raymond Buchanan was a child trafficker?'

'I felt dreadful, of course, but there was something I didn't want to mention in front of Alice.'

'Fair enough. And what was that?'

'Those "peeps", or whatever they are. Sister Lazarus has one.'

His head swung towards her. 'Sister Lazarus? Are you sure?'

'Positive. She wears it on a chain attached to her pocket. I saw it two days ago.'

'Interesting, but what does that prove? Not all stanhopes contain dubious images. As you saw from Mr Buchanan's collection, some are quite innocent.'

'Call me cynical, but I doubt this one is.'

'It might simply have been a gift from Buchanan? No, don't glare at me like that. It's possible. Just because you don't like the woman doesn't make her a villain.'

'I don't like her, but suppose she discovered what it contained and is using it to blackmail him?'

'Blackmail? That's quite an assumption. Buchanan keeps his collection at the house, so how did she get hold of it?'

'I've not worked that out yet. It's something I'll ask Alice when I next see her without implying everyone she works with is a suspect.'

'She's a mature woman, Flora. I doubt she hasn't already entertained the possibility.'

'We need to concentrate on this Salvation Army couple. See if we can find out who they are. The Army tour pubs for donations all over London. Identifying them will be almost impossible.'

He drummed the fingers of one hand on his knee. 'I told you. I have an idea about that.'

'Which you're being very secretive about.' Flora leaned to one side as the taxi took a corner, her voice raised against a cacophony of hoots and the rumble of wheels passing within inches on either side.

'I'm not ready to reveal it yet as it needs more thought.'

'What about this Swifty character? Unfortunately, the only person who saw him at the hospital when the children went missing is now dead.'

'Someone must have seen him. We're talking about six children, not counting Isobel Lomax.'

'I'm still trying to see a "peep" as an effective blackmail tool,' Bunny said. 'Plenty of respectable public servants and wealthy men own private rooms full of erotic artwork that they show to male guests at dinner parties. Then there are those with postcard collections secreted away in innocent looking books in libraries.'

'Oh?' Flora raised an eyebrow at him. 'What do you know about such things?'

Bunny smiled. 'Never you mind, but it doesn't ring true Buchanan would submit to blackmail over a few compromising photographs. No, something else is going on, and it's connected with the *SS Lancet*.'

Flora stared out of the window as Marble Arch came into view. Bunny could be right, in that there was a more serious reason for Mr Buchanan's out of character cooperation with these villains. And why would they need his ship if it was not to transport children?

22

At Eaton Place, Stokes informed them with a grave shake of his head that there had been no callers all morning. 'Nor has Miss Pond returned.'

Bunny thanked him and collected his post from the hall, pocketed a letter, then disappeared into his study, leaving Flora to fret until luncheon. Helpless to do anything but wait, she took to walking past the telephone in the rear hall, willing it to ring, though the contraption remained obstinately silent.

During an early dinner that evening, the chime of the doorbell brought them both into the hall without waiting for Stoke's announcement.

'Hope you don't mind my stopping by,' Harry said, as Stokes relieved him of his cashmere overcoat. 'Lydia is still frantic and asked if I would call in. She would have come herself, but she had an NUWSS meeting tonight. Have you heard anything from Inspector Maddox?'

'No, nothing.' Flora presented her cheek for his air kiss.

'I'll wager they're still at the docks,' Bunny said. 'The ship is due to leave in a couple of hours. If they have found anything, we should learn about it soon.' He followed Harry into the sitting room, where Bunny poured brandy for them both.

Bunny brought Harry up to date on their discovery of the stanhopes Mr Buchanan kept in his home, and Flora's conviction that one was in Sister Lazarus' possession.

'It occurs to me there might be some sort of relationship between this Sister Lazarus and this Buchanan chap,' Harry said. 'If not, then why did she have one of his stan things?'

'Stanhopes,' Bunny corrected.

'Maybe he gave it to her as a gift?' Harry suggested.

'I cannot imagine that.' Bunny strode to the sideboard where he poured coffee. 'Why wear it at the hospital? What if she lost it?'

'To taunt him?' Flora turned and faced him, one arm draped along the back of the sofa. 'Maybe she found it, not knowing what it was at first. Then realised and used it against him.'

'Are you sure you don't want her to be guilty because you don't like her?' Harry suggested?

'That's what Bunny said.' Flora tutted. 'But Buchanan looked stricken when he opened that envelope with the concert ticket. He didn't want to cooperate, but was compelled to.'

'By whom?' Bunny cradled his glass. 'Sister Lazarus? That doesn't seem likely.'

'Why not? She's cold and not exactly civil. Not like any nurse I've come across.' Flora sipped from her cup without enthusiasm. She wouldn't sleep tonight if she drank too much coffee. Not that she expected to, with Sally still missing.

'I still cannot see a man like Buchanan involved in child abduction over a few risqué photographs,' Harry said.

'You know of him?' Flora asked, surprised.

'Only by reputation. I believe he's quite the philanthropist.'

'A pity we weren't privy to Buchanan's reaction when Maddox told him he planned to search his ship. That would have told us if he's guilty or not.' Bunny swapped his brandy for his coffee and leaned against the mantelpiece; one foot crossed over his other ankle. 'Harry is right, Flora. Buchanan is no socialite. He has wealth enough to live the rest of his life like a king. He also doesn't care that the whole of London is aware he shares his home with a single lady.'

'Single lady?' Harry's cup froze in mid-air. 'That sound interesting, what have I missed?'

'Oh, nothing. Just idle gossip which has been exaggerated. It's an innocent relationship.' Flora glared at Bunny, then dropped her gaze to her lap.

'There's more to this affair than risqué photographs,' Bunny said, thoughtful.

'What then?' Harry leaned forward to return his glass to the table. 'Unless you think he was responsible for that nurse's death. What was her name?'

'Nurse Prentice,' Flora supplied. 'I'd love to know what she found out that got her killed.'

The room fell strangely silent as they fell into their own thoughts, interrupted only by the rhythmic tick of the mantel clock.

'We appear to have exhausted the subject.' Harry slapped his thighs and rose. 'So I'll leave you both in peace to enjoy the rest of your evening.' Flora glanced up at him quickly and he realised his mistake. 'Sorry, Flora, that was insensitive of me. I know how fond you are of Sally. I sincerely hope nothing bad has happened to her.' He paused beside her chair and pressed her hand. 'You will let us know immediately if you hear anything, won't you?'

'Of course, I'll call you—' she broke off at a ring of the doorbell, followed immediately by a loud pounding on the front door. Flora followed Bunny into the hall where Inspector Maddox barged past Stokes, forcing him against the wall.

'It's all right, Stokes,' Bunny forestalled the butler's dumb-founded protest. 'Do come in, Inspector.'

* * *

Inspector Maddox marched past them into the sitting room still occupied by Harry.

'Have you found Sally?' Flora followed him in. 'And the children, were they on the ship?'

'All in good time, Mr Harrington, Mrs Harrington.' Inspector Maddox still wore his coat and hat, and declined Bunny's gesture for him to take a seat. Instead, he sent an enquiring look Harry's way and in response, Bunny made a brief introduction.

'Ah, yes!' Maddox nodded. 'I questioned you in the Evangeline Lange case. Thought I'd seen you before.'

Harry's eyes narrowed, but he didn't respond. Flora imagined he remembered too, having been viewed as a suspect in his own fiancée's murder the year before.

'The raid on the *SS Lancet* was a fiasco.' Maddox glared at Flora, then belatedly snatched off his hat. 'And I hold you, Mrs Harrington, entirely responsible.'

'What do you mean?' The anticipation that had knotted Flora's stomach all day turned to crushing disappointment. 'What about Sally? And the children?'

'Flora,' Bunny cut her off. 'I'm sure the inspector will explain. However, sir, before you go any further. Would you kindly remove your men from my porch? Having two policemen outside my door will do nothing for my status in Eaton Place.'

'I'll ask Stokes to take them to the kitchens for a cup of tea.' Flora skirted her husband and pressed the bell.

'What happened, Inspector?' Bunny asked, having re-established authority in his own house.

'Nothing at all.' Maddox sniffed. 'There was no sign of either Miss Pond or any children. The cargo hold was full of farm machinery, and the captain possessed the required documentation for their transportation to New York.'

Flora kneaded her forehead with one hand and slowly paced the room. She had been so convinced they would find Sally on that ship. Now they had no idea where to look next.

'Based on the flimsiest of evidence,' Maddox continued in a low tone that did nothing to conceal his frustration, 'I took a dozen policemen off the streets. My Superintendent has demanded I issue a formal apology to Mr Buchanan for inconveniencing him.'

'Mr Buchanan was there?' Flora demanded, no longer intimidated by him, policeman or not. 'What did he say?'

'As the legal owner of the vessel,' Maddox clasped both hands behind his back and rocked on his heels, 'his permission was sought to visit the ship, which he gave without hesitation.'

'You asked him first?' Flora said, incredulous. 'He must have warned them, thus ensuring there would be nothing for you to find. How could—' Bunny's arm tightened around her shoulder and she swallowed her next remark.

'If you would allow me to finish, madam,' Maddox went on, 'I doubt Mr Buchanan had time to make the arrangements. He accompanied us to the dockyard and made suggestions as to likely hiding places.'

'I see,' Flora murmured through gritted teeth, still convinced that if Mr Buchanan knew about the raid, he would have sent Swifty and his cohorts some sort of message to warn them.

'A complete waste of time,' Maddox growled. 'This escapade of yours has caused me no end of trouble.'

'Escapade?' Flora met his furious gaze without flinching. 'Is that all you think it was?' Was being reprimanded by his superior all he cared about?

'I understand the raid proved ineffective, Inspector.' Bunny placed a possessive arm around Flora's shoulder. 'However, I don't appreciate you haranguing my wife for her perfectly reasonable concern over these missing children.'

Maddox flushed, stared at his feet and cleared his throat. 'Well, um, I didn't mean to be disrespectful, and I'm not unsympathetic to your wife's desire to be a good citizen.'

'It's more than that!' Flora snapped. 'Have you forgotten my maid is still missing? And please don't say she's run off on a whim to join the circus.'

Harry smothered a laugh, hurriedly turning it into a cough.

'Forgive my saying so, madam.' Maddox dropped her name in favour of the more ingratiating address. 'Do you have any idea what taking a dozen men off routine duties could mean on the streets? Word gets round fast in that part of the world. I imagine many crimes were committed tonight, and I had no men available to deal with them.'

'I'm sure Mrs Harrington regrets the inconvenience, don't you, Flora?' Harry said.

Flora looked to where Harry now lounged in his chair, one brow raised in mild enquiry.

'I, I suppose so,' she mumbled, swallowing against the tension that tightened her throat.

'The fact remains,' Maddox turned back to Bunny, 'this venture was entirely ill-advised. We could have spent our time in the search of the Lomax girl.'

'That was a low blow, Inspector. Made to muddy the fact that even with all your considerable resources, you have not located the child.' Bunny's eyes flashed fire as he squared up to the man. Flora could have hugged him.

'We have no proof the Lomax girl's disappearance is connected to these children you claim are missing.'

'Don't you believe they are?' Flora's anger dissolved a little when she realised he was right. There was nothing to suggest Isobel was taken by the same people.

'I've had officers visit all the addresses you supplied me for those children. Their families maintain they are alive, well and living elsewhere. Without checking every county in the south, for which we have neither the resources nor the authority, we cannot verify their stories. Without an official report, we have no cause to investigate.'

'I know all that, Inspector,' Flora said through gritted teeth. 'But the families are cooperating with these people.'

'I'm afraid we also appear to have lost track of Swifty Ellis.' The inspector eased his collar away from his throat. 'He hasn't been seen in any of his usual haunts for days.'

'Doesn't that tell you something?' Flora asked, no longer apologetic. 'He's been alerted to your investigation, and he's gone to ground.'

'Which could also be for any number of reasons.' Maddox appeared determined to gain some professional superiority. 'We still wish to question him about Nurse Prentice's murder.'

'You think he was involved?' Flora asked.

'I'm not at liberty to say, madam.' He twisted his hat in both hands and cleared his throat. 'I'll, uh, take my leave now.' He nodded to each of them as he left, then turned back at the door. 'If you should come across any more conspiracies, I would advise you to be sure of your facts before coming to the police.'

Flora waited for him to be out of earshot before she murmured, 'I am sure of my facts.'

23

'How could we have got it so wrong?' Flora addressed Bunny's reflection in her dresser mirror as she got ready for bed.

'Ignore Maddox's posturing.' He dropped a kiss on top of her head. 'More importantly, why didn't they find anything on the ship when someone went to all that trouble of giving that note to Buchanan?'

'Is it possible this gang were too clever for them and hid the children somewhere else?' Flora pulled pins from her hair, releasing the heavy tresses down her back.

'Either that, or they were never there at all,' Bunny murmured.

She twisted around in her chair to face him. 'You still believe in my theory, don't you?'

'I do, but so much of this case is supposition.' She opened her mouth to contradict him, but he forestalled her. 'That's not to say there isn't some sort of conspiracy going on, but we don't have much evidence.'

'Sally is still missing.'

'I'm aware of that, but I can understand why Maddox was angry.' Bunny perched on the bed and untied his shoelaces. 'That he raided that ship on our word alone will have his subordinates nudge and whisper to each other for some time.' A shoe hit the floorboards with a dull thump, as if it took Maddox's reputation with it.

'The ship has probably sailed by now, and we'll never know what happened to those children.' Flora propped her elbows on the dresser and dropped her chin into her palms. 'And Inspector Maddox thinks Buchanan is the injured party,' she sighed, before beginning to brush her hair.

'Which means we're missing something.' Bunny draped his trousers over a chair, dropped his socks on the polished floor and kicked them aside as an afterthought. 'Did the Buchanans have other children apart from the daughter who died?'

'I don't know.' Flora halted her hairbrush in mid-air as she pondered the question. 'Alice didn't say. What made you ask that?'

'You said Buchanan told her he couldn't bear to leave the house where they had raised their children, which suggests they had more than one.' He climbed into bed, his arms folded on the pillow behind his head, the covers bunched at his waist.

'Hmm, you might have a point. Perhaps Mr Buchanan is listed in Debrett's. His family would be mentioned, wouldn't they?'

'I cannot be bothered to go back downstairs and look.' He leaned back against the piled-up pillows, sighed and closed his eyes. 'I'll wait till morning.'

'No need.' Flora rose from her chair and slid open a drawer in the nightstand. 'I have a copy here.' She perched on the side of the bed and flipped through the pages. 'Banderlege, Bander, Bannalea, ah, here it is. "Buchanan, Raymond E. Married Mary Frimley, daughter of Bishop and Mrs Frimley of Wisbech, 7th May 1868, son Victor born 1873, daughter Alice born 1876, died 1888."'

Alice. His daughter was called Alice. Did that mean something? That Alice Finch wasn't Flora's mother after all, but a natural child of Raymond Buchanan? She shook her head to dislodge the thought. No, he wasn't old enough to be Alice's father and his daughter Alice was listed as dead at the age of twelve.

'Flora, are you listening to me?' Bunny nudged her gently. 'I said the son must be about thirty now. Has Alice ever mentioned him?'

'Not to me. He's probably married and has a life of his own.' She turned to the next page. 'There might be an entry for him here, too.'

'Never mind that.' Bunny took the book from her, returned it to the nightstand and turned down the wick of the oil lamp until it guttered and went out. 'I didn't suggest an early night so we can sit in bed and read Debrett's together.'

'It was your idea; about the book I mean.' She discarded her robe and climbed in beside him. 'You know, you really ought to wear pyjamas. I'm sure Stokes is uncomfortable when he counts the laundry and doesn't find any.' She trailed her fingers lightly down his bare breastbone into the soft skin of his belly.

'To the devil with Stokes.' He released a soft grunt and lunged sideways, pulling her into his arms. 'I hate to waste the moonlight.' He flicked a glance at a harvest moon visible in a shaft of silver beyond the casement window, then slid down the strap of her nightdress, running his lips lightly down the side of her neck and across her bare shoulder.

'I cannot stop thinking about Sally.' A tremor ran through her as the thin garment fell to her waist in a whoosh of silk. Her lower belly pulled in anticipation of familiar sensations as his lips nuzzled her neck, his hand sliding across her now naked back.

'I won't let Maddox forget about her. I promise,' he whispered as his lips slid across her cheek and claimed her mouth.

'I know.' Her throat prickled with tears as she relaxed into the comforting circle of his arms.

Later, she lay staring up at the moonlight playing on the ceiling with Bunny's even breathing and the odd creak and thump of the house in the darkness.

The day had made perfect sense until Inspector Maddox had barged into the room with his foul temper and accusations. The note Buchanan was given had to mean something. Why detail the *SS Lancet*'s departure time if it wasn't real? Or had they wanted Buchanan to lead the police to the ship? No, how could he have known he was being observed and why not go to them himself? And then there was the man in Salvation Army uniform Sally said she recognised. Or did she? Perhaps she only thought she did and was mistaken? Though that wouldn't explain why she had not come home.

Abel's concern for Sally was clearly genuine as Stokes reported he had called at the house several times over the last two days asking for news of her.

Her instincts couldn't be wrong, could they? Admittedly, she could never have guessed Alice Finch lived in Mr Buchanan's house, but then if they were in it together, whatever this was, why involve Flora in the first place?

Or could she trust only what she had seen for herself? Sister Ruth Lazarus had heard Lizzie Prentice ask Alice for time alone to talk. What did Lizzie want to tell Alice that Ruth didn't want her to hear?

'Lizzie had to know something,' Flora said aloud. 'It's too much of a coincidence that she was killed within an hour of that conversation. Did she guess Buchanan was being blackmailed into helping this Swifty character?'

Bunny turned over and mumbled something sleepy, but thankfully didn't wake.

Details circled in her head of the day when she and Sally had been locked in a killer's cold, damp cellar huddled together for warmth, with every expectation of becoming his next victims.

At least then they had been together on that occasion. This time, Sally was alone and faced a second night in captivity. Who knows where? If only the police would find her. And if not the police, then who?

Flora had fallen into the semi-consciousness languor before full sleep claimed her before she remembered she hadn't asked what was in the letter Bunny had received earlier. It must have been important, because he put it into his jacket pocket instead of leaving it on his study desk when they arrived home.

She had been about to ask when Harry had arrived, followed by an angry Inspector Maddox. She would ask him in the morning.

* * *

Flora stared through the window as the motor taxi trundled along the Victoria Embankment and into Queen Victoria Street, the dome of St Paul's Cathedral visible between the buildings.

'Where exactly are we going?' she asked Bunny for the third time since leaving Eaton Place. 'I don't wish to be ungrateful, but I'm not in the right frame of mind for an outing. I ought to remain at home in case Sally returns.' *If she does.*

'You cannot hole yourself up inside the house forever, my love. We have to have faith that she will be found, safe and well.' He removed a letter that had arrived the previous day from inside his jacket. Written on plain paper in a rough brown envelope, it was unlike most of Bunny's correspondence, which made it all the more intriguing. 'I meant to ask you about that at breakfast,' Flora said. 'You looked rather pleased to receive it?'

'It's from a friend of mine who is a captain in the Salvation Army.'

'Really?' She turned to face him. 'I didn't know you had those sort of connections.'

'The Blakes were neighbours of ours in Richmond when I was younger, but we haven't been in touch recently.' He returned the letter to his pocket. 'Captain Blake works in one of their shelters and has agreed to see us this morning.'

'Where is this shelter?' Her enthusiasm lifted a notch.

'In Whitechapel.'

'Whitechapel? Isn't that where the Ripper killed his victims?'

'That's not the only thing that happens in Whitechapel.' Bunny eased his collar away from his throat, a gesture which told her he was uncomfortable.

'It was over twenty years ago. I doubt the Ripper is still lurking about the place.' Flora shrugged and went back to looking out of the window.

'Don't joke about it, Flora. He was never caught, remember?'

'Sorry.' A thought struck her. 'Are we going anywhere near where the murders happened?'

He nodded. 'We are going to the Hanbury Street shelter.' He grinned. 'Right in the heart of Ripper country.'

'Which of his victims was found there?'

'Really, Flora, and I thought you were the expert.' He tutted good-naturedly. 'Annie Chapman, his second victim, was found in a yard behind number twenty-nine.'

Flora smiled, promising herself she wouldn't make a point of looking out for it, but the idea still intrigued her.

With Threadneedle Street and Bishopsgate behind them, the shops and houses took on a rundown, unkempt look with broken windows and piles of rubbish in the streets. Brushfield Street took them past the chaotic clamour of Spitalfields Market, where men in overalls wielded brooms and buckets of water to clear spilled blood and discarded offal from the road and the busy market shed.

Bunny closed the cab windows against the smell, which seemed to be entrenched in the stonework.

The driver made a left turn into Commercial Street, then a right into a narrow road only wide enough for two hackneys to pass.

'Is this it?' Flora stared up at a line of red brick buildings with the gable ends over the street, shaped like a row of tiny steps leading up to a single window in the peak.

'Hanbury Street.' Bunny nodded. 'The shelter is further along here on the right.'

Flora was about to say she meant number twenty-nine, but thought better of it. Instead, she spotted a sign with a number on the centre panel and counted upwards until she identified the door she was looking for.

Number twenty-nine was a shabby shop front with a red wooden door to its left and a black one beside it, which she assumed led into the rear yard where the poor woman's body was found. The shop had been roughly boarded up some time before; the two rows of windows on the floors above giving every sign of the property being vacant.

'How many did he kill?' Flora kept her gaze on the red door as they passed along the street, which didn't improve much in appearance and smelled of cooked cabbage and manure.

'Ah, back to Jack the Ripper, are we?' Bunny sighed. 'If you must know, five were attributed to him, but between '88 and '91, eleven murders occurred in this area. The body of a woman called Martha Tabram was found in George's Yard Buildings in August eighty-eight. She had been stabbed thirty-nine times, but the police refused to attribute her killing to the Ripper.'

'Why ever not?'

'Because,' Bunny said reluctantly, drawing out the word. 'Her throat wasn't cut like the others.' He slewed a sideways glance at her. 'Do you wish you hadn't asked?'

'Of course not.' Flora swallowed as unwanted images crowded her head. 'I can be objective about violent crime. I've had more than a little experience.' *Even if Inspector Maddox treats me like a useless novice.*

Bunny tapped on the glass partition, signalling the driver to halt. They alighted on a narrow, cracked pavement in front of a red brick building. Despite its unimposing façade, the shelter stood out among the surrounding dilapidated shop fronts and houses. A hardware store stood two doors away, its goods piled into wicker baskets on the pavement beneath a torn awning. Several ragged women huddled near the entrance to the shelter, some of whom carried bundles, though there was not a pair of shoes between them.

The women certainly looked in need of charity. One woman's skirt was badly torn and barely covered her modesty, while others were no better clad; their clothes patched and darned. The colours faded to an indistinguishable shade of murky green. A young woman of about eighteen in the distinctive black bonnet and cape of the Army conversed with a woman who held a small child in her arms.

'Why are they standing out here?' Flora whispered, aware of the odd sideways looks they had attracted. 'If it's a shelter, why don't they go inside?'

'This is a night shelter,' the female in the bonnet had apparently heard her. She turned from her conversation with the group to address Flora. 'They have to leave in the morning, but may return at night.'

'That sounds harsh,' Flora said without thinking. 'I'm sorry. I didn't mean to sound uncharitable, but where do they go all day?'

'Flora,' Bunny warned.

'It's all right,' the woman actually smiled, though it was a reserved crack in a stony façade. Not conventionally pretty, the girl possessed clear olive skin and wide brown eyes that glowed with good health, in stark contrast to the sad, weather-beaten figures clustered on the street. 'It's understandable. But if you think about it, allowing the homeless to laze about all day in front of a fire simply makes them more dependent. At least outside they have to make some effort to make a living.'

'Now, Peggy, you know the rules,' she turned away again, her tone matronly as she spoke to a figure with a scarf tied over her wispy grey hair. 'It's well past eight, so you shouldn't be here.' The woman called Peggy mumbled something Flora couldn't catch, but the girl remained unmoved. 'If you've three pennies, you can come back at six tonight. But not a minute before then, mind.'

Grudgingly, the woman moved away from the door, taking the small group with her. The child grizzled, and was rewarded with a rough jiggling on the woman's hip, which didn't appear to help matters as the mewling turned into a full-blown wail.

The girl's expression softened. 'Is there something I can help you with?'

'I hope so.' Bunny cast a last look at the creatures who had paused a few paces off. 'We've come to see Captain Blake.'

'Follow me, please.' She stood aside to allow them into the main part of the building, which comprised a long hall of bare, but recently swept floorboards with an enormous fireplace at one end. The girl slammed the door and shot the large bolt on the inside. In response to Flora's surprised look, added, 'We have to keep this locked or they'll sneak back in when we aren't looking.'

Flora exchanged an uneasy frown with Bunny, but the girl seemed unmoved.

In the hall were rows of long wooden benches covering the entire floor, each with a number painted roughly on the end. Apart from an odour of damp wood and dust, the room was clean without any of the unpleasant smells she had detected outside.

'Where are the beds?' Flora murmured, only half expecting an answer.

'This used to be a women's shelter, but now is known as a "sit up",' she explained. 'For a few pennies, the poor get a bowl of soup, a warm fire, and a bench to sit on.'

'They sit up all night?' Flora gaped at her.

'Did you think they were given feather beds and bathrooms? If you'll wait here a moment. I'll ask Captain Blake to come and speak to you.' The girl's smile faded and with a gesture that they were to wait there, she disappeared through a door.

'She didn't have to be sarcastic,' Flora snapped, more in shock than genuine anger. 'I didn't know what to expect.'

'I suppose this place is a shock,' Bunny said. 'Was I wrong to bring you with me?'

'No, I'm glad you did, but it's so—' She broke off as the door opened again to reveal another young woman. More Bunny's age, she wore her plain black dress with obvious pride. The unflattering bonnet was absent, her hair pulled back from her face in a severe, perfectly smooth bun. A wide forehead and widely spaced hazel eyes above an enquiring smile held Bunny's gaze as she approached.

'Bunny.' She ran the last few steps and took both his hands in hers in a relaxed, almost intimate gesture. 'How wonderful to see you again! It's been so long.'

24

'And you, Emily.' He grasped both her hands in his and stared into her eyes for long seconds, the skin on his neck flushing slightly.

Emily turned an enquiring smile on Flora as natural and charming as her lilting voice.

Bunny started and recovered himself. 'Oh, yes. Er – allow me to introduce you to my wife, Flora. Flora, I would like you to meet Captain Emily Blake.'

Flora shot him a brief, accusing sideways look, then thrust out her hand, forcing Emily to release one of Bunny's. 'I'm delighted to meet you. Though until this moment I knew nothing about you.'

'Emily and I lived next door to each other in Richmond when we were young,' Bunny said. 'When we were about, oh, when was it, Emily?'

'Ten. And when did you stop calling me Emmie?'

'Have you worked here long, Captain Blake?' Flora asked, eager to break the invisible bubble they stood in.

'Oh, please, call me Emily. I joined my brothers and sisters almost ten years ago now. My army ones, that is, as no one else in my family understood my calling. Only Bunny understood.' They continued to regard each other with an easy warmth born of long intimacy that made Flora uncomfortable.

'I thought if anyone could help with our problem, it would be Emily.' Bunny smiled again while still keeping hold of her hand.

'We could take tea while you tell me what brings you here.' Emily gestured them into a small rear room where a welcoming fire crackled in the tiny iron grate. A plain pine table surrounded by four wheel-backed chairs and a rag rug brought colour into an otherwise stark room. The girl who had shown them in acknowledged them with a nod as she stacked blankets on a set of racked shelves.

'I admit to being intrigued by your letter.' Emily gestured them to sit in other chairs arranged around a black leaded range, where flames danced behind a grille in a small door.

Bunny held out a chair for Flora, but she sidestepped him and took the second, pointedly not looking at him, though from the corner of her eye she caught his wry smile as he sat.

Emily set a kettle on top of the range before joining them. 'How can I be of assistance?' She folded her hands in her lap and sat in contemplative silence without interrupting while Bunny explained about the death of Lizzie Prentice and her connection to the missing children.

'I know of St Philomena's,' Emily said, when he had finished. 'It has an excellent reputation.'

'Which this affair will do nothing to enhance,' Bunny said.

'I appreciate that.' Emily twisted her hands on her lap as if nervous. 'You said the children went missing directly from there? They weren't taken from their homes?'

'As far as we know,' Flora said. 'They were collected from the hospital on discharge. Some in the company of their family, but in one case a man took an eight-year-old girl away in a taxi.'

'It's uncertain this child was removed by the same man, but if not, it's a strange coincidence.' Bunny gave Flora a warning look.

'And your maid?' Emily asked. 'How is she involved?'

'That was my responsibility.' Flora stared at her lap as shame heated her face. 'I asked her to watch someone whom we believed was involved. This person met with a couple in a Salvation Army uniform. Sally followed them and she hasn't been seen since.'

'You think one of our soldiers is involved?' Emily's face paled slightly, but the look she split between them was guarded rather than surprised. 'Is that why you came here?'

Bunny's response was interrupted when the kettle rattled on the range and spat a stream of steam into the air.

'Keep talking while I make the tea.' Emily rose and filled a plain brown teapot with a grace that would not have looked out of place in a Kensington drawing room presiding over a silver pot and bone china cups.

'We aren't sure,' Bunny said carefully. 'Nor do we intend to insult your organisation, which has an exemplary reputation of course, I—'

'You cannot insult us in any way I haven't already heard.' Emily held the kettle in the air, a smile playing over her full lips. 'Simply say what's on your mind, Bunny.'

'As you wish.' He rubbed his hands across his thighs. 'Is it feasible someone, maybe even two someone's, are impersonating your officers?'

Emily returned the kettle to the range and brought the teapot to the table where she filled three cups with careful deliberation.

Flora swallowed, hoping she wasn't about to take offence and order them out, despite her previous assurance.

'I'm sorry about your maid,' Emily said, at last, handing Flora a full cup of murky brown liquid.

Flora took refuge in adding milk into her cup, which made little difference as the brew remained a dark brown. She took a tentative sip and choked.

'Oh dear, is the tea all right?' Emily's eyes widened in alarm.

'It's fine,' Flora's voice lifted, but she recovered herself quickly. 'Perhaps a little stronger than I'm used to. Might I have some sugar?'

'Of course.' Emily pushed the sugar bowl across the table towards her, then lowered herself into a chair opposite.

Bunny frowned at a point somewhere on Flora's chin, pulled a handkerchief from his pocket and held it out. Wordlessly, she took it with more force than was necessary and used it to wipe her face.

'I'm not avoiding your question.' Emily's knuckles whitened on the tabletop as if she was preparing herself to speak. 'Have you heard of the Emigration Bureau?'

Flora shook her head, and Bunny crossed his arms over his chest, but remained silent.

'The Bureau was established twenty years ago by our founder, General Booth. He advertised in the Social Gazette, offering free passage to domestic workers prepared to travel to Queensland, Australia, for work. Recently, the bureau has arranged for children to be moved to rural homes in Canada. Farms mostly.'

'Where do these children come from?' Flora asked.

'All over London.' Emily fiddled with her teaspoon. 'I regret to say we keep records of the adults, but statistics for children were not begun until last year.'

'That's somewhat lax?' Flora fought to keep her voice neutral but doubted she had succeeded. 'Shipping children thousands of miles from their homes without knowing where they came from or where they have been sent?'

'It's not as random as that, I assure you. Few children have been sent without their parents.'

'But even so—'

'Let her finish, Flora.' Bunny placed a hand on her forearm, silencing her.

'The reason for our – circumspection – is that we have our enemies in the Government who disapprove of sending our labour force abroad.' Emily became defensive. 'We don't publicise the service too widely to avoid scrutiny.'

'Where is this, Bureau?' Bunny asked. 'It might be worth paying them a visit.'

'I doubt it. They don't have a proper office yet, just a few clerks working out of a corner room at our headquarters. It's a philanthropic practice, so I doubt any of our members would be involved in anything untoward.'

'Isn't kidnapping maids considered untoward?' Flora snapped, only to find herself on the sharp end of Bunny's angry look. 'I'm sorry,' she blurted, horrified to find her eyes welling. 'I'm finding this more emotional than I thought. Sally means a lot to me and she could be anywhere, even hurt, and...' She inhaled a deep breath to compose herself. Bunny slid his arm across the back of her chair, his fingers stroking her nape. His touch calmed her, and her breathing slowed.

'I apologise for my lack of control.' She swallowed, embarrassed at her display in front of this young woman who shared a past with Bunny. 'How can you be certain these children are going to suitable homes? That they are not simply being used as cheap labour on farms and treated as no better than slaves?'

'Isn't a life of hard work in healthy surroundings preferable to being maimed in a badly equipped factory, or even starving to death in a city slum?' Emily asked, seemingly unaffected by Flora's outburst.

'Is that true for your entire organisation?' Bunny asked, an edge to his voice that made Flora proud. It appeared he did not much like her answers, either.

'The Bureau searches out candidates among the poorest, it's true,' Emily continued. 'Although we've never recruited from hospitals.' She peered at them over the rim of her cup, then set it down again with a firm click. 'Which leads me to your original question.' She leaned forward, her hands clenched on the tabletop. 'A little while ago, a woman arrived at another of our missions with a request. She asked if her nephew might be added to the list for emigration. At thirteen, the boy was a bit of a handful. He had joined a street gang known to be involved in local burglaries and she wanted to prevent him being sent to a training ship.'

'I'm sorry, I'm not familiar with that term,' Flora interrupted. 'What is exactly is a training ship?'

'They are prisons for young men,' Bunny said. 'Decommissioned navy vessels are moored on the Thames at Purfleet and Chatham. Boys in their teens convicted of less serious crimes are sentenced to what is euphemistically called training.'

'Euphemistically?' Flora stared at him.

'The regime is beneficial to their rehabilitation,' Emily began. 'But life on board those ships is harsh. To be plain about it, those young men are sent to be broken. They are worked relentlessly and suffer punishments for minor infractions, almost like the sailors were in the Napoleonic wars. This woman I mentioned cared for her nephew enough not to let that happen, but she had no income to support the boy and came to us for help.'

'Couldn't he have been given employment?' Bunny asked. 'I believe there are several major employers in this area?'

'That was attempted, but he was dismissed after a week.' Emily's wry look showed it was not a pleasant experience. 'He hated being inside, so his aunt thought life on a farm would suit him. Anyway, the reason I mentioned her is she appeared under the impression that the Army paid a fee for sending young people to positions in Canada where they were wanted.'

'I take it that isn't the case?' Bunny asked.

Emily shook her head. 'The Bureau pays their travelling expenses, but never offers money to families. When my colleague asked her who had told her this, she said a friend of hers received an amount of money off a couple from the bureau to send her daughter to a farm in Canada to work as a lady's maid.'

'A lady's maid? On a farm?' Flora said, sceptical.

'Exactly. This woman had been sworn to secrecy because there was a waiting list. If she revealed she had been given preferential treatment, the offer would be withdrawn.'

'And the fee paid to her was subject to return, I gather?' Bunny said. At Emily's grave nod, he added, 'An effective way to keep their activities secret.'

'Indeed,' Emily said. 'And if this woman hadn't tried to help her friend, we might never have discovered the fraud. Word has gone out to our other missions to keep an eye out for this couple, but it's difficult. The pair wear authentic-looking uniforms and carry collection boxes. They have only been seen a few times and by the time we go looking, they have gone.'

'The couple who were in the Lamb and Flag two nights ago,' Flora exchanged a knowing look with Bunny. 'We must tell Inspector Maddox.'

'In good time, though we aren't popular with him at the moment.'

'You mean I'm not.' Flora sniffed. 'Emily. Has your organisation reported this to the police?' Bunny asked.

'Ah, no.' A flush bloomed in her cheeks. 'We're hoping to discover the culprits ourselves. The police disapprove of our methods in the spread of God's word. They claim that our bands and parades cause disruption in the streets and anger from the more conservative denominations. If the story about this couple gets into the newspapers, the scandal could ruin us.'

Flora prepared to ask if the army's reputation was worth more than the children, but Bunny caught her eye and gave an imperceptible shake of his head.

'Thank you for being so candid with us, Emmie.' Bunny rose, retrieved Flora's still full cup and placed it with his own on the tray. 'I would have understood had you refused to speak to us.' A remark, Flora assumed, was aimed at her. 'If we discover any more about this couple, we'll be sure to let you know. And should you hear—'

'I'm sorry, Bunny,' Emily stopped him. 'I'm obliged to obey the tenets of the army and, my superior will insist on total privacy.' She must have seen the disappointment on their faces, and her expression softened. 'But I'll do what I can.'

'Our address is in my letter,' Bunny said. 'As is our telephone number.'

Emily laughed, a girlish, charming laugh which made her quite pretty. 'I'm afraid we don't run to such luxuries here in Whitechapel.'

Flora noticed she didn't promise to get a message to them by any other means either.

* * *

Once out on the street, their presence acted like a source of entertainment, prompting Flora to regret not having asked the cabbie to wait for them. Doors opened and ragged children spilled onto the street to stare at them as they passed by. Women in none-too-clean, creased and darned clothes leaned against doorframes, aiming half-threatening looks their way, while others held contempt or hopeful expressions.

Flora could not resist pressing coins into several cupped hands as she walked towards Brick Lane where the traffic was heavier.

'You didn't tell me Captain Blake was a woman. And an attractive one at that.' She eased closer to Bunny as two urchins ran past her; both being shouted at by an indignant greengrocer. The boys disappeared into an alley, leaving the disgruntled shopkeeper to retrieve the apples the boys had dislodged from a pyramid on a trestle outside the shop.

'I didn't think it was relevant,' Bunny said, though the corner of his mouth twitched.

'How would you feel if I produced a presentable young man, held his hand and called him by a babyish name and announced we had known each other for years?'

'If I thought the occasion warranted, I would challenge him to a duel in Hyde Park.' He cast a sideways look at her from beneath lowered brows, though his eyes behind his spectacles glinted with amusement.

'Don't mock me.' She pouted, aware there was no real threat in Emily's existence. 'I'm unaccustomed to having your former paramours paraded before me.'

'Hardly a paramour, and I refute having paraded her. We haven't seen each other since we were sixteen.'

'Old enough for the pangs of first love, then?'

'You are my first love, Flora. My only love, so you have nothing to worry about.' Bunny took her hand in both of his and squeezed. 'Although I adore that you are jealous. I also forgive you for being less than your normal polite self.'

'I'm not jealous!' Her cheeks flamed, though at the same time she acknowledged to herself that she had been rude. A little.

'Silly me.' He squeezed her hand, hard. 'I must have misunderstood. Oh, there's a hansom cab.'

'Thank goodness.' Flora sighed. 'I thought we would have to walk all the way to London Bridge.'

The tension left her as she settled on the seat in the glass cab, relieved to be inside and separate from shabby streets that made her feel exposed in a way she had not experienced in Southwark.

'Captain Blake is an intelligent, dedicated young woman,' Flora ventured a doubt that had niggled at her as they sat in the plain little room at the mission. 'But her loyalties aren't the same as ours.'

'I know. Which makes me feel we are on our own if we want to find this couple.' Bunny adjusted the blanket over Flora's knees. London hackneys were still cold and the better drivers provided blankets inside for the use of their passengers.

Flora sneaked an admiring look at his profile, a rush of pride running through her. In previous cases, Bunny always took the stance she should leave the real investigating to the police.

She liked to think his involvement this time was because children were at risk, although perhaps he was finally beginning to enjoy the excitement of the chase?

Occupied with their own thoughts, they studied shabby buildings and roads beyond the windows, where most of the shopkeepers' goods spilled onto the pavements and manure sweepers were scarce.

Whitechapel possessed an air of desperation, where no one smiled, and every eye Flora looked into stared back expressionless or slid away. Everything from the buildings to the clothes they wore merged into an amalgam of black or brown as if colour and life had been leached from its inhabitants and buildings.

A young woman like Emily Blake, attractive, intelligent and lively should have been mistress of her own home, but chose to spend her days in such a depressing, joyless place. But then who would help those people if not women like Emily?

'You've gone quiet,' Bunny said after a few moments. 'I feel we are getting closer to solving this mystery.'

'I wish I possessed your confidence. We still don't know what Lizzie Prentice saw, or who the couple masquerading as Salvation

Army soldiers are. Even the ship information was a dead end. Where does that leave us now?'

'Do you still think Sister Lazarus killed Lizzie to keep her quiet?'

'Is that so hard to believe? When Sister Lazarus entered the office with the tea tray that day, her skirt was wet. She had no reason to go outside as the kitchen was a few doors down from Alice's office.' Bunny opened his mouth to speak, but she forestalled him with a hand on his arm. 'I know you thought she had to find a handyman to fix the boiler, but we only have her word there was anything wrong with it.'

'Normally I would say you have quite an imagination, but there's every chance you could be right. But under no circumstances must you confront her. If she killed Lizzie Prentice, she's dangerous. If you see her at the hospital, promise me you'll be discreet and not even hint that you suspect her.'

'That won't be easy.' She caught the look on his face and sobered immediately. 'No, you're right. I won't say a word.' *But it won't stop me looking for proof of her involvement.*

25

Flora woke to the sound of rain pounding the window glass of their room and a slate grey sky that meant the gaslights stayed lit into late morning. Water dripped from the eaves and overflowed the gutters to rush down the front of the houses and pool at the base of the area steps.

Affected by the oppressive weather, the baby became fretful and would not settle on Flora's lap. His chubby body went rigid in her arms, his dimpled fists clenched as he made his unhappiness clear in a long, unrelenting scream.

Conscious she was making things worse, Flora left him to Milly, whose murmured endearments followed her out of the room. She had barely gone halfway along the hall before the wails turned to gurgles, so by the time Flora reached the ground floor she had sunk into self-pitying despair. Milly was the one Arthur wanted when he was unhappy, tired or hungry, not her.

But then, what could she expect when she wasn't the one who cared for him all day? Perhaps she could make up for her failings by devoting her free time to finding these children? The alternative was to dismiss Milly and take over Arthur's care. The notion appealed for all of five minutes, then the sound of raised voices in the hall prompted her to increase her stride down the last few steps into the rear hall.

Her first thought being that the confrontation concerned Sally, but she found cook arguing with a laundry maid. On seeing Flora approach, the older woman shoved the younger one behind her and smoothed down her skirt. 'I didn't see you there, Missus.'

'Is something wrong?' Flora sighed, her question perfunctory. She was not in the mood for domestic squabbles today.

'Just that the silly girl hung the washing out this morning and now it's soaked again. She's giving me gyp about her having to do it all again. I told her it would be a lot worse when the weather gets colder and fog comes in, then anything hung outside will be covered in blacks. She's threatening to give notice and go home.'

'She's a country girl,' Flora replied, referring to the Sussex-born maid. 'This will be her first winter here, and the fog can come as a shock.'

When she and Bunny moved to London, Flora hated the cold winter days that turned dark and gloomy in the middle of the afternoon; the foggy air a mustard yellow, filled with soot specs and felt greasy in her skin 'She'll get used to it.'

'Well I 'ope she does afore them sheets are scrubbed to ribbons.' Cook dropped an awkward curtsey, mumbling to herself as she left.

'This rain is relentless.' Flora said when she joined Bunny in the sitting room, hurrying towards the crackling fire and staying there until her cheeks stung, though her toes remained numb with cold. 'Cook reminded me just now that it won't be long before the fog sets in for the winter.' Flora shuddered at the thought of Arthur's tiny lungs being attacked by the thick, choking fumes that made it difficult to breathe. 'The baby is so fretful, and it's going to get worse. There is always something to worry about where he's concerned.'

'Don't be so hard on yourself.' Bunny looked up briefly from a newspaper that looked suspiciously damp. 'Everyone is miserable today; thus your mothering skills are not in question. I've instructed Stokes not to bother with any outside work and keep the fires banked up all day. The staff can also make tea whenever they feel inclined. At least we'll all be comfortable indoors.'

'You're too generous.' Flora shivered, both hands held out to the flames though didn't bother to add that the kettle was always on the boil in the kitchen. What he didn't know wouldn't hurt him. 'What would your mother say?'

'Whatever she likes, she's not here,' he mumbled. Discarding the newspaper, he rose and advanced on the sideboard, where he rifled through the pile of letters on a silver tray. Selecting a stiff white envelope, he expertly slit it open with a paper knife.

'Listen to it.' She nodded to the window, beyond which the oppressive rain fell in a continuous, low roar. 'When will it stop? Cook was complaining earlier that the butcher's boy hasn't yet brought the delivery.'

'I'm sure we'll not starve to death,' Bunny replied, distracted, his forehead creased as he focussed on the letter in his hand.

Flora stared out at the street again, as unbidden, an image of Sally entered her head. She had been missing for three days. Was she warm and being fed? Surely if she was still alive, they would have heard something? 'I don't suppose Inspector Maddox called when I was upstairs?'

'Unfortunately, not.' Bunny pulled a face. 'Shall I telephone him? It might make no difference other than remind him we still expect some effort on his part.'

Flora sighed and was about to say that might annoy rather than encourage him but was forestalled by Stokes' appearance with the news that Alice Finch was on the telephone asking for Mr Harrington.

'Are you sure she said Mr Harrington, Stokes?' Flora asked when Bunny had gone to take the call.

'Absolutely, madam.' Stokes gave her a look as close to a glare as he dared before withdrawing.

'What did she want?' Flora asked when Bunny returned a few moments later.

'That she would like us to call in at the hospital tomorrow. She has something she wants to show us. I could only just hear her. Goodness, it's freezing out there in the hall.' He strode back to the hearth, both hands held out to the orange flames.

'The rain must be affecting the lines,' Flora said, though with no idea if this was true. 'Did she indicate what it was?'

'No.' Bunny sank onto the sofa Stokes had placed in front of the fire. 'She sounded nervous and kept dropping her voice. As if someone was listening.'

'Perhaps we should go now?' Flora cast a quick look towards the window. 'Although it would take us a while to get there. If we could find a cab willing to take us.'

'And I have no intention of driving, not in this.' Bunny flapped a hand at the window. 'Miss Finch said St Philomena's has had an influx of patients with chest infections since yesterday, so she insisted we go tomorrow.'

Anxiety tightened Flora's chest, but she kept her voice neutral. Why was Alice being so mysterious? What couldn't she say over the telephone?

The butcher's boy finally arrived and after a supper of pork loin that seemed to go immediately cold between the kitchen and the dining room, Flora suggested an early night. 'It's getting colder by the minute down here and I can see my breath.'

'It's not long past nine, Flora.' Bunny looked up from the book he was reading.

'You don't normally complain.' She tightened the shawl around her shoulders, running a hand across the back of his neck as she passed his chair on her way to the door.

'Perhaps it isn't such a bad idea.' His lips twitched in one corner, he snapped his book shut and leapt to his feet. He took her cool hand in his. They ran up the stairs, making exaggerated shivering noises. Giggling, they burst into the brocade draped bedroom made cosy by a lit fire and drawn curtains.

It might have been a romantic night spent in her husband's arms had not Bunny refused to remove his woollen dressing gown or his fishing socks. Though she had little reason to complain, as Flora had layered her oldest flannel nightgowns to ward off the cold. The room closed in on them, private and cosy while they huddled into bed beneath extra covers and giggled away as they lay like spoons in the frigid cold that pinched fingers and made their noses red.

* * *

The next morning, after a good ten hours of 'sleep' which left Flora no more refreshed than an afternoon nap, she rose with a mild headache. After a desultory breakfast, she counted the minutes until it was time to go to St Philomena's, her head full of questions about why Alice wanted to see them. Had the police found Isobel Lomax? If they had, there would have been no requirement to inform her or Bunny. Or had something else come to light in the hospital?

Dressed in a thick navy-blue gown that buttoned to the neck against the damp October cold, Flora descended the stairs into the hall at the same moment Stokes hurried from the rear hall to answer the door.

'I'm sorry for the intrusion,' Lydia burst inside. 'Abel is frantic about Sally. We wondered if you had any news?'

Abel almost entirely filled the doorframe, where he hovered until Stokes gestured him to move so he might shut out the cold. He stomped inside reluctantly and shifted his feet while he stared at the floor. Flora experienced a surge of sympathy for him. Abel still felt guilty for having 'lost' Sally, though she also knew his feelings went deeper than that. If they didn't find her, Abel would never forgive himself, though the thought sent a shudder of alarm through her. Surely they would find her? It was only a matter of time – wasn't it?

'I'm sorry, Abel. I wish things were different, but we haven't heard anything new.' His unkempt hair and evidence of a careless shave made Flora's heart ache for him.

'S'not your fault, Missus.' Abel took a deep breath. 'It's more mine. I was supposed to be looking after her.' Flora was about to protest, but he waved her away. 'I went back to The Antigallican yesterday. Not sure why, but I couldn't think of anything else to do. The barman recognised me so I didn't ask too many questions, but I heard someone say the police had been looking for Swifty Ellis.'

'I know.' Flora walked down the last few steps into the hall. 'Inspector Maddox told us they were looking for him, but he's not been seen.'

'Not by them, maybe.' Abel sniffed. 'But some blokes in the pub said he was at St Saviour's dock yesterday.'

'Where is this dock?' Flora's heart skipped a beat.

'It's in the Jacob's Island area, near Tower Bridge,' Lydia said. 'Not that it's an actual island any more. After the cholera outbreak in the middle of the last century, the Neckinger stream that flowed into the creek was built over.'

'Was there any sign of Sally?' Though Flora knew her question was redundant. Had Abel found her, he would have said so.

Abel shook his head. 'Swifty's barge was all locked up and empty.'

'Did you say he has a barge?' Lydia interrupted. 'How does a small-time crook like that afford to buy a barge, not to mention cover the mooring fees?'

'I was gettin' ter that.' Abel split a look of frustration between the two women. 'A couple of the bargees told me Swifty stopped signing on for casual work a year ago. He bought his own barge and does private work. I didn't ask what, but my guess is he has a side-line in stolen goods from the ships. The crews often help themselves to bits and bobs from the cargo and sell 'em private.'

'You are sure it was empty?' Flora hoped he was wrong, but if Sally was there, she was clever enough to let someone know. If she still could.

'I'm not daft.' He glared at her with lowered brows. 'The hull was well above the waterline. I kept watch for several hours. It was empty all right, and no one came near.'

'I apologise. I didn't mean to belittle your intelligence.'

Flora's thoughts whirled again. This time in a different direction. 'Is it possible this barge is where he keeps the children before they are taken aboard ship?'

'That is an interesting thought.' Lydia bit her bottom lip, thoughtful. 'However, the first child disappeared two weeks ago. How could Swifty have kept them hidden during that time what with dock workers and bargees coming and going? Children don't sit still for long, they make noise.' She shook her head. 'I doubt he keeps them there.'

'Then where?' Just then, Bunny wandered into the hall, giving a start at the sight of Lydia and Abel. 'Good morning, Miss Grey, Mr

Cain. I had no idea you were here. Have you brought news by any chance?'

'They came to ask us that.' Flora removed her coat from the stand and shrugged into it while Abel repeated his story for Bunny's benefit.

'Ah, I see. Disappointing, I know.' Bunny placed a comforting hand on Abel's shoulder, a gesture prompted, Flora assumed, by the man's downcast expression. 'We were about to leave for St Philomena's, summoned by the inimitable Miss Finch. Perhaps she has something new to impart.' Bunny gave Abel's shoulder a last pat and reached for his hat.

'You're going now?' Lydia split a hopeful look between them. 'Could we come with you?'

* * *

The heavy rainfall forced their motor taxi to little more than a crawling pace, so it took them over an hour to reach Southwark. Flora felt claustrophobic as the steady downpour drummed the cab roof where she was squashed into the seat beside Abel Cain.

'She'll think we aren't coming,' Flora fretted.

'Miss Finch will understand with rain this heavy.' Bunny wiped condensation from the window, the annoying squeak making Flora wince.

It was well past noon when Bunny paid off the driver outside St Philomena's Hospital. Flora stepped out of the taxi into rivulets of water that reached mid-ankle, her dash for the main door sending water into the hem of her coat. 'Miss Finch is expecting us,' she explained to the porter who attempted to delay them.

Her boots squelched as she pushed open the door to the corridor which led to Miss Finch's office, glancing back to where Abel hovered by the porter's desk. 'Aren't you coming, Abel?'

'I'll wait here if it's all right with you, Miss Flora.' He held his cap in one hand and brushed water off one shoulder with the other. 'I don't much like 'ospitals.'

'I sympathise.' Bunny patted his arm before walking on. 'Wait here if you prefer. We shouldn't be long.'

Alice rose from her desk as they entered, a look of relief mixed with anxiety on her face. 'I apologise for summoning you here like this.' She nodded in acknowledgment to Lydia, but before they had taken their seats, handed Bunny a small silver globe. 'After what we discussed the other day, I thought you should see this.'

'Where did you get it?' Bunny weighed the object in his palm.

'It looks like one of Mr Buchanan's peeps.' Flora noted this one was different to the one Sister Lazarus had, in that hers was spherical and gold, not egg-shaped and silver. This one was about the size and shape of a quail's egg, a thin silver chain hung off the wider end.

'That's exactly what it is.' Alice wandered to the window, her gaze on the far distance as if removing herself from the situation. 'I was given Lizzie Prentice's things this morning. She has no family to speak of, so the poor girl will be buried in a pauper's grave. This,' she pointed to the object in Bunny's hand, 'was among them.'

Bunny turned the object over in his fingers before holding it up to the light, squinting while he talked. 'This is indeed similar to the others, and—' He blinked and jerked his chin back. 'Oh, dear.'

'What is it?' Flora went to take it from him.

'No, Flora.' He pulled his hand out of her reach. 'I don't think you should see this. It's rather, er, explicit.'

'Don't be silly.' Flora blew air through her lips in an impatient tut. 'It cannot be worse than the ones we saw in Mr Buchanan's office.' She wrestled the silver object from his hand and lifted it to her eye.

The edges were fuzzy, but the image showed two naked figures wound around one another, making it impossible to see which body parts belonged to whom. 'It's a photograph of a couple,' Flora said. Squinting, she twisted the frame, then when she realised what she was looking at, lowered it again. 'Oh, I see.'

'Precisely.' Alice exhaled slowly; her eyes closed.

'Which puts an entirely different slant on the matter,' Bunny said.

'Well?' Lydia demanded. 'Isn't anyone going to explain?'

'It's a picture of two naked men,' Flora whispered, uncomfortable heat flooding her face.

'Surely not?' Lydia gasped, with more surprised fascination than shock. 'Let me see.' She extended a hand towards Bunny and gestured he pass it over. He didn't.

'This item is hardly suitable for a married woman, Miss Grey, let alone an unmarried one.' Bunny eased his collar away from his throat, laid the object on the desk and placed his hands flat on either side as if he expected it to explode.

Lydia pouted, but gave in with a resigned shrug.

'I've never heard—' Flora broke off as she tried to form the words, 'I mean, I knew about... men and other men, of course, but as to a photograph of them actually—'

'Indeed.' Alice's tone declared the subject closed. 'The existence of which convinces me Mr Buchanan is no child trafficker. He was being coerced with *that*.' She gave the silver egg a severe glance but made no move to touch it. 'What makes you say that, Miss Finch?' Bunny asked gently.

'Because a man in that photograph is Victor Buchanan, Raymond's son.'

The room fell silent, a strange anticipation in the air as the occupants tried and failed to think of something to say. Then the door opened and Raymond Buchanan strode into the room. 'Miss Finch, might I have a word with—' he halted mid-sentence.

26

Buchanan's face paled, his eyes widening as they focussed on the object on the desk. His mouth opened, but no sound came. He exhaled slowly and checked the corridor outside, then closed the door and leaned against it.

'Raymond, I, er,' Distaste and anxiety warred on Alice's face as she took a step towards him. 'We never meant—'

'You don't need to say anything, Alice.' His voice was only a rush of air. 'I know what that is.' He gestured vaguely at the silver egg in mild disgust. 'How many of the blasted things are there?'

'You've never seen this one before?' Bunny held it up between thumb and index finger.

'No, never.' His Adam's apple bounced as he swallowed. 'Where did it come from?'

'I don't want you to think—' Alice began, but broke off when he held up a hand.

'It's all right, Alice. I knew I couldn't keep all this to myself for much longer, but I was hoping to sort out this – mess – before it became public knowledge. It seems I miscalculated.' He slumped into the remaining vacant chair, propped his elbows on the desk and dry washed his face with both hands, making his carefully coiffed hair stick up at the front. 'All I ask is that you allow me to explain before you condemn me.'

'How did you become involved, sir?' Bunny asked gently.

'And what exactly is it you are involved in?' Flora added.

'I wasn't sure at first.' He raised his head and met Bunny's gaze unflinchingly. 'Smuggling perhaps, or maybe helping criminals escape the country? I didn't ask too many questions.'

'Because of these photographs?' Flora asked, wishing he would get on with it.

'When Alice told me children had been taken from this hospital, I thought she was exaggerating.' The look he gave Alice pleaded for forgiveness. 'Then when that Inspector Maddox demanded to search my ship for kidnapped children, I was horrified at my duplicity.'

'But you still didn't tell him what you knew?' Flora said, losing sympathy.

'Enough, Flora, you're getting ahead of yourself,' Bunny stopped her with a pressure on her arm. 'Start at the beginning, Mr Buchanan. How did these people first contact you?'

'It began before that. When Ruth Lazarus found the gold stanhope I kept in my office here.'

'One of your staff has one of those?' Lydia asked.

'Yes. She goaded me with the fact I was unlikely to report her for theft because of the contents. That if I wanted it returned, I should meet a friend of hers.'

'What friend?' Alice asked.

'Look, might we all sit down?' He waved them into the chairs and placed both hands on the desk. 'I'll explain everything as best I can.'

A general scraping of chairs followed as they arranged themselves into a semicircle around Alice's desk. Bunny remained standing, his hip against the mantelpiece and a foot on the fender as if he presided over a social gathering.

'About two months ago,' Buchanan began. 'Ruth brought a man named Lieutenant Brodie to see me.'

'Our imposter friend,' Flora murmured.

'He claimed he was an officer in the Salvation Army,' Buchanan insisted, apparently having heard her. 'That he wished to discuss the aims of their Emigration Bureau.' He lifted both hands, palms upwards. 'What reason did I have to doubt him?'

'The fact Ruth was forcing him on you, perhaps?' Flora said, but was hushed by Bunny.

'Go on, Raymond,' Alice urged him gently. 'Tell us what happened then.'

'He explained that their organisation advanced passage money to the poor so they might travel to the New World to build more prosperous lives. That army policy is that this passage money is refunded once the immigrants secured employment. Which he told me can take years.' Buchanan broke off and took a long breath, as if marshalling his thoughts. 'This man... Brodie... said they would subsidise these fees through private donations.'

'Oh, Raymond!' Alice chided. 'You didn't give the man money as well?'

'I wasn't to know it was a fraud.' Buchanan brushed a hand through his hair nervously. 'It was only when he demanded I give free passage aboard my ship for these families that I knew something was off. I threatened to see his commander, but Sister Lazarus reminded me about the stanhope she had in her possession. I had no choice.'

'Which is when Inspector Maddox told you he wanted to search the ship for these children?'

'Something like that. I imagined if he could arrest Brodie, I could negotiate with him over the stanhope for my cooperation. However, I didn't get the chance.'

'Because the children weren't on the ship?' Bunny mused, stroking his chin with one hand.

'Exactly. I swear to you, those emigrants were supposed to be adults with children, not small children travelling alone.'

'I have to say that all sounds plausible.' Bunny came to stand beside the desk.

'To me too,' Buchanan issued a cross between a snort and a laugh. 'The *SS Lancet* is a cargo ship and doesn't normally carry passengers. I set aside part of an upper deck and fitted them out as bunks and washing facilities for a few travellers.' He ran a hand around his neck and back again. 'The scheme sounded genuine, so I complied.'

'What changed?' Flora asked. 'How did you find out they were kidnapping children and sending them on their own?'

'I did not make the connection until a character in a long brown coat was seen hanging about the hospital when the first two children went missing. A boy called Albert Farnell and a girl, Martha Fox. Forbes spotted him on two occasions and so did one nurse.'

'Lizzie Prentice?' Flora exchanged a look with Bunny, which told her he had concluded the same thing. Swifty Ellis.

'I took you seriously, Alice.' He turned to look at her, but she had trouble meeting his eyes. 'But when I checked with the police, they had received no complaints. When I tackled Brodie, he said he had planned it with the families.'

'They did,' Bunny said. 'The families might even be liable to prosecution together with Brodie and his cohorts. Selling children is now illegal.'

Buchanan slid his arm away from Alice's hand as if guilt prevented any contact. 'When other children went missing, I didn't like the way things were going, and I confronted Brodie.'

'You knew how to contact him?'

'Er, no.' He looked confused for a moment. 'Ruth arranged a meeting at a pub in Fleet Street. We never use the same one. I told him he couldn't use my ship any more, but he just laughed. That I had to agree to one more voyage, after which Ruth would return the stanhope, and that would be an end to it.'

'And you believed him?' Flora's voice rose, sceptical.

'He's a persuasive man. He convinced me those children were going with the full blessing of their parents. That they would be given a trade and live in the country.'

'Some of them are only six or eight years old.' The distress in Alice's eyes was clear. 'What trade would they learn?'

'The younger ones would be adopted by wealthy, but childless families in Canada.'

'You just went along with it and kept silent?' Flora's anger, mixed with disbelief, came through in her tone.

'Excuse my interrupting, Mr Buchanan.' Lydia's voice brought their attention towards her. 'Considering the subject, why did you have the stanhope in the first place?' She gave the room a swift, embarrassed glance. 'Or is that insensitive of me?'

'Not at all, my dear. I would like to reassure you I do not seek – novelties – for my amusement.' He massaged his forehead with one hand, his eyes closed as he took a deep breath. 'My son is less than discreet as to his – proclivities. In fact, he appears proud of them in a way no decent person should be. He gave me the one Sister Lazarus has as a gift.' He gave a ragged laugh. 'He knew about those I had collected and imagined it would amuse me. An act of defiance to show he rejected my principles and my way of life.' He dropped his hand to the desk again. 'I didn't want the thing in my home, so I hid it in my office here, but not well enough, apparently.'

'How did Sister Lazarus know about the stanhope in the first place?' Flora asked, as a thought occurred to her. 'They are innocuous objects unless examined closely. Does she know your son had given it to you, what it contained and used it to manipulate you?' It seemed something of a coincidence that anyone would stumble upon it accidentally. Bunny had had to explain what it was when they first discovered them in the cabinet in Mr Buchanan's house.

Buchanan's head jerked up, his haunted gaze alighting on Flora. 'That didn't occur to me. And how did you know she knew Victor?'

'I didn't know she did either.' Alice had reverted to staring out of the window as if distancing herself from the conversation, but now Buchanan received her full attention. 'Why have you never mentioned it?'

'I don't think she does, not as an acquaintance, I mean. She's the daughter of his cook, I believe.'

'I know your class regards servants as invisible, Raymond, but they aren't deaf!' Alice exclaimed, exasperated. 'How could you have been so careless where Victor is concerned?' She waved a vague hand at the silver egg on the desk. 'Was this one in Ruth's possession before it came to Lizzie's?'

'The reason Lizzie was killed do you mean?' Flora asked, having no thought of that before. But it made sense.

'I had no idea there were others of those – things – floating about.' Buchanan fisted his hands on the desk. 'Much less who has them. Victor probably had others made, but he certainly didn't tell me.'

'Maybe it's not important either,' Flora said. 'Could we get back to Mr Brodie?'

'Yes, yes, of course.' Buchanan ran a hand through his salt and pepper hair in a nervous gesture. 'I should have known I wouldn't escape them so easily. When that concert ticket for the Bechstein Hall arrived with my instructions, I was horrified. It said that I was to go to the Lamb and Flag public house during the interval, where Brodie would give me orders when the *SS Lancet* was to sail so I could fill out the manifest for customs.'

'Why didn't you tell the police what you suspected when Inspector Maddox spoke to you?' Bunny asked. 'You let a perfect opportunity to stop these men pass you by.'

'I was going to, but when Maddox came here to ask for my cooperation, Sister Lazarus showed him in. I dismissed her, but she whispered she would be listening to every word from the next room.'

'Where does this man Brodie keep the children before they take them to the ship?' Flora asked.

'I don't know.' His eyes told her he was telling the truth. 'They arrive on Ellis's barge an hour before the ship leaves.'

'Why didn't you tell Inspector Maddox this story?' Bunny asked.

'I haven't had a chance since the search. Sister Lazarus appears every time I even consider it. She wears that blasted stanhope on her belt to remind me.'

'You could have told me,' Alice said, anguish in her voice. 'I would have helped you.'

He shook his head. 'When I realised what sort of people they were, I couldn't risk them hurting you. And besides, it wasn't just my reputation I had to protect. If that photograph became public, Victor could go to prison.'

'I doubt this Brodie person would have gone to the police voluntarily,' Alice said. 'They have as much to lose as you.'

'I couldn't take the chance, Alice. For Victor's sake.' He stared at the stanhope that still lay on the desk as if it might bite him. 'Nurse Prentice's inquest came as a terrible shock. Like Dr Reeder, I thought her death was a tragic accident. Brodie or one of his gang must have killed her.'

Flora believed Lizzie's death could be put at Sister Lazarus' door, but without incontrovertible proof, she kept silent.

'However she came by it, poor Lizzie found herself in the middle and suffered the ultimate penalty.' Alice's clipped tone showed she was fighting to restrain herself. 'And what about the Lomax girl? Is this Brodie responsible for her too?'

'I swear to you I have no idea. The police think she wandered away from her home when her nanny was courting.'

'A nice, convenient theory which has produced nothing.' Flora's breathing quickened as her anger matched Alice's.

Buchanan groaned and his complexion took on a grey tinge. These revelations were clearly hard on him, though Flora got the impression he was also relieved to talk about something which had become an unendurable burden.

'Victor is a grown man, Raymond.' Alice placed a sympathetic hand on his shoulder, her voice softening. 'You aren't responsible for his choices.'

'Perhaps.' Buchanan sighed. 'But he's still my son.'

'I cannot believe it of Ruth.' Alice covered her mouth with one hand. 'I knew her mother was a cook, but not where she worked. She raised Ruth alone in difficult circumstances. Ruth seemed to like it here and gave every sign of appreciating a rewarding career.' She stared at Buchanan as if she expected him to contradict her, but he remained silent, his eyes closed as if he couldn't bear to disillusion her.

'Not everyone can put their past behind them, Miss Finch,' Bunny said gently. 'Nor do they wish to. It's possible her scars run too deep, and she's incapable of normal emotion. These children have become nothing to her but commodities.'

'But... children!' Alice's features twisted in anguish. 'She works with them every day. She sees how frail they are, how helpless. How could she *sell* them?' She glared at Buchanan again, anger replacing pain in her face. 'And you. How could you cooperate with such a scheme, even for Victor's sake?'

'There will be a time for recriminations, Miss Finch.' Bunny placed his arms on the desk and leaned closer to Mr Buchanan, who looked as if he had aged a decade in the last few minutes. 'If you wanted these men to be discovered, why give the police false information?'

'I – I don't understand.' Buchanan blinked. 'What false information?'

'That note Lieutenant Brodie gave you listed the date and time of the ship's departure. Yet, according to the police, it is still berthed at Tilbury.'

'Perhaps they switched ships?' Lydia suggested. 'Maybe they plan to take the children on another vessel.'

'They don't have another vessel. Only mine,' Buchanan said. 'That note was Brodie's instruction on what I was to include in the official manifest for the voyage.' His face cleared as he looked from Flora to Bunny and back again. 'I mislaid it somewhere between the concert and home that night. Did someone find it?'

'Something like that.' Bunny looked at Flora but offered no explanation. 'You mean it was Brodie who decided when the ship left, not you?'

'Exactly. When the police searched the vessel, I assumed they had changed the arrangements because it was too dangerous.'

'Do you still have the note, Flora?' Bunny pushed away from the desk and skirted Lydia's chair to where Flora sat.

'Er, yes, I think so.' She rummaged in the tapestry bag hung on her wrist until her fingers closed on the edges of the paper.

'I thought you had given it to the police?' Lydia said.

'No. Bunny recited it to Inspector Maddox over the telephone.'

Bunny took the note from her and spread it flat on the desk, smoothing out the creases gently with his fingers so as not to smudge the handwriting. 'The writing is spidery and difficult to read. What are these letters "TS" scrawled in the bottom corner?'

'I told you, I didn't write it,' Buchanan insisted. 'I don't recall seeing those letters. I only had the thing a short time before I lost it.'

'Nor did I,' Flora said. 'We gave Maddox the name of the ship and the time of sailing on 4th October.'

'Did you say the fourth?' Buchanan straightened. 'No, that's not right. The *SS Lancet* was scheduled to sail for New York on 7th October.'

'The seventh?' Flora frowned, 'But I'm sure—'

'It's a simple mistake,' Bunny interrupted her, running his thumb across the page. 'The horizontal line on the number four doesn't meet up with the top line. This isn't a four, it's the continental way of writing a seven.'

'So not the fourth, but the seventh! That's today!' Flora grabbed Bunny's arm. 'They haven't cancelled the voyage, they never intended leaving until today. Maddox must be told. He has to go back and find those children.'

'Maddox is unlikely to instigate another raid on our say so.' Bunny straightened. 'Especially after the trouble, he got into last time. I'll wager those children are being kept elsewhere until the last minute, in case the dock is being watched.'

'They could be anywhere,' Lydia said. 'There are dozens of deserted buildings, warehouses, even empty houses where a group of children could be kept with no one knowing.'

'They'll still need to be taken to the ship before it sails tonight.' Flora scraped back her chair and made for the door.

'Where are you going, Flora?' Bunny demanded.

'Abel! He said Swifty owns a barge. He even knows where it's kept. That's how they plan to get the children to the ship.'

'He also said it was locked up and empty as recently as yesterday.' Lydia stood too, leaving only Mr Buchanan slumped in his seat.

'Well, perhaps they're there now. It's worth a look.' Bunny dropped the silver egg into his pocket and made for the door, leaving the others to follow.

Abel rose smartly from the wooden bench when the group arrived in the entrance hall, his face a picture of apprehension. After a brief introduction to the benefit of Alice and Buchanan, Bunny asked him to describe the barge.

'It's got a black hull with a red lighthouse in a white circle painted on the stern. The tarpaulin is a deep green colour where most of them are black or brown. Let me come with you and I'll show you exactly where it is,' Abel pleaded. 'They might hold Sally down there, too.'

'Very well, Abel.' Bunny strode to the porter's desk, talking as he went. 'I suggest you come too, Buchanan. We'll take a cab to the police station and talk to Maddox in person to give us the best chance of his taking us seriously. Flora, you remain here with Lydia and Alice.'

Flora opened her mouth to protest, but he held up both hands, palms outwards.

'I'm not trying to exclude you. If we find these children, you need to be here to help.'

'Raymond, you will be careful?' Alice pleaded, halting him. 'The police aren't known for their capacity for forgiveness. You could be in a lot of trouble.'

'I'm not entirely ignorant of my culpability, Alice, my dear.' Taking his silver-topped cane from the porter with one hand he put his hat on with the other. 'I'm prepared to accept the consequences. Somehow, it's a relief to have it out in the open. The main thing is we must stop the ship from leaving.'

* * *

Flora watched them disappear through the glazed doors into a steady downpour, their shoes splashing through the water that had continued to gather onto the cobbles.

'I admired him, you know,' Alice said, her voice small and sad. 'I still cannot believe him capable of such a thing.' Porters, nurses and visitors flowed past them on their way to the wards, kitchens and consulting rooms, oblivious to the drama taking place around them.

'He was trying to keep his son out of prison,' Lydia said, compassionate as ever. 'When he realised what he had done, it was too late.'

'It's never too late. He could have stopped it,' Alice snapped, her breath forming a mist on the cool glass.

'This rain doesn't help either,' Flora sighed. 'It's been falling all day and with no sign of stopping.'

'Which doesn't bode well for a search of the docks,' Lydia murmured.

'We aren't achieving much here.' Flora forced a lighter tone into her voice amongst all the gloom. 'We can only go back to the office and wait.' She sneaked a look at Alice, hoping her admiration for her patron did not extend to the romantic. Her conviction that Alice Finch was Lily Maguire had not diminished, but that was not a possibility she had time to contemplate.

27

On their way back to the office, Alice waylaid a passing nurse, from whom she requested some tea. 'Nothing like a cup of hot tea to help order one's thoughts,' she gestured the ladies into the room ahead of her.

Flora and Lydia resumed their seats, while Alice hefted the coal scuttle and shook shiny black lumps onto the dying fire. 'I owe you an apology, Flora. I had my suspicions about Ruth Lazarus but told myself they couldn't be true. I mentored that girl through her training and thought I knew her.'

'Her choices, much less her actions cannot be laid at your door,' Flora said.

Alice set the scuttle beside the grate, and then plucked a brass poker from the stand, stirring with vigour into the glowing embers.

'But to blackmail Raymond. He's the kindest man. She must have put him through agonies.'

Alice almost hurled the poker into the rack, making a sharp rattle, which made both Lydia and Flora wince.

The nurse arrived bearing a tray, and while cups were passed around and enquiries made as to who wanted milk or lemon,

Flora's head spun with questions. Would Bunny convince Inspector Maddox to search the ship again? Would he even be at the police station when they got there? Where were the children now?

'I hate sitting here just waiting.' Flora's composure cracked, and she set her cup and saucer down almost hard enough to break the china. 'What happens if they don't find anything this time? The police will never take us seriously again.'

'If the plan is to leave this evening, where else would the children be?' Alice asked.

'What if they're keeping them somewhere else until the last moment?' Flora said. 'The ship won't leave for hours yet. Hiding children away successfully isn't easy. They'll need food and water, somewhere to sleep and be kept quiet. That isn't possible on a ship with a crew coming and going. So where have they been all this time?'

'It's hopeless.' Alice splayed her hands on the desktop and leaned backward. 'Even if they are being concealed at the docks, they could be anywhere. It's a maze down there.'

'Children make noise,' Flora reasoned. 'It would have to be somewhere they can neither be seen nor heard. Where no one would think of searching.'

Lydia straightened. 'Flora, have you still got that note?'

'What? Er, no. Bunny took it with him to show to Inspector Maddox. Why, have you thought of something?'

'Possibly. Apart from the date and time of departure, there were two letters written on it.'

'The letters "TS" in capitals?' Flora shrugged. 'We don't know what they stand for.'

'I should have realised it before.' Abandoning her untouched tea, Lydia grabbed her bag and gloves from Alice's desk and stood. 'I know where they are. The Tower Subway.'

'Of course,' Alice said, releasing a breath.

'Well, is one of you going to tell me what that is?' Flora split a confused look between them.

'It's an old railway tunnel that runs beneath the Thames. It hasn't been used for several years, so it's the perfect place to hide a group of children.' Lydia pulled on her gloves, only sparing a few seconds to glance at the clock. 'Miss Finch, could you telephone Camberwell Church Street police station and tell Inspector Maddox the children are being held at the Tower Subway, not Jacob's Island.'

'Wait.' Alice halted her at the door. 'They'll still have to get the children to the ship. If we re-direct them and they find nothing, Maddox might refuse to continue with another fruitless search, and then we will have lost them.'

'What do we do?' Flora's heart jumped in her chest.

'We can reach the Tower Subway before this Lieutenant Brodie transfers them to another vessel,' Alice said. 'If they aren't there, well, we'll think about that later.'

'We're still guessing,' Lydia said.

'I don't intend sitting around waiting,' Flora replied. 'They still have Sally, remember? Bunny might not be happy, but if they found the children, he would understand.'

'Well, don't think you are going without me.' Alice unhooked her coat from a rack by the door and shrugged into it. 'The subway is about a mile from here, most of it is alongside the river. We'll have to watch our step in the fog and it's getting dark.'

'That doesn't sound easy.' Flora's nervousness made her fumble with her coat buttons.

Lydia smiled and lifted her chin. 'Don't worry, I know the way.'

* * *

By the time they entered the main reception hall, young children and old people with hacking coughs on foot or in wheelchairs were being escorted through the corridors by harassed nurses. Some lay near motionless on trolleys, their skin grey and chests barely moving, while others crowded chairs in the reception hall.

Flora's heart twanged with sympathy, but her thoughts remained on the children whose fate lay in her finding them before the *SS Lancet* sailed off into the estuary on its way to Canada. She jumped smartly aside as a trolley containing a wan-faced child rushed past her, accompanied by a frowning nurse and a serious-faced doctor, who let the double doors to the wards flap as they passed.

'They look so desperate,' Flora said, following the trolley with her gaze. 'You can help them can't you?'

'I would like to say yes, but some are already too weak to fight off the effects of the polluted air. Then if you factor the damp and cold they have to contend with in their own homes, their chances are not good.' Alice lowered her voice. 'If we're right about the subway, we might save those children who were taken.'

'I'm sorry, I don't mean to appear weak.' Nodding, Flora drew herself up to her full height. 'You're right, that's what we must do.'

'Good. Now I need to collect a few items from the storeroom.' She strode to the porter's desk where she held an earnest conversation with Forbes.

'We'll find them, Flora. I feel sure of it.' Lydia pressed her hand.

'I hope so, but I feel we are running out of time.'

'You wait here and I'll see what Alice is doing.' Flora was about to say she would go too, when a shadow appeared at Flora's shoulder and Dr Reeder stepped into her path.

'Good afternoon, Mrs Harrington. You look lost. Is there anything I can help you with?'

'Not at all, Doctor.' Flora was surprised he had remembered her name. 'I'm well, and how are things with you?' She wondered if he'd had any more success in moving his X-ray machine out of the damp basement, then remembered Alice had a strategy to prevent that.

'Excellent, though this cold spell has made us much busier.' He nodded towards the porter's desk where Alice and Lydia stood talking to Forbes with three hurricane lamps on the desk beside them. 'Miss Finch looks as if she's equipping herself for an expedition. Might I ask what is going on?'

'I don't have time to explain, I'm afraid,' Flora sidestepped him to leave, unwilling to complicate the situation. 'I'm sure you'll understand, but we are needed elsewhere.'

'Surely you can spare me a moment?' he insisted. 'I could probably be of help to you if only you would tell me how.'

Flora debated whether to include him. After all, a strong young male might be an asset.

'Flora, we need to go.' Alice cocked her head, her eyes wide.

'I don't think so, Dr Reeder, but thank you for your interest. I'm sure Miss Finch will explain everything in due course.' By which time she hoped they would have the police involved as well.

'Are you sure?' He grasped her upper arm, his face close enough she could make out a fine stubble on his chin and the smell of antiseptic on his hands. 'I consider myself a gentleman and the idea of three women alone out in this weather is abhorrent. Whatever you intend might bring you into danger.'

Flora hesitated, but it would take too long to explain. 'I'm sure we'll manage, but thank you again.' She tugged her arm free from his hold and hurried out onto the front drive where Alice stood with Lydia, their shapes lit by the hurricane lamps that swung gently from their hands.

'What did he want?' Lydia handed her a lamp by its thin metal handle, the wick inside the contained glass box burning steadily with a yellowish glow.

'I'm not sure. Playing Sir Galahad, I think. He offered to help us with whatever we are doing.'

'Maybe he's taken a shine to you?' Lydia giggled.

'Our Dr Reeder is quite the gentleman,' Alice said, her lamp held up in line with her eyes. 'The rain has stopped, but mind your step on the slippery cobbles and wrap your scarves around your faces. The chemicals used in the tanning factories in this area make the air quite pungent, though the rainstorm has damped it down somewhat. We can't have you contracting bronchitis.'

'You sound like my mother,' Flora said with a laugh. Her cheeks heated in the cold air as she realised what she had said. She sneaked a glance at Alice but she had already set off towards the gates with Lydia close behind.

Although only early afternoon, daylight had faded and despite the three oil lamps, visibility was low. Flora's boots splashed through streams of water that had gathered in the gutters and dips in the road, though once they were outside the hospital gates, the cobbles gave way to packed dirt, which helped increase their pace.

It wasn't until the cloying stench of sulphur caught the back of her throat that she remembered to cover her mouth. Taking only shallow breaths, she picked her way across puddles and slippery paving stones, careful to keep the others in sight.

'We'll stick to the road as far as London Bridge, then take the river path.'

The muted orange glow from the lamps bobbed as they trudged along deserted pavements most people weren't foolish enough to venture onto on such an awful night.

Gas streetlights barely lifted the gloom as they walked along Southwark Street, where shopkeepers had set out lamps and candles by their doorways to help light the way. Pedestrians scurried past, their heads down, some offering profuse apologies when collisions occurred, while others cursed and muttered to themselves. 'You were going to tell me where we are going,' Flora said, tugging her coat collar higher. Although the rain held off, the air was damp and a fine mist peppered her head and shoulders with moisture.

'Years ago, they built a tunnel beneath the river between Vine Lane and Tower Wharf,' Alice replied, keeping her voice low.

'Like the underground?' Flora said.

'Not quite,' Alice said. 'The carriage wasn't electric, but pulled along a track on a cable. It was expensive to run, so they closed it down and turned the tunnel into a walkway instead.'

'Until Tower Bridge was opened,' Lydia added. 'Then it closed for good. No one wanted to pay to walk a mile beneath the river if they could cross an open-air bridge for free.'

Flora clamped her mouth shut at the thought of venturing into a dark tunnel on such a cold, damp night when she could barely see a foot in front of her face. Unwilling to show her fear in front of the other two she kept silent.

With each step, the damp cold seeped through Flora's coat, though it was her best and heaviest. Her scarf grew damper as she breathed into it, forming a rough, wet rope round her neck, but discarding it was unthinkable when the alternative was to breathe in soot and sulphur. Pushing aside her discomfort, she followed Lydia through the greenish yellow mist as she left the road and took a path beneath brick archways.

'Keep close,' Lydia warned, her lamp bobbing as she walked.

A sour odour of silt, combined with the sulphur and coal smoke showed they had reached the river. The hairs on Flora's neck prickled, and she cast a fearful look behind her, but all she could make out were the blurred outlines of the warehouses that loomed above them; a lattice of spidery walkways running between the buildings high above their heads.

'There's a hansom at the end of the street,' Alice called, just as Flora made out the twin lamps of a vehicle about twenty feet away; that it was indeed a hansom was confirmed by a whinny and the scrape of a shifting hoof. The driver did not appear to notice them as he attached a sacking hood to the horse's nose. The sacking acted like a filter to help the animal breathe in thick fog.

'Excuse me,' Alice called. 'Would you take us take us as far as the bridge?'

'My gawd.' The man jumped back, startled. 'I din't see you there, Miss. Wot you doing out on a night like this?' He turned back to the horse, dismissing her.

'We need to get to Tower Bridge. Or at least close to it. Can you help us?' Lydia pleaded. 'It's urgent.'

'In this wevver?' The man tugged his cap further down his forehead, sending a trickle of water down onto his saturated cape, not unlike the ones they wore, but shorter. 'I ain't going anywhere tonight.'

'It's only a mile or so,' Alice pleaded, joining them. 'We'll pay you double.'

'Why didn't you say so in't first place?' He retrieved the reins and moved past them to mount the step onto his perch. 'Puts a different slant on it, I s'pose.'

'Thank you, you're most obliging.' Alice hung her lamp on a side hook where the carriage lamps were fixed, though the extra light made no discernible difference.

Flora climbed onto the hard seat and scooted into the corner, quickly joined by Alice and Lydia.

'It's a bit of a squash for the three of yous.' The driver observed from his perch above them.

'We'll manage.' Lydia slammed the wooden doors with a thud. 'If you could just get us there as quickly as possible.'

He clicked his tongue, and the horse lurched forward and clattered onto the road.

The muted orange glow from the lamps bobbed as the horse trudged along narrow pavements, snorting now and then, his mane hanging in wet rats' tails. Flora hoped the animal wasn't in too much distress, but he kept moving, as if accustomed to the conditions.

28

Flora grabbed the handhold above her as the hansom made a sharp right turn before London Bridge, where Southwark Cathedral sat on their far left; the top half covered by fog. They negotiated the steep incline of Duke Street, which bounded the approach to the railway station, confirmed when a high-pitched whistle cut through the fog. Almost immediately, the shadowy black snake of a train careered along beside them for only thirty seconds before disappearing into the mist.

Because of the poor visibility, their driver ambled, rather than trotted, along Tooley Street, where the majority of shops appeared to be river related. Chandlers and candle makers, merchants, salesmen, ship's biscuit-bakers, store-shippers, block-makers, and rope sellers jostled beside second-hand clothes stores, grocers and bakers.

'Are you sure we couldn't have walked quicker?' Flora had no idea how much time had passed since leaving the hospital; it was disorientating being swallowed up by the fog, which made buildings loom out of the grey mist, taking on substance only when they were feet away from them.

'It's not far now,' Lydia said with confidence, though Flora suspected she was trying to reassure herself just as much as her. As if to confirm her words, the hansom drew to a halt at the side of the road. His head appeared over the side of the canopy, visible only as a blurred black circle. 'This here's Pickle Herring Street. I'll stop this side o' Potters Fields. That close enough, Missus?'

'Perfectly, driver, thank you. We'll walk the rest of the way.' Alice pushed up the trap above her head and handed him his inflated fee.

'What is Potters Fields?' Flora asked, the name somewhat incongruous in this industrial place where cranes and pulleys were a constant feature.

'At one time they made pottery here, but it's been a burial site for the poor for a long time. There are a few old gravestones there still, but it's mostly a park. Adds a bright spot to this depressing place, anyway.'

Flora chose not to remark on the fact that where else could an old graveyard be viewed as a bright spot?

The rain had eased considerably during the cab ride, though drops fell steadily onto their heads and shoulders as they stepped down from the cab.

Alice retrieved their lamps, the metal handles slick with water, so Flora was in danger of losing hers. The cold pressed down, cutting through Flora's clothes, the scarf becoming damper by the second as she breathed into it. The cab set off again back the way they had come, and Flora threw it a longing look. Pushing aside her discomfort, she followed Lydia through the greenish yellow mist beneath brick archways and paths that turned from slippery cobbles back to packed dirt.

'Keep close,' Lydia warned, her lamp cast a bobbing light as she walked. 'The path is firm now, but less than a hundred years ago this entire area was a marsh criss-crossed with streams that ran into the major river. Most of it has been built over, but it can be marshy in places, so watch your step.'

'Where are we?' Flora asked, shivering. Dim lights shone from the rows of warehouses on the other side of the river, where the medieval Tower of London lay squat and forbidding.

'This is the entrance.' Lydia slapped the side of a large wooden box with a flat metal roof.

'That thing?' Flora eyed it suspiciously.

'The tunnel is directly below us.' She swung her lamp in an arc that illuminated a low metal door bordered by metal rivets.

Alice placed her hurricane lamp on a dry spot on the ground. 'Someone has been here recently. There's a new lock on this door.'

'How do we get inside without a key?' Flora rattled the hasp with stiff fingers.

'Stand aside.' Alice eased between them, an object in her hand which she had removed from inside her coat. From the weak light from a nearby streetlight it looked to be a leather sausage about two feet long, rounded into a ball at one end.

'You brought a sap?' Lydia's voice held admiration. 'How practical of you, Miss Finch.'

'More of a blackjack actually.' Alice tucked the metal end into the hasp and leaned her full weight on it. The padlock cracked and sprung open, hitting the kerb with a clang. 'It's a metal core encased in leather.'

'You've done that before, haven't you?' Flora widened her eyes, impressed. 'Did you get that from the hospital storeroom?'

'Not exactly.' Alice threw her a brief, sideways look. 'Although I find they have their uses in situations like this.' She tugged the door open on well-oiled hinges, revealing the railing of a circular metal staircase that dropped into black nothingness. Flora's heart thumped painfully at the thought of descending into that dank, dark hole, the bottom of which could be flooded from all the rain that had fallen in the last hours. She decided not to mention that until it became a real problem.

'I suppose it was too much to expect the gas lighting would still be working.' Lydia sighed, holding a lamp over the hole. 'There used to be lifts here when the railway carried passengers,' she whispered. 'I'll lead the way, but watch your step. It's likely to be slippery.'

Flora suddenly felt dizzy at the prospect, but the alternative would be to wait there, alone and with the possibility of the rain starting again. Summoning her courage, she tried not to think about the black steps that wound into the earth.

'The walls are wet, but at least they aren't running with water,' Lydia said, as if it were something to celebrate. 'Shows some maintenance has been kept up on the shell of the tunnel. There might be some water below.' She voiced Flora's own fear, the lamp in her hand bobbing like a disembodied yellow ball as she took the first steps down. In single file they descended the steps, the metallic ring of each one resounding on the brick walls. 'They had to bring water down by the bucket during the building work. The Thames is mere feet away, but it's all sand and heavy clay beneath us.'

Flora squeezed her eyes shut against an image of millions of gallons of dirty water being so close, but snapped them open again, fearing she might miss a step.

'This tunnel has been here forty years and hasn't leaked once.' Lydia sounded as if she was enjoying herself. Or was it bravado to get her through this dark, oppressive place that took them further into the bowels of the earth with each step?

'Which means it's about due,' Flora murmured to herself, then almost missed a step. Her stomach lurched. She grabbed the cold but dry metal handrail with both hands to steady herself, then released a long, relieved breath. The last thing she needed was to slip and twist an ankle.

Minutes passed slowly as Flora found her own rhythm on the triangular steps. A shadow rushed past Flora's foot, disappearing so fast she couldn't be sure what she had seen. She froze. Was it a rat? No, she mustn't think of rats.

'What's wrong?' Alice asked at Flora's back.

'We're almost at the bottom, and there are lights below.' Lydia's voice drifted back up to them. 'Listen.'

Flora cocked her head, but all she could hear was an intermittent drip of water and their own steady breathing. 'I can't hear anything.'

'Neither can I,' Alice whispered.

'Then it's safe to say we are alone. But keep a lookout. Those lights haven't been left on for nothing.' She held the lamp out in front of her and descended the last few steps that opened out onto wooden floorboards in a cavernous room, where high-backed wooden benches were affixed to the walls on either side. The lights Lydia referred to came from a row of oil lamps arranged around the edge of the room; they did little to lift the gloom.

'This was once the waiting room, where passengers gathered before boarding the train.' Lydia moved past them, her lamp held up to throw an arc of yellow light into the barrelled ceiling.

Flora squinted, waiting for her eyes to adjust. Her fears about leakage returned as the walls seemed to sweat like those of an aqueduct. Pools of water puddled on the dirt floor, but not enough to be described as even a light flood.

Alice had picked up one of the lamps from the floor and strolled the benches that ran along the left side of the room. Thin mattresses covered with striped ticking had been arranged on the seats, partly obscured by piles of blankets. At one end stood a chamber pot, which by the acidic smell had been used and not emptied recently; a stack of plates scraped clean of food sat at on the floor at the end.

Flora took a step forward and something cut through the sole of her boot. She bent and picked up a tiny metal object, which on closer inspection was a toy soldier. 'They're here,' she whispered.

Alice approached a pile of draped blankets, lifted the top one and moved it aside. She moved to the bench, lifting blankets as she went. Flora gasped as low moans came from beneath, and some of the bundles grew arms. A tousled head emerged, issuing an annoyed whimper of disturbed sleep.

Wide eyes in youthful faces stared at them, confused at first, and then with growing interest as the children pulled themselves upright from where they lay head to toe on the old waiting room seats. One by one, they stretched and eased upwards, rubbing their eyes and yawning.

'They are so listless,' Lydia said as she moved along the line; the lamp held up to view each face. 'They're conscious, but barely moving. They must have been drugged.'

Alice sniffed the air, her head tilted to one side. 'Laudanum. There are too many to carry. If we have any chance of getting them out of here, we'll have to wake them.'

'No wonder they didn't stir when they heard us come down the stairs,' Flora said.

'Laudanum's an effective way of keeping them quiet and coop-erative.' Lydia moved to the end of the bench, where a girl beneath a pile of blankets had not moved. 'I only hope they haven't been given too much. Given in too high a dose it can be fatal.'

'I doubt that,' Flora said. 'Ruth Lazarus would know how much to use.'

A tow-headed boy, apparently disturbed by the sound of voices, emerged from a pile of blankets, scratching his head. 'Who're you?' he asked, his voice thick, sounding only mildly interested.

'It's Jack Hobbs, isn't it?' Alice rubbed each of his hands

between hers. 'Don't you remember me? I'm the matron at the hospital.'

'Didn't recognise yer wivout that funny 'at.' He yawned and slumped back against the bench, his eyelids drooping.

Flora moved to where a girl of about eight lay, her cheek against her hands, eyes closed. She wore a floral printed dress, over which a thick woollen coat had been draped. Flora shook her shoulder gently, then a little harder until the girl yawned and stretched, blinking unfocussed brown eyes.

'What's your name?' she whispered, so as not to alarm her.

The girl pulled herself upright, dislodging a mass of uncombed and grubby ringlets, her pupils wide and confused. 'Isobel.'

'Isobel,' Flora repeated gently. 'We've been looking everywhere for you.' Flora stared into wide, but unseeing eyes. 'How do you feel?'

'Hungry,' she whispered.

Beneath the coat which smelled of stale food and sweat she wore a grubby blouse under a pinafore which was delicately embroidered and definitely expensive. Her heeled boots looked new, but although the soles were barely worn, the uppers were badly scuffed from her sojourn underground.

Flora eased Isobel to her feet, though the girl submitted to her touch without enthusiasm. Flora led her to where Alice stood with the others in a quiet group at the far end of the room, where she knew the staircase to lie in deep shadow.

'Wake up now. It's time to go.' Alice gently tapped the cheeks of a boy of about nine who kept batting her hand away. Her voice was firm but reassuring as she coaxed him onto wobbly feet. 'We have to get them back up to the surface before someone returns to fetch them. I assume this Swifty chap intends to take them to Tilbury on his barge.'

Flora retrieved her lamp from the floor and held it up to

shoulder height, the flame probing the shadows in the faint hope she had missed something, but the bench now lay empty. Her stomach lurched with disappointment that the one person she had been so sure to find was not there. The flame slid across a circular hole that covered the entire end of the room, beyond which looked like a metal snake that stretched away along the bottom of the river; the curved walls lined with circles of wrought iron about two feet wide bolted together with rivets as big as her fists to form a tube. The snake undulated to the right and into a dip and then up again, disappearing into the darkness where the lamp flames could not reach.

'It's fascinating and yet frightening isn't it?' Alice said from behind her.

Flora jumped and swung to face her. 'I've seen nothing like it before.'

'Now there's a woman who's never been on the tuppenny tube.' Lydia laughed, easing the arms of a fair-haired girl into a shabby jacket at least two sizes too large. Apart from Isobel, they all wore clothes which looked as if they had been made for someone else. The two boys wore trousers that halted at half-mast, while another's flapped over his feet, and skirts and cardigans ended before reaching ankles and wrists.

'You're right, I'm afraid.' Beatrice had scorned the idea on the first and only occasion Flora had suggested it as a novel way of travelling in the city.

'The underground railways are only for working people,' she had said, dismissing them.

'Are you all right, Flora?' Lydia said from her shoulder. 'It's pretty grim down here, I know, but you look so pale. You aren't going to faint, are you?'

'Of course not,' her voice hitched. 'Lydia, Sally's not here.'

'Oh, Flora, I'm so sorry, I forgot. Look, wherever she is, we have to believe she's alive and well.'

'I know.' Flora bit her lip and stared around. 'I was so convinced she would be kept with the children. Maybe she was never here at all.'

'You talkin' 'bout Sal?' The boy who had commented on Alice's hat started towards her but halted a few feet away.

'Yes.' Flora scooted to his side. 'You've seen her? Do you know where she is now?'

'She was 'ere yesterday. But when we woke up this morning.' He scratched his head again frowning. 'I fink it were this mornin'. Can't really tell down 'ere. Anyways, she was gorn. Dunno where.'

'You didn't see her leave?' Flora crouched beside him; her face close to his. His lips parted and a spark appeared in his eyes, showing he longed to tell her what she wanted to hear. Then it died again, and he shook his head. 'I'd tell yer if I knew, but I were asleep.'

'It's all right. It's not your fault.' Flora reached a hand to smooth down his hair but thought better of it and patted his hand instead.

Had Sally managed to escape? But if so, then why hadn't she raised the alarm? Or had the boy's sense of time been confused and Sally had been removed hours before, not yesterday?

'Oh, 'old on.' Jack thrust a hand into his pocket from which he pulled out a fob watch on a brass chain. An old, dented thing, but Flora could hear it ticking. 'It's me dad's. I didn't nick it or nuffink.'

'I'm sure you didn't.' Flora kept her voice steady though she had to resist the urge to shake the words out of him. 'Jack. When did they take Sally away?'

'I'm not sure.' He held up the fob for Flora to see. 'The little 'and was on the two and the big 'and on twelve.'

Flora gasped. 'Alice, they were here less than an hour ago.'

'Will the monster come now?' One girl asked as she cowered

behind Alice, around whom the children had gravitated in various stages of wakefulness, their eyes trained on the opening to the tunnel.

'What monster?' Flora asked.

'The bloke said the monster would come out and get us if we made a noise.' Jack swiped his sleeve beneath his nose.

Flora's hand drifted to his shoulder, mentally condemning whoever would leave them alone in a place like this and then add monsters to their fears.

'We have to go, Lydia. Now.' her voice rose in panic as the thought came to her that whoever put these children down here would be back anytime.

Alice nodded and lined the four girls and two boys up at the bottom of the steps, giving each one words of gentle encouragement interspersed with praise. They were more responsive than they'd first been and muttered among themselves.

'Let me go up first,' Lydia said. 'I'll check there's no one above unless it's Bunny with the police. Give me a few moments, then you send the children up.' She clattered up the metal steps, while Alice bent to give the children instructions.

'Hold on to the handrail and take the steps one at a time. The lady will wait for you at the top and we'll be right behind you.'

In single file, the children shuffled forward, the only sound their light footfalls, scattered with the odd frightened exclamation when one girl claimed she had seen a rat.

'Rats are the least of our problems,' Alice murmured, following behind.

Flora retrieved the lamp and took up her place at the back of the line. The oil had almost run out, and only a half inch of liquid swirled in the bottom of the glass bulb. She hoped they would reach the top before they were engulfed in total darkness. She contemplated bringing more of the lamps that lined the walls with her, but decided she needed to keep her hands free. The decision made, she had rounded the first curve when a bang came from above, followed by a metallic clang and a masculine yell.

'Who the 'ell are you? And what are you doin' 'ere?'

Flora froze and Alice issued a colourful curse under her breath.

—————

29

A series of thuds and shouts followed by a feminine scream reached them through the metal stairs. Then silence.

'Lydia must have walked right into them.' Panic lifted Flora's voice. 'Now, what do we do?'

One girl turned and whimpering, tried to force her way back down the steps past Flora. Her fear rapidly transferred to the others, who followed. 'No, stay where you are!' Flora extended her arms, blocking their flight. 'The stairs are too narrow. You might fall!'

Alice gathered the children into a huddle around her, flicked a look at Flora and mouthed the word, 'Listen'.

Flora froze, then came the unmistakable sound of boots on metal.

'It's them,' Jack said, the most talkative of the group.

'Who?' Flora whispered.

'Them wot brung us the food. Told us we're going on some big ship.' His lower lip quivered. 'I don't wanna go to sea.'

'You won't be going to sea.' Alice's calm, matronly manner was almost believable, had not the reality been staring them in the face.

'We could go back down and escape through the tunnel?' Flora whispered.

Alice shook her head. 'It's almost a mile to the other side. These children are still drowsy, they cannot move fast enough. Besides, the door at the other end is most likely locked. We're trapped.'

Flora stooped awkwardly on the step so her face was level with Jack's, his eyes large and fearful in the gloom. 'Do you know how many of them there are?'

'Two. But they ain't 'alf big.' He wrapped an arm round Flora's waist and buried his face in her skirt. With Isobel clinging to her other side, she was in danger of slipping off the step and hooked one foot round the railing to regain her balance.

Above them, footsteps rang on the steps, coming closer, accompanied by the glow of a lamp that filtered through the handrails and gaps in the steps.

Flora held her breath, waiting.

'Well, and what 'ave we 'ere?' A pair of scuffed workmen's boots loomed into Flora's line of vision; the lamp held too high to see his face. Despite this, Flora sensed he was smiling.

Isobel whimpered again, and another girl started to cry.

A second figure loomed behind him on the stairs, not so bulky, but equally intimidating. He too carried a lamp, its arc of light bouncing off the walls as he lumbered closer. 'Who're they?'

'I dunno, but we'd better get them all up top.' He hurried down with his companion, grabbed Alice by the shoulder and shoved her roughly in front of him. The children fell silent and filed past him, their eyes averted, evidently accustomed to taking orders from these men.

'Cm'on you lot. Move!' The second man growled, using a boot to urge them forward quicker.

Fury rose in Flora's chest and she stomped past him up the steps, trying not to flinch when he fell into step behind her. He didn't say a word, but she could feel his eyes on her back all the way to the top.

The door clanged open and the thug behind Flora shoved her into line where the children had been gathered beside the kiosk. Two hurricane lamps had been left burning on the ground, but barely penetrated the fog, while a third had been knocked over – evidenced by a pile of broken glass in a puddle of oil.

'Are you all right?' Alice whispered at Flora's shoulder.

Flora nodded, her eyes probing the heavy mist for signs of Lydia. What had they done with her?

Frustration and anger combined as she mentally chastised herself. They had come so close to saving these children, but now it could all be for nothing. She had brought not only Alice, but Lydia, into danger. Would she ever be able to make it up to them?

'Where's the other one?' The man who was evidently the leader pushed his way to where his accomplice stood.

'You told me to come with ya, so I tied her to that iron ring on the—' He held up his lamp, the light illuminating a dull iron ring attached to the wall. A short length of rope hung from it, but no Lydia.

'You didn't tie it tight enough!' He strode to the ring, lifted the end of the rope, then dropped it again in disgust.

'She can't have gone far,' the first man whined. 'With any luck, she's fallen in the river and drowned.'

Flora kept her head down, unwilling to let the thugs see her smile as hope flared.

Please, God, let her have got away.

'We don't have time ta worry 'bout her,' the first man growled. 'We've gotta get them kids onto the barge or Swifty'll 'ave our guts.' He shoved Alice onto the path that ran along beside a stony beach slightly below them, from which came the rhythmic slap of water.

The whir and clatter of machinery came from the buildings

opposite, where figures moved in the blurry light from windows, but at ground level was deathly silent and deserted with no sign of life.

'In case yer thinkin' of calling fer 'elp,' a man's voice growled in her ear. 'The ware'ouse shift is readying the cargoes for the early morning. At this time o' day the river's quiet, so shouting won't do yer no good.'

'Thank you for clearing that up.' Flora hid her disappointment and turned her attention to the river. A short wooden jetty dipped down to where silent barges were tied up side by side against the stone quay, forming a raft that spread into mid-river, the vast support of Tower Bridge looming above like a great iron monster, only its bottom half visible.

At least the rain had stopped, though it was scant comfort, her unease made worse by the mournful sound of foghorns that cut through the fog. It wouldn't matter how much she waved and shouted, no one beyond a few feet out on the water would notice them.

'Where are you taking us?' Alice demanded, though Flora suspected she already knew. 'We're going on a little trip.' The larger man issued a low, menacing chuckle, then without warning, gave her a hard shove between her shoulder blades that sent her off the stone wall and onto the beach.

Flora gasped as she lost her footing, but regained her balance and turned to help the children down onto the shingle. Alice was given similar treatment and hit the ground knees first with a whoosh of stones, though she made no sound.

Shingle crunched beneath her shoes, the uneven ground making progress slow as Flora rushed to help her to her feet.

'I'm all right,' Alice whispered. 'Help the children down.' She nodded to where some children had started to cry but were ordered by the second man to be silent.

Between them, she and Alice helped the children onto the beach and led them towards the wooden jetty. 'Hold each other's hands and move slowly. Don't run.'

Isobel hung back, so Flora took her hand and urged her gently towards the narrow wooden planks that shifted with each movement of the barge. 'I won't let you fall.'

'Just get going!' the thug in the lead growled, giving Flora's back another hard shove, which sent her onto the jetty that creaked and rocked beneath her feet. Isobel whimpered at her side and, ignoring the thug behind her, Flora helped her onto the deck of the nearest barge. The barge dipped again, and she staggered to regain her balance as the deck slid sideways beneath her feet.

Below her, she could make out the crudely painted image of a lighthouse within a circle on the hull, which fitted the description Abel had given them.

'Well, don't just stand there. Get down below!' The first man snarled from beside the edge of the hole where a sliding roof had been moved back to reveal a short set of wooden stairs lit by a sulphurous glow.

Teeth gritted, and with Isobel's hand in hers, Flora descended the narrow steps sideways, but instead of the cold, dark and damp space she had expected, the cabin opened out into a comfortable sitting area. Two oil lamps hung from hooks on opposite walls, making the cramped space almost cosy. The floor had been laid with grey linoleum, which quickly became slippery beneath the wet feet of the children, who clambered and slid down the steps to join her.

A low door sat at the far end; beside which a potbellied stove with a metal chimney made a crooked path through the barge roof. Upholstered benches lined both sides on which the children huddled together in silent rows. Had they all been told they were going to sea? Is that what had frightened them so much?

'You don't have to manhandle me,' Alice snapped at the nearest thug who had pushed her roughly onto the bench seat. 'I'm perfectly capable of seating myself.'

Flora admired her strength, though at the same time braced herself for some sort of retribution which never came. Instead, the brute simply snorted, turned and stomped back up the steps, where he slid the hatch shut with an ominous bang.

'Come and sit down, Flora,' Alice urged. 'I know you're restless and angry, but there isn't anything either of us can do.'

'I don't want to sit down.' Flora paced the cramped space. 'Had we got to the subway twenty minutes earlier we would have been away before those thugs found us.'

'I know. But what's done is done. You'd do well to conserve your energy for the time being.'

'Why?' Flora halted and turned to face her. 'Do you think there will be another opportunity for us to escape before we reach Tilbury?'

'It occurs to me that's where the children are being taken,' Alice whispered, gesturing for Flora to keep her voice down. 'What makes you think we'll be going with them?'

'I hadn't thought of that.' Flora's breath hitched. She and Alice weren't part of their plan. Did these men intend to throw them into the river before they reached the ship?

'Where are we going, Miss?' A girl with a mass of curly brown hair asked.

'I don't know, dear.' Alice rubbed the child's hand between both of hers. 'Though it looks as if we shall be here for a while, so we may as well get to know each other. Now, tell me your name.'

Despite her own terror, pride surged in Flora at Alice's calm demeanour, focussing on each child's face while she coaxed out their names and where they lived. Information the police would need in order to return them to their homes. If they were rescued. Raised voices above sent Flora back to the hatch.

'They're still up there. I can hear them talking.' What were they waiting for?

She crouched on the top step, making sure she could not be seen by a casual glance from above. The lead thug sounded as if he was arguing with another man, whose face was not visible, though Flora could clearly see his floor length brown tweed coat. Swifty...

Were they preparing to leave? She did a quick calculation in her head. 'Tilbury is over twenty miles away. Bunny will guess that's where they will take us, but will he get there before the ship leaves?' The thought of him on the quayside as the SS Lancet pulled into mid-ocean made her want to cry.

'S'pose she's gone to fetch help?' a male voice she assumed to be Swifty's asked, bringing Flora's attention back to the conversation.

'She don't know where we've moored,' an impatient voice answered. 'How's she going to lead anyone back here even if she gets a policeman to take her seriously?'

'You dolt,' Swifty's voice came again. 'Look up there. Even if you can't see that ruddy great iron bridge over your thick head, she would have.'

'Stop panicking. We'll be halfway to the ship by the time they get here. 'Sides, the filth won't never find this barge amongst all these others. Now look lively, here's the boss. Get ready to cast off.'

Flora frowned as a third voice hailed them, followed by steady footsteps directly overhead.

'Can you tell what's going on?' Alice whispered.

'It seems Lydia got away, but they plan to be gone before she can summon help.' Flora held up a finger, her head tilted. Another voice was speaking. One which sounded familiar, but different. She released a sigh as she realised her instincts had not failed her. 'I think we are about to meet the mastermind behind this grubby little business.' She had barely spoken before the hatch slid open again, sending Flora scrambling off the steps and back to the bench seat.

A pair of shiny black shoes appeared, followed by a tailored brown tweed suit and the hem of an immaculate dark overcoat as its owner descended into the cabin.

'Good evening, laydees.' Claude Martell's sparkling black eyes regarded Flora with the same expression with which he had tempted her to try his famous madeleines. 'Forgive the accommodations, but I did not expect your presence here.'

'I've been expecting you.' Flora's voice remained calm, though her stomach churned with a mixture of fury and fear.

'You knew?' Alice stared at her.

'I had my suspicions when we misread that note. Who else do you know who would write a number seven like a four?'

'A Frenchman, of course.' Alice sighed. 'Why didn't I see that?'

'It seems.' Martell delivered his oily smile, 'that no matter how well one plans and practises, one always misses the teensiest details.' He held the thumb and index finger of his right hand up to his face. 'Fortunately, this one will not matter until it is too late.'

Jack had his arm around Isobel, her head bent into a blanket, gently sobbing. One girl drew up her legs and cowered in a corner, while the others simply stared, wide-eyed at Martell.

Flora left her seat again and halted two feet away from the smug Frenchman. 'How does someone go from serving tea to selling children?' She hoped her fierce whisper could not be heard among the fearful faces that stared up at them from the bench seats.

'Life is not as simple as you imagine, Madame Harreengton.' He held both hands out, palms upwards, in a gesture of surrender. 'I merely help these poor unwanted cheeldren. And they are unwanted, or 'ow could I have persuaded them away from their guardians so easily? They will 'ave better lives in a new and beautiful country. Would you rather they died of lung rot and malnutrition?'

'Isobel Lomax was wanted. Is wanted.'

'Ah, yes.' He flicked a glance over her shoulder to where Isobel had buried her face in Alice's neck. 'A most attractive child. I could not resist. They are always the easiest to place.'

'How do we know you aren't sending them into slavery for cruel masters?' Flora demanded.

'Because I tell you they are not.' His dark eyes flashed with anger. 'My friends in New York will arrange their adoption to respectable families. So much more lucrative than what cat houses offer. Don't concern yourself, my dear. These children shall enjoy lives they could not dream of in a Bermondsey slum.' He gave the Gallic shrug that was such a part of his tea shop persona, though now his whole demeanour emanated fakery and corruption. His jutted his chin, narrowed black eyes and caricature moustache repelled her now. 'Whatever their fate, it is of no consequence to you.'

He nudged Swifty with an elbow. 'Your friend on the dock said you've let one of these meddling women get away.'

'Wasn't my fault, Mr Martell. I told you not to employ those too. Daft they are,' he reverted to grovelling mode. 'They said the girl slipped the rope and took orf.'

'I hope you weren't as careless with the mouthy one who was unwise enough to follow me the other day?' He flicked Flora another knowing glance. "As she been taken care of?'

'Don't worry 'bout her.' Swifty tugged the peak of his cap. 'I've got her stowed nice and safe.'

Flora stiffened. They were talking about Sally. She's still alive.

'What do you mean stowed?' Martell's eyes flashed fire. 'I told you to get reed of that beetch two days ago. If she's still breathing, there'll be consequences.'

'I know what you said, but I've made me own arrangements for 'er.' Swifty tapped the side of his narrow nose and winked. 'She's too nosy by half and crafty, that one. I can get a good price for her from a madam I know in Kentish Town.' He aimed a gap-toothed grin at Flora and Alice. 'If I take these two far enough out of London, I could get even more for them.'

'Don't be stoopid!' Martell cuffed Swifty's ear, sending him back a pace. 'It's much too reesky. These women aren't nobodies.' He stroked his thumb and forefinger down either side of his moustache. 'Non, they must be disposed of once we have delivered the cheeldren. When it is done, leave them in the tunnel. No one will come looking there for a long time, if ever.'

Flora held her breath. Bunny would come for her, wouldn't he? He knew where they were going, but if he found the Subway empty, might he think to return there later for another look? Possibly not if they had searched for it once. The thought they would miss each other by minutes while she and Alice died of cold and hunger in that dank tunnel made her heart flutter.

Without sparing Flora or Alice another look, Martell turned and left. Swifty followed, still rubbing his ear, slamming the hatch shut behind him.

With no weapons left in her armoury, all Flora could think to do was to mount the short flight of wooden steps and tug at the handle attached to the hatch, which remained firmly shut. Delivering a final, angry thump with her fist, she retreated and slumped onto the seat. 'We might as well be some cargo being shipped for a profit.'

'Lydia will fetch help,' Alice whispered, her chin cocked at the children as if to warm Flora to watch her tongue. 'Let's hope she is in time.'

Flora attempted a smile but doubted she convinced anyone. Her head whirled with scenarios, some hopeful, others despairing. Lydia had been brought up in this neighbourhood. She knew her way around, unlike Flora. Had she been able to raise the alarm with someone who would listen? Or had the thug above been right, and she had fallen into the river in the growing dark and the thick fog? No, Lydia was smart and fearless. She would survive. She had to. And what of Sally? She was evidently still alive, but where? Had she already been taken to the *SS Lancet*?

The children huddled together on the seat opposite, while Alice spoke gently to each and adjusted a collar or wrapped a blanket tighter round a pair of small shoulders. Restless, Flora rose and moved to the far end of the cabin where the potbellied stove clicked as it cooled. She looked around for something to replenish the embers visible through the small door on the front of the stove, but there was nothing to hand.

'What are you doing, Flora?' Alice asked in a harsh whisper.

'I can't bear this waiting. Perhaps we can still get out before we leave the dock.' She tried the handle on the door in the end wall, which gave with a scrape of warped wood against the frame. Beyond lay a small inner cabin, this one unlit, the window covered by a square of canvas nailed to it that allowed weak light through.

'Anything?' Alice asked.

'I don't know yet.' The room held a low pallet set against a wall covered with clothes and a blanket, its length taking up the entire width of the cabin. There was no sign of a door to the outside and the ceiling was flat and solid. She was about to leave when the pile on the bed shifted. Or could it have been a trick of the light? Flora frowned and waited, but when nothing happened, she turned to go, halting when she heard a sound. A groan, or was it an exhalation of breath?

She swung back, narrowing her eyes to focus in the low light.

As her eyes adjusted, she made out a cloud of wavy brown hair fanned out on a grubby pillow. Flora uttered a curse under her breath that the evil Martell kept more children there, when an arm fell away from a pale, oval face with the eyes closed.

Sally!

Flora dropped to her knees beside the pallet and peeled away the top blanket. The same smell she had detected on the children clung to her. Sally had been drugged, too. Flora shook a shoulder, but Sally didn't stir. 'Sally, Sally, can you hear me?'

'Did I hear—?' Alice's head appeared round the door. 'Oh, my goodness. This is your maid?' Without waiting for an answer, she eased Flora to one side, though in the tiny space she could only press herself against the cold bulkhead. Alice pressed two fingers to her wrist, then prised open one eye. 'Drugged. And heavily, by the look of it.'

'Is she all right?'

'Her pulse is steady, but she's barely conscious.' Alice turned back the covers, her head bent as she listened to Sally's chest. 'Her breathing is shallow. They must have given her a large dose.'

Flora exhaled through pursed lips as relief flooded through her. 'How do we get her out of here?'

'We don't. Not yet. Give her time to regain consciousness. Then maybe she can move on her own.'

'That might be too late,' Flora said, aware that Jack and another child stood at the open door, staring at them.

'Is Sal all right, Miss?' Jack asked.

'I hope so, Jack. Now go back into the other room and sit with the others.' Flora frowned, her head cocked, while she listened. 'I can't hear the noise of an engine. Didn't Martell say we had to leave straight away?'

She had barely got the words out before thumps and shouts

came from above, then heavy footsteps tramped across the deck above their heads.

'Wass 'appenin'?' Jack cried, his voice high with fear.

'I'll see.' Alice gave Sally a last pat, rose and disappeared through the low door and ushered the curious boy out with her.

Flora replaced Sally's covers and perched on the edge of the pallet set inches from the floor. The girl's breathing seemed more regular, deeper. Or was Flora's imagination born of hope? Guilt tore at her for sending her to watch Buchanan at the concert. Not that Sally would have wasted time attributing blame or feeling sorry for herself. She was glad the children had had Sally to comfort them. She would have had them singing songs to banish the dark and told them stories at night. With these thoughts uppermost, Flora took a moment to realise the banging had stopped, and the children had fallen silent.

Too silent.

* * *

'Is everything all right, Alice?' Flora rose and pulled open the door. When no answer came, her nerves prickled.

'Fleur, watch out.' Alice cried, just as something heavy hit the bulkhead where Flora's head had been a second before. She staggered sideways, regained her balance and looked up, straight into the face of Ruth Lazarus, her upraised hand wrapped round a wicked looking wooden club.

'Good afternoon, Ruth.' Flora forced calm into her voice. 'Is that what you used to kill Lizzie Prentice?'

A wry smile tilted the corner of Ruth's thin lips, though the expression in her eyes remained flat. 'Think you're clever, don't you?' She lowered the club. 'She asked for it.'

'Ruth!' Alice snapped, obviously horrified. 'Think about what you're saying. This isn't you.'

'Of course it's me!' Ruth swivelled to face her. 'It always has been. It was the obedient, never speak out of turn Sister Lazarus who was the sham. Always having to bow and scrape to the likes of you.' Her top lip curled and she switched her gaze back to Flora.

'Lizzie saw me and Claude when we were Sally Army recruiting. We only stopped into the Cork Galleon to collect a few quid. I had no idea Lizzie worked there.'

'Recruiting? Is that what you call persuading families to sell their children?' Flora could not look away from the club, the wood stained with what could have been grease. Or blood.

'I made her swear she wouldn't breathe a word or she'd regret it. But I didn't kill her. You'll have to look elsewhere if you want someone to hang for that deed. Not that it wasn't convenient.'

'You were blackmailing Mr Bannerman with that photograph, weren't you? The one Lizzie found.'

'She was no angel, I caught her going through my locker. Claimed she was going to return it to him, but more like she was hoping to sell it.'

Ruth laughed, a harsh, cruel laugh. 'We knew Bannerman would do anything to stop us handing them over to his precious Board of Governors.'

A shout followed by a thump came from above, followed a few seconds later by a sound which made Flora's heart lift.

A whistle.

'So you kept it with you to taunt him, in case he got any ideas about defying you?' Flora said loudly, hoping Ruth hadn't heard it and determined to keep her talking.

'Worked, didn't it?' Ruth raised a sardonic brow. 'Lizzie refused to tell me what she had done with the other one. Not that it really mattered. Bannerman was right in it with us by then.'

'I see.' Flora licked her lips, though her mouth was so dry, it made little difference. 'Did Lizzie know what was on it?'

'Don't know, don't care,' Ruth snorted. 'I would have killed her too. I even followed her into the yard that day, but someone beat me to it.'

Isobel began to sob and Jack muttered something under his breath Flora didn't catch.

Alice gently shushed the children, gathering them into the corner, far enough to avoid any flailing arms. Thus far Ruth had ignored the children, but Flora had the impression she was beyond threatening them to get her way.

If she could catch Alice's eyes, maybe one or both of them could rush her, or would it be more efficient to act alone? With barely space to move in the small cabin, suppose they hurt one of the children? Scenarios played through Flora's head, immediately rejected when the hatch slid open with barely a sound. Flora's breath caught in her throat and she forced herself not to look up, praying a friendly face would appear and not one of the thugs.

'Look!' one of the children gasped.

Ruth jerked her head up and back, and thus distracted her arm which held the club lowered.

Flora lunged, but before she closed the gap between them, Alice sprang from her seat and brought the sap down on the woman's head.

Ruth let out a surprised moan and crumpled to the floor. Flora jumped back to avoid being dragged with her.

'Blimey!' Jack exclaimed, his eyes wide, while the other boy let out a delighted whoop.

'Do you think you've killed her?' Flora asked.

'I didn't hit her hard enough.' Alice sniffed as she returned the sap inside her coat. Flora wondered briefly if she had a special place for it, but knew she would never ask.

'Flora? Are you there?' Bunny's voice came through the grey mist that hovered over the hatch. He paused half way into the cabin, his hands braced against the edge of the hatch. His gaze went to the prone figure on the floor then back up at Alice. 'Goodness, it seems you've managed without our help.'

Flora released a relieved sob and threw herself toward him, grabbed his face in her hands and planted a resounding kiss on his lips.

'Steady on.' He adjusted his glasses with one hand. 'You know I can't see much without these.'

'Spectacles can be replaced.' Flora kissed him again. 'Your wife cannot.'

He chuckled, descended the remaining steps and wrapped her in a suffocating embrace. He smelled of coal smoke with hint of sandalwood. Smuts sat on his face and hair, and his glasses were askew, but nothing mattered other than he was there.

One of the girls giggled. Jack muttered something that sounded like a disgusted snort.

'I'm exceedingly glad to see *you*, Mr Harrington,' Alice said from behind them, putting emphasis on the 'you'.

'I'm delighted to see you too, Miss Finch,' Bunny said over Flora's shoulder. 'You're not hurt are you, Flora?' he asked, his lips against her forehead.

'No one is hurt. Just cold, scared and extremely relieved you are here.' She hugged him again. 'You aren't alone are you?' she murmured.

As if in answer, the whistle sounded again, followed by shouts above that steadily increased in volume. Footsteps pounded across the roof and a police Sargeant stuck his head through the hatch. 'This the right barge, Mr Harrington?'

'It is, Sargeant.' Bunny called out without looking up. 'Everyone appears to be safe and unhurt, apart from Sister Lazarus here.' He nodded to where Ruth had pulled herself onto all fours, groaning. 'You might send a couple of men down here to fetch this member of the gang.'

'Nice work, Mrs Harrington.' Sargeant tipped the edge of his hat in salute.

'I wasn't responsible for that, but thank you anyway.' She gave Alice a grateful smile. Alice inclined her head, her calm demeanour restored. No one would ever guess she carried a crowbar inside her coat.

'Have you found Lydia?' Flora's breathing quickened at the thought. How could she have forgotten her? 'She got away from those brutes, but we don't know what happened to her.'

Bunny gripped her upper arms in both hands. 'Calm down, Flora. Don't worry, we found her.'

'You did?' Relief flooded through her. 'How? You're here and her note said we would be at the subway.'

'She was standing in the middle of the road waving down the Black Maria. We almost ran her over in the fog. She followed the men who brought you here and told us where you were. We had to search several barges first or we would have been here sooner.'

'Where is Lydia now?' Flora asked.

'She was shivering with cold, so we put her in the police van. She wanted to come and find you but Maddox insisted.'

'This is all very gratifying.' Alice insinuated herself between them. 'However, before you do anything else, we need to get these children onto dry land and somewhere safe. This touching reunion can wait until later.'

'Ah, yes, yes of course.' Bunny released Flora and stepped aside as Alice passed Isobel through the hatch to a policeman on the deck.

Ruth sat with her back against the bulkhead, cradling her head and groaning. The other children circled her, eyeing her, some fearful, others defiant.

'I don't hafta go to sea now, do I?' Jack asked, when his turn came at the bottom of the steps.

'Not unless you want to.' Alice handed him through the hatch into the policeman's waiting hands. 'And not until you are a lot bigger.'

Inspector Maddox slid down the side rails on the wooden steps; a technique Flora suspected he had used before. He shoved his hands in his pockets, clicking his tongue over Ruth, who stared back at him, unflinching. 'Constable!' he called to a shadowy figure above the open hatch. 'Get down here and fetch Miss Lazarus out would you?'

'I didn't know you were acquainted with Sister Lazarus, Inspector,' Flora said.

'I interviewed her when this first started. Callous sort of woman. Didn't think much of her at the time. Dead eyes.' His lip curled as he turned away, then he paused and ducked his head down again. 'Oh, and, Harrington, you'll never guess who the boss is.' Without enlightening him, he disappeared into the fog.

Bunny frowned. 'What did he mean by that?'

'Mr Martell, whom I sincerely hope has been apprehended by now.'

'Martell?' Bunny's frown deepened. 'Claude Martell who owns the tea room?'

'Yes, but never mind him. Sally's in the rear cabin. She's been drugged. Someone will have to carry her out.'

Bunny's frown cleared, and he sighed. 'Well, that's a relief. I wasn't looking forward to telling Abel we still hadn't found her.'

'Where is Abel?' She stared up through the hatch, but all she could see was a curtain of grey mist.

'He caught one of the thugs who brought you here. Threw him

down on the beach, and before anyone could stop him, Abel started pounding him, demanding to know what he'd done with her. The police had to drag him off, though they didn't seem in much hurry to do so. It appears they don't like child abductors.'

'Which is as it should be.' Flora spared no pity for either of the men who had taken such pleasure in tormenting small children.

He glanced up at the open hatch where the policeman waited. 'We should let these gentlemen do their work.' Two burly policeman clattered noisily down the steps where they hauled Ruth to her feet and shoved her roughly in front of them. Bunny tapped the second one on the shoulder. 'When you've dealt with her, please tell Inspector Maddox we've found my wife's maid, but will need some help getting her out of here.' The policeman smiled and tipped his helmet in a salute and left.

Bunny groaned and pulled Flora back into his arms. 'How do you manage to keep getting yourself into these scrapes? I'm beginning to feel I should confine you to the house from now on. At least I would know where you were.'

'An action some would say is justified, but you won't.' She buried her face in his coat and fought the tears in her eyes which welled up. 'Though I must say I do appreciate you always coming to my rescue.' Her throat closed and her last words ended on a sob. She mustn't crumble, not now. Emotions and recriminations would have to wait.

More footsteps sounded above them and seconds later, Abel appeared. 'That copper said Sally's here.' He landed on the floor with a thump, his head bent to clear the low roof. 'Where is she?'

'In there.' Flora couldn't help smiling when Abel had to fold himself almost in half to get through the door. His soft voice drifted back to them as he talked soothingly to Sally.

'Is she awake?' Flora called out from where she stood, aware that the tiny cabin wouldn't hold the three of them.

Abel ducked his head through the opening, his face dark with concern. 'No. She's still out. I'll have to carry her.'

'Can you manage?' Bunny asked, though the offer was impractical because there was no room for manoeuvre inside the cabin. Abel would have to manage alone.

Leaving him to it, Bunny climbed out onto the deck and reached a hand back to assist Flora. He led her across the jetty and onto the dock, where Inspector Maddox stood beside a police van with several of his men. He sauntered towards them, giving Flora a head-to-toe look of admiration mixed with disdain.

'I'm pleased you're safe, Mrs Harrington, however I'm not comfortable with the fact you ignored my advice to leave this matter to the professionals.'

'Had I not done so, Inspector, these children would be on their way to the Americas by now.' After all she had been through she wasn't going to accept chastisement from Maddox. Not when he had refused to take her concerns seriously. Let him explain that to his superintendent.

30

Alice handed Isobel into a waiting taxi on the dockside, into which the other children sat shrouded in blankets, their excited faces pressed to the windows.

'Where are they going?' Flora asked. 'Miss Finch wants them taken to St Philomena's,' Maddox replied. 'A doctor will examine them to ensure they have suffered no ill effects.' He cleared his throat, and then addressed the policeman closest to him.

'Is Miss Pond off that barge yet? We'll need to talk to her.' Maddox nodded to the open hatch from which shadows moved and the odd scraping noise came.

'That will have to wait, Inspector,' Flora said. 'She's still suffering the effects of the laudanum, which is why Abel is having such difficulty. She's in no state to be questioned.'

He accepted this with a curt nod, then turned his attention to two of his men. 'We've got another villain somewhere on this dock,' he shouted. 'I want him caught, sharpish. It's cold out here, and this fog plays havoc with my chest.'

'How did he get away?' Flora shuddered as Martell's unsavoury plans for herself and Alice repeated in her head. The thought that he might escape made her breathing quicken along with her heartbeat.

'Gave us the slip.' Maddox stared out over the water, where the blurred outlines of men leapt from one barge to the next, their lamps bobbing like large fireflies through a light drizzle that settled on Flora's nose and any curls that had broken free from her hat. The six-inch hatpin she had used to secure her hat had done its job well and, the hat was still in place, even if flat and askew.

'Don't worry, he won't get far.' He offered her his hand. 'Might I assist you off this barge?'

Flora shook her head. 'I'd rather wait until Sally has been brought out, thank you. I want to make sure she's safe.'

'As you wish.' Maddox made his way back across the barges, where he became a moving shadow on the dockside.

'Would you mind if I left you for a moment, Flora?' Bunny asked. 'The other Black Maria has arrived, but the men seem to be having trouble with the horses. I'll give them a hand. I won't be long.'

'You don't have to explain, just go.' She waved him away, then rearranged her scarf over her nose and mouth, partly for warmth and to keep smuts from irritating her face.

A sound behind her brought her gaze to where Abel emerged with Sally draped over one shoulder. Her dark hair hung down Abel's back and her arms swung as he manoeuvred his bulk awkwardly through the hatch.

'Is that you, Miss Flora?' Abel raised his other hand to his eyes.

'Yes, it's me.' Flora held up the lamp, so it threw an arc of weak yellow light over his face.

'Sorry I bin so long.' He lifted his shoulder to settle Sally's weight. 'I thought she was going to wake up a few minutes ago, but she drifted off again. She can't walk, so I had to drag her out of that cabin.'

'This way, Abel.' Flora held up the lamp, so it shone on where the wooden jetty stood. 'I'll light the way over these barges, but watch your step. They shift with the incoming tide and the decks are slippery.'

Just then, a shout went up on the far side of the dock.

'What's happening, Miss Flora?'

'I don't know, I—' Flora broke off as the policeman who had shouted was knocked over the edge of the dock by a figure, who jumped the three feet onto the barge below. A man in a long coat that flapped round his ankles scrambled across the deck and sprinted onto the next barge. A whistle sounded, but the man leapt and scrambled from one barge to another – straight for them.

'It's Swifty!' Flora gripped Abel's arm. 'He's heading this way. Quick, get Sally off.'

'Can't, Miss Flora. If I go, he'll start up the engines and leave. We can't let him get away.'

'The police will get here before he can do that,' Flora said, though from what she could make out they were busy hauling their comrade out of the river.

'Go on, Abel,' She shouted just as Swifty reached the barge and ran towards them, shouldering her roughly aside as he leapt for the hatch.

She gave a cry of anger and surprise as she fell, her arms flailing for something to hold on to, but all she grasped was air. The lamp slipped from her hand and shattered on the deck with a tinkling crash, followed by a small whoosh as the flame drank up the spilled pool of oil on the wood.

She heard Abel's gruff roar of anger as she hit the deck. Pain lanced through her side yet instinctively she scrambled backwards away from the flame. But it had already gone out.

Abel gave another guttural growl and with his free arm, took a wide swing at Swifty, but was hampered by the fact he still held

Sally. The smaller man ducked smartly away and bent to pick something from the boards. It looked like a long pole with a hook on one end. He raised it to shoulder height and brought it down on Abel's exposed shoulder. Had he not been holding Sally, the blow might not have had much effect, but taken off balance, Abel slammed onto the deck, taking her with him.

Flora watched in horror as Sally landed with her head and shoulders over the side, one hand trailing in the oily black water.

Abel lay still for a few seconds before staggering clumsily to his feet. He threw a punch at Swifty, but it went wide, unbalancing him. His left knee collapsed, and he fell face down onto the stern. His breath left him in a grunt, but he immediately hauled himself onto all fours, shoulders heaving.

She edged slowly round the narrow ledge, just as Swifty swung his weapon again. Abel must have sensed the blow coming and scrambled to one side with surprising agility for such a big man and pulled himself to his feet just as Swifty raised his arm to strike again. At the last second as the blow came, Abel turned his upper body sideways and the pole landed on the deck, gouging a dent in the wood. Abel took a step forward and kicked the weapon from Swifty's hold, sending it rolling across the deck.

Flora's gaze went to Sally, who lay between her and the two men. She scrambled to one side, circling the deck to reach her, hoping Swifty was too focussed on getting Abel away from the engine housing to worry about her.

The deck tilted again, a combination of the tide and the frantic shifting of the fighting men's weight. Flora grabbed the side to prevent herself from slipping off into the murky water, not daring to move again until the barge righted itself. Swifty ran forward to attack Abel again, who was now balanced precariously on the edge of the barge.

Abel's weight and height would count against him if Swifty

landed another blow. As she watched, Sally slipped a little more towards the water. Flora gritted her teeth and held on, praying the barge wouldn't tilt again and throw her off. The wooden jetty had straightened out since they had climbed aboard; the tide was coming in fast, spreading across the shingle beach towards the quayside.

The barge steadied, and Flora made a lunge for the pole Swifty had dropped. It was about six feet long and heavy, making her wish she had thought to ask Alice for her sap instead, but she would have to make do.

She slid the pole through her hands until she gripped it near the middle and swung it in a wide arc from her waist, grunting as it contacted the back of the smaller man's knees. A shudder ran through her arm and the pole jerked from her hands, clattered down and rolled across the tilting deck, landing against the bulkhead with a gentle thump.

Swifty howled with shock and pain as he crumpled, but recovered quickly and rolled away from Abel's retaliatory blow. The smaller man lunged again, throwing both arms round the bigger man's thighs and dragged him to the deck where they merged in one black shadow as they grappled to get the upper hand.

The barge shifted again, and losing her balance, Flora crashed to the deck, expelling the air from her lungs as pain seared through her already sore ribs. She tried to take in a breath, but her chest felt frozen and refused to work, the pain increasing with each try. The pole had rolled away and lay against the lip of the deck, too far away for her to reach.

After what seemed like minutes but could only have been seconds, her muscles obeyed and she gasped in a lungful of sulphur-laden air. It didn't matter, dirty air was better than none. She flexed an arm, then the other, taking inventory of each limb as she eased herself upright, gasping as pain stabbed through her left side. Taking a few shallow breaths to test the limits of what she could tolerate, she judged her limit, then slowly clambered upright.

Abel had Swifty in a headlock, and taking her chance while they were distracted, Flora crawled across the roof to where Sally lay face down, one leg bent beneath her, her hair draped over the side of the boat, the ends trailing in the oily water. 'Sally!' She shook her, but there was no response.

Flora braced a hip against the hatch, placed one foot on the lip of the barge and hauled Sally back onto the deck, but her dead weight proved more awkward than Flora had imagined. She would move an inch and then slip back two, slipping perilously closer to the edge.

Swifty rolled to one side to throw off Abel's hold, but the big man refused to let go and together, they crashed back onto deck.

The barge rocked dangerously and Flora's grip loosened.

Sally slid further over the edge, but at the last moment before momentum took her the rest of the way, Flora reached out a hand, her fingers closing over Sally's wrist.

Behind them the fight continued, interspersed with grunts and shouts of pain as blows landed. Swifty located the pole and raised it above his head, but giving a furious roar, Abel grabbed it from him and flung it overboard. Sally slipped, and Flora stretched her arm until her shoulder screamed, but hooked a hand into the waistband of Sally's skirt. She hung on, but couldn't get any purchase to pull her into the barge. All she could do was cling on and hope someone came to help her. Another six inches and Sally would go into the Thames and they might never find her.

Somewhere to her right, Swifty put his head down and barrelled into Abel, sending both men crashing onto the hatch. The barge swung to one side. Sally slipped again and Flora's fingers cramped, her gaze on the fuzzy outline of the dockside in search of help.

'Hold on, Flora, I'm coming!' Bunny's voice reached her through the mist, though she couldn't yet see him. 'Don't let go!'

'That's easy for you. You're not wearing the corset!' she shouted back through gritted teeth. The garment cut into her and her ribs screamed with pain; her fingers continued to cramp until she could hardly feel them, but she refused to let go.

Bunny reached the jetty and prepared to jump for the barge, but hesitated. The gap was too wide; the rope securing the barge to the jetty was strung tight. A tense few seconds passed as he gathered himself to make the jump, during which Abel pulled back his fist and aimed a punch at Swifty's face. The smaller man ducked to one side to avoid the blow, but lost his balance. He gave a sudden, terrified yell and toppled over the edge just as the stern of the barge swung back again and crashed into the jetty at the same time as Bunny leaped, landed on deck and strode to where Flora sat, both feet braced against the edge, her lips pulled back in a grimace.

'I can't hold onto her for much longer,' she gasped. 'I can't feel my fingers.'

Bunny sank to his knees, leaned down and grabbed Sally by the shoulders. In a series of slides and awkward lifts, he eased her limp form onto the deck.

'She's still breathing,' Flora said, brushing Sally's damp hair away from her face.

As if she had heard her, Sally gave a moan and her eyelids fluttered. Her skin felt clammy, her lips blue, and though freezing to the touch, she was beyond shivering. She wore the same clothes as on the night of the concert, but her beloved wool coat was missing.

Two policemen thumped across the deck.

'Where have you been?' Flora demanded. 'You lot disappeared as soon as Swifty turned up.'

'Don't blame them, Flora.' Bunny chuckled. 'It was tougher than they imagined getting the man out of the water. Then the others couldn't get close enough without putting you in more danger.'

'That's not what it looked like from where I was standing.' Flora huffed a breath, glaring at the policemen who had lifted Sally onto a stretcher.

Abel elbowed the policemen out of the way and staggered towards them, one hand clamped against his head, and a frown distorting his features. 'Is she all right?' he demanded, dropping to one knee beside the stretcher.

'Let them take her to the hospital, Abel.' Flora said through a laboured breath, her gaze fixed on the dark trickle of blood that worked its way down the side of his face. 'We'll get a doctor to look at that cut as well.'

'Never mind me. I've had worse.' Abel lumbered to his feet and followed the two policemen who loped off down the jetty, the stretcher slung between them.

Several others swung lamps over the edge of the barge, peering into the dark water for signs of life, their task hampered by the fact it was fully dark, which made shadows everywhere.

'Do you think he's gone?' Flora asked, aware they searched for Swifty, from whom there had been no sign since that last terrified shout. Perhaps he couldn't swim?

'He could be three feet away from the boat and he'd still be invisible in this dark.' Bunny cocked his chin at one policeman. 'Perhaps his body will wash up somewhere downriver.'

Flora winced and squeezed her eyes shut, then remembered what he had planned for Sally and her heart hardened – a little.

'Has Alice left yet?' Flora bobbed her head round Bunny, searching the gloom for her.

'I'm here!' A shadow detached from the gloom and came to her side. 'When I saw that man Swifty attack you on the barge, I couldn't leave.'

'I thought you had gone with the children.'

'I sent one of the young policemen with them in the hackney. I'll go along later. When this is over.' Alice stamped her feet and rubbed her upper arms with both hands.

'How many children have they sent abroad before you thought to ask questions?' Flora asked.

Alice sighed and pulled up the collar of her coat. 'According to Inspector Maddox, this all started with a simple fraud. No one examines a Salvation Army couple shaking collection boxes too closely. Those reluctant to contribute are intimidated by their persistence and preaching about the deserving poor. No one likes to be seen as uncharitable in public – well, most people don't.'

'I suppose not.' Flora's smile was admiring and resentful at the same time. She should have thought of that. 'It's the perfect subterfuge. No one remembers their faces; we only see the uniforms. When did they expand it to child abduction?'

'Don't punish yourself.' Bunny rubbed his upper arms with both hands and stomped his feet. His hair was plastered to his forehead by the misty rain. He must have left his hat somewhere 'It's not as if these missing children are wearing poke bonnets and playing trombones on street corners. I wish they were that easy to find.'

Flora laughed despite herself. A mixture of relief and having defeated death, perhaps? Then a thought struck her that she had been struggling with since Alice had first told her about the children. 'Do you believe they were being sent for adoption by childless couples and living in wealthy homes?' Flora asked.

'Do you?' Alice's smile wilted around the edges. 'What distresses me the most is that they preyed on children who weren't really wanted. Those who had been left with uncles, grandparents and sisters who could ill afford another mouth to feed. So brutal and calculated. What better place to select candidates than my hospital, where they are made fit and healthy before they took them? I feel as if I was culpable. By the way, Lydia is wet and cold, but safe and half asleep in the police van.'

'Thank you. She was wonderful leading them here, I must thank her.' They moved towards where the van stood against a towering wall of the wharves that lined the dockyard. Bunny gave her waist a squeeze before he stepped to one side and addressed a young policeman.

Flora grabbed the older woman's arm, keeping her voice low. 'When we were on that barge and Ruth was about to brain me, you-' she broke off as the solid bulk of Inspector Maddox loomed up behind Alice, his face wreathed in smiles.

'I don't do this often, Mrs Harrington and as I said earlier you ignored my advice.' Maddox tipped his hat back on his head as he grinned down at her. 'However, I feel I ought to thank you for your help in this investigation. We had nothing until you put us onto the link between the Nurse Prentice murder and Swifty Ellis.'

'I'll see you soon,' Alice whispered, removing her hand from Flora's. She stepped away, leaving her with the policeman.

The silent dock was full of the heavy tread of feet and shouting; the scrape of hooves on gravel and an idling engine of a motor taxi on the road below Tower Bridge; unreal images that melded together in Flora's head, together with the chill of the river and the continued mournful wail of foghorns.

A policeman directed Flora to a police van parked behind a Black Maria which contained the two thugs from the subway and Mr Martell, whose scowling face appeared in the metal grille of the door. His black eyes caught hers and froze, narrowing slightly.

Flora shivered; her lip curled as it came to her he might make himself useful baking madeleines in the prison kitchens.

'Sorry about the transport,' Maddox said, appearing at the open van door. 'We couldn't find another cab in this murk.'

'It's unimportant.' Flora tore her eyes away from the French-man. Though at the same time wondered what her mother-in-law would say if she saw them arrive at Eaton Place in a police van.

Sally lay lengthwise on the bench seat inside the police van, her head on Abel's lap and his coat draped over her, with Lydia huddled at the far end, her face visible above a blanket. She grinned when she saw Flora, pushed one hand through the wool and gave a weak wave. She looked as tired as Flora felt.

'I'd better let you all go home now.' Maddox turned to leave. 'We can get everyone's statements in the morning.'

'Inspector.' Flora summoned him back. 'Ruth Lazarus said she didn't kill Lizzie Prentice.'

'That doesn't surprise me.' He snorted, but didn't react. 'She's not likely to admit to something that would be guaranteed to get her the rope. I'll question her later, but she's in no fit state right now. We had to tell her that Swifty was probably dead. She's in some sort of shock.' His tone suggested he was more irritated at the inconvenience than Ruth's feelings.

'No, I suppose not.' A yawn cut off further talk as a combination of pain, relief and weariness overwhelmed her. She slid along the seat to make room for Bunny, just as the door slammed shut.

'Sally's breathing is better and her colour is coming back.' He adjusted a blanket around her shoulders and dropped a kiss on her forehead. 'Alice thinks she won't need to go to the hospital. She only needs to sleep off the laudanum. We could call a doctor when we get home if you prefer.'

'I would, thank you. Just to be sure.' Flora leaned into him, drawing comfort from his presence. 'Maddox said Ruth was bound to deny killing Nurse Prentice to avoid being hanged. Buy why deny it at this stage when they have all been—'

'Hush.' Bunny placed a finger on her lips. 'It's over. Forget them, and Maddox. I simply want to go home, have dinner, and go to bed. We'll sort out the finer details in the morning.'

'That sounds like an excellent idea.' Flora snuggled into his side, sore in places and tired but happy to be safe, though deeper worries filled her head. Had she saved those children, or condemned them?

What if she was wrong and, apart from Isobel, what if Martell was telling the truth and the children would have had a much better life in America? Had she ruined their chances of escape from the slums?

What would happen to them now?

31

The police van trundled through the streets in the darkening afternoon, where Flora huddled against Bunny to keep warm in the unheated interior, a single lamp balanced on the narrow strip of floor emitting the only light.

'What happened on the subway after those thugs caught you, Lydia?' Flora asked, mainly to distract herself from the fact her ribs hurt every time they went over a bump in the road. 'I was certain we were finished at that point.'

'They tied my hands, but the knots were loose, so I waited for them to go back for you, then got away.' Her nonchalant shrug implied she had done nothing unusual. 'I hid behind the kiosk and then, when they brought you all out of the tunnel, I followed down to the river. When they made you climb onto that barge, I ran back to the main road and waited for the police.'

'We owe you a lot, Lydia.' Bunny reached forward and squeezed her arm. 'Without your local knowledge, we might never have got to those children in time.'

Their voices woke Sally, who had spent most of the journey

propped against Abel's shoulder. She groaned and rubbed her eyes. 'Where am I?'

'We thought you'd be out until morning,' Flora said, relieved. 'Welcome back. I can't believe you're awake.'

Sally yawned, and stretched her arms, easing her shoulders. Her eyes snapped open, then her face suffused with alarm and she jerked upright. 'What am I doin' in 'ere? I ain't under arrest, am I?'

'If that's the case, then we all are.' Bunny's laugh was only slightly uneasy.

'Where are the nippers? I was with them in the tunnel.' She stared around, panicked.

'Hush,' Flora soothed. 'They're safe and the gang has been captured. We're taking you home now.'

'That's a relief. For a moment I thought—' she broke off and glanced sideways, then stiffened as she realised she was cradled in Abel's arms. Not that there was much alternative when she, Abel, and Lydia shared a narrow bench with little room to move.

'We've heard Lydia's story. Now what about yours, Sally?' Bunny prompted.

'I shouldn't have left the pub the way I did.' Sally smiled apologetically at Abel. 'But when I saw it was Martell in that Sally Army uniform, I knew straight away he was up to no good.'

'You recognised him?' Bunny said. 'I had no idea you had been to that tearoom.'

'Miss Flora took me, when we spoke to that nurse that time in the Evangeline Lange case.'

'Ah yes, so I did. What an excellent memory you have, Sally,' Flora said.

'He must have spotted me, 'cos when I reached the corner, one of those heavies pushed me into a shop doorway. Next thing I knew, I was down in that subway.'

'Martell was the brains behind it all.' Lydia sighed and rubbed her upper arms with both hands.

'Brains, eh? Well, I never.' Sally yawned and leaned against Abel's shoulder. 'And him such a poncy little man an' all.'

Tired as she was, Flora had to bite her lip to prevent a full-blown laugh.

'Did you see anyone else, other than Martell and the two thugs?' Bunny asked, Flora assumed to discover more evidence to pass to Inspector Maddox.

'Just them and that Swifty bloke.' Sally's accent sounded more pronounced, and she slurred her words a little. 'I was in the tunnel a couple of days, maybe more, but it was difficult to tell. I took one lamp they left with us and went into the tunnel to find a way out, but the kids got scared I was going to leave them, so I came back. Then when the big one brought in food, I kicked him in the you-know-what's. After that, they forced sherry down me and I went spark out.'

'That sherry had laudanum in it,' Lydia said.

'I thought it tasted funny.' Sally grasped Abel's arm as the van rocked whilst they took a corner. He tenderly brushed a strand of hair away from her face.

'You should really go to the hospital, Sally.' Watching them, Flora wondered if she might have to find a new maid before too long.

'Nah. I've been worse'n this after a Pond family wedding.' She rubbed the heel of her hand into one eye. 'I'll be fine after a good sleep. And if it ain't too much trouble, a bath would be nice.'

'Abel's head is as hard as yours.' Lydia pointed to the makeshift bandage he wore, courtesy of Alice. 'He wouldn't go to the hospital either.'

The van pulled to a stop and a policeman's face appeared in the internal window. 'Was it Kinnerton Street you wanted, Miss Grey?'

'Perfect, thank you.' Lydia eased from the corner seat, stretching. 'I too am looking forward to a bath, a hot supper, and a good night's sleep. Come on, Abel.' She nudged the big, handsome man, whose attention was still focussed on Sally. 'We'll both come and see you at Eaton Place tomorrow, Flora. We'll have a proper postmortem over tea.' Lydia reached for the hand of the policemen who handed her down onto the road.

Flora touched Abel's arm who seemed reluctant to leave. 'Thank you for all your help, Abel.'

'If it's all right with you, Miss Flora, I'd rather stay with Sally so I can 'elp her indoors,' Abel said while looking shyly at Sally, whose eyelids were drooping.

Flora looked at Bunny who nodded. 'All right Abel, if that's what you want.'

The van door slammed shut and through the rear window, Flora watched Lydia's outline fade into the darkness.

'Alice declined my invitation to come back with us.' Bunny slid both arms around Flora, his chin against her forehead. 'She insisted she had to go to St Philomena's to make sure the children are all right.'

'She told me. She feels responsible because this happened at her hospital. I also think Lizzie Prentice's death weighs heavily.' Flora recalled the look of determination in Alice's eyes when she wielded the sap above Ruth's head, though it had lasted only a second.

Word must have reached Eaton Place that Sally had been found, for when the van pulled up, several curious faces were lined up at the basement windows. Stokes emerged from the house and hurried to the rear of the van. Together he and Abel helped Sally from the van but as Stokes took a step towards the house, he hesitated. 'Oh, sir, do you wish me to—?'

Bunny waved him away. 'I'll manage, Mrs Harrington.'

'I've a feeling the neighbours are watching us,' Bunny said, helping Flora along the multi-coloured tiled pathway to their front door. Lamps glowed behind almost every window in the darkened street where the policeman slammed the rear door of the van, then climbed up next to his driver, urging the horses to move off with a shout and a crack of his whip.

'I wouldn't be at all surprised.' Smiling, she leaned into the comfort of Bunny's one-armed hug.

32

Flora examined her face in the sitting room mirror, rubbing hard at a smut that had settled beside her eye. 'I feel such a wreck, I'll think I'll take a bath *before* dinner.'

Her hair had lost half its pins and hang in untidy ringlets down her back. Her dress was torn at the hem after her struggle on the barge, the wool damp to the touch. It also smelled funny; a mixture of silt and sulphur. Bunny looked immaculate as always, with only a streak of sand on his trouser leg below the knee.

'I quite like the tousled look.' He eased his shoulders and came to stand at her side, his hands stretched out to the fire.

'You worry me sometimes.' Flora cocked her head. 'Is that the doorbell?'

Bunny turned a frown on the front window as the sounds of male voices reached them from the hall and the butler appeared at the door.

'A Dr Reeder is here, sir, and insists on seeing you,' Stokes announced, his lips clamped into a straight line and with obvious reluctance, stood aside to allow Dr Reeder into the room.

'I hope I'm not intruding?' the newcomer said. 'I apologise for simply turning up like this, but I heard what had happened to you.'

'Good evening, Dr Reeder.' Flora patted her hair, then abandoned the idea, realising she would only make it worse. 'How unexpected.'

'Poor Miss Finch, what a dreadful experience it must have been for her,' he said, apparently not noticing Flora's dishevelment. At Flora's surprised look he added, 'And you, of course, Mrs Harrington. You were quite the heroine, I am told.'

'By whom?' Bunny retrieved his hand from the doctor's handshake, then crossed to the sideboard where he poured three glasses of sherry.

'Why, Mr Buchanan himself. There are rumours going around the hospital, so I called in at Birdcage Walk to see if I could be of assistance. I must have caught him at a vulnerable time, as he blurted out everything.'

'Everything?' Flora asked.

'Indeed, yes. How yourself and Miss Finch helped the police round up the villains who had kidnapped those children.' He accepted the glass Bunny held out without looking at it.

'You heard about this at the hospital?' Bunny's expression was guarded. 'I'm surprised news reached it so quickly.' Bunny took a slow sip from his glass, his gaze fixed on the doctor.

'When Mr Buchanan said he had been blackmailed, well.' Reeder took a perfunctory sip from his glass, though seemed to have trouble swallowing. 'I could hardly believe it.'

'Mr Buchanan told you about the blackmail?' Flora asked, surprised.

'Why, yes? About his son, and the uh – photographs, the threat to his governorship of the hospital. He's relieved it's all over.'

'I imagine he is.' Bunny caught Flora's eye, a simple message in his look that matched her own thoughts. Reeder knew far more than he should.

'I hope the photographs which have caused all this upset have been located?' He tried to appear disinterested, but failed dismally. 'Mr Buchanan explained the source of the strain he has been under these past weeks,' Reeder said. 'I, uh, assume the stanhopes are in the possession of the police now?'

'You know about those?' Flora said. *So that's what is worrying him.*

'Not all of them.' Bunny came to stand beside Flora. 'No one is sure how many of the wretched things exist.'

'Ah, I see.' Reeder hand shook as he brought his glass to his lips. 'Mr Buchanan was under the impression one was found in Nurse Prentice's belongings. Is that in your possession?'

'I believe we have it, don't we, Bunny?' Flora ignored her husband's warning look, and the almost imperceptible shake of his head. 'We'll return it to Mr Buchanan in the morning. More discreet, don't you think, than involving the police?'

'I agree, and I would be more than happy to do that for you. After all, we don't want it falling into unsympathetic hands.'

'We, Dr Reeder?' Bunny asked gently. He placed his glass on a nearby table and came to stand at Flora's shoulder, his closeness giving her confidence. Why did Reeder want that photograph? Was he involved in the blackmail scheme and wanted the evidence removed before he could be implicated?

'That's kind of you to offer, Doctor.' Flora eased closer to Bunny. 'However, we're due at St Philomena's in the morning, as Inspector Maddox requested.'

'The police? What for?' A trickle of sweat ran down the side of his temple, though the room was barely warm from the newly laid fire.

'To take our statements.' Flora tried not to make her smile too triumphant. 'There are a few details he needs to cover. It appears there are more elements to this affair than anyone imagined.' *You being one of them.*

'Would you like more sherry, Dr Reeder?' Bunny strode to the sideboard, whispering in Flora's ear as he passed, 'I know what you're doing.'

'Good,' she whispered back. 'When he makes his move, be ready.'

'This decanter is almost empty,' Bunny exclaimed, with more volume than was strictly necessary. 'I'll ask Stokes to refill it. Won't be a moment.' Shielding the crystal container with his arm, he strode to the bell and summoned the butler.

Stokes must have been hovering outside, as he appeared immediately. For once, Flora didn't resent the butler's busybody ways. Although she couldn't hear what Bunny said to him, the man gave a single, swift nod and withdrew rapidly.

'Now, what were we talking about?' Bunny strode back to Flora's side. 'Ah, yes, you seem inordinately concerned with one of Mr Buchanan's peeps, Dr Reeder.'

'I beg your pardon?' Perspiration beaded on his forehead. 'I was merely—'

'Is it the stanhope itself which interests you? Or the contents?'

'I, er, I'm not sure what you mean.' Reeder stared at the floor, his Adam's apple bobbing like a fishing float. 'Mr Buchanan merely expressed a wish to have it returned to him and I offered.'

'It was you in that photograph with Victor Buchanan, wasn't it?' Bunny took a leisurely sip from his glass and pointed it at the doctor. 'Ruth Lazarus knew, but then she wasn't going to tell anyone while it was to her advantage.'

'I really don't know what you're talking about. I—'

'Lizzie Prentice was another matter entirely, though, wasn't she?' Flora's lower belly pulled as she realised where Bunny was taking the conversation. *Lizzie Prentice*. 'She found the silver peep and saw what was inside? Is that why you killed her?'

'Really, I—' He studied each of their faces for a long moment, then sighed. With a fatalistic nod, he set his glass down on the table beside Bunny's.

'That stupid girl. If only she had minded her own business.' He kept his voice low as if talking to himself, his tone changing from affable to angry. 'She saw it in the X-Ray room and couldn't resist looking at it.'

Flora eased closer to Bunny and reached for his hand behind the folds of her dress.

'I thought Lizzie and me were friends.' Reeder lifted his chin, defiant. 'I thought she would understand, but she was disgusted with me.' He retrieved his glass, downed the contents in one gulp and set it down again, hard enough to crack it.

Flora gripped Bunny's hand tighter but dared not look at him while Reeder was still engrossed in his story. Having begun, he seemed unable to stop.

'That was when she told me Ruth Lazarus had one too and we must both be involved with those children who went missing. She couldn't have been more wrong. I knew Ruth was blackmailing Mr Buchanan, but I thought it was extortion, not kidnapping. Anyway, it was nothing to do with me. I had my own problems. Lizzie threatened to take my stanhope to the Board of Governors if I didn't tell them where the children were.'

'How inconvenient when if, as you claim, you didn't know anything about them?' Bunny said.

'When I confronted her in the yard that day, I tried to explain, but Lizzie didn't believe me. She said I deserved to be publicly disgraced. That once the police knew, they would make me tell them where the children were.' He gave a short, scornful laugh. 'She didn't realise Victor was the other man in the picture. For his sake and mine, I offered to pay her, but she pulled away from me and...' He shrugged, as if what followed was inevitable. 'I grabbed a stone from a flower border and hit her. I barely remember doing it. When I looked down I saw her, lying on the path, bleeding.'

'Lizzie didn't have the peep on her though, did she?' Bile rose in Flora's throat at his casual violence. He exhibited more anger than remorse. Or did he believe that as a man who helped save lives, he had the right to take them, too?

'No.' He stared at the carpet. 'I searched her pockets, but found nothing.' He spoke as if he had forgotten they were there. 'I slipped back inside, and when someone else found Lizzie, I pretended I had come out to see what the commotion was about.'

'Then you tried to convince everyone she must have died from a fall?' Bunny twisted his glass in one hand, his voice calm.

'They would have taken my word had not that idiot of a coroner disagreed.'

'All that, and you still didn't have the photograph,' Bunny said. 'And its existence could cause a great deal of trouble for you and Victor Buchanan.'

'I'll go to prison.' He brought a fist down onto the table, rocking it. 'I'll never be able to practise again.' His eyes flashed with fear, then narrowed, sending Flora backward a step.

'Inevitable, I'm afraid.' Bunny squeezed Flora's hand hard, then released it. 'Besides what the police call indecent practices, you did murder a young girl.'

'I was afraid you might say that.' Without warning, the doctor produced a small pistol from inside his coat. So small, Flora had to look again to make sure it was real.

'I hadn't expected that,' Flora whispered.

'Nor me.' Bunny stepped in front of Flora, shielding her.

'I hoped I wouldn't have to do this.' Reeder lifted the weapon slowly. 'But you leave me with no alternative.' He eased sideways towards the door, drawing a wide arc around them, the weapon pointed at Bunny's chest. 'Now, I want my stanhope back if you please.'

'You'll have to allow me to fetch it,' Flora thought quickly, playing for time. Could they bluff it out? 'It's locked away in a safe in the butler's pantry.'

'Don't lie.' His eyes flashed, and the gun jerked. 'I'd be willing to wager it's in this room. Now give it to me.'

He had barely finished his demand when the door opened behind him, and a shadow loomed in the doorframe. Flora's lips parted, but before she could speak, Dr Reeder stiffened, a look of startled confusion on his face. His eyes rolled up in his head and he crumpled to the rug like a puppet with its strings cut. The gun fell from his hand and skittered across the polished floorboards, coming to rest against the hearth.

Abel Cain stared at the prone form on the floor. 'Stokes said you had a bit of trouble in here, Mr Harrington.'

'Not any longer, Abel,' Bunny said. 'That was most efficient, thank you.'

'Yes, thank you, Abel.' Flora released a breath she didn't realise she was holding. 'I had forgotten you were still here.' Her gaze went to his hands, which were empty. 'What did you hit him with?'

Abel held up his right fist, clenched into the size of a plucked chicken. 'Once the cook settled Sally in her room, she was making me a cup of tea when Stokes came running and said I was needed.'

'I shall have to raise that man's wages.' Bunny pointed to the motionless figure on the floor. 'I doubt he'll stay unconscious for long. Find something to tie his hands together, would you, Abel?'

Stokes appeared in the doorframe. 'Shall I telephone Inspector Maddox, sir?'

He stepped smartly aside as Abel dragged the unconscious Dr Reeder along the floor by his ankles.

'Straight away if you would, Stokes.' Bunny untied a silk cord from the curtains and wrapped it around the doctor's wrists, which he then wound round the leg of the sofa. 'Tell him we have another candidate for his cells.'

Bunny chuckled and while Abel shared in their private joke, Flora bent to retrieve Reeder's pistol from the floor. The weapon was tiny, only three inches long, and sat neatly in her palm, the metal smooth, cold, and comfortably heavy; the curved handle inlaid with mother-of-pearl etched with gold.

'Bunny,' she hefted the object in her hand. 'Can I have one of these?'

'What the devil?' Bunny snatched the gun from her hand. 'Goodness, Flora, what do you think you're doing?'

'I wasn't going to use it!' Her hand felt strangely empty without it. 'I thought it would fit perfectly inside my bag.'

'This, my darling is a Webley Bull Dog.' Bunny held the gun with reverence. 'Small but powerful, and certainly not for inexperienced hands.' He placed it inside a drawer of the bureau and, narrowing his eyes at her, slid it firmly closed.

33

'How are you feeling?' Bunny asked when Flora joined him in the sitting room, concern obvious in his expression. 'Did you enjoy your breakfast?' He leaned a shoulder against the long window that overlooked the street, his arms folded across his chest.

Flora had slept late that morning, took a second bath in twelve hours to rid herself of the damp filth of the Tower Subway and enjoyed the luxury of being served her breakfast in bed.

'I slept better than I thought I would.' The only legacy of her struggle on the barge and the episode with Dr Reeder were scraped knees, sore fingers, and a residual ache in one hip. Her dreams had been full of replays of the previous night's events, especially one defining moment which stuck with her. 'I thought I would never get the taste of soot and sulphur out of my mouth after yesterday, so spoiled myself and ate two slices of toast loaded with blackcurrant jam.'

'And Sally? I heard her regaling a maid with her heroics when I came downstairs.'

Flora eased into her favourite sofa and sifted through the mail that Bunny had left on a low table. 'I've given her a couple of days off to recover, but you would think nothing had happened to her. Have you heard from Inspector Maddox yet?'

'He telephoned first thing to inform me all villains are now under lock and key, including the captain of the *SS Lancet*. The children are to be returned to their families this morning.'

This news did not please Flora as it should have. Having seen some homes the children had come from, it occurred to her they had been saved from one type of horror only to be returned to the original one. Then there was the child called Annie, of whom there was still no sign.

'Isobel Lomax's parents wanted us to accept a reward,' Bunny continued, oblivious of Flora's disquiet.

'I hope you refused.' She looked up from the pile of letters and frowned.

'Naturally. I thanked them politely, but said that virtue was its own reward.'

'You didn't!'

'Of course not. I suggested they make a donation to St Philomena's Children's Hospital instead.'

'Excellent solution.' Flora picked up an envelope. 'I'm sure Alice will be grateful. I can only imagine how she feels about harbouring a villain like Ruth on her staff.'

'I doubt anyone will blame her for Sister Lazarus' actions. Talking of Alice...' His gaze shifted from his contemplation of the street. 'I've concluded you were right. Her features in repose are like yours. There's definitely a family resemblance.'

'What made you think of that, specifically?' Flora halted, taking out the letter inside. She had not told him the entire story of their captivity in the barge for fear of his dismissing what she had heard as her imagination.

'Because I'm looking right at her. She's at the front gate.'

'What?' Flora dropped the letter onto the sofa and rose slowly.

So she hadn't imagined Alice's oblique promise of the day before. Fearful that Alice might change her mind and vanish again, Flora ran to the front door and yanked it open.

Alice stood on the top step, her hand reaching for the bellpull. She blinked in surprise at seeing Flora and lowered her hand. 'Good morning, Flora. I... I think we need to talk.'

'I agree.' Flora stepped back to let her pass into the hall, her heart thumping uncomfortably in her chest. The fact she had not actually pressed the doorbell meant Stokes had not appeared, so Flora took Alice's coat and hung it on the hat stand.

'Come into the sitting room. It's the first door on your left. Have you had breakfast?' Flora's throat dried, making her words high-pitched.

'Yes, I was up early, but I would welcome some coffee.'

Bunny greeted Alice with his usual charm, as if she was the one person in the entire city he wished to see.

'Actually, I have to leave you,' he said, easing towards the door. 'Inspector Maddox has asked me to write a full account of what transpired yesterday. I think I'll do that now, while it's all still fresh in my mind.' He backed away, but paused at the door, directing a slow, conspiratorial wink at Flora.

'That was tactful of him.' Alice licked her lips as if nervous, then paused beside the sofa Flora had left a moment before, her gaze on the opened letter and the pile she had left on the cushions.

'Excuse me a moment and I'll move these.' Flora gathered them into a pile and placed them on the nearest table.

Alice sat and arranged her skirt around her, as if waiting for Flora to take the seat next to her.

'I have so much to tell you, Flora,' she said when their eyes were level. 'Now I'm here, I'm not sure where to begin.'

'Then let me.' The question Flora had asked herself all night sprang to her lips. 'When Ruth was about to attack me, you called me Fleur.'

'Yes, I did.' Alice twisted the metal clasp of the bag in her lap. 'It was the name I gave you when you were born.' She swallowed, then released a light, almost derisive laugh. 'Riordan hated it and insisted you be called Flora.'

'He did?' Flora frowned. She had been told her grandfather had changed her name because he considered a French one pretentious, but perhaps she had misunderstood.

'I reacted purely by instinct when I believed you were about to be hurt yesterday.' Alice shrugged. 'Yet, I was terrified I had revealed something you wouldn't welcome. Or accept.'

'I'm not imagining it then?' Flora whispered, barely able to breathe. 'You really are Lily Maguire?' Excitement sparked through her nerve endings and sent blood rushing through her veins. Her instincts hadn't betrayed her after all. Finally, she was about to have every question that had plagued her all her life answered. Before she could summon any of them, the door clicked open to admit Stokes with a tray.

His knowing smile as he set the coffee pot between them told Flora he was aware this was no ordinary social call. 'I assume you wish to pour madam, and would rather I withdraw?'

'Um... Oh, yes, thank you Stokes.'

'A tactful manservant too,' Alice's lips twitched. 'My, you are a fortunate young woman, Flora.'

'I believe I am.' *Even more so now.*

'I want to – I mean I need to explain,' Alice said when the door closed again. 'It's a long story.'

'One I dearly wish to hear.' Flora concentrated on pouring coffee, mainly to stop her hands from shaking. The rich aromatic brew filled her senses and calmed her, but her heart fluttered in her chest.

'My father was a minister, and when I was fifteen, I went into service to train as a lady's maid to Lady Vaughn.' Alice accepted the cup Flora handed her. 'I had a – liaison with a young man in the family. We were both young, and well, you still have hope then that the impossible might work out well.'

Flora took a mouthful of coffee, smothering William's name that sprang unwittingly to her tongue.

'The young man was as impetuous and romantic as I was – at first. He told his family we wished to marry. I won't go into the drama which erupted then, but Lady Vaughn made sure the wedding did not take place, and instead, they sent him to America to complete his education. Although everyone knew it was to remove him from me.'

Flora's hand shook as she returned her cup to the saucer, reminded of a similar conversation she once had with Lady Vaughn after Riordan's death, when the secrets about Flora's parentage had come out.

'Riordan Maguire was a kind, upstanding man, if a little proud. He was a little older than me but I knew he admired me, so when he offered to give my child a name, I was flattered. Not to mention relieved.' Alice sighed, and in that one sound, Flora heard a life-time's anguish. 'I accepted him mainly to spite the father because he allowed money and social position to part us when he had always claimed those things weren't important to him. It took me a while to admit that to myself, but I can see it now.'

She raised her cup to her lips. Possibly, Flora suspected, to give her time to compose herself. During the brief silence, Flora's gaze traced several strands of grey she had not noticed before that wove through Alice's chestnut hair.

'I was fond of Riordan,' Alice said after a moment. 'But there was never love between us – not the kind I felt for...' She broke off, her lips pressed together in a hard line. 'Anyway, he said that didn't matter and from the moment you were born he adored you. We both did. This might sound selfish, but he spent every free moment he had with you and it might sound odd, but I felt pushed aside. Ignored.'

'Are you saying it was my fault you left?' Flora blurted. 'Because you were jealous of me?'

'No, oh no, that wasn't it at all. You were never to blame for anything.' Alice's features twisted in anguish. 'I'll answer all your questions afterward, but I need to tell this without interruptions, or we'll become side-tracked by misunderstandings and accusations.'

'I understand. I'm sorry, go on.' Flora fought a mounting desire to scream at her. Demand to know why she had walked away and left her to grow up without the most important person in her life. A mother. Instead, she folded her hands in her lap and fought down the emotions that threatened to overwhelm her.

'I was eighteen when you were born,' Alice said. 'I was romantic, high-spirited, and loved to dance. Riordan became... possessive, overbearing. If I joined in the country dancing at the summer fair or talked to a young man, any young man, he would drag me aside and say my behaviour was inappropriate. That it reflected badly on him.'

'All the servants at Cleeve Abbey respected him,' Flora jumped to Riordan's defence, a man she still missed. 'He most likely wanted to keep their respect, and if he thought his wife was...' she trailed off. 'I'm sorry. I promised not to interrupt. Please, go on.'

'I'm not trying to cast him as a cruel or a wicked man. He wasn't. However, the other house servants took their cue from him and treated me accordingly. They thought I didn't deserve Riordan because I was no better than I should be. I wasn't grateful enough that he had saved me from disgrace. Riordan never defended me, so I felt alone.'

Flora frowned as memories crowded her head. Riordan was

proud, certainly; maybe over serious, his smiles rare and precious, but Flora had always known she was loved.

'Your father,' Alice's voice pulled Flora back to the present. 'Your real father returned from America and came to see me at the lodge when you were young. He said he had made a mistake in leaving me – us. That he had been bullied into it. He was doing well in America and begged me to return there with him.'

Flora was about to demand why she had not done so, but held her tongue.

'I don't know why I refused,' Alice said, as if she read her thoughts. 'I was tempted, but Riordan was my husband, and he was good to me in his own way. I felt I had to stick with the choice I had made. Besides, I couldn't have shamed him like that in front of everyone he knew.' She laughed then, a self-mocking, hollow laugh. 'I thought I was being noble, although my pride had a lot to do with it. How dare your real father run away and then crawl back and say he was sorry?'

'When he came to see you at the lodge, there was an argument wasn't there?' Flora blurted, unable to stop herself. The temptation to use William's name remained strong, but she acknowledged that that was Alice's prerogative. She would wait and see if she volunteered it before admitting she already knew.

'Why yes, he did.' Alice met Flora's eyes. 'How could you remember that? You were barely walking.'

'I do. Bits and pieces anyway. Won't you tell me what happened?'

'He pleaded with me to leave with him, and when I refused, he got angry. He kept saying we belonged together, that we had a child. Then to persuade me he lifted you into his arms. I had this terrible thought: he was going to take you away. I reached for you, but he wouldn't let go, so I flew at him. In the scuffle, I fell and hit my head on the table and was knocked out.'

'I can still see you lying on the flagstone floor.' The images that had plagued Flora in dreams returned. 'There was a brightly coloured rag rug on the floor. I was frightened because you weren't moving, and the awful silence. I remember the silence most of all. Then came shouting. Lots of shouting.'

'I'm so sorry.' Alice reached for Flora's hand that sat in her lap. 'I thought you would be too young to understand.'

'So he – my father, returned to America alone?' Flora swallowed, her ears popping with the tension bottled up inside.

'Yes, yes, he did.' Alice withdrew her hand. 'After that, any disagreement I had with Riordan ended the same way. He accused me of wanting to leave, even though I had stayed. A rift developed between us; a polite, silent one, but a rift all the same. I think we both knew I should have gone.'

'I began helping at the women's refuge in town, mainly to get away from the Abbey. Riordan couldn't understand why I spent my time with people who regarded me as a do-gooding busybody. I tried to explain that I wanted to help downtrodden and abused girls who had brutish fathers, many of whom saw them as only useful to earn money.'

'Like Amy Coombe?'

'Exactly.' Alice's eyes widened. 'How do you know about her?'

'I met her after Father died. I'll explain how it came about later.'

'Riordan didn't understand that I too felt abused.' She brought a hand to her bodice, her eyes moist. 'In here. Six years of being treated like an errant child made me feel worthless. When Sam Coombe raised his fist to me, I believed it was only what I deserved.'

'Everyone thought Coombe had killed you and hidden your body.'

'I'm not surprised. He was a violent man, and I was determined to get Amy away from him. Such a scrawny, frightened little thing. He hit me with something. I don't know what, but I still carry the scar.' She lifted an artful curl away from her face, revealing a jagged white line a half an inch long on her temple. 'I staggered into the street, and walked and walked. I don't know where or for how long. It snowed that night, but I hardly felt the cold. The next thing I remember was being shaken awake by a bad-tempered guard at Paddington Station who kept demanding my ticket. The carriage had emptied and this kind lady spotted blood on the collar of my dress. She told off the guard saying it was quite obvious I was hurt. She paid my fare for me and took me to her house where she looked after me. Her name was Mary Buchanan.'

'Raymond's wife?' Flora gasped as disjointed pieces of the puzzle clicked into place in her head. No wonder Alice wouldn't hear anything against him.

'She summoned a doctor who diagnosed a serious head injury. For a long time, I suffered from headaches. Mary insisted I remain with them to recover and until they could contact my family.'

'Why didn't they? Did you lose your memory?'

'No, but I allowed them to think I had.' Alice's cheeks flushed a deep red, and she mangled the tapestry bag in her hands.

'But the Buchanan's tried to find out who you were, surely?'

She nodded. 'Raymond hired a private investigator. The train I was found on started its journey at Exeter, so when Raymond began enquiries there I didn't correct him.'

'I don't understand. Why did you mislead them?'

Alice shrugged. 'My recovery was greeted with happiness and celebration. I found myself in a beautiful house with kind people who seemed to want me there. No one to tell me I wasn't worthy and that to dance was a sin. I almost forgot I ever had a former life.'

'And me? Did you forget me?' Bitterness edged Flora's voice.

'No, never.' Her eyes pleaded for understanding. 'I knew there was a price to be paid for my actions. You were that price.' She grasped Flora's hand and hung on. 'I was a weaker, more cowardly person then. I was selfish and restless. I know what I did was wrong.'

'What about the nursing?'

'I'm coming to that.' Alice drained her coffee cup, setting it back in the saucer with a firm click. 'I needed a name, so Mary suggested I use that of their dead daughter, a child they had lost a year before. Alice.'

'The one who drowned in the Serpentine?' Flora gasped.

'Yes, they wanted to hear her name in the house again. To a real person and not a ghost. That might sound maudlin to some, but I liked it. You see, I wanted to be more than the ghost of Lily Maguire.'

'And the Finch part?'

'During my recovery, I would sit and watch the greenfinches gather in a tree outside my room. At certain times the tree moved without the wind as if the leaves were alive with tiny green birds. So I chose Finch.' She shrugged as if what was perfect sense at the time might seem odd now. 'As time went on, the past haunted me. I realised I couldn't take everything and give nothing. Not after what I had done, so I became a nurse at the London Hospital. I signed up for training and went to live in the nurses' home, which was a trial and different from Birdcage Walk. Not that I'm complaining,' she added. 'Those were good times, and I worked hard in a profession I came to love. Over the years I worked my way up to Ward Sister and then three years ago I was made Matron.'

'And the Buchanans?' Flora asked.

'They were my family.' Her features softened as memories ran through her head. 'I spent every Sunday with them. Mary died of consumption three years ago, which was when Raymond begged me to return to live at Birdcage Walk. Can you blame me for accepting his offer?'

Flora shook her head. 'And you never married again?'

'How could I? I was still married to Riordan. In fact, I wrote to him...' Her face took on the meditative look of someone wrestling with a memory.

Flora inhaled sharply. 'He knew you were alive? When was this?'

'I might have known he hadn't told you.' Her gaze hardened as it met Flora's. 'It was ten years ago. I asked him to forgive my leaving, and that I would understand if he divorced me for desertion. I asked if I might see you again occasionally, away from Cleeve Abbey, if he didn't want anyone to know.'

'What happened?' Flora's throat tightened.

'He refused. He said he would never divorce me, and I must never ask to see you again. That I had deserted you and I didn't deserve to be part of your life.'

'You did. Desert me, I mean.'

'I know.' Alice's eyes welled. 'Which is why I replied, accepting his terms. I asked for only one thing. That he was not to poison whatever memories you had of me.'

Flora frowned as she searched her memory. Riordan never mentioned any letters. Nor were there any among his things when he died. 'I don't understand. He did everything he could to find you when you went missing. He wrote to the newspapers and—'

'Are you sure about that?' Alice's eyes softened with resignation. 'He made it clear to me he thought he was well rid of me.'

'No! That isn't true, he always—' Flora had been about to say that Riordan always spoke kindly of Lily, but her memory was flawed. He never mentioned her mother at all. Not once in all the years she was growing up. Flora had always interpreted his reluctance as the pain of never having found her, but was what Alice said true? That Riordan had consciously wiped Lily from their lives? The fact Flora only had two photographs of her mother had never struck her as odd. Photographs Riordan had never asked to see, and none of Lily had ever been displayed in their home.

'I can see by your face you're beginning to accept reality.' Alice's voice held no rancour.

'I... I think I am.' The signs were there, but she had simply ignored them. None of what she had always believed was real.

'He never replied to my second letter,' Alice said. 'Not that I ever wanted a divorce, although I've had offers.' A hint of pride lifted her voice. 'Besides, had I remarried, I would have had to give up nursing, which I had no intention of doing.'

Flora was alert for deceit, but why would Alice lie after all this time? What had she to gain now?

'Are you all right, Flora?' Alice's eyes darkened with concern. 'I realise this must be a dreadful shock.'

'I'm quite well, just, let's say I'm rearranging my memories.' She took a deep shuddering breath and fought down the pain that lanced through her chest. 'What made you decide to resume contact after twenty years?'

'I always wanted to but lacked the courage. Then I found these when I was helping Raymond sort out Mary's things after her funeral.' Alice delved inside her handbag and withdrew two yellowed newspaper clippings, handing them to Flora. One bore the heading 'Woman disappears from Cheltenham leaving, husband and child'. The other dated a year later with 'Still No News of Missing Woman on One Year Anniversary.'

'The Buchanans had known who you were all along?' Flora gaped at the pages, looking from one to the other in disbelief.

'It seems so. Those reports stirred everything up again. What I had left behind, whom I had hurt.' Her eyes met Flora's for a heartbeat then slid away. 'I even took a train back to Gloucestershire, though I wasn't sure what I would say to Riordan when I got there. I was too late. The landlord at the hotel in the village told me Riordan had died the year before.'

'I see.' Flora did not think it was the right time to mention he had in fact been murdered.

'The landlord didn't know me, but he was happy to gossip about the family up at the Abbey. He said your name was Harrington now, and that you had moved to London, so I let things lie for a while. For all I knew, your husband knew nothing of either your past or mine, so I risked making things worse.'

'What changed your mind?' Flora asked.

'I read the account of the Evangeline Lange case in the newspapers, where your name was mentioned. Then there was this.' She dipped into the bag again and handed her a much-folded newspaper clipping. Newer than the others, it bore the announcement of Arthur's birth five months before, together with their London address.

'I tortured myself for weeks over whether I should contact you. I even walked past this house several times, and once, I saw you come out pushing a baby carriage. I hurried away before you saw me. When I finally plucked up the courage, I...' She closed her eyes and a tiny frown appeared between her brows. 'What I did next might seem a little, well, sinister.'

'Why? What did you do?' Flora stared at her for long seconds, then the truth hit her. 'You sent us the invitation to St Philomena's Hospital?'

Alice nodded. 'I instructed the porter to tell me when you arrived so I could be sure I was the one to show you round. I planned to tell you who I was over tea, and take the consequences of whatever you felt about me. Then Lizzie Prentice was killed and the story of my past had to wait.'

'What if Bunny had not known Riordan wasn't my real father? Suppose he couldn't accept it?'

'I'm not a callous woman, Flora.' A wry, almost familiar smile appeared on her face. 'I pride myself on being an excellent judge of character. Ignoring the fact, I failed miserably with Ruth Lazarus. I told myself that if Bunny struck me as the unforgiving type, I would remain silent and let you go on your way. The moment I saw your husband, I could see what sort of man he was. Nothing I said could change his love for you. Had it been otherwise, I would have never spoken.'

'I'm grateful for that at least.' Flora swiped her hand across her eyes as tears welled. Though if Bunny had been a different sort of man, Flora might have spent the rest of her life in ignorance.

'You must feel angry and confused,' Alice said. 'I've had twenty years to reconcile myself to what I did, but this is all new to you.'

'You're right. There's a great deal I have to think about.'

'Is there a chance you could find it in yourself to forgive me for the past?' Alice's smile was the same one Flora knew intimately from the photographs she had of her. 'I would understand if you wished to have nothing to do with me.'

'The only person who could be hurt is gone, and to be candid, I need a mother.' She almost added that she always had, but that would have been a cruel barb, which Alice didn't deserve. Didn't she try to find a way back and Riordan had cruelly refused her?

'You don't know how much this means to me, Flora. And if I may, I have a request of my own, which I hope you'll view kindly.'

'You'd like to meet your grandson,' she finished for her.

'I would.' Alice bit her bottom lip, nervous. 'If you agree of course. I never imagined that I would be a grandmother.'

'I was going to suggest that myself.' Flora rose and approached the bellpull. 'I love showing him off and I have a feeling he is going to take to you.' That Arthur would receive more loving attention from Alice than he did from Beatrice was a minor triumph. 'He has an excellent nursemaid. Unfortunately, she doesn't seem to like me much.' Flora relayed her request to Stokes then resumed her seat.

'That's not uncommon,' Alice smiled knowingly. 'At the hospital, we experience similar situations. When a nurse sits up for four nights with a desperately sick child, she can become critical of the mother, even resentful when it's time for the child to go home.'

'Milly hasn't had to deal with anything like that. She knows how much I love Arthur. I would do nothing to jeopardize his health.'

'With the sole charge of a young baby, it's hard for her not to become attached. She might feel she's the only one who has his true interests at heart. She might even come to regard you as an intruder.'

'What should I do?' Flora asked. 'I don't want to dismiss her. She's a good nurse, but I feel she disapproves of me.'

'Might I suggest you ask her for advice from time to time? Even if you don't need it. She knows your son as well as – even better than – you in some ways. Discuss his sleep patterns and teething remedies. Involve her rather than treat her like an ordinary servant who should disappear into the walls when she isn't required.'

'I doubt any of my servants would accuse me of that. Ask Sally.'

The door opened and Flora turned towards it. 'Ah, here he is now.' She sought the nursery maid's gaze and held it for long seconds. 'Milly, this is Mrs Finch, Arthur's grandmother. You'll be seeing much of this lady in the future.' Flora changed her title so as to avoid even more gossip in the servant's hall.

To her credit, Milly displayed no reaction other than a widening of her eyes before she bobbed a curtsey and murmured a polite greeting. Having handed the baby to Flora, she was on her way out again when Alice called her back.

'Milly, as you have a unique relationship with young Arthur,'

Alice began. 'I wonder if you would mind telling me about him?' At Milly's surprised frown, she added. 'Is he a good sleeper? Does he fuss when he's tired? What are his favourite toys?'

Milly shot Flora a concerned look, but at her nod crept closer. 'He's a good baby, Missus. He sleeps well and rarely fusses. He's never ill other than a cold and he's got five teeth now.' Her voice held pride as if taking credit for it.

Alice asked gentle, non-critical questions about the baby's care, even congratulating Milly on Arthur's obvious intelligence, as if this was due to her.

Fortunately, the baby proved to be in an excellent mood, welcoming the strange new face with chuckles and a close examination of Alice's hair and clothes.

While they talked, Flora took the role of silent observer, delighted with both her son's reaction to her mother and Milly's slow blossoming beneath the older woman's attention.

This was what she had missed all her life; a mother's advice and gentle guidance on subjects she could never have broached with anyone else. Even Bunny, for all his practicality and kindness, didn't always understand that Flora often felt ill-equipped to be a mother. Like most men, he regarded motherhood as instinctive; but in truth, she floundered, with panic and doubt taking turns.

Alice made baby noises against the baby's plump cheek, and was rewarded with soft looks and endearing smiles from a chuckling Arthur. As she watched, Flora felt warmth leave her and something else took its place. Alice must have done the same for her when she was a baby, so how could she have walked away from the small, wriggling body that needed her so much?

Flora kept her expression neutral, but she knew with certainty that she could never have abandoned her child, no matter how difficult her life became. Or was she being unjustly critical? Alice had been badly hurt by Mr Coombe, so was it possible her maternal instinct did not return with the same intensity as before?

After six years, had living with Riordan's verbal pounding that Lily was an unworthy mother had an impact? Maybe she had convinced herself Flora would be better off without her? The questions circled in her head with nowhere to go, until she decided they should be left in the past, or she would never be at peace with her mother's return. No one can truly guess the hearts of others, and all that mattered was she was back in her life now.

Despite her calm reasoning, a tiny worm of resentment sat at the back of her mind, which repeated over and over. *I was her child. How could she have left me?*

34

Bunny went ahead into the house, leaving Flora on the doorstep aiming a last wave at the rear of the taxi taking Alice back to Bird-cage Walk. The vehicle disappeared round the corner and with a contented sigh, she closed the front door and leaned against it.

'Do you really think I look like her?' She turned her head side-ways to study her profile in the hall mirror.

'I do.' Bunny came to stand behind her, his hands on her shoul-ders. 'Not so much in individual features, but your laugh, and the way you bite your bottom lip when you are worried. Then there's that tiny hiccough when you—'

'Enough!' She elbowed him gently, making him chuckle.

'I take it your talk went well?'

'Yes,' Flora replied carefully, not wishing to raise doubts at this early stage. 'She had a complicated story to tell. I need time to let it settle in my head.'

'I admit I'm intrigued to know what kept you apart for so long, but I'm happy to wait until you are ready.' His steady gaze met hers in the glass. 'Do you think you'll be able to forgive her?'

'What makes you think I haven't already?'

'Because for whatever reason, she left you. You might be all grown up now, but that abandoned little girl still lives inside you.'

'I will forgive her. Eventually.' She would not admit it, but his keen perception sometimes frightened her. 'Though I will never tell her that.' The implication that he shouldn't either sat heavily between them.

'I understand.' Bunny nodded slowly. 'What should I call her?' he asked, changing the subject. 'Mother-in-law, Miss Finch or Mrs Maguire?'

'She wants me to call her Alice.' Flora leaned her head back against his shoulder, her hands clasped over his at her waist. 'She says she isn't Lily Maguire any more.'

'Which in a way makes perfect sense.' He propped his chin on her shoulder. 'You both need to give yourselves time. Her to get to know you, and—'

'For me to forgive,' she finished for him. 'Yes, I see that now. I was so bound up in the excitement of wanting her to be my mother, I forgot how I might feel if it turned out to be true.'

'I expect she'll be relieved to hear Maddox will not prosecute Raymond Buchanan.'

'Truly?' She met his gaze in the mirror. Bunny nodded. 'With a child trafficking gang in custody, the police are feeling magnanimous. Not to mention Maddox getting his name in the papers as the lead investigating officer.'

'What about the peeps?' Flora stiffened slightly, prepared for bad news.

'What peeps?' Bunny blinked behind his horn-rimmed spectacles. 'I doubt they will see the light of day again. Nor do I imagine anyone connected with the case will wish to reveal they ever existed either.'

'Did you have something to do with that?'

'Whatever gave you that idea?' His lips twitched as he drew a small silver egg shape from his pocket, swinging it gently on the end of its chain.

'You kept it?' she said in a whisper. She reached for it, but he moved it nimbly to one side.

'Call it a memento. Reeder won't want it back now, especially when I have had the photograph replaced with something less, er, controversial. An image of my wife, perhaps?'

'Sounds perfect. Is that possible?'

'I don't see why not.' He slipped the silver egg into his pocket again, grasped her hand and drew her along the hall. 'It's chilly out here. Let's go back to the sitting room where there's a fire.'

'I hope Victor Buchanan doesn't have any more of those photographs floating about to cause trouble.' Flora skirted the sofa, which had been placed closer to the hearth than normal and sat, a wave of heat enveloping her from the banked-up fire.

'Not if he has any sense,' Bunny plonked down heavily beside her, making the cushion dip on her side. 'Or he could find himself penning verses in Reading gaol.'

'Not funny.' Flora narrowed her eyes at him, but his grin persisted.

'You know, there's still a chance for them.' She relaxed her head against the upholstery and addressed the ceiling. 'They still have years ahead of them, so why shouldn't they spend them together? After all, it's where they should have been all along?'

'I gather you're referring to Alice and William?'

'Who did you think I meant?' she replied without looking at him.

'It's been twenty years, Flora. Years which must have changed them both beyond recognition. Perhaps they aren't right for each other now?'

'I don't believe that.' She recalled William's face when he talked about Lily, and Alice's when she explained she had parted from her child's father. Hope sat in both of them, deeply set maybe, but it was still there. William was still away on his mysterious trip, which she hoped was as innocent as he had claimed.

'You mean you don't want to believe it?'

'It isn't only that.' Flora shifted closer, lacing the fingers of her left hand with his. 'Alice has always regretted not going to America when William asked her to. She still loves him, and I know William loves her.'

'You cannot write their story for them, Flora.' Bunny released her hand and rested his chin against her hair. 'We'll just have to trust that to luck and nature.'

'Luck and nature,' Flora repeated. The crackle and spit of the fire combined with their steady breathing. 'And perhaps a little help from me.'

ACKNOWLEDGMENTS

I would like to thank the brilliant team at Boldwood, specifically Caroline Ridding for her vision in helping me bring Flora to life. My thanks go to Isobel Akenhead, Sarah Ritherdon, Sue Lamprell and Debra Newhouse, and also to Boldwood's creative department for the stunningly beautiful covers.

ABOUT THE AUTHOR

Anita Davison is the author of the successful Flora Maguire historical mystery series.

Sign up to Anita Davison's mailing list for news, competitions and updates on future books.

Visit Anita's website: www.anitadavison.co.uk

Follow Anita on social media here:

X x.com/anitasdavison
f facebook.com/anita.davison
g goodreads.com/anitadavison

ALSO BY ANITA DAVISON

Miss Merrill and Aunt Violet Mysteries

Murder in the Bookshop

The Flora Maguire Mysteries

Death On Board

Death at the Abbey

Death of a Suffragette

Death by the Thames

Death on a Train

Poison
& Pens

POISON & PENS IS THE HOME OF
COZY MYSTERIES SO POUR YOURSELF
A CUP OF TEA & GET SLEUTHING!

DISCOVER PAGE-TURNING NOVELS FROM
YOUR FAVOURITE AUTHORS &
MEET NEW FRIENDS

JOIN OUR
FACEBOOK GROUP

BIT.LYPOISONANDPENSFB

SIGN UP TO OUR
NEWSLETTER

BIT.LY/POISONANDPENSNEWS

Boldwood

Boldwood Books is an award-winning fiction publishing company seeking out the best stories from around the world.

Find out more at www.boldwoodbooks.com

Join our reader community for brilliant books, competitions and offers!

Follow us
@BoldwoodBooks
@TheBoldBookClub

Sign up to our weekly deals newsletter

https://bit.ly/BoldwoodBNewsletter

Printed in Dunstable, United Kingdom

72655760R10211